The Golden Thorns

The Golden Thorns

Leigh Ronald Grossman

The Wildside Press

Rockville, Maryland

The Green Lion
www.wildsidegame.com

Cover design by Stephen H. Segal

Edited by Amy Goldschlager
Special thanks to Sean Wallace and Seameus Bethel

ISBN 0-8095-7181-1
ISBN-13 978-8095-7181-9

Published by:
Wildside Press
9710 Traville Gateway Drive #234
Rockville, MD 20850
www.wildsidepress.com

First Wildside Press edition: January 2008

10 9 8 7 6 5 4 3 2 1

For Rowena Sandoval
who understands when I stay up writing until dawn

Contents

Acknowledgments

In their earliest form, *The Green Lion* and *The Golden Thorns* were the first books I finished, completed in the mid-1990s. John Betancourt, a friend since college and at the time a science fiction editor in New York, pushed me to write the novel, which grew into two books in the storytelling process. The books landed me my first agent and got some favorable attention from publishers, but ultimately were never published, unlike the ten books that followed. Years later, Betancourt, now head of the Wildside Press (which also publishes my gaming books), asked if the novels were still available, bringing the books full circle.

Over the last year, I've had the opportunity to revisit the writer I was more than a decade ago, at a very different time in my life, while substantially rewriting the books to reflect how I've grown as a writer since that time. As an author I've written a number of collaborations, but collaborating with my own past self is certainly one of the more interesting writing experiences I've ever had.

I owe thanks to many people, particularly to John Betancourt for his roles at both the beginning and end of this saga; my first agent, Don

Maass, who made a number of suggestions for shaping the narrative; current agent Val Smith, who keeps me focused and writing; to Lois Garrett, who believed in the earliest version of this book more than anyone; to Rowena Sandoval for her love and support; proofreader Penelope Stowe; and most of all to editor Amy Goldschlager, who first saw these books as an editor at Avon Books, but had a tremendous hand in helping to reshape them a decade later, and whose friendship over the years has helped even more than her editorial guidance.

The Golden Thorns

PROLOGUE
A Touch of Thorns

❖

Summer, an hour after sundown
1014 years After the Death of Mara
On a hillside overlooking the Calambrian River

From outside the tent, the noises of battle had begun to subside. The occasional horn still blew, but mostly the cries of wounded men, and a few women, dominated the dusky hillside.

Inside the tent, a dozen women planned their own battle. A few of them wore Cathanese armor and colors—the only one of the contending armies below that numbered women among its ranks. These women were committing treason simply by their presence in the tent. The other women wore a broader variety of clothing than might be expected at a social gathering, everything from noblewomen's gowns, to servants' castoffs, to the motley of muscians and circus performers.

None of them would have long survived discovery by any of the forces fighting below, either.

Members of the Thorn Cult seldom met in such numbers, or in such a risky venue, but the need for speed and efficiency was beginning to outweigh the need for secrecy.

Within the next year, most of them expected to be either dead or helping to rule the world.

"Now is the time to act," one of the armored women was saying. "The cardholders are all weak or dead below us."

"Not yet," their leader answered. "We must not show our hands here yet. All is as it should be. The battle has weakend and confused our enemies. It's possible that it has strengthened our pawns."

"We can't risk that," said the soldier.

"On the contrary, we risk nothing yet." The leader adjusted the cowl that covered her face. "The cards must be brought together, but we need not be the ones to do that. All that is required is that we control how they come together, and that the cards are in our hands at the right moment. We have no armies like the ones below." The leader gestured toward the noises from below the hill. "For the moment we will let the armies fight, and prepare to step in after the prize they fight over is snatched away."

The soldier seemed unconvinced. "How can we be sure that we will have the cards when we need them?"

"There are prophecies," the leader answered. "But also, we have an agent in place. Not all of your sisters are within this tent. One of us watches the cards, and there are others in place to watch her, in case she does not succeed, or wavers in her purpose. She will do what is necessary to bring the cards together. In the meantime we will prepare to take advantage of today's events."

By the time full darkness had fallen, the tent was empty again, and the magic that had concealed the meeting from unwelcome eyes had dissipated as well.

"Quite the hero, your son."

"It was the worst moment of his life, I think."

"Bah," said the interrogator. "If he still lives, after all that followed that battle, he'll be proud of it someday. Perhaps not now, but in years to come, when people whisper about him and give him special seats at the theater, and when his children are accepted at the University without initiation or sponsorship." Something sounded a little unreal about the interrogator's remarks, as if the words came secondhand, rather than from personal experience.

"He's a long way from that, Councilor."

"Not enough pride, that's all. He comes from a fine bloodline; it's to be expected that he'd be a great warrior. Don't you think?"

The interrogator received no response.

"Pity he's probably dead now."

Still no response. Night had long since fallen. Lamps illuminated the parlor.

"Perhaps we should take a break and you can continue your story when you're feeling more talkative."

The parlor remained silent, except for the occasional noises of gulls outside on the moonlit docks.

The interrogator got up to leave. As he reached the door, he turned to ask a final question.

"So tell me, what did he get out of all of it? He didn't care about the money or the titles or the battles. So what did he accomplish?"

"Nobody lies to him anymore."

The interrogator laughed at that. He seemed genuinely amused.

"Everyone gets lied to."

"Not in the same way. Some people chase after their destinies, or let the world rule them. My son came to make his own choices. Slowly, to be sure, painfully at times. He may have started out as my pawn, or someone else's, but now no one rules him. Here you are with all the wealth of the University behind him, and you have no more control over him than I do. You haven't even figured out where he is."

The interrogator nodded. "That's true. But that's why you are here. Good night, captive. We will speak of this again tomorrow."

The door closed on the parlor, with its velvet cushions and barred windows.

Outside, noises rose from the docks: fishermen unloading, and always the gulls.

Tomorrow he would stretch the story out a bit more, and give another day of freedom to his son. He wondered if the boy knew that the woman who'd been both his greatest enemy and his biggest benefactor still lived. Until recently, of course, Falorn had ascribed those roles to different women.

The interrogator had asked surprisingly few questions about his son's judgment, instead seeming to look for some sort of clues in the events that had transpired around him: the events that had reached a certain climax in the battle along the Calambrian River.

1

The Price of Knighthood

Summer, the same day
1014 years After the Death of Mara
Along the banks of the Calambrian River

When no one remained to kill, Falorn let Cirque lead him away from the battlefield. They seemed to walk forever. Cirque supported Falorn as he stumbled over bodies on the hard-packed field, or slipped on pools of men's and horses' blood.

Finally, he lay down at his companion's urging. Falorn blinked his eyes until tears came again. He saw nothing, even with his eyes open. He felt blind, and crippled, and very, very sad.

"Sart's Breath! Look at him," he heard someone say from nearby. Falorn had no idea how much time had passed. He wanted only to be left alone to die.

"Leave him," said another. "He'll never live with those wounds. Tend to another."

"He fought well, though. The queen wanted . . ."

"Damn you, do as I say! What do I care for some foreigner dragged in on the arms of a stinking elf? They can both rot together with the Seven Kingdoms corpses, for all I care. If they live, they should be burned as heretics."

"Priest," he heard another voice say. "Those were not wise words. Too many of your betters have died today. I will not allow this one to do so as well. I saw friends die today. *You*, I must point out, are *not* a friend. It would bother me not at all to see you die. Am I understood?" Falorn felt certain he had never heard the voice before.

"Yes, Lord Alex," the second voice replied. "I will have my surgeons do what they can."

"You will do nothing of the sort. You will order your lackeys to free the elves immediately, return their possessions—*all* their possessions— and allow them to minister to this one. I will send my personal physician to look in on him as well, and *I will be back to make certain you have done everything I said*. Am I understood?"

"Yes, Lord Alex."

"Good. I suspect I may be saving your life. Imprisoning those two elves was a very, very foolish thing to do. They would have given you cause to regret it." The voice grew louder, as the man speaking approached closer. Falorn felt something cold touch his lips, then something wet them. A few drops of liquid trickled into his mouth. "I have little enough of this elixir," the voice said again, this time a whisper in Falorn's ear, "but you have earned it today. A fine mess these cards have pulled you into; I only hope I can lend you a little of the strength to pull yourself out of it. We will meet again soon."

With that, the voice quieted, and Falorn slept.

For a long time, Falorn dreamed. In his mind, he saw Sera again, although part of him still remembered that she had run away from him. She wore the same clothing as on the first day he had seen her: a blue velvet dress, worn over dark leggings and belted with a chain of thick gold links. Light brown, shoulder-length hair framed her face. She had strikingly deep brown eyes.

Sera looked as if she'd been crying. She seemed to be in a small room, although Falorn couldn't see the walls clearly. She kept glancing around, but he couldn't tell what she expected to see. The walls themselves seemed to be moving, but she didn't seem to notice them.

Soon, Falorn noticed that the walls were made up of growing, moving thorns.

They wound closer to Sera, but still she saw nothing.

He wanted to warn her, but his voice didn't work at all.

She kept looking around, but somehow the thorns eluded her sight. The plants grew closer. Now they touched Sera, and Falorn saw blood flow as the thorns pierced her legs and twined upward. She kept looking frantically to all sides as the plants enveloped her, but she never seemed to understand what was happening.

Soon she vanished from sight beneath the thorns. In her place, Falorn saw only a single deep red rose.

He awoke underneath a diffuse red sky. Gradually Falorn realized that he lay inside an old, worn tent. The sun shone redly through the thin, dyed cloth of the roof.

Someone sat on a campstool beside him.

His eyes took too long to focus. A green-eyed woman sat on the stool. Most of her blond hair had been cropped off raggedly at the nape of the neck, except for a single, very thin braid that hung a third of the way down her back, slightly off to the left. Her white linen tunic fit loosely over broad, strong-looking shoulders. The tunic gapped open slightly as she sat, revealing a thin gold chain with an enameled rose pendant.

"Elise," he finally said. The name came out in a hoarse croak.

"Yes, it's me," she said. "You shouldn't talk. I'll get one of the elves."

"Wait," he rasped. "The battle. Did we win? Tell me what happened."

"I will. Just let me get one of the elves first. I'll be right back." He noticed she walked with a slight limp.

His eyes lost their focus as soon as she exited the tent, and only gradually regained it after she and Ryal returned a few moments later.

"It's fine," he heard Ryal saying. "Tell him everything if he wants. If he were going to die he would have done it by now. He's half healed already."

Elise sat back down on the stool. While she talked, Ryal puttered around, probing Falorn's half-felt injuries, rubbing him with ointments, changing bandages. As always, the black-haired elf's hands moved constantly. *Hellein*, Falorn remembered, as if from very long ago. *They call themselves the Helleinen. People who don't like them call them elves.*

"I'm not sure I would say we won the battle," Elise began, "but we didn't lose it. The armies are still facing each other, and we may fight again. But I think we won't do so this season.

"You saw part of the battle. We started the fight with about 20,000 men. Calathan's army had about 25,000 men and mercenaries, and the

Seven Kingdoms sent 20,000 more. So we faced more than two of them for every soldier of ours. The wizards fought first, and killed a few of each other off, and a few hundred men, but neither side was able to gain much of an advantage. Then they kept sending waves of men at us.

"The Queen and her generals kept us in it; maybe our soldiers fought harder, too, since their families and lands were at stake. Anyway, we held out for three days before our cavalry was swept away and both flanks were pinned down by enemy troops. Then they just hammered at the center, knowing there was nobody else left to reinforce them. Eventually, our lines had to crumble.

"General Stennet commanded in the center, and your friend Zaren had his men link their shields to form a wall along the front of our lines. Between the two of them, they fought off everything that came at them, but each time they lost more men. Finally, the enemy attacked with everything they had left, putting all their reserves—thousands of fresh troops—into another attempt to break the center. They destroyed Zaren's shield wall and cut almost all the way through our lines."

"But you charged," said Falorn feebly. "You countercharged against them."

"You did more than I did, Falorn. You fought your way through to Stennet's banner when it was about to fall. People saw that, and kept fighting. And because they kept fighting, they held out long enough for the Rohnan army to arrive."

"The horns I heard . . . ?"

"Were the vanguard of an army of soldiers led by the God-Emperor of Rohn in person, and commanded in the field by his brother, Alex of Rohn. By the time they got here, the attack on the center had failed, but we had nothing at all left to defend with; the next attack would have wiped us out. But they didn't dare attack with the Rohnans guarding our center. They skirmished for another day, realized that neither side could win, and then retreated back onto their side of the Calambria River. That's where their army is sitting now."

"While the Queen of Cathan and the God-Emperor of Rohn haggle over the price of his help like a couple of fishwives at market-time," said Ryal, drawing a fierce look from Elise.

Elise would say no more about the battle, and urged Falorn to sleep.

When he woke again, darkness had fallen, and Cirque sat on the bed-side stool. A troubled look darkened the Hellein's blue eyes. In the lantern light, his light hair looked like burnished gold.

"What day is it?" Falorn managed to ask.

"Sleep," said Cirque, and Falorn obeyed without difficulty.

Falorn awoke in daylight. Pain rippled through his chest and arms, like dozens of needles jostling and fighting to free themselves from beneath his skin. He moved a hand, delighted to find it still worked. Painstakingly, he forced his arm to move, until his hand settled over the pouch which still sat on his chest. The cards inside the pouch gave off a soothing warmth, but combined with the pain and the heat of summer, he barely felt the sensation.

"You look much better this afternoon," said Cirque from the stool beside him.

"I feel like I visited Kerion's ovens."

"You came as close as a mortal can to doing just that, if he wants to stay alive. Those ovens singed you a bit, I think."

"Are they still fighting?" He remembered someone telling him something about the battle, but a haziness still filled part of his mind.

"No. The fighting on the battlefield is over for the moment, I would think. The Seven Kingdoms army is departing. I suspect the Calathanese army cannot by itself prevail. The disputes of these last few days have occurred between Cathan's Queen and the God-Emperor of Rohn. They still argue over the price of his aid."

"Let them. I never want to be in a fight like that again."

"No. I should hope not. You did terrible things out there, Falorn. The singers will say they were glorious, but you and I both know how minstrels lie. You did terrible things. I pray you never grow to like them."

"Never. I never could." A vision of a young, brown-haired man standing on a pile of dead men surfaced inside his head. "I only remember a little of what happened, but it's very hard to think about."

"You must not forget it, though. You did what you had to do, and you were guided by a dark magic, but you must never forget."

"No. You're right."

"I think . . ." the Hellein paused. "I saw how you fought. I think it must have looked very much like my kinsman's fight that you described to me before we came to Cathan, when those soldiers killed him for his card. I am glad that your battle had a happier ending, at least for you."

Falorn caught a dark undertone in Cirque's words. *There was something about that place I fought, something I was looking for. I wanted to find somebody there.* The name came to him suddenly.

"Zaren?" he asked.

Cirque's look told him the answer.

"You fought to the spot where he stood, but not until long after he had fallen. At the end, you stood on top of his body and cut down everything that came near. I think that you never knew it was him. I could do nothing to save him, nor could you. He and his friend Stennet fell nearly together, and he laughed nearly to the end. I have been told that he had, in human terms, an honorable death."

"He didn't *want* an honorable death," said Falorn. "He wanted to live. He had settled down until he met me. I dragged him into this."

"Nobody forced him to the very front of the action. He died trying to save his friend, and he did save many others. Would you judge him by his words, or by his actions?"

"He told me never to fight fair. He fought like a demon. Why did he have to die?"

"That is a question for religious authorities. I have very little opinion on the subject. The local religious authorities are not, at present, speaking with either of us, so you will not have an answer from them. Perhaps you can honor the man, without questioning his end."

"I'm sorry, Cirque." Falorn felt tears in his eyes. "It's just that . . . I just feel very . . . very alone." He saw a dark look flicker through the Hellein's eyes. "No, I don't mean that exactly. I'm glad you're here, and Ryal, and Elise. But I'm going to miss Zaren an awful lot. He was the only one who didn't want to make me do something because of the cards. He just tried to help me. And I've lost Sera, too. . . ." He couldn't hold the tears any longer.

He felt arms on his shoulders when he finally regained control of his body. Elise sat next to him on the bed, holding him. Cirque still occupied the stool, his face impassive.

The next morning Falorn could move a little more. He could see a battered pile of possessions sitting on top of a chest: torn clothing and boots, both muddied with blood-soaked dust. *My own blood*, Falorn realized. His sword lay across the top of the pile, cleaned, oiled, and sharpened.

"I'll fix the clothes when you're ready to wear them again," Ryal told him. "If I do it now, you'll just want to get out of bed."

"I feel much better."

"Good. We have a lot to talk about, when you've healed. There are things that must be done."

"I suppose this has to do with the . . ." He quieted at the look on

Ryal's face. After that, they spoke little; Falorn wondered who the Helleinen wizard thought might be listening.

The bandages came off for good a week later, and only then did Ryal let Falorn out of bed for more than a few minutes at a time. He felt sore, but strong again. A network of thin scars covered his chest and arms, giving his skin the appearance of a much-patched shirt. His face remained unblemished—whether from luck or Ryal's craft, Falorn didn't know.

He began to walk around the camp, at first only short distances, but later at much greater length. Elise always accompanied him, sometimes with one or both of the Helleinen; she insisted he wear his sword whenever he left the tent.

"If I'm so dangerous that I have to be guarded closely," Falorn asked, only half-jokingly, "then why do you let me run around armed?"

"Oh!" said Elise, "Is that what you thought? That's not what I'm doing at all."

"Then what are you doing? Not that I don't enjoy your company."

"I'm watching your back. You have enemies in this camp."

"Enemies? I thought you said I was some kind of hero?"

"You are, but not everyone else is. You lived, and a lot of others died. You took two banners by yourself, when old noble houses lost their colors to the Seven Kingdoms. And you have powerful friends. Alex of Rohn himself interceded on your behalf when the priests wanted to let you die, and . . ."

"What?"

"I said Alex of Rohn . . ."

"No, I heard that. I just don't understand." Elise guided him to a makeshift log bench, and gently sat him down.

"When Cirque brought you from the battlefield, the priests refused to treat you because you weren't a churchman. They ordered the elves locked up."

"Where was the queen?"

"I don't know. Busy trying to pull together her victory, I imagine. Alex himself came to the church hospital-yard—I don't know how he even knew you were there—and he insisted they treat you. I hear he threatened to kill the Archbishop himself.

"Then the priests said they would treat you, but you would have to wait, since they were treating nobles before commoners. If they waited much longer, you would be dead, of course. So Alex sent a messenger to the Queen, asking that you be knighted for your bravery. She couldn't, of course, since you're not from Cathan. When he heard that, he pulled out his sword and knighted you himself, on the spot. Then the priests had to treat you, or at least let the elves treat you. Especially with the greatest swordsman in the world standing there, with his sword out."

"Alex . . . *knighted* . . . me?"

"He did," she said. "He didn't give you a title, but you're a knight and a noble, as surely as I am. Welcome, Sir Falorn."

"Please . . . just Falorn."

She smiled, a little sadly. "You're a knight now, whether you want it or not. You've earned it, no matter what anyone says."

"That's not it. I'm very honored. I . . . I never expected anything like this, never even hoped for it. It's just that I'm still the same person. I don't want you to treat me any differently, just because someone touched me with his sword to keep someone else from letting me die. I'm still just Falorn. I'd hate it if you started calling me something else."

"Whatever you want," she said, but her eyes disagreed with him.

Falorn shifted his position on the log slightly, and looked up at the camp around them. A grassy valley had turned to a wide field of mud, filled with worn-looking canvas tents and rock-lined firepits. Few of the knights or noble officers lived in the valley encampment; most stayed at one of the two small Cathanese castles which lay in the hills nearby, overlooking the best river crossings from Calathan. The camp held mostly common soldiers and convalescents, people who had no alternatives.

"Wait a minute." Something suddenly occurred to him. "Doesn't knighthood make me obligated to him, or something?"

"Only if you want to be," Elise answered. "You were unconscious, so nobody could ask you to swear any oaths. I swore an oath of service to my Queen. You don't owe anything to anybody but yourself. Though I imagine there are people who will try to convince you otherwise."

On the way back to the tent, he spotted a familiar face.

"Tirya!" he called, as the black haired woman disappeared into a cluster of tents at the edge of the camp. "Elise, that was Tirya. She might have news of Sera."

"So?"

"So I'd like to know how she is. Is something wrong with that?"

"Falorn, if you want to know how Sera is, why don't you just ask her?"

"I'm trying to. She's over there."

"Not Tirya. Just ask Sera."

"What are you talking about?"

"Sera's staying in Southriver Castle, with Alex and his party. Who do you think brought them here?"

"What . . . do you mean . . . ?"

"Sera's been here since the God Emperor's baggage train arrived. She offered to ask Alex and his brother for help when she met with the Queen. The Queen sent Tirya to help her."

"So she didn't disappear. And you knew!"

"I had orders not to tell. The court was full of spies, and if any of them suspected, she might have been killed."

"Well, let's go see her, then."

"I'm not sure that's such a good idea. You're still not well, and it's not just a short walk."

"So we'll ride." He pointed. "There's a whole string of cavalry horses over there that are barely getting exercised anyway."

"Why don't we let it wait a little while, Falorn?"

"Because I want to see her. I miss her."

"You'll have plenty of time to see her, but I think you ought to wait until you're feeling a little better."

"Elise? What are you trying to tell me?"

"Falorn . . ." He waited. They had reached the front of the tent, walking as they talked. Elise fidgeted nervously with the canvas tent-flap.

"Elise, you might as well tell me. Is Sera all right? Has something happened to her?"

"As far as I know, she's fine. But I'm not sure she wants to see you."

"What do you mean? Of course she'll want to see me. We haven't seen each other in months."

"Then why didn't she visit you the whole time you were in bed?"

"I don't know," he said. The question hurt a little to think about. "I've been almost killed two other times since I left home, though, and she's the one who saved me both times."

"I just don't want to see you hurt, that's all. You're my friend and I care about you."

"Thanks. I still want to see her, though. If it has to wait until tomorrow morning, that's fine, but I want to go visit her."

"Whatever you want to do, Falorn. You're a knight now." Elise turned and walked away from the tent. Once again, Falorn felt very alone.

2

The Sword Without a Name

Long after Falorn had fallen asleep that night, he felt a touch at his shoulder. He woke instantly. Cirque stood by the bed, holding a hooded lantern. Its shutters closed off all but a shard of candlelight. Ryal stood by the entrance to the tent, as if watching for anyone else awake and moving nearby.

"There are things we must talk about if you are awake," said Cirque. "I apologize for the hour, but some things are best discussed in the dark of night, and out of the presence of royal agents."

"What's going on?"

"That, I think, is what we must decide." Falorn sat up in bed as Ryal handed him a mug of steaming liquid. The drink tasted harsh and bitter when he sipped at it, but it cleared the lingering fog from his head.

"First," said the Hellein, "there is something I must give you." He spread an embroidered red cloth, a square the length of Falorn's forearm, across the quilt. When he produced a flat pouch, Falorn began to suspect the nature of the gift. The pouch shimmered and glowed with a not-quite-translucent green light. A burst of heat seared his chest; Falorn nearly cried out before he realized the cause of the eruption.

"Cirque, you can't," he said, when the heat subsided to the cards' normal soft warmth.

"Please do not presume to tell me what I can and cannot do, particularly when it concerns the wishes of dead men. Zaren and I spoke at length before the battle. He made it clear that if he died, he wanted Stennet to have this, and if Stennet also died it was to go to you. It belongs to you. Unless you would prefer the queen to have it?"

"No, not that. Zaren would have hated that. It's just that . . ."

"It is among the last wishes of your friend. He put it in writing in case anyone disputed it; The man was somewhat more learned than he preferred others to know. I have one copy of his last will and testament in my possession. Would you like to see it?"

"No. You're right. I just still can't believe he's dead. He was more alive than anyone else I knew. I wish I'd known him longer, or better."

Cirque said nothing in reply. Instead, he reached into the pouch and removed a pair of small, ivorylike plaques, and laid them face up upon the red cloth.

On the face of the first card, a green-armored knight stood on a grassy hilltop, his hand touching the flank of the emerald-colored steed beside him. The knight's eyes looked downward, toward something at the base of the hill, but the object of his attention lay beyond the face of the card. The card seemed to pull at Falorn, as if the knight longed to join his crimson fellow within the pouch at Falorn's chest.

The second card he'd seen before. A blue serpent twisted and writhed across its smooth, polished surface like a maggot invading a plate of meat. The sapphire eyes stared at him with an expression that brought him suddenly back to the darkness of the deadly tunnels beneath Windford, where Zaren had shown him the card.

Falorn gave Cirque an odd look.

"Zaren only had one card," he said.

"That's true," said the elf. "The other one belonged to Stennet. If the queen's people were to find one on the battlefield, they would wonder where the other was. If both are missing, they will have fewer doubts."

"Won't she know that I have them? Will she be able to sense them?"

"She knows you have some. She and her agents will not be able to judge one from another, unless it is a mate to one she already owns."

"But if we stay here for long, she may rethink her generosity of allow-ing me to keep the cards." He wondered about what Elise had told him—how the queen had refused to knight him. Nobility carried with it certain rights, Falorn knew, rights that the queen might prefer he not have. Did that include the right to arbitrarily take his cards?

"Certainly she may—which brings us to the crux of our conversation."

Falorn had begun to get that feeling.

"We were approached recently by Lord Dianeme, the chancellor to the queen. She made a proposal of sorts to us, which we would like your help in pursuing."

"Does this proposal have anything to do with a trip to the Seven Kingdoms?"

"I told you he'd know," said Ryal.

"We did agree to discuss the matter again after the battle." Falorn nodded slightly as Cirque continued. "According to Lord Dianeme, the queen feels much of the current situation stems from the cards. She would very much like to have the ones in the Seven Kingdoms removed from their present owner. . . ."

"Who *has* been trying to kill you," Ryal pointed out.

"Why would she send us? Doesn't she think I'll just keep the cards for myself? Anybody else would."

"I believe she is willing to take that risk. With Ryal's magic and your cards, we would have a better chance than a force she might send, and if we fail, it can't be traced directly to her. If you succeed and keep the cards for yourself, she's still better off than having them in the Seven Kingdoms, where Jhodric can keep using them to improve his soldiers and assassins. I suspect she thinks you are a bit more . . . pliable . . . and if she sends the right agent along, you might be persuaded to give up the cards."

"So she wants the three of us and Elise to go into the Seven Kingdoms to hunt down Jhodric and bring back his cards."

"That is the substance of what she wants, yes."

Falorn thought for a few minutes. Neither of the Helleinen said anything. *They won't pressure me*, he knew. *They would probably be happy to wait all night if it takes me that long to make a decision. And they did stay for the battle, even though I didn't make any kind of formal commitment to help them afterward. I might not really owe them anything. But I can't stay in Cathan indefinitely, either. And nowhere else will be safe for me as long as Jhodric has as many cards as he does.*

"I don't want to kill him," Falorn finally said. "If we have to go take his cards away, that's fine, but I won't hunt someone just to kill him."

He expected the Helleinen to argue, but they just nodded, as if they expected no less from him. *Or as if they're just humoring me.* Another thought struck him: *I wonder why they want to make this journey so badly. Why would they put so much effort into a dangerous trip that helps them only indirectly? It's almost as if they have a personal grudge.*

"I shall make the arrangements with Lord Dianeme," Cirque said. "I think it might be best if you stayed out of the queen's presence before we leave. There's no reason to remind her of your cards, and you are fast becoming a major cardholder."

Am I? he thought. *I suppose that's true. If there are eighty-four of these cards and I have seven . . . how many people can there be with this many?* He suddenly realized something he'd almost forgotten.

"I'll have to see Sera," he said. "She may want to come with us. Even if she doesn't, I want to see her again. To say goodbye, if nothing else." He remembered Elise's words on the subject, and wondered how much Sera wanted to see *him*. She must be happier with an emperor's brother than an innkeeper's son, albeit a recently knighted one. *I hope she'll talk with me, at least.* He felt a tightness in his throat at the thought that she might not, might have good reasons not to.

Once again, the Helleinen both nodded in agreement, however.

"I'll take you to see her in the morning if you'd like," said Ryal. "Cirque can see Lord Dianeme at Northriver Castle while we ride to Southriver."

"Thank you," Falorn said. "I asked Elise, but she didn't want me to go. She didn't think it was a very good idea."

"Maybe it isn't," said Ryal, "but it's your choice. I do get the feeling that Sera and Elise might not be so terribly fond of each other."

"Well, Sera can take a little getting used to. She grew up in a very strange place."

"It's a very strange place we all grow up in, Falorn," Ryal answered, but his eyes looked elsewhere, very far away, as he said it.

The look made Falorn think of the home he'd left behind. *Maybe when things settle down I can find a way to send word home,* he thought. Not that there'd been many settled moments since he'd taken the armor from that dead man on the road and unwittingly started himself on the road to knighthood.

Elise looked in on him in the morning at breakfast time, but she left hurriedly, claiming duties for the queen. Shortly afterward, Falorn walked to the string of cavalry horses with the two Helleinen. He and Ryal rode southward together. The morning still felt young and fresh when they reached the walls of Southriver Castle.

The soldiers who guarded the lowered castle drawbridge wore the red surcoats of Rohnan troops over their armor. Black trim edged the surcoats, and a black owl emblazoned their sergeant's shoulder. Falorn wondered if the owl symbolized Rohn itself, or if the man bore a partic-ular noble or region's symbol. He knew little about Rohn, or about any of the other countries he'd traveled through or encountered soldiers from. His talks with Helleinen in Delerian had touched only a little on geogra-phy, and Elise's reading lessons had avoided the subject except where it directly touched on Cathan.

The sergeant waved them onto the drawbridge and through the open gate. More soldiers ran toward them as they entered the sunny courtyard within; men led their horses away as quickly as he and Ryal could dis-mount. Then, an officer arrived, armed and clothed in red like his men, but wearing a gold-plated helmet. A neatly trimmed black beard outlined the man's round face.

"Welcome, Sir Falorn," the officer boomed out in a cheery voice, surprisingly loud coming from such a small-framed man. "I'm Kennemen of Dark River, one of Lord Alex's household knights. These are my men on duty," he added, waving expansively around the courtyard and walls.

"That's quite a few men," said Falorn.

"Well, thank you, it is. My lands have prospered these last years. My family has a tradition of serving the Empire, and the Empire's done well for me and mine."

Falorn nodded and smiled slightly, uncertain how to reply. The man went on talking.

"I'm glad you're well enough to finally come visit. Lord Alex's inter-vention on your behalf has been the talk of the camp—well, of this cas-tle, anyway, maybe not of the Cathanese camps. He made the most dire threats if you didn't make a full recovery; I'm glad we don't have to see him carry them out. Let me take you to see him; he'll want to talk with you himself, right away, of course."

"Is . . . is Sera here also?"

"I'll say she is. The Lady Sera will be with Lord Alex, of course. You can see them both at once."

Falorn had trouble keeping up with Kennemen's pace. The man's short legs whirled like wagon-spokes, moving as rapidly as his words. He continued his animated conversation, only gradually realizing that Falorn no longer walked alongside him.

He began talking again as soon as Falorn caught up, although this time he moderated his pace somewhat.

"So are you well acquainted with the Lady Sera? You must be if you ask after her so quickly. Maybe you're kin even? Perhaps by marriage? She's a brave one, riding through a war without an escort. Not many ladies would do a thing like that, and no one but Lord Alex seemed to know her at court, either. I don't know what she told him, or what he told His Majesty the God-Emperor, but we were on the march in a matter of days. I couldn't believe the orders when I first heard them. . . ."

Kennemen chattered on. Falorn nodded now and then, content to keep silent and listen. He wondered if the friendly knight even noticed.

New red wall-hangings decorated the spartan stone halls of the narrow castle. Everywhere Falorn saw Rohnan soldiers. Unlike the Cathanese castles and camps he'd seen, few servants or camp-followers littered the halls. The only women in sight looked like the wives or mistresses of nobles and their maidservants; he saw none of the female soldiers who accompanied the queen, nor the prostitutes and camp-women who populated the outskirts of the valley camp.

Only when they reached the black-stained doorway of Alex's chambers did Falorn realize that Ryal no longer accompanied him; the wizard had slipped away silently sometime during the long walk through the stone-floored hallways.

Kennemen's knock went unanswered for a long moment, before a voice inside called out to come in. Falorn wondered where Alex's servants were; he doubted the brother of an emperor sat alone in his chamber. *Perhaps not even if he wants to.*

The door opened into a long, narrow room. Sun filled the chamber. Tall, thin, leaded-glass windows lined an entire wall, and sun streamed through them, spilling onto the faded furniture and carpet. Sera sat at the edge of one reddish-pink couch. A sandy-haired man lay across the couch, his head in her lap; she stroked his hair as the man looked across at Falorn and Kennemen. He had the saddest eyes Falorn had ever seen.

"Welcome, Sir Falorn," the man said, sitting up as he spoke. Sera smiled at Falorn faintly. Her hair had grown in the last few months, and she wore it in a short braid now.

"Hello, Your . . . your . . ." Falorn stumbled, unsure of the proper title.

"'Alex' will do just fine. I don't really care for titles. They just give people something to fight about."

"It seems like there are a lot of things people will fight about around here," Falorn ventured tentatively.

"Not just here. People kill for more than cards or titles or lands, young Falorn. People will kill everywhere, for anything. And if you've nothing worth killing for, they'll kill you for your name, or your reputation. Remember that. You're becoming known, Falorn, especially after this battle. If people know your name, they will want to kill you. You're probably used to people chasing you for your cards. Soon, people will be chasing you for no reason at all."

"Lord Alex?"

"Please, just Alex. I want no titles between us."

"Why?"

"Why no titles, or why will people try to kill you? No titles because you don't need them and I don't want them. Your reputation will be title enough soon. I think you're brave enough and lucky enough to live that long. And people will try to kill you because of that reputation. You're a good swordsman who fought like a demon in battle. The man who kills you will be able to say that he's an even better swordsman. They'll try to surprise you, or ambush you from behind. You will have to kill them, or they'll keep trying to kill you, and one day you will be sick, or unlucky, and they'll do it. And every time you do kill one of them, your reputation will get that much bigger, and even more people will want to kill you. I think you will be very famous, Falorn, but for the sake of your soul, I hope you are not very happy."

Sera stroked Alex's arm as he spoke, but the man seemed to take no comfort in it. Falorn wondered if Sera's gesture was for Alex's benefit, or for his.

Falorn saw Alex's sword leaning against one arm of the faded couch. Black cord covered the long hilt, long enough for a two-handed grip. The tapered blade appeared almost black as well. The steel thinned to an incredibly fine edge; near the tip, it looked too frail to survive contact with an opponent's blade. He wondered how many blades had shattered under the apparent weakness of Alex's weapon.

The blade glowed faintly blue to Falorn's eye.

"It's a fine sword," Alex said, noticing Falorn's look. "We used to be like best friends, that sword and I. Now, we tolerate each other's company. We're like a pair of old fishmongers married for too many years. All they ever do is fight, but you know somehow they'd be lost without each other."

"Does the sword have a name?"

"No. Not anymore. It used to, but that only made people want it more. It's not worth killing people over a sword with a name."

"I guess."

"You'll know, soon enough. Have you named your sword?"

"No, it seemed. . . ." Falorn trailed off. He hadn't named the blade because he felt he hadn't earned the honor of a named blade, and because a part of him thought the weapon still belonged to the green-clad corpse he'd robbed it from.

"Don't. It will only make you unhappy. Don't give it a name that you'll only have to take away again."

"I think I understand," said Falorn. Alex stared at him with pale blue eyes. His face looked very worn.

"Do you?" He held the stare for a moment before breaking eye contact. Falorn felt like an old, thin lion had just examined him thoroughly, deciding whether he merited the effort of killing and eating. "I'm sorry, young Falorn. I don't mean to upset you. You'll learn all of this for yourself soon enough, but it has been a painful lesson to me. I have few friends alive anymore; I find myself unburdening my feelings on near-strangers."

Falorn glanced at Sera to see her reaction to Alex's remark. She looked back impassively. He noticed the glint of gold from a thin chain around her neck.

He and Alex talked for nearly an hour; mostly Falorn listened while Alex spoke sadly. Kennemen had quietly gone elsewhere, but at the end of the conversation, he returned to announce Alex's luncheon with the Queen of Cathan and the God-Emperor of Rohn.

Alex turned his sad blue eyes toward Falorn just before he stepped through the door. He held the gaze for a moment, then walked out without a word.

Falorn found himself alone in the room with Sera. *I have no idea what to say.*

"It's nice to see you on your feet again," she said, finally. "I missed you."

"I missed you too," he answered. "I thought I would never see you again."

"You'll always see me again, Falorn."

"You keep saying that, and then you keep going away."

"I always come back."

"That's not the point."

"I had to go. The queen ordered me to, and she wouldn't let me tell anyone, not even you. Alex was the only chance she had of winning the battle, and she was afraid spies would chase me if they found out where I was going."

"I wouldn't have told anyone."

"I know that, but the queen ordered me. And then when I got to Alex . . . well, you see what he's like now. He needs a friend."

"Just a friend?"

"Of course! You don't think . . ."

"I don't know what to think, Sera. I don't know what to believe. You didn't even come visit me once while I was hurt. What am I supposed to think?"

"I did come to visit you! I came twice. Both times Elise said you were too sick to see anyone." She paused. "Why don't you ask her?"

"I don't know what to believe. I just wish you wouldn't leave again." *But this time, I'm the one who will be leaving*, he realized.

"I hope I don't have to. But right now, Alex needs me. I can't leave him when he's this upset; he might do anything."

"Sera, I need you, too."

"You don't, Falorn. I'd like to stay with you, but I can't right now. You're a hero now. No one will call you a peasant anymore." She laughed. "Not even me. You'll be fine. And after this is all over, we can be together again."

Falorn wondered how much he could believe. He wanted everything she said to be true. Before he could answer, her eyes seemed to focus behind him. He turned, and saw Ryal standing in the doorway.

"I'm sorry to interrupt, Falorn, but there is something you must see."

"Can it wait a few minutes?" He had an awful feeling that he might not see Sera again for a long time once he left this room.

"I'm afraid it cannot wait. You must come now."

Falorn walked over to Sera and tentatively held out a hand. She closed the distance between them and held him tightly, burying her head in his shoulder.

"You take care of yourself, Falorn," she said fiercely. "I want to see you again."

"I hope it's soon."

"I do too, but it won't be. Please be careful."

"You too."

"I will be. Remember, we'll be together when this is all over."

He followed Ryal out the door, looking over his shoulder to see Sera's expression. For a moment he thought she cried, but then she straightened and stared out one of the windows. Her face bore no tears in the sunlight, nor any expression at all.

3

Endings and Beginnings

❖

"Where are we going?" Falorn asked Ryal as they hurried down the passageway.

"You will see in a minute. Keep an eye out for the guards, please."

"Do the queen and Alex know where we're going?"

"I think that will become clear very shortly."

Falorn looked carefully around the hallways as they walked through the castle. In many places, walls glittered with faint blue light, illuminating hidden seams. His head barely ached anymore when he used the blue thief card, despite the lingering weakness from his injuries. *Either I'm becoming more used to its magic, or it gets easier the more cards I have.*

Falorn turned to help when Ryal reached toward one of the hidden portals. The Hellein seemed momentarily surprised, and then grunted slightly as if in remembrance. Ryal pressed a finger to his lips as they passed into the secret corridor. Falorn focused on walking silently; neither of them made any sound at all as they moved forward. A thin coating of dust covered the floor, broken only in a few places by the tracks of Ryal's boots leaving. Falorn wondered how the Hellein had entered the chamber without leaving marks of his passage.

They heard conversation ahead: three voices from beyond a thin plaster wall. He recognized the queen's and Alex's. *The third voice must be the God-Emperor of Rohn.*

"Surely you see the justice of my position," the stranger said in a loud, harsh bass voice. "My army saved you. Without my men, you and your girl-knights would be sitting in some memorial harem to the Immortal King."

Falorn winced at the words, but the queen sounded unruffled as she responded.

"Perhaps, but then, perhaps not. Your men never actually *fought* on my behalf. The tide of the battle had already turned when they entered the field. While their presence is welcome, and I was very glad of their arrival on the field of battle, you and they have hardly made great sacrifices. You have lost only three of your ten thousand men: one who drank himself to death, and two whom your brother hanged as rapists."

"The battle was lost. We both know it. You might have lasted another day or so, but do you think the Seven Kingdoms forces would have withdrawn without the encouragement of my ten thousand fresh soldiers who you mock? Ha!"

"Certainly your troops contributed to Cathan's victory, by their presence, if not their actions. And I have offered ample compensation for their services. I am willing to grant the trade terms you request. The land grants you ask are impossible, of course. If I wanted to give up Cathanese land, I wouldn't have fought this war. Too many of my people have died."

"The real question concerns the five cards which you hold, though, doesn't it?" asked Alex. Falorn had nearly forgotten the swordsman's presence at the table.

"I must have them!" the God-Emperor shouted.

""You cannot. The price you demand is too high. It would cost my people a great sacrifice, and you have made no such sacrifice on my people's behalf. The trade terms are more than ample price for your soldiers' service, along with my offer to pay the costs of your expedition."

"That is not enough. I will have the cards and the lands as well. You have enemies enough as it is. You ought not be so anxious to create another antagonist out of one of your only friends."

"I think that will not happen," the queen said in a silky voice. "My kingdom has its troubles, to be sure. But we have had good harvests these past three years, and we will get the harvest in this year despite the fighting. Even with the price of feeding my army and yours, and the cost of all the blood spilled along the Calambria this summer, my people will not starve. But some of your folk ought to have a care for their livelihoods, I understand."

"What are you saying?"

"Rohn is a large country. Your wealth is your land, more wealth than you have folk to tend to. So much virgin, wild land: who knows what might live there? Who knows what might come out of the forests along the long, long frontier, especially if the flower of the Rohnan knighthood were far, far away fighting in another land. Trolls might ravage whole villages, for instance, or carry off children and sheep. Fishermen might return home with their boats and catches to find that merfolk had risen from the sea, destroying homes and stealing away wives and daughters to replace what the fishermen took from the waters. Why, anything at all might happen."

"Someone has been talking," said Alex, quietly.

"Someone will die for those words. I'll kill the messenger who told you myself," said the God-Emperor

"Your troops are half packed up to leave already. How could it be a secret? Your men would go by themselves if you didn't give the order. They will fight to protect their homes and loved ones as my soldiers did, men *and* women. The stories are all over camp and castle; every servant knows the telling of them." The queen said the words very matter-of-factly, as if it really were common knowledge. Falorn wondered how much of what she said was true.

"I have not left yet. My men will obey me."

"Of course they will. They know that you are a good ruler, who will hold the well-being of his people ahead of his personal interests."

"You are wrong. My men will obey me because they fear what I will do to them and to their families if they fail to please me. You want people to love you. It will cost you your throne. Let them *love* your half-wit husband—make them *fear* you. Only fear will keep you on the throne."

"We each rule as we think we must."

"This is not over."

"Of course it is not. We will be talking a great deal, particularly with the increased trade which will result from the terms I am giving you. Ruinously unfavorable terms, as you well know."

"We must go, brother," said Alex. "The terms are good. The cards will come to you if you are meant to have them."

"The cards are my due!"

"Later, perhaps. Not now."

"This is not over," the God-Emperor said to the queen. "We will talk again. I will have them whether you like it or not."

"Perhaps," the queen answered. "As you say, we will talk of it again. We will have many, many months to talk of it."

Falorn and Ryal kept silent until long after the rulers finished their luncheon. He and the Hellein returned to the courtyard circuitously, without attracting the notice of any Rohnan soldiers. To Falorn's relief, Kennemen's troopers no longer held the watch. Their replacements wore blue roosters appliquéd onto their red surcoats.

The new guardsmen returned Falorn and Ryal's horses without question or incident, and the two of them rode on their way quickly.

Cirque awaited them in the tent. While they rinsed off travel-dust, he set out a meal of cold sausage, fruit, and cheese, as well as a bucket of ale. The three of them sat down to eat and quietly discuss the events of the day.

"I spoke at length with Lord Dianeme," Cirque told them. "She seemed quite agreeable to my proposal, and assured me that the queen favors it as well. I suggested we leave quickly, to take advantage of the weather. She proposed we wait until after the Rohnans leave, so as not to arouse suspicion. She agreed to provision and equip us as well."

"What do we need?" Falorn asked. "We still have most of the supplies from our trip in, other than food. I checked it all before we left the Summer Palace."

"I think we may need somewhat different provisioning for a trip into a hostile country in secret. A mule train might be a bit more . . . conspicuous and cumbersome than we would prefer. And you will want new armor, I am certain."

"What happened to mine? I've been meaning to ask."

"What little of it remained unpierced or unbroken was cut from your body, somewhat unwillingly, by surgeon-priests of the Cathanese church. A number of links they removed from within your wounds. No doubt it has been melted down for scrap by now."

"Oh." A part of him felt sad at the loss, one more thing that had not survived the battle.

"We will be taking two of your acquaintances along, Lord Dianeme assured me: the Queen's Knights Elise of Whitecliff and Tirya Huntmaster." It took a second for the names to register in Falorn's mind;

Elise had never mentioned her home or lands, and he'd never asked her full name.

"I'm glad," Falorn said.

"I am glad as well, although I think neither of them has much love for Helleinen. You will be able to continue the reading lessons you have been forced to neglect. A knight should be educated. Too many people listen to his words."

"Not you, too, Cirque. I'm the same person I was. I haven't changed."

"We all change, Falorn," said Ryal. "You humanfolk change faster than Helleinen, but we change as well. You were knighted by a great man. It would change anyone."

"I was unconscious!"

"Falorn," said Cirque, in a different tone of voice, "there are lessons you should learn here. Lessons you *must* learn, I think, if you want to keep hold of what is valuable in yourself. Whether you were aware of it or not, you have surrendered much of your freedom through your actions. If you wish to keep what little is left, you ought to be more aware of the consequences of what you do."

"What are you talking about?"

"You fought very well in what the Cathanese are now calling 'The Battle for Freedom' or 'The Battle of the Calambria.' This was a very important battle, for more reasons than you will have thought of. Many people fought in it, from many nations, which means a great many more will want to hear about it. A number of kings, princes, and powerful nobles fought and acquitted themselves well. This is precisely the sort of battle that songs are written about: a battle which nobles and common folk are both interested in, so minstrels will have an audience whether they play for princes or for taverns. Do you understand so far?"

Falorn thought of the battle songs he had listened to growing up in his father's inn. Traveling musicians often stopped on their way through the Free Duchies; even beyond his quarrels with his secretive father, much of Falorn's desire to leave home grew out of their songs about heroes and battles and monsters and kings. He nodded slowly.

"Good. Now how much do you remember of your role in the battle?"

Falorn remembered the first three days, when he'd mostly watched and guarded—he remembered everything up until he and Elise rode into the thick of the battle. Only snatches of what followed remained. He described his memories to Cirque: guarding the low stone wall with a handful of unarmored levies for days while the battle raged around them without touching their position; cavalry troopers overrunning his soldiers, who turned and ran without a fight; killing three troopers and chasing after the others; reaching the rear of the battle just as the Cathanese lines began to crumble, and plunging inward into the thick of the fighting, following Elise's mad charge. After Falorn finished, the Hellein looked at him expressionlessly and began speaking again.

"There is much that you did not see, or could not know, even if your mind remained clear. Although I doubt anyone could have fought as you did with an unclouded head, except at the price of madness. Many people saw the battle from the surrounding hills: soldiers not in the fight, wizards and their retainers, servants, nobles too old to fight, a few wives and children, as well as the scribes and minstrels who came for the sole purpose of recording what happened along the Calambria. I saw a great deal myself, and some of those people have told me many things that I did not see.

"Zaren and Stennet fought boldly and well, but they were being pushed back. Calathan had broken their line in the center and almost cut it in two. Just at the point when the whole center seemed ready to break and run, a handful of knights charged into the advancing enemy, with you at their head."

"Elise led the charge, not me."

"That may be true, but already no one remembers it. Elise fought bravely, but she is not the hero minstrels want. She is not the sort of woman whose story brings a great many coins thrown into one's hat. People will see the parts of a story that they can believe. And they also saw you fight on even after the rest of that handful of charging knights— including your Elise—had been stopped. You fought your way through a duke's household guard, killed the duke and his son, and took their colors. Then you killed every man of his household who tried to take them back from you, until none of them remained.

"Even that was not enough. You kept on fighting until you reached the last of Zaren and Stennet's men who still stood in the center. They rallied around you, even though they'd been beaten a moment before. With you at their head they fought off attack after attack, and after all of them went down you kept on fighting from on top of a pile of bodies. You took another set of colors before the Rohnans came onto the field and the Calathanese and their allies withdrew. Beneath the pile of bodies, the queen's men found Stennet's colors and the Queen's Own Standard which his soldiers held in the center of the battle; you saved them both from being captured."

"Cirque, you were there, too. You make it sound like I did all of these things by myself."

"I was there at the end, but no one except for my own people will remember my presence in the battle. For the same reason, no one will remember that you were unconscious when Alex knighted you."

"I don't understand."

"You are a hero. In songs, heroes either die or are rewarded. Since you did not die, it is only fitting that you be given honors by the greatest living hero present on the battlefield, especially since he arrived on the hills with the Rohnan vanguard, in time to see you charge and fight. Had Alex not rewarded you, I suspect eventually the queen would have. Since so many people witnessed your actions, she would have had little choice. No one, however, will sing about the murky circumstances under which Alex granted your title, or that you weren't conscious to accept the honor, or to agree to any of the obligations that would normally accompany a grant of knighthood.

"The Church and its archbishop are important patrons of the arts in Cathan," continued Cirque. "No one would dare offend them with a story that would not be believed anyway. For the same reason, any references to Helleinen will be removed from songs in Cathan. I suspect that a more appropriate tale of you meeting with Alex on the field of battle will be substituted in place of the inconvenient course that events actually took.

"What little freedom you had was based on anonymity. You have lost that in Cathan. Before, people only pursued you because they wanted your cards. Now they will follow you for other reasons as well."

"Alex said that."

"Alex remembers only the people who pursue with swords. He has had to kill too many of them. Most of the people who follow you will not want to kill you. Many will want you to marry their daughters, or will want to borrow money from you, or will want you to take their children on as apprentices. Others will want you to endorse their causes or political factions. Only a few of them will try to kill you."

"Not much of a future for a hero, is it?" Falorn asked.

"It's not that bad," said Ryal. "You're only a hero in Cathan, and a villain in a few other places. If it makes you feel any better, you're still nobody in our land of Delerian."

"Thanks, Ryal," said Falorn

"It's not that bad. Sometimes when it seems like everyone hates you or is trying to kill you, it's nice to know you're a hero somewhere."

"Which shall prove a comfort," said Cirque, "as we prepare to go into a country where everyone hates you or is trying to kill you."

"Don't worry too much, Falorn," Ryal said. "Word doesn't travel that quickly. Most of the people we meet will never have heard of you, and the ones who have won't know what you look like. Especially since we'll all be in disguise."

He dreamed of Sera that night. Not of Sera as she was now, emotionally distant and soon to be gone from his life, but of Sera as she had been, vulnerable and lethal and loving and evasive all at once. Falorn dreamed of the nights he'd spent half-conscious in her bed after she'd rescued him from attackers in the city her now-dead father had ruled so brutally. He dreamed of the first night they'd made love, and of how he'd woken up the next morning to find she'd abandoned him.

Why do all the people I care about lie to me? But it wasn't just the people he cared about, Falorn knew. Zaren had never lied to him. Nor Elise or the Helleinen, as far as he knew.

Mostly, it was his father's lies and evasions he'd run away from, only to find the rest of the world just as full of half truths. When the lions entered his dreams he slept more peacefully, but Falorn still awoke with a generalized longing to be with Sera again, or with his family. *Neither of those things is going to happen for a while*, he forced himself to admit. *And then only if you're very lucky or get a lot more skilled.*

He spent the day on the practice fields.

The horse's neck quivered slightly, and its ears twitched. The twitching distracted Falorn momentarily from the long files of soldiers trudging through the mud below the hill. He reached down and scratched the soft brown hair on the horse's neck; the animal shook its mane by way of encouragement. He went back to watching the Rohnan soldiers below as he continued to scratch the horse's flank absently.

The sun sat low and red against the western horizon. Falorn had been on the hilltop since just after dawn, sometimes watching from horseback as the troops passed below him, other times dismounting and sitting on the low stone wall where the militiamen under his command had died. It had drizzled all morning, giving way to a fine mist by afternoon. Now though, an hour before sunset, the rearguard of the Rohnan army marched under a clear sky, toward the orange and pink surrounding the fading sun.

Falorn had seen Sera only in passing in the days while the Rohnan army prepared to leave. Once she waved at him from a distance when they saw each other across a well-trampled field of half-loaded wagons. On two other occasions he saw her at Alex's side. On this day, although he had spent all day watching the soldiers and wagons push their way through the trampled mud left behind by the Rohnan cavalry, he had not seen her at all.

He pulled his wet cloak more tightly around himself. Although the fabric shed most of the warm rain which had fallen earlier, he still found himself shivering, even in the late summer heat. The horse whickered as Falorn started to shake slightly; it nosed his leg for attention and he rubbed a hand through the animal's mane, not bothering to wipe the tears from his face. He felt a deep emptiness in the pit of his stomach. In the morning he had wanted to ride down and meet Sera, to tell her he would follow her anywhere, that he never wanted to lose her again. But as the day went on, and the stream of troops below eddied and flowed away toward the distant plains of the Rohnan Empire, he just sat and watched, either from the horse's back or the hard, wet stones of the wall.

A horse snorted nearby. He turned in the saddle and saw Elise and her mare a dozen feet away, silhouetted against the sun. He thought to wipe away the wetness on his cheeks, but then left it. Her eyes focused on the troops below, and he wondered what she thought about the withdrawal of the God-Emperor's forces.

Neither of them spoke for the next two hours. Long after sunset, when nothing could be seen below them and even the clattering of baggage wagons had faded away into the darkness, they rode down the opposite side of the hill together. Their mounts carefully picked their way over the damp loam toward the cookfires of the camp. When Elise extended her hand, Falorn took it, and held it as they rode side by side.

4

Mountain Paths

Two weeks later Falorn found himself in the mountains on Cathan's northern edge, although far to the west of the pass which had brought him from Delerian the previous spring. He, Ryal, Cirque, Tirya, and Elise had left the horses with their escort of troopers from the Queen's Own Guard in the foothills a day behind them. Now the five of them walked along a wide path carved into the jagged rock.

"This was a trade road, once," Elise told him as they trudged forward. The two of them walked together while Tirya scouted ahead. Behind them, the Helleinen watched the rear and handled the mules. Despite Ryal's talk of disguises, they carried equipment much like that which had served them on their trip from Delerian, where the Helleinen lived; at the moment, food and relative ease of travel seemed more important than deception. They planned to leave the mules on the other side of the mountains, and exchange their clothing for the more inconspicuous Seven Kingdoms-styled garb on the creatures' backs. Falorn thought of the new shirt of chain links one of the mules carried as well, and smiled wistfully, remembering all that he'd gained and lost along with the other two sets of armor he'd briefly owned.

"There's not much travel this way anymore," Elise continued, "but once, this led to one of the richest lands in the world."

"Aren't the Seven Kingdoms still rich?"

"They're big. They're rich in some ways. But I'm talking about long before the Seven Kingdoms. This used to be dwarven country."

"Dwarves? Like in the carnival?"

"Like in the *legends*. They were fantastically rich. They had cities made of gold and precious stones. They built this road, and it's still standing a thousand years later. They could make anything: swords like you can't imagine, covered with silver and sapphires, but lighter than any steel and impossibly sharp. They made chalices and crowns and jewelry and lamps which burned for weeks at a time with barely any oil. The dwarves were the most remarkable craftsmen in the world, and Cathan fed them. In return for grain and animals, the dwarves sent caravans of treasure over this road and down the mountain. They gave us the crowns which the kings and queens of our country still hold sacred. They made Cathan rich, and together Cathan and the dwarves were strong."

"What happened?" Falorn asked. He realized that he'd never seen the king or queen wear a crown at all.

"I'm not sure. Some of the dwarves are still here. A few of the mountain shepherds still trade with them. The rest of them . . . I don't know. Maybe they found some other source of food, or the gold from their mines gave out and they moved on, or they died of a plague . . . I just don't know. Trade gradually slowed down, and then almost stopped completely. Cathan turned to other countries for trade, and forgot about the dwarves, mostly. I think the dwarves mostly forgot about us, too. There's no bad blood between Cathan and the dwarves; we're more like sisters that have drifted apart over the years, married to different men and raising different families. Lives grow apart, and so do countries."

"That's sad," said Falorn.

"That's life."

They set up camp an hour before dark on a flat open space to the side of the road. An old firepit remained in the center of the clearing, as well as a stone-lined well, dry for many years. A roofless shed of unmortared rock had once held charcoal for travelers, but now yielded only a nest of field-mice, which Cirque accidentally disturbed.

While the Helleinen prepared a fire, Tirya unpacked and strung three bows. Falorn watched the tall, black-haired huntmaster as she worked. She wore thigh-high boots which accentuated her height and her leanness. A long, thin rapier always hung at her side. *I wonder what passed between her and Sera,* Falorn wondered as he looked at Tirya. *They seemed to like each other instantly, traveled together—and now Tirya never even mentions Sera's name. Is it just that she got what she wanted from Sera when she brought Alex's troops? Or did something else happen? I wonder if I'll ever know?*

Falorn waked over at Tirya's signal. She and Elise had begun teaching Falorn to shoot, in addition to his reading lessons. The Cathanese shortbow came to him less easily than swordsmanship, but he worked hard at it.

"Come on Cirque," Falorn called out as he picked up a bow. "You should try it." He couldn't resist needling the Helleinen warrior a little. *I don't think I'll ever understand what he has against bows.*

"I have tried it," the light-haired Hellein replied, "many times. Before you were born. I find the bow to be an . . . inelegant weapon. It lacks grace. Politeness dictates that you at least face whomever you are trying to kill at close quarters."

"What's politeness got to do with fighting?"

"Your late friend Zaren's philosophy of fighting is not the only way, Falorn. We Helleinen live a long time. We must be able to live with the consequences of our actions for many, many years."

Falorn winced at the mention of Zaren. *You're alive and he's dead— that's what you're saying. There's so much I could have learned from him, so much more I wanted to know about him. Why did he have to die?*

Or is it that you don't want to hear what Cirque is really saying?

Falorn lifted his bow and began shooting, loosing arrow after arrow to distract himself. Elise and Tirya stood to either side, shooting as well. Elise spoke only a few words to him, correcting errors in form. Tirya said nothing at all as she buried arrow after arrow into the center of her target. The Helleinen found things to do around the camp, and quietly ignored the whole process. Although they worked together willingly enough, Falorn suspected the Helleinen and the Queen's Knights still loathed each other.

They shot at targets until full darkness enveloped the campsite. "Come on," Elise said afterward. She walked over to her pack, which lay on top of a waist-high pile of rocks. A bullseye lantern sat on a slightly higher stone, so that its light shone over Falorn's shoulder as he sat next to Elise on the rocks. Elise reached into her pack and removed a battered, cloth-covered book. She unwrapped the waxed sailcloth that pro-

tected it, and set the volume on Falorn's lap, opening it to where he'd finished the previous night. "Time to read," she said.

She watched over Falorn's shoulder as he found his place and began
to read. The book was a ponderous volume of Cathanese history, filled
with intricately illuminated text and painstakingly rendered scenes of
heroes and battles. Based on the covers, worn from heavy usage, he suspected the volume to have been a favorite of hers as a girl. He read slowly, pronouncing the words out loud. He still had to carefully sound out
most of the words, but a few he now recognized on sight. He caught
many of his own mistakes now and corrected himself when he could.
Elise talked very little, content to listen to his painful rendering of the
Cathanese past. She helped only when he became hopelessly lost in a
word or passage.

Sometimes he caught a faraway look in her eyes, as if she remembered other times, when other voices read the book aloud to her.

Midway through their third afternoon on the mountain, Tirya found a
city. She waited for them at the end of a smooth stretch of stone path,
accompanied by two short-legged men. Both of the men wore iron helmets and heavy suits of chain mail over their barrel chests. Dark, full
beards concealed what little of their faces showed through the nasal-
guards of their helmets. Axes hung at their sides. They carried crossbows,
and spoke in a throaty language that only Tirya seemed to understand.

"The dwarves welcome us to their mountain," she translated, "this
tribe of dwarves, at least. Their city, Vazkara, lies only a few hours ahead.
They invite us to dine and shelter within their city walls tonight, before
we resume our journey."

"Should we accept?" Falorn asked her, fingering his bowstring
absentmindedly. He had taken to carrying one of the bows with him until
he became more accustomed to it. He needed more practice before he'd
be able to bring down the sort of small game they saw on the mountain,
but he thought it best to try as much as he could now. They'd brought
plenty of arrows along, and he wanted to be at least a passable shot
before they reached the Seven Kingdoms.

"I have already accepted. To refuse their hospitality would be the
worst sort of insult." Falorn thought of the cannibal Baron of Golden
Reeds's hospitality that he'd experienced a few months previously, but
said nothing.

They walked behind the dwarves, at first following the main road but soon turning onto a secondary thoroughfare. The trail narrowed, although it remained wide enough for four men to walk abreast. High stone walls towered on either side of them; the road seemed to have been carved into the heart of the mountain as if a river had cut a channel into yielding stone. In places, the stone cliff-walls which loomed above them had been polished, or even carved. Mostly the rock appeared rough, but the surface of the road felt smooth as river pebbles beneath their feet.

If the dwarves told Tirya their names, she didn't pass the information on to the rest of them. She spoke to them easily enough, it seemed to Falorn, although sometimes she or one of the dwarves had to repeat something a few times before the meaning became clear.

"That's a shepherd's dialect she's speaking," Elise told him. "Her people come from this part of the north, and they've always traded a little with the dwarves. It's an old, old language; many of the children no longer learn it at all. It dates back to before the foothills of these mountains were part of Cathan at all. Her people had their own country once."

He looked at the black-haired Tirya, talking quietly with the thick-bearded dwarves, and wondered how many secrets her people still held.

The secret of the approach to the city held a little longer, at least; by the time they arrived, darkness had fallen, and the dwarves led them through featureless, impenetrable gloom. Even with the cards' help, Falorn could not say where they left the trail, nor could he find a single landmark in the darkness. They stopped at a heavy wooden door, iron-bound and framed in stone against the very side of the mountain itself. The front entrance and visage of the city—if anything like a city gate existed—remained hidden to them.

"This way," Tirya told them, as the dwarves led the way through the door and into a wide passageway of raw stone, which yawned forever onward in front of them. One of the dwarves retrieved a torch from some hidden receptacle, but the dancing flame barely illuminated the corridor for a few paces on either side. The second dwarf spun a long, brass key in the elaborate locking mechanism of the door behind them. A bolt clicked into place, and the dwarf tucked the key back within the metal links of his byrne.

The mules' shoes clattered and echoed as the Helleinen led them inward. The corridor bored straight into the mountain, but passages broke the walls on either side at frequent intervals, so many passageways that Falorn quickly gave up counting them.

When they finally turned into one of the side corridors, he had lost track of the time they had spent in the darkness. Falorn focused on the thief card in his pouch as they walked. The now-familiar spindly blue lines appeared along the stone walls and floor, tracing out hidden patterns in the smooth-seeming stone. Hallways shifted and twisted around him, like the burrowed paths of snakes or ants, seemingly without reason or pattern. Some of the passages were smooth, with friezes and chiseled carvings that danced and shifted in the flickering torchlight. Other walls looked rough, like natural fissures with added stone floors. The tunnels might have been recently carved, or they might have been older than the road outside; even with the aid of the blue thief card, Falorn could distinguish no signs of wear.

They passed door after door in the patternless halls. Sometimes doorways gaped open into more of the endless twisting passageways, or into great vaulted chambers whose contents the torchlight only hinted at. In other places they passed a baffling array of doors placed in the hallways with seeming randomness: a round, green-painted door placed three feet above the floor; another in the shape of a massive pair of lions struggling—fighting each other with fangs and knife-edged claws—carved of some exotic wood; a wide square panel with brass hinges at its top, intended to be pushed outward rather than opened; an intricately carved series of panels depicting armored dwarves, all crowned with gold or laurels, the finely worked wood inset with gems and gold leaf. Falorn lost count of the splendid doors as quickly as the side passages, and could only begin to guess at what might lay behind them.

The dwarves finally paused in front of a wide, round portal plated in polished metal. The door's convex surface glittered, reflecting glimpses of their faces back at them in the wild light of the torch. Falorn's eyes widened as he looked at the door more closely: *silver* covered it, more silver than a rich man's table would hold. A blue glimmer outlined the edges and center of the metal hemisphere.

One of the dwarves fished a key out from within his armor—not the same key which had sealed them in the caverns, Falorn noticed. The knobbed brass wand slid into the middle of the silver mirror where it bulged slightly outward, although no keyhole marred the center of the polished door. Without any further visible motion on the dwarf's part, the silver panel opened noiselessly outward. The dwarf motioned them inside, and one at a time, they stepped through, each ducking slightly to pass the circular entrance. The mules followed reluctantly, coaxed by Cirque and Ryal.

They walked into darkness, but as Falorn and the others crossed the doorway, light suddenly bathed the chamber. A glow emanated from the polished gray-black of the stone ceiling, brightening gradually till they might as well have stood in daylight. Bits of quartz and silvery metallic minerals in the walls reflected the light, making the room glitter.

Tirya and the dwarves remained in the hallway. When Elise looked quizzically at the black-haired hunter, Tirya shrugged and gestured slightly toward their hosts.

"They want me to come and get the food," she said. "They tell me we are to eat and sleep here, and that their leaders will talk with us in the morning before we leave." One of the dwarves pushed the doorway closed. When it shut against the rock wall, no seam remained—only smooth, polished stone, without a trace of silver.

Falorn glanced around the rectangular chamber. To his right, a trough carved of some jadelike stone extended across one of the shorter walls, the length of two tall men. Fluted decorations covered the front of the trough, twisted designs interwoven like knotted clumps of earthworms, but bearing no chisel-mark or other sign of their carving. He assumed that water filled the pale green stone of the basin, and when Cirque led the two mules over to water them, the animals confirmed his suspicion. Falorn walked over to help the Hellein unload their supplies and set out fodder for the mules.

While the pack animals ate, he walked around the room. Tables and wide, low chairs littered the floor, all carved from the same translucent green stone. Intricate patterns embellished all of the furniture, although not the same carvings; they seemed to be the work of many dwarven artists, or a few extraordinarily diverse ones. Velvet and satin cushions covered the chair-seats, and deep green velvet curtains allowed for a few alcoves of privacy along the long rear wall. Piles of velvet cushions and thick, quilted blankets leaned against the far left wall.

All of them wandered the room, but no one spoke. Falorn wondered if the others shared his unvoiced suspicions of the dwarves. As if catching his thoughts, Cirque looked at him and nodded grimly. The Hellein walked over to Falorn's side, and spoke quietly in his ear.

"Odd that they take the trouble to walk us through such a roundabout maze and then lock us in, is it not? They do not seem to be the sociable sort; even the Queen of Cathan invited us to dinner."

"I wondered myself," said Falorn. "Tirya seems to think they're being hospitable, though it's an odd way to treat guests."

"An odd hospitality indeed," Cirque replied.

"Best to speak softly of it, though?" Falorn asked.

"It is nearly always best to speak softly when one is a guest. I doubt anyone will overhear us now, but speaking softly in strangers' houses is a good habit to cultivate." Cirque looked like he might say something else, but the swish of the door opening halted his words.

5

Mountain Hospitality

Falorn looked up as Tirya stepped through the doorway, carrying a silver tray piled high with covered dishes of silver and gold. She set the tray down on one of the tables and returned to the door. One of the dwarves handed through a second tray, and soon a third. After the third trip, the door shut quietly behind her, once again fading into the stone as if nothing but solid rock backed the polished surface of the wall.

More than a dozen covered plates and bowls filled two tabletops. A third table held pitchers of wine and mead, as well as silver mugs.

Ryal lifted the first of the covers and breathed deeply in the steam that rose from within the golden bowl. The smell of lamb and roasted nuts filled the room. His expression suddenly took on an odd character; the Hellein's nose quivered like a rabbit's, and Falorn couldn't help but wonder if he were about to witness another transformation like the time Falorn had seen him turn into a wolf.

"Falorn, would you come here for a moment?" Ryal asked, waving Elise and Tirya away from the food. "I would like to show you something."

Falorn walked over to the table, mystified.

"Tell me," said Ryal, "what do you smell?"

Falorn thought for a minute before answering. "Lamb . . . nuts of some sort . . . mint, I think . . . I'm not sure of anything else. The mint's pretty strong."

"It is strong. There's a reason for that. Do you smell something else, almost like the mint, but not quite the same?"

Falorn realized he did. A sharp scent distinguished itself from the mint when he concentrated on the odors. When he focused on the steam rising from the dish, he could tell the two scents apart easily.

"It's strong, I think," he said. "It fades into the mint if you're not looking for it, though."

"*Fool's mint*, it's called, for just that reason. My people have a longer name for it, and there are other words as well, but *fool's mint* will do nicely." Ryal smiled wryly. "It is because of this herb that a wise man will not sit down and talk with his enemies over a mug of mint tea, or a leg of lamb with mint jelly."

"What does it do?"

"When it smells as strongly as this? It kills, quickly. I think perhaps we should eat from our own stores tonight."

"This can't be!" said Tirya. "They promised hospitality. My people and they are friends!"

"You're welcome to try it," Ryal answered. "I might be wrong. If not, I have an herb which counteracts fool's mint in my pack. Allow me to fetch it before you sample the food, please. And avoid the other dishes, if you can. I may not have antidotes for all of them."

Falorn noticed that Tirya came no closer to the plates as the elf walked over and began rummaging through their baggage. He withdrew several pouches and fastened them to his belt before returning with one in his hand.

"Here," he said, pushing the small leather pouch into Falorn's hand. "You should have this in case I'm not here the next time someone tries to poison you. The leaves inside should be crushed and boiled in water. The tea which results must be drunk before the final stages of fool's mint poisoning; once the convulsions set in, it is very difficult to induce the victim to swallow anything, and it may do little good anyway." Falorn looked at him almost blankly.

"But. . . ."

"Don't worry, take the pouch. I have more, and it grows commonly where I live. Besides, you're far more likely to be poisoned than I am."

A thrashing sound from across the room distracted them. One of the mules lay on the ground, its limbs flailing helplessly. The other had sunk to its knees. A mask of foam clung to its muzzle.

"That," said Ryal, "is what the final stages of fool's mint poisoning looks like. It affects many animals as well as humans, although it's a rare animal that will eat it in the wild state. It's a sad way for faithful animals to go, although I doubt we'd have been able to bring them out of this place anyway. Odd that they would poison the animals, too, and not just us. Unless their goal is to keep us from leaving this mountain, rather than just to rob us."

"We have a little time, I think," said Cirque. The blond Hellein gathered up his weapons and began adjusting the fit of his belt and boots. "The dwarves will give the poison time to work before they arrive to finish us off."

Falorn checked his weapons, and reflexively felt for the pouch at his chest. The cards continued to give off a reassuring warmth, but Falorn felt the need to touch their container as well. He looked around the room while Cirque and Elise began sorting through their equipment, pulling out things that might be easily carried. *I wonder what Cirque has planned. A fight would be ridiculous; we can't stand against a city full of dwarves while trapped in the center of a mountain. That means we have to escape.*

He looked closely at the wall behind the vanished silver door. No trace of a seam remained. The blue glow had disappeared, as if the magical door did not exist on this side of the wall at all. Falorn stepped over to the long inner wall and began slowly walking along its length. He ran his hands along the smoothly polished stone face as he stepped, feeling for subtle gaps or uneven surfaces, while focusing all his senses on the gray-black rock.

He found the first door within one of the alcoves. A hidden panel in the floor flashed blue for a moment, then slid aside as his hand found the catch that freed it. The space beneath led nowhere, a narrow shaft no longer and wider than a man's coffin. Thickly piled sacks filled the hidden closet. Falorn slit the edge of a seam with his knife and a thin stream of pale green powder trickled out. The powder smelled of mint, or something very like mint. A search beneath the sacks revealed nothing; Falorn snorted in disgust and moved on. Elise stopped for a moment to investigate his find, but she quickly gave up as well and returned to sorting their packs.

"Over here," he said, ten minutes later. The wall behind the now-scattered column of blankets and pillows revealed a faint horizontal seam, wide enough for a small man or dwarf to pass through easily. When Falorn sprang the catch, a section of wall slid upward in near silence, the stone revealed as a thin veneer. Beyond, a narrow staircase spiraled downward.

"We should move quickly," said Cirque as they began descending the stairway. "They will not be long in following, once they fail to find our poisoned bodies. You should lead, Falorn. You seem to have a talent for discovering paths." Tirya glowered somewhat at this last statement but said nothing. They all bore light packs of salvaged supplies; Ryal and Elise carried lanterns for illumination.

A profusion of passages branched out from the stairwell, no less confusingly than the hallways they had passed through on their way into the mountain. A slight blue flash caught Falorn's eye, and he left the stair to follow it. Other glimpses of blue led him further into the warren of dark tunnels, deep within the mountain. Sometimes the color appeared only for an instant. At other times the blue aura outlined a section of wall or floor where a hidden door lay, or a pitfall which needed to be avoided. As they continued through the tunnels, Falorn found himself moving more confidently. Now and again he picked out an obstacle before the telltale blue flash.

The blue light began to grow stronger as their walk through the twisting paths lengthened. Finally, Cirque motioned for a rest. Falorn sat along with the others, but he felt no fatigue. Only a thin coating of sweat touched his forehead. *I could do this forever*, Falorn thought, and knew it was the lion cards that gave him strength. Blood sang within him, warming muscles and making his face flush slightly. The others looked tired, though.

"We need not worry so much about pursuit for the moment," Cirque said. "I think we have passed far enough away from where they left us that the dwarves will not find us quickly. We can now concern ourselves less with pursuit, and more with escaping the mountain itself." Cirque pulled himself to his feet and checked his weapons before motioning for Falorn to take the lead as they walked onward. The lions and other cards seemed to tug him forward, although Falorn's mind wandered through the tunnels around them. *We have enough food and oil for days, if necessary, but these tunnels look endless. I wonder where all the dwarves live in these endless catacombs. I wonder how many dwarves are left inside this dungeon of an underground city. There can't be that many of them anymore. Surely not the thousands and thousands who must have spent generations digging the miles of tunnels, stopping to polish and ornament the rock walls as they mined.*

The cards are leading me somewhere, Falorn realized. The blue glow seemed to magnify and direct his path. He remembered the way Sera's fiancé had caught him, and hoped he wasn't walking into a similar trap. *I can't sense any other cards like mine ahead, but that doesn't mean anything. For all I know, I might be leading all of us straight to the hall of some dwarven king or war-leader.*

The tunnel narrowed until they had to crawl through it; even a dwarf would have had to crouch as he walked. The passage angled downward sharply. In places Falorn had to brace himself to keep from sliding forward on the rough stone floor. Raw, unfinished rock scraped and irritated their exposed skin as they crawled along it. No decorations or flourishes marked the walls or floor of the tunnel. Even the labyrinth of side passages had vanished; the tunnel twisted like a hooked fish trying to escape, but they could only leave by turning around and crawling back through the narrow way they had already come.

Ahead, the blue light grew stronger. The color became a steady mask through which Falorn's vision filtered.

Only gradually did he realize that the others saw light ahead as well. At some point while they crawled forward, the illumination had subtly shifted from blue to a shimmering golden glow.

The tunnel ended abruptly in a ragged pit. Twenty feet below, a wide room glowed from the illumination of dozens of lamps, each emitting a steady, flameless light. Falorn saw sacks and barrels and piles of chests heaped against the sloping rock walls of the chamber. Stands of spears leaned against the walls. Gemstones reflected back at him from the hilts of swords that sat gathered in bundles and corded like so much brushwood. Nowhere, in all the vast chamber which spread out below him, could he see any sign at all of a living thing.

"What is it, Falorn?" Elise whispered from behind him, blocked from the view by his body. "What do you see?"

"It's . . . I think it's what we came here to find."

"Then what are we waiting for?"

"I'm not sure how to get down."

Falorn inched backward and allowed Elise to squeeze past.

"Oh, for the love of Marré!" she said. "This is easy." She slithered backward a few feet and unfastened her pack. A coil of thin cord sat on top of her supplies. She quickly looped the end around an outcropping of rock and fastened it with an odd sort of knot. After refastening her pack, she carefully maneuvered around and began crawling backward toward the edge of the hole, the cord gripped loosely between her hands.

"Elise," Falorn said, "look out. You're getting close to the edge."

"Of course I am. Haven't you ever climbed a rope before?"

"No."

"We'll lower you down, then." With that, she seemed to drop herself through the hole. After what seemed like too long, he heard a voice.

"It's all right. I'm down," said Elise from below. "It's all clear down here; no sign of dwarves. Let Tirya come down next, and then have the elves lower you."

All of the others knew how to climb. After his dizzying journey to the cavern floor—he had to jump the last few feet when the cord ran out—he watched the Helleinen scurry effortlessly down the rope. Falorn felt as if he traveled within a company of squirrels.

Gold littered the floor. The luminous glow of the lamps reflected from coins which had escaped from long-rotted sacks. Throughout the broad cavern, the floor shimmered with an uneven carpet of coins and bars of gold, silver, copper, and other metals Falorn didn't recognize. Chests of silver plate and gilded oddments lay in uneven columns stacked against the rough, unfinished walls, heaped around with sacks and piles of loose treasure. Here and there bright colors broke the solid sheen of precious metal: rolled tapestries and thick rugs, spilled bags of rare dyes. None of the silver or brass coins or implements scattered around the vast cavern looked tarnished at all, as if the air itself cleaned and polished the treasures within the storeroom constantly. From the puff of breeze at his cheek, and the faint blue glow which permeated the whole room, Falorn wondered if that might actually be the case.

Unlike some of the tunnels, the walls of the storehouse remained unpolished, unsmoothed rock. Except for the lamp-sconces, Falorn saw no obvious signs of construction or improvement in the chamber. The floor felt smooth and even beneath his boots, but he couldn't tell how much of the cavern had been carved out by dwarves, and how much by forces of the gods and nature. No attempt had been made to keep the storehouse secure or secret; dozens of tunnels and corridors honeycombed its walls, none of them barred or sealed in any way. Treasure filled some of the side passages as well.

No one seemed to have used the storehouse in many years. Everything within looked old but unworn, the accumulated detritus of long-forgotten wealth.

Without thinking about it, they spread out in the room and began looking through the vast layers of treasure. Falorn made certain to remain within sight of the Helleinen. *I wonder how long it will be before the dwarves find us? It could be moments*, he knew, *or it could be never.* He looked around hurriedly, wanting to drink in the sight of so many precious things before they again had to flee.

Something glinted blue at his feet. He picked up a small pouch and poured it out into his hand. Rubies glowed back at him: deep, deep red like blossoming roses in the golden light of the room. Falorn replaced them in the pouch and tucked it into his pack. He took a double handful of gold coins as well, as payment for the dead mules and the new armor he'd left in the room above. *That's the third mail shirt I've lost since the beginning of the spring.* He shook his head ruefully, then looked back down suddenly. *There may be better armor down here*, he realized, and began poking through the chests.

He found human-sized armor in the second chest below a half dozen dwarf-sized byrnes: a pair of mail shirts studded with gold and crested with silver eagles at the shoulders. *That's too much*, Falorn thought. *I couldn't wear those.* He kept looking, poking through an endless sea of copper coins and long-lost signet rings of washed electrum. A telltale blue flash drew him to a decaying sack at the foot of a nearby wall. For a moment, a loud voice distracted him. Looking to his right, he saw Elise and Tirya marveling over a sword of some sort. The sack flashed again, this time a brighter blue, as if insisting he investigate its contents.

Mostly, more old coins filled the sack. They poured out when the decaying cloth fell away at his touch, a river of copper stamped with the faces of long-dead kings. Falorn sifted the coins aside. A small wooden box remained within the ruins of the sack. Untarnished brass ornamented the corners of the box. It had a brass lock as well, but no carvings or ornamentation.

Falorn concentrated, wondering how to work the lock mechanism. Something flashed blue, leaving spots dancing in front of his eyes. When his vision cleared, no glow remained around the box's edges, but the lock no longer looked complex. Looking at it, Falorn traced the course of its mechanism within his mind. The lock released at a quick twist of his knife blade.

Sapphires glittered, dazzling Falorn as he opened the container's lid. Cut stones filled the box: square emerald-cut sapphires the size of his thumb; cabochon-cut star sapphires; round stones and triangular stones and one long oval stone half as long as his index finger. He almost closed the box again, but then the stones suddenly began to glow from beneath.

Carefully, Falorn set the box down. Removing the pack from his back, he took out the pouch of rubies, and carefully emptied the sapphires into it as well. Only after he had drawn the cord and replaced the pouch within his pack did he dare look at what now lay revealed on the blue velvet bottom of the wooden box.

Storms moved across the ivorylike faces of the four new cards. On the first, wind-tossed, sea-green ocean attacked emerald-masted ships. Beside it, sheets and torrents of blue rain tore through a cobalt thicket of blue trees, tearing at foliage and ripping wooden giants from their blue forest moorings. On the third card, a thick red snow fell on a buried crimson mountainside, endlessly falling from the billowing red clouds that enveloped the mountain's top and threatened to swallow the world. The fourth card held a golden wall of windborne sand that blew across the rolling golden dunes of a vast desert. The sand scourged away everything in its path, sweeping off tents and golden-thatched roofs, and scouring the flesh from men and animals till nothing remained but the bleached gold of their bones, half buried in the engulfing gilt sand. Falorn looked at the four cards, and the storms carried him away.

Gradually, he emerged from the hold of the tempests that buffeted his soul. The other cards asserted their presence as well, after being momentarily lost in the power of the four storm cards together. He found himself on his knees. Falorn shook his head, and felt drops of sweat run down his brow as he did so. Only after he had put the cards safely with their fellows against his chest did he dare look up once more.

Cirque stood above him. The Hellein extended a hand to help Falorn stand up. He took it gratefully, surprised at how much the cards had weakened him.

"Thanks," he said. He accepted a sip of water from Cirque's flask. "I don't quite know what happened."

"So once again, the cards seem to find you, young Falorn. They all seem to find you."

"I hope not. Maybe you're right, though. Do the others know?"

"Only Ryal and I. The other humans are busy looking at swords and other weapons. Ryal will give warning if they notice you."

"I didn't mean to keep it a secret. . . . I just meant . . ."

"Better, perhaps, if you keep a few secrets, Falorn. Your friends will understand, and the enemies disguised as friends will use fewer of your own words against you."

"You and Ryal and Elise and Tirya are friends," Falorn said. "I'm certain of it."

Maybe Cirque is right and I shouldn't be so trusting, Falorn thought. *But I have to trust someone, and these are people who have had my life in their hands. If I don't trust anyone, I'm not really any different from my father, keeping secrets from his family, never telling anything unless he had to. It's no way to live.*

"Better, perhaps, to be a little less certain of your friendships as well." He put an arm around Falorn's shoulder. "Come now. It is time to fetch the others and leave this place."

6

Mountain Voices

❖⋮❖

Once they left the treasure room, Falorn found tunnels to lead them from the mountain. The web of blue lines seemed to illuminate the underground passages before his eyes, as if he had traveled the subterranean roadways for years and learned their every nuance. In the two days that passed before they emerged from the depths of the ancient city, they saw no dwarves at all.

"I wonder how many dwarves live there anymore," Elise speculated to no one in particular. "Maybe only a few of them are left."

In the dark closeness of the tunnels, even her quietly spoken words echoed faintly. Privately, Falorn half-agreed with Elise, but none of them kept watch any less vigilantly as a result of it.

Once they left the inside of the mountain, they did see dwarves again. Small shadows stole from faraway rock formations to shoot bolts from long crossbows, and then returned to hiding before Elise and Tirya's arrows could reach them. These dwarves looked nothing like the underground city dwellers. They wore furs, even in the mildness of the mountain summer, and kept their beards trimmed short. The dwarves seemed more interested in keeping the travelers moving than in seriously attacking; the occasional crossbow shots never hit, and the mountain dwellers never pursued their quarry in any numbers.

After the third day, Falorn saw no more dwarves. That night, a familiar howling disturbed the darkness.

"Not wolves again," Falorn said to Ryal as they sat on watch around a low fire. They wore cloaks against the slight chill of the mountain evening. Around them, the others slept.

"I'm surprised we haven't heard them sooner," Ryal answered. "The dwarves must have driven them away from their settlements."

"I suppose I should be glad we're through with the dwarves," said Falorn, though wolves seemed only a marginal improivement

"Until the trip back, anyway. Unless we decide to try and cross the other border, into Delerian. I suspect your Cathanese friends will want to travel back to their queen, though."

"That's a long way off. We'd best finish the trip out before we worry about the journey back." Falorn rubbed his hands together to warm them. "The wolves don't seem to be getting much closer."

"No. Give them a little time, though. We have another week in the mountains yet."

"That's comforting."

The wolves remained distant, but their howling continued throughout the night. Even later, when Falorn lay wrapped tightly in his cloak and trying to sleep, he found himself lying awake, listening to the faraway, plaintive music of the wolves.

Tirya waited in the middle of the path. The sun shone high in the sky, above the peaks which surrounded the high, rock-strewn valley they walked through. The mountains teemed with summertime life along their little-used route. Mountain goats grazed peacefully on the slopes. A single ram eyed the travelers warily, but otherwise the animals showed little fear. Plants colored the mountainside a thousand shades of verdant green, poking up between every rock, and taking over some of the pebbly slopes entirely. Everywhere, Falorn saw hares and birds, as well as the occasional bear.

"There's trouble ahead," Tirya said as they drew close. "The pass from this valley is full of traps. I'm not certain whose."

"What sort of traps?" asked Elise.

"All sorts. Pitfalls, springing spikes, hidden nooses, flying spears, bear-killers, everything. Someone likes to catch travelers."

"But there aren't very many travelers through here," Falorn said.

"Well, someone doesn't like to miss any of them. Be careful and stay close to me from here on. Don't step anywhere I haven't told you is safe."

They walked forward carefully, Tirya in the lead. She picked her way across the broken ground carefully, probing grassy patches and pausing to check rocky clumps for hidden triggers. Falorn walked a little behind her, concentrating all his attention on the ground ahead. He spotted the first obstruction just before Tirya threw a hand up and called out to the rest of them to stop.

"These rocks are rigged," she said, gesturing with her bow. She stepped back and extended the bow once more, this time tapping one of the rocks slightly. Falorn jumped as a spear leaped from the ground. Tirya nodded when he looked to her, and he walked over to investigate. Five feet of wood protruded from the ground, a roughly trimmed sapling thicker than his arm. Whoever set the trap had carved the end of the spear into a barbed point, and coated it with some dark, viscous substance, which looked and smelled like tree-sap.

"What kind of poison is that?" he asked Tirya.

"I don't know. Why don't you ask your elf friend? He seems to know all about poisons."

Falorn looked over at Ryal, who just shrugged.

They walked on until nearly sunset. Tirya picked a rocky, easily guarded campsite, partway up a slope and walled on three sides. From the only approach to the camp, Falorn could look down the overgrown, rock-strewn hill. From below, they could not be seen easily. Anything coming at them would have to pick its way up the slope, exposed all the way to bowshots. They built only a small fire, back in the rocks where it would attract no attention.

Falorn lay awake late, listening to the wolves. In the sheltered campsite, he could see only the rocks around him. He considered all that had happened since he had left his father's inn, what he had gained and what he had lost. All the while, the howling continued. *I wonder what it would feel like to spend my nights running free, with no cards to worry about, and with all the woods and mountains to howl defiance at? I left home to learn about the world, but I still don't seem to have many choices. Other people want to make my decisions for me, or force me into doing what they want. I wonder how much freedom there really is out there?*

When he finally slept, Falorn dreamed of lions. One of them stood on either side of him, guiding his way along a narrow, mountain path. He tried to force the lions away, to negotiate the rough trail by himself. Shaking their manes sadly, the animals finally walked away from him. They sat down to watch him from a few paces down the trail. But as soon as they left, he realized he could no longer move at all. Falorn swayed uneasily, knowing that if he took a step in any direction, he would lose his balance. He wanted to call the lions back from where they sat quietly gazing at him, but even opening his mouth might throw him off balance. Falorn stood there terrified, teetering at the edge of nothingness.

He woke at dawn, and instantly clutched at the pouch of cards hanging around his neck. Sweat had dampened the leather, and he felt clammy all over. Hurriedly, Falorn used water from one of the waterskins to wipe away the perspiration, and with it the memory of his dream.

That morning they continued their cautious journey, stopping frequently at Tirya's insistence to disarm and destroy traps.

"But won't that tell whoever set them that we're on the mountain?" Falorn asked.

"Of course it will. But it will also make him work a little harder to catch the next person."

"You sound like you want us to get caught."

"We'll handle whatever we find. It will be good practice for you with your bow, or with that sword of yours." She patted the hilt of her new saber, a sleek-bladed weapon she had found in the dwarven treasure hall.

"What if they're Seven Kingdoms soldiers? Won't that give us away?"

"They'd have to live long enough to report us. And besides, it would be worth it to have a shot at whoever set these traps."

Falorn wondered how the Queen of Cathan would feel about her knight's sentiment, but surprisingly the Helleinen agreed with Tirya.

"People can't be allowed to set traps like this," Cirque told him, although the Hellein would not elaborate further. Falorn had a feeling that Cirque *hoped* Seven Kingdoms soldiers were responsible, although they remained miles from the empire's border. He remembered the hatred the Helleinen had for the Seven Kingdoms—the only thing the Helleinen and Cathanese knights held in common, and the only thing that allowed them to cooperate.

Late that afternoon, Falorn spotted the answer to the mystery of the traps. He had become good enough at spotting the traps that he wandered slightly wide of Tirya's path, to give himself more practice with the blue thief card. He stiffened suddenly, and shivered as he recognized the shape of the wide footprint in the soft ground in front of him.

"Tirya, come here. You should see this." He stood completely still, looking down at the mark near his feet.

"What is it?"

"Troll spoor."

"It is, at that," she said. "A big one."

"A smart one, too," Ryal added, coming up beside her. "Most trolls don't build traps in their spare time."

"We'll have to be sure to tell it how smart it is before we kill it," she said with a grimace. "Do you have any other useful suggestions?"

"How about you tell us where to find it, now that Falorn's found something for you to track it by."

"I think I'll do that. It's a pity you're not much use in a fight."

"I'm useful enough, when it's necessary. I prefer to leave the fighting to those who have no other craft."

"Enough, Ryal," Cirque said, putting a hand on the wizard's shoulder. "Save the anger for the troll." Tirya stared hard at both of them for a long moment, then turned sharply away to begin following the tracks. Elise followed closely behind her. The two whispered urgently back and forth, but Falorn could make nothing of the words.

The trail took them upslope, away from the path they had been following. Falorn stepped awkwardly up the rocky incline, unused to walking with an arrow on his bowstring. Elise and Tirya moved more smoothly, prepared to straighten, draw, and shoot in one fluid motion. Falorn found himself envying their relaxed poise in the face of danger; he had to stop and focus to bring his mind back onto the troll itself.

He wondered where they would find it. Falorn scanned the rocks around them as Elise and Tirya walked up the slope ahead of him. Cirque stood twenty paces to Falorn's right, looking equally vigilant.

As Elise and Tirya reached the top of the slope, the creature leaped out from behind a rock. With both arms, it swept a massive branch in a broad arc. Falorn heard a sickening thud as the club crushed Tirya's side. The force of the blow sent her into the air. She hit Elise, who fell down, her bow and helmet flying in opposite directions. As the creature lifted its club for another blow, Falorn stood, drew, and shot.

The arrow flew wide.

The troll didn't even seem to even notice as it landed another blow.

Falorn dropped the bow and pulled out his sword. Cirque charged beside him as he ran forward. The club swung again and again. Tirya's body jounced with the impact of each stroke.

The creature looked up as Falorn drew near. Falorn and Cirque spread out slightly, to prevent both of them from being hit by the same blow.

Ducking the first swipe, Falorn ran closer, swinging his sword as he lunged within the creature's guard. His blade bit into the troll's side. The creature dropped its club and reached for Falorn with thick, gray-taloned hands. At the same time, Cirque slashed at the back of its knees.

Falorn batted at the creature's hands with his sword. Blood sprayed and dripped on his face. The troll drew his hands back; Falorn saw he'd cut them badly. He swung again, before it could connect with a crushing blow. His blade opened a wound on the creature's chest. The troll swung with a giant open hand.

Before the blow fell, Falorn knew it would hit.

The paw slammed into him, and time stopped.

All the breath rushed from his lungs.

He flailed his arms as he flew through the air, somehow holding onto his sword. The ground rushed at Falorn. He twisted; time passed with incredible slowness. His shoulder banged on the grassy dirt, barely a hand's length away from the edge of a wide rock. The rest of his body hit the ground, and he bounced once.

His head fogged. Falorn wondered when time would speed up again.

He could see Cirque battling the troll, darting in and out with agonizing slowness. Nothing hurt, but Falorn knew any moment pain would come. He tried to move his arm, and found that it responded, but much too slowly. His ears rang. He heard someone speaking to him, but he didn't know who, and the words meant nothing.

Falorn sat up slowly, and his head began to clear. He flexed his shoulder, and forced it to move in spite of the stiffness. His sword arm still worked for the moment. He would worry about the extent of his injuries later. Pushing himself to his feet, Falorn began staggering back toward Cirque and the troll. His ears still rang, and dizziness pushed at him.

The battle had shifted. Cirque still fought, but someone else had joined him. *Or something*, Falorn realized as he sank to his knees, unable to fight back the dizziness any longer.

The wolves are here, he thought, trying to make sense of his still-muddled vision. *No, they aren't wolves. They can't be wolves. Wolves only have four legs.* He wondered if he had fallen unconscious, and was imagining the fight. Delirium brought on images like this. But his head ached too much, and he had to fight hard to see at all. What he saw had to be real.

Three other creatures had joined Cirque in the fight. They had bodies like enormous grayhounds or whippets, wide ribcages tapering into narrow abdomens. Each had six legs, like a dog's legs, but somehow more flexible. They leaped in and out of the fight with impossible agility, biting and worrying at the troll and then jumping back before it could turn its attention to them. They had heads like wolves, but longer. Their tall ears stood straight up, and pointed forward. Short brown hair covered the animals, except at the top of their backs, where an iridescent stripe ran down the ridge of each creature's spine. The colors shimmered and shifted as the sun caught them; they seemed to glow in impossible ways, each one differently. Falorn had never seen anything like those colors or patterns, or heard of any animal that bore them.

The three animals tore at the troll. Next to them, Cirque's sword dipped and flashed and bit at the creature, drawing blood again and again. A fine mist of blood covered the Hellein, and red ran freely off the muzzles of his canine allies. The ground shook as the troll fell. Another wave of dizziness slammed into Falorn, and his head lolled on his shoulders. His hand hit the ground as he fell, scraping the rock. This time he felt the pain, and as he lay on the ground, his shoulder and side began to throb as well. He cried out in spite of himself as the pain grew. Even with the cards, the tearing at his side threatened to overwhelm him completely.

Somehow, it didn't surprise Falorn at all when the first voice began speaking in his head.

Who are you? the strange voice asked. *Are you dying?*

"I'm . . . I'm . . ." He realized he had spoken out loud, without knowing where the voice had come from. He looked around, and saw no one. Had he imagined the soundless words?

A cold, wet nose poked at his side, where exposed skin showed through a tear in his ruined tunic. The nose tickled, and he almost laughed as he turned. Pain shot through him, stifling the laugh. Dark brown eyes looked at him, concerned.

Can you speak? the voice asked. *Are you mute?*

"I just said. . . ." The doglike face looked at him quizzically.

Can you understand me at all?

The voice is coming from the dog! Falorn realized. *No. It can't be. There must be someone hidden. This must be magic.*

What's a "dog"? the voice asked.

A dog is . . . why am I answering my own thoughts? I'm going crazy. I must have hit my head when I hit the ground.

You didn't hit your head. You hit your shoulder.

Who are you? Falorn asked.

I asked you a question. What's a "dog"?

A dog is a creature that looks like whatever is in front of me. Only with fewer legs and without the glowing stripe. Who are you and where are you?

I'm standing in front of you. I have six legs and a stripe. I assume from your tone that you don't like these "dogs"?

I like dogs well enough. But I've never met a talking dog before.

That explains your confusion. I'm not a dog.

Oh. What are you?

I might ask you the same question. I and my people live in these mountains. You and your companions are strangers here.

Falorn shifted slightly and sat up, wincing as he did so. *Thank you for helping Cirque kill the troll.*

Cirque is your companion?

Yes. Haven't you talked with him? Where is he?

One of my companions speaks with him now. The concept that appeared in Falorn's mind wasn't exactly "speaks." He understood that the creature meant the kind of conversation they were having now. Apparently, they could only communicate with one other creature at a time. *Cirque is tending to your wounded companion. She has regained consciousness.*

Elise . . . or Tirya? He remembered the horrible pounding of the club after his missed bowshot. He knew the creature could only be referring to Elise.

I do not know how they are called, except for Cirque. What are you called?

Falorn. My name is Falorn.

Welcome to the mountains, Falorn. My name is Sbashe.

Falorn struggled to his feet, ignoring the pain. Warmth surged in his chest. He hoped the lions would help him heal fast, that his injuries weren't serious. An arm steadied him.

"It's all right," Ryal said. "Lean on me. I'll help you."

Falorn allowed Ryal to support him. The six-legged animal walked on Falorn's other side, but no more voices appeared in his mind. He concentrated on setting one foot before the other. He could see Cirque in front of them, leaning over a woman's still figure. Another of the six-legged creatures sat beside the two of them, legs folded beneath itself.

The Hellein looked up as they approached. Elise lay on the ground, her lower body covered by a cloak. Cirque had bandaged her head and propped it up. The knight's eyes remained closed, but her chest rose and fell with even, regular breathing.

"I'm glad you are with us again, Falorn. You should be lying down alongside Elise, however. Ryal looked at your wounds earlier, and I think they are not serious. But they could become so without rest."

"When did he look at me? I thought . . ." Falorn realized that the sun had moved in the sky. He must have lost consciousness from the pain.

"You slept for a few hours after the fight. I looked at you, and attended to a few other matters, while Cirque spoke with the corgets."

"The . . ."

"Our allies are called corgets. I have heard of their people before, although I had never met them."

"The one I met is named Sbashe."

"I met her as well. She helped me earlier, while you slept."

"Tirya . . . ?"

"She is buried. The troll's body is gone, and his lair searched. A camp has been set up nearby, where the rest of the corgets await us. We will move there as soon as Elise awakens. Until then, you should sleep as well."

"But I . . . but . . ." Falorn had trouble forming his words and thoughts. He felt someone helping him as he lay down, but he had no idea who. The images in his mind became muddled, then seemed to break up. Soon, he saw only lions, one on either side of him, once again guiding him along a narrow trail. *You're back,* he thought. *Praise be to Mara, you're back.*

Sleep, traveler, said the voice in his head. It took a while before he realized the voice did not come from one of the lions. Almost against his will, Falorn found himself obeying. The lions settled beside him and someone covered him with a cloak as he slipped into darkness. Throughout the night, lions prowled his dreams, green and blue and gold creatures who tossed their manes impatiently as they stalked the cold, rocky ground around his sleeping body.

7

Freedom

Falorn woke up to near-darkness, as the last sunlight faded from view behind the surrounding mountains. One of the corgets lay beside him.

Hello . . . ? he thought. *Sbashe?*

Yes, he heard the familiar voice in his mind, recognizing the subtle undertones now. Sbashe's voice had a slight lilt to it. He wondered if the corget was a he or a she. *Didn't Ryal say something about . . .*

I'm a she, the voice answered, *but you're hardly my type.*

I'm sorry. Falorn flushed red. *I didn't mean to speak out loud.*

You didn't. But I read your surface thoughts. You may as well get used to it.

It's a little embarrassing.

Embarrassing? The corget seemed unfamiliar with the concept.

I'm not sure I could explain. I'm just not used to it, that's all.

You'll explain some other time, perhaps? Now we must walk a little ways. Food and a warm bed are waiting.

Falorn stood up slowly. He stretched out his arms carefully, grateful that the pain in his side had subsided somewhat. He felt warmth against his chest, and reached reflexively to touch the pouch.

71

What is that you wear around your neck? Sbashe asked. *I can see that it is magical, but your pouch and tunic hide it.*

You can see that it is . . . ?

Magical. Something created by a wizard, or by supernatural forces. Surely you've heard of magic?

You can see magic? asked Falorn.

Certainly. Can't you? How can you wear something you cannot see?

I can see them, but I can't see magic, Falorn said.

You are a strange creature, said Sbashe, then lapsed into mental silence as they walked toward the prepared camp.

The camp sat in a narrow, sheltered valley, between two high rock faces. Dozens of corgets prowled between the stone walls and in and out of the caves that lined the rocks. A fire glowed from one of the cave mouths, and Sbashe led Falorn toward it. Cirque and Ryal sat at the fire, across from a triad of corgets who sat back on their haunches. In the darkness, the creatures looked as much like upright leopards as dogs. Elise leaned against a cave wall nearby, a thick cloak wrapped tightly around her.

Cirque looked up and waved as Falorn and Sbashe approached.

"Welcome, Falorn," the Hellein said. "There is food here for you. Come, sit by the fire. We are talking of our journey, and of what we have seen."

They sat around the fire and talked for hours. The conversation followed curious paths; voices appeared in Falorn's head, and for a long time he could not distinguish from which of the corgets each voice originated. All of them had an unnerving way of staring into him with deep canine eyes. They asked about his travels and he told them everything. He could hide nothing from them, and he tried to recall events as fully as he could to avoid confusing them. Most of all, the corgets asked about the cards, and their magic.

Falorn spread the cards out in front of the fire, where the corgets could see each one as he told them of its discovery. *They see far more than I do*, Falorn knew. Magic appeared clearly to them, detected by senses he and the Helleinen did not possess. They nosed and sniffed at the cards, but revealed nothing of what they discovered. Falorn asked what they could tell him about his cards, but Sbashe and her fellows seemed not to understand the question; they could not explain what they knew to someone bereft of their sensory ability.

By morning only Elise had gotten much sleep. She dozed near the fire, fading in and out of consciousness. Although she responded to Ryal's healing attempts, nothing could take the place of rest. Falorn and Cirque gladly accepted the corgets' offer of another day or two of hospitality. They slept, and continued the discussion with the corgets when they awoke. Other corgets hunted for them all, and guarded them against mountain predators.

In two days, Elise felt nearly strong enough to travel. Tirya's death had made her somber, although the Helleinen seemed strangely unaffected. Falorn wondered if they would care about his death. He supposed not; long-lived creatures like the Helleinen probably accustomed themselves to deaths among their shorter lived fellows, sudden or otherwise.

Falorn walked with Sbashe among the hills at the valley's edge. The corget's odd, six-legged gait had taken a while for him to get used to. Despite Sbashe's canine appearance, she walked more like a cockroach than a dog, with the front and back legs on one side moving together with the middle leg on the other. When she ran, she moved all three legs on each side together.

Falorn had been practicing with his bow while he and the corget conversed. The memory of his missed shot lay heavily in his mind.

You couldn't have saved her, you know, said the voice in his mind.

What do you mean? I missed the shot, Falorn answered.

I can see that. Do you really think you could have killed a troll with one shot?

I don't know. I might have distracted it, at least, Falorn said.

Maybe, said Sbashe. *That's not much of a bow, though. Not for a troll, anyway.*

It's all I had.

I think the troll's first blow killed her.

Then why did it keep hitting her?

Trolls aren't very smart.

This one was smart enough to set traps all over the mountain.

You're right. Probably she was still alive.

Falorn sat on a rock, dropping the bow beside him. He buried his face in his hands.

Death comes to us all, Sbashe said.

I could have saved her. If I'd looked a little harder, I might have seen the troll before it attacked her. I have the thief card. I could have used it a little better.

These things are true, said the corget. *Your carelessness prevented*

73

you from saving her life. But there's little you can do about it now except practice harder to prevent its happening again. The Helleinen suspect that you let her die on purpose.

What! Falorn jumped up without thinking.

They thought you might want to eliminate one of the people spying on you, or to prevent the Queen of Cathan's knights from betraying you when you finished your trip.

No!

I can see that, said Sbashe. *It was simply a faint suspicion. Nothing they would ever tell you, I'm certain.*

Elise would never steal the cards. I can't believe it. She wouldn't, would she?

I don't know. I can read nothing in her mind. She can speak to me, and hear what I say, but I and the rest of my people hear nothing of her thoughts. We heard nothing of Tirya's thoughts before she died, either. I can't tell you whether or not they were plotting against you, only that the Helleinen think they might have been, and suspect that you let Tirya die because of it. The corget didn't seem to think there was anything unusual about being unabloe to read Elise's thoughts.

Even if they were planning something I wouldn't have let her die if I could stop it, Falorn said. *The cards aren't worth it.* He thought of the troll's club falling again and again. *I don't know if anything is worth it.*

I can see that is how you feel. I hope you choose companions worthy of your trust and fellowship.

Everybody keeps telling me that!

You are a focus of great magical forces, Falorn. You can't see them, but you cannot escape them, either. Something is gathering around you. It draws the cards to you, and it draws people to you, some of them friends and some enemies. It draws us to you.

Does that make you friends or enemies? Falorn might have kept the bitterness from his voice, but not from the thoughts that underlay his words.

I am a friend. I have kept the wolves away from your camp, and my people have guarded you these last three nights. You have traveled a long way, and done well with the magic you have been given. I see great forces around you. I would like to observe them further. You will bear watching in the days to come.

Does that mean you're coming with us?

You will need a companion and watcher on the path you are traveling. I could use another friend.

I will be a friend to you as long as you use your magic well. The forces in your hands could twist you like that troll if you misuse them. I would tear out your throat before I would allow that to happen.

Sbashe bared her fangs, and Falorn felt a sudden stab of fear. The feeling vanished just as quickly. Falorn reached down and picked up his bow before standing up.

I think I'd better practice some more while the light holds, he said.

That's a good idea. The next troll might find you in front of it.

Falorn said nothing. He shot at practice targets until a few minutes before sunset, leaving only enough light to recover his arrows one last time. Even after the light faded away, he practiced drills with his sword, stopping only when darkness covered the valley completely.

The journey resumed two days later. Elise walked normally with no signs of injury, although she seldom spoke. The Helleinen spent much of their time on the trail conversing with Sbashe. Falorn scouted ahead for long hours, as Tirya had.

He let the power of the thief card fill him as much as he dared. It showed him hidden groves and trails, allowed him to follow animals to their lairs if he wished, illuminated the mountain more plainly than the inks that colored the thick history book Elise had left behind in the dwarven mountain. Falorn had to catch himself constantly to keep his mind on the trail, rather than follow the tantalizing glimpses of hidden places and things the magic of the card revealed.

After three days of walking, they found themselves descending from the mountains into a series of ridge-lined valleys. Occasional villages appeared, wherever the soil could support farmers.

The fourth valley was wider than its predecessors. A castle guarded its far edge, where a road cut through the hills. A slow-moving river ran through the center of the green valley. Falorn could see a pair of villages along the river's edge, and a few clusters of houses elsewhere.

"Is this the Seven Kingdoms?" Falorn asked Elise.

"I don't think so," she answered. She'd spoken a little more in the last day or so. "There's no flag above the castle, and a Seven Kingdoms castle would have a garrison unit's flag, and the commanding officer's flag if he was a noble. Besides, the path from the mountains isn't guarded at all. I think it's one of the little independent principalities the Seven Kingdoms tolerates on its borders."

"It's an awfully small country, if that's what it is."

"I imagine we'll find out soon. We have to go through it."

They left the trail before it wound down into the valley. Falorn saw no shepherds or guardsmen in the hills nearby, but the presence of the path implied occasional traffic. As they skirted the valley, he saw no activity at all, however. A miller's wheel turned in one of the river villages, but no smoke rose from smithy, forge, or oven.

"Where is everyone?" Falorn asked Elise. She shrugged in response.

They walked less easily as they neared the castle. Falorn kept the power of the thief card in his mind, looking for ways to approach the fortress undetected. He found himself slipping from one hidden place to another, always staying under cover. The others followed behind him, spread out just a little, while Sbashe ghosted close behind him.

Falorn kept his bow out and strung as he walked. Elise held her bow at ready as well, and the Helleinen walked with swords drawn.

The castle—a small shell keep—guarded the valley's only outlet, overlooking all approaches to the road through the hills. A drawbridge stood open, bridging the weed-filled moat. No sentries stood on the walls or on the parapets of the castle's lone tower; if any guards patrolled the keep, they hid themselves well.

A thin wisp of smoke rose from a single chimney within the castle.

"Where *is* everyone?" Falorn said again, but then he spotted a flicker of movement from the corner of his eye. A small, dusty flag flapped in the wind beyond the castle, near where the road began.

"That is a Seven Kingdoms military flag," Cirque said. "One belonging to the Kingdom of Ilessa within the Seven Kingdoms. It signifies a small unit of footmen in a provincial garrison troop."

"How do you know that?" asked Elise.

"I have fought in and around the Seven Kingdoms for many years. It seemed prudent to learn their signals, insignia of rank, and military structure. They take exceptional pride in their organization and seldom deviate from it."

"They're organized, all right," Elise said, spitting onto the ground. "Like a cancer."

"Cancers can be fought. One must be very precise about which tissue one removes, however."

She ignored him and turned to Falorn. "Let's see what those soldiers are doing. Can you get us close?"

Falorn looked at Cirque and the Hellein nodded slightly. "I think so. Stay right behind me."

He began crawling quietly through the underbrush, following the tiny blue flashes the card gave him, working his way toward the flag without showing himself to any observers. Elise and the Helleinen followed him closely. Sbashe made her own silent path, out of their sight.

Fewer people than he expected stood beneath the worn leather pennant. Two soldiers circled the perimeter of a small temporary camp: three tents, a firepit, and a cleared area at the edge of the packed-earth road. The sentries carried loaded crossbows and wore short broadswords at their sides, but they paid little attention to the camp's edge.

Beneath the flag, an officer and a man in an unadorned black robe spoke with three old, bearded men. Three other soldiers guarded a cluster of seven or eight children just at the edge of young adulthood. Around their necks, the children wore leather collars with brass rings. Nearby, on the road itself, someone had laid out a length of chain, crossed at regular intervals by yokes. Each yoke contained an open brass ring with two holes in it, so that a pin could be hammered in to seal it closed.

Four more soldiers sat at a fire nearby, roasting pieces of chicken on spits. The soldiers wore boiled-leather cuirasses over black tunics and quilted black skirts. Their boots looked worn, and their uniforms bore signs of patching and repair. Falorn crawled carefully back, until he and the others passed beyond hearing of the sentries.

"Bretek damn them for fake soldiers," Elise hissed urgently, "They're *slavers!*"

"Slavery is against the law in the Seven Kingdoms," Cirque said.

"What did that look like to you, elf?"

"I saw what you did," Cirque responded.

"Well, are you with me?"

"What are you going to do?" Falorn asked Elise.

"We can't just let them take those children."

"What can we do about it? Don't we need to sneak into the Seven Kingdoms without anybody noticing?"

"We could be long gone before anyone knew. In this remote place, it might be months before anyone missed these soldiers." Cirque's eyes shone with an odd, predatory gleam as he spoke.

I wonder what hurts feed his hatred of the Seven Kingdoms? thought Falorn, not for the first time.

"We'll spread out and shoot first," Elise said, "starting with the sentries. Then we take the others out before they know what hit them."

"I'm not sure this is what we're here to do," Falorn said quietly.

"We're here because there is a war on," Elise answered. "We have to fight that war when and where we have the opportunity." For once, she and Cirque seemed to be in agreement. Ryal and Sbashe said nothing.

They're going to attack with or without me, he realized. Reluctantly, Falorn nodded his head. "I'll do it."

As he drew close to the camp again, the sight of the huddled children saddened him, but he still had no wish to kill the soldiers.

The officer's discussion with the bearded old men had finished, and the soldiers had begun to strike camp. The officer and the black-robed man spoke quietly together as the guards packed the weathered tents and other equipment, stowing them on four tethered mules. One of the guards drew his sword and prodded the collared prisoners to stand up with the flat of his blade.

The soldier whistled as a well-developed girl stood up.

"Look ha' this," he said, waving a pair of his companions over. He touched the point of his sword to the back of the girl's neck. Sliding the blade downward, he slit the seam along the back of the tunic.

A thin trail of blood glistened in the wake of the weapon, catching the afternoon sun where it shone on the pale skin of the girl's back.

The soldier put his free hand around the girl's neck, forcing her head up with his thumb. Her eyes rolled back in fear as he caressed the side of her face. She had bound her light brown hair up with a ribbon, the same black color as the soldiers' clothing. The soldier's hand slid downward along her collarbone.

He pulled it forward suddenly, and her tunic ripped with a loud tearing noise. He continued to pull until the garment hung in two shredded pieces from the girl's shoulders, revealing her breasts and belly.

The soldier stepped back a pace and bowed while the girl stood shivering.

"Hain't she a piece?" he said. He stepped forward again and cupped one of the girl's breasts in his hand. "An hain't this somethen' ta make the march home a little happier?" Someone clapped nearby. Falorn looked away from the soldier and realized the girl had captured the sentries' attention, as well as that of everyone else in the camp. The officer and robed man watched silently. Neither seemed inclined to stop the proceedings. The old men stood a little apart, with their backs turned.

I have to act now, Falorn knew. Cirque and Elise waited on his signal. Steeling himself with another look at the shaking girl, Falorn stood, drew his bow, and shot.

The arrow lodged in the first sentry's chest. The man fell, gurgling, as Falorn shot again. His second shot flew over the officer's head. He heard a scream from the second sentry as Elise's arrow struck. A hurried third shot grazed the officer's arm. Falorn dropped his bow and charged into the clearing, drawing his sword as he ran.

"Bandits!" the officer screamed. "Get the bandits!" He lacked the thick accent of the soldiers.

Falorn ran for the group of children. The soldier fondling the girl gaped at Falorn. He barely raised his sword as Falorn swung, slicing him open from throat to belly. Blood sprayed Falorn and the girl.

He turned to face two other soldiers, who advanced on him with swords drawn. One jabbed at his guard. Falorn feinted at the man's side, drawing the soldier's blade down. The second soldier stepped forward, inadvertently blocking his fellow's retreat. Falorn switched his grip and swung his sword two-handed. The blade sliced through the first man's arm and collarbone, and into the second guard's unprotected face. Both men went down.

He looked around for another opponent.

All of the guards had fallen or fled. The black-robed man lay dead beneath the flag. Falorn saw no sign of the officer. Near the fire, Sbashe worried at an armored corpse. The children still huddled together, the one girl holding both arms over her chest and shaking as if with a palsy. Blood leaked from between her hands.

The dying soldier lay at her feet, still twitching slightly.

"Falorn! Come here," said Elise. "This man says he is the leader hereabouts."

"Some leader," Falorn muttered, not loud enough for anyone to hear.

He walked over to where Elise and the elves stood with the three bearded men. He could hear the oldest one speaking, a tall man of about seventy years, his face spotted and wrinkled where the thick white growth of beard failed to cover it.

"I am the Hist of Tasaria," the man said as Falorn drew close. "By whose leave do you trespass on my lands?"

"What?" said Falorn, in spite of himself. "These are your lands?"

"You dare to question my authority?"

"Are these your people?" Falorn asked, pointing to the children in their collars.

"Not anymore."

"What do you mean, not anymore? Either they are or they aren't."

Part of him knew that he had no business talking to a born noble this way, but he was too angry at the sight of the chained children to care. *I could have been one of them a few years ago*, he knew. He had left behind friends in his father's village who looked very like the terrified boys who stood rooted in place at the edge of the road.

One of the other old men began reaching for a weapon at the sound of Falorn's words, but the sight of Cirque's drawn blade stayed him.

"They grew up on my lands, but they have been given over for service elsewhere. They are my people no longer."

Wait, Falorn realized. *I'm a knight. I have every right to talk to him this way.* "What are you talking about?" he asked the old man.

"Have more respect when you speak to your betters, little man."

"I'll decide who my betters are. Hist or no Hist, no man who sends his own people off for slaves is my better."

"You know very little of the world," the old man said. "Sometimes the price of freedom is high. I choose to pay in flesh. You prefer payment in blood. Sooner or later the blood will be yours."

"Fine words for a slave dealer. What do they pay you to pimp your own people? Or do you just like to watch the soldiers play with them?"

"Have a care what you say, little man. I am still a ruler, and you are a traveling sword. My kingdom may be small and poor, but yours is smaller still. You carry your wealth on your back, but I must do what I can to protect mine."

"What are you saying?"

"I have a very powerful neighbor, one which could easily swallow me, despite certain treaties signed in my grandfather's time. They allow my Tasaria its freedom, as long as it pays just tribute every two years."

"Tribute in slaves?"

"There are no slaves in the Seven Kingdoms. Every second year they require all children who have reached the age of thirteen winters, for thirty years' service at the discretion of the Immortal King. At the end of their service, they are free to return, or to accept a grant of land elsewhere."

"Have any of them ever come back?"

The old man said nothing.

"What will you do with them now?"

"They are mine no longer. I will turn them over to the nearest soldiers. If need be, I will march them down the road myself. Their freedom is already forfeit, for the next thirty years. If I do otherwise, the freedom of the rest of my people will be lost as well."

"You mean your own freedom."

"Call it what you will. I cannot fight you. I have no young men left. But I have to live in this land after you leave to find your deaths. When you're gone from my country I will have to find a life for my people."

"I care more about their freedom than yours," said Falorn, pointing at the children.

"You have done nothing to save them." The old man drew himself up to his full height, as if trying to summon whatever shards of dignity remained him. "I am the Hist of Tasaria," he said. "You have trespassed on my lands and insulted my person. Take your contraband with you if you must, but leave my lands now. I will not warn you again."

Falorn turned and walked away in disgust.

"We will leave presently," he heard Elise say from behind him. "I fear you have saved your kingdom only at the cost of your soul. That is a hard trade to make."

"I fear it is the only trade I was offered. Any man would do the same in my place."

"Perhaps," said Elise, "perhaps."

Falorn walked over to where his pack sat in the brush, retrieving his arrows on the way. Tearing a strip of cloth from one of the bodies, he wiped his blade clean and sheathed it. He carried the pack over to where the children still stood. None of them had moved more than a few inches, as far as he could tell.

"What's your name?" he asked the girl, as gently as he could. She had pulled up the front of her ripped tunic so that it concealed her chest once more. Drying blood covered the tunic, and her hands.

"Th . . . Th . . . Thea, milord."

"You're free now, Thea."

"You won't hurt me, milord, will you?"

"You're free. I don't own you."

"Then we are lost. The soldiers will kill us when they come back." She bowed her head. When she raised her face again, tears glistened at the edges of her blue eyes. "Won't you take me with you, please?" She reached her arms out to him. The ruined tunic dipped, once again revealing her blood-soaked breasts. "I'll be so very, very good. You won't ever have to beat me."

"Thea, I . . ."

"I know," she said, bowing her head again. "We will wait here, and the soldiers will take us. There is nowhere else for us."

Falorn reached into his pack and pulled out his second tunic. He laid the white cloth on her shoulders, wrapping it around her. She began to shiver, and huddled against him suddenly.

"Please don't make me go," she cried out, and then began sobbing against him. The other children looked on silently.

Falorn felt a hand on his shoulder. He looked up at Ryal hopelessly.

"We can't take them where we're going," he said to the wizard. "But I can't leave them here. We'll have to turn back."

"I'm afraid we can't do that either," Ryal said. "You wouldn't be welcome in Cathan without the cards and with more mouths to feed. The war made enough orphans."

"Then where?"

"Delerian."

"Delerian?" The Helleinen country had never occurred to him as a possibility. He remembered the other humans he had seen on his stay in Helleinen custody. *Maybe there would be a place for them. At least it will be better than anything they have here.* After a moment, he nodded.

"I'll take them myself." Ryal said. "The border's not far from here and I know the countryside."

"Can we risk splitting up?"

"I think there is little choice. I talked with Cirque about it and he agreed. I'll be a week or so getting them to Delerian and another week getting them settled in and sheltered, while you travel to Jhodric of Northfall's lands. You can visit them when you pass through Delerian next. I'll meet you in Northfall in two weeks and a day."

"How will you get there?"

"Birds fly freely and quickly," he said, winking at Falorn, "and there are many other shapes that travel faster than slow, two-footed men. I'll be there to meet you."

"We'll be there," said Falorn, and embraced Ryal fiercely. "We'll be there."

Thea looked up from his side shyly. "Thank you, milord," she said. "I promise we'll be good. We won't let you down."

"You're free, Thea," he said. "Ryal's going to take you someplace where no soldiers will follow you." He looked into her deep blue eyes, and he could see she understood nothing of what he had said.

8
Following Trails

❖

"We must go quickly," Cirque told Falorn. "The man in black was an inquisitor. He will be missed shortly. The officer will be back soon with more troops."

"I guess we can't keep taking the road."

"For a little while we can," said Cirque "It is the quickest way into the Seven Kingdoms. Anyway, we want the troops to see us."

"We do?" Falorn glanced toward the road, where Sbashe kept watch.

"If they see us, they will give chase, but I think they cannot catch us. If they do not see us, they will pursue Ryal. The children's trail is plain enough."

"Oh," said Falorn. He thought for a moment. "How do you know the man in the robes was an inquisitor? He looked like a village priest to me."

"I looked at his papers." Cirque withdrew a sheaf of documents from his belt and waved them at Falorn. "In the Seven Kingdoms, papers are everything."

"That's true enough," said Elise, walking on Falorn's other side as they traveled uphill on the cobblestoned road. "I'm surprised there was an inquisitor at this remote of an outpost, though."

"Maybe someone in the Immortal King's court had reason to doubt the piety of the locals. Maybe there is a civil officer in this district that needed to be counterbalanced. Who knows? We will get nowhere by trying to understand the church of this unholy empire."

"Also true," Elise replied. She and Cirque seemed to have reached an understanding of sorts. *I wonder if it's because of the fight, or just because we're finally getting to the Seven Kingdoms?* The two of them continued to talk of Seven Kingdoms organization and politics while Falorn walked ahead to join Sbashe's scouting.

He soon left the road, preferring the comparatively thick cover of laurel and blueberry bushes that covered the upward slopes on either side of the cobblestones. Here and there, dogwood trees spread their canopies close to the road; the forest thickened on the hills which surrounded the road.

Are you tired of conversation, then? a voice asked in his head. He turned his head. Sbashe loped beside him.

No. I don't think so. I just wanted to walk in the hills a little and think. They know more than I do about what we're getting into. Things change so much and so often. Sometimes I need time to get used to the changes, said Falorn.

I can leave you alone, if you'd like, Sbashe answered.

No. I'm glad of the company, actually.

I know, said the corget.

The two of them walked through the forest's edge silently, never leaving sight of the road although they never showed themselves. When the sun drew close to the horizon, Falorn chose a camp in a clearing two hundred paces back into the hills. He began to set up shelters as Sbashe went back for the others.

The four of them ate cold rations that night. Fire seemed like a senseless luxury, despite the early autumn coolness.

Falorn took the first watch. He used the blue thief to help him spot birds in the forest blackness surrounding the camp. After two hours watching silent owls swoop down on wood-mice and other small rodents, he felt vaguely queasy. With relief, he turned the watch over to Elise and bundled himself into his cloak to sleep.

He dreamed, and in his dream he saw the soldier and the girl again. Again he watched the soldier tear off her tunic, but this time Falorn found his hands empty. He could do nothing to stop it. The other soldiers looked at him and laughed as he watched them all fondle the girl's breasts and caress her face. Falorn looked at the girl's face again, and he saw Sera's face. He screamed as the soldiers' hands moved downward.

He awoke to find Elise cradling his head in her hands.

"It's all right, Falorn," she said, over and over. He looked up at her face, still foggy from the dream.

"Did I shout out loud?" he asked.

"You called out Sera's name."

"I'm sorry," said Falorn.

"I don't think it was loud enough to attract anyone. I hope not, anyway."

"I had the most awful dream. I thought that . . ."

"Shhh," said Elise, putting a finger over his lips. Then, after a minute, "You really miss her, don't you?"

"Yes," he answered.

"That's too bad. I don't think you'll see her again."

"I know. But I miss her anyway."

"She's not worth it, Falorn. There are a thousand nobles' daughters just like her. If that's what you want, you can find another one easily enough."

"I don't know what I want. But I miss her."

"Time heals," she said. "See how you feel in a year or so." He grunted noncommittally and closed his eyes. The dreams stayed away, but sleep remained just as elusive. He rose in the morning unrefreshed.

Elise transformed herself in the morning before they set out again. She produced a roll of cloth from her pack, and wrapped it around the outside of her undertunic, binding her small breasts tightly to her chest. She slipped a thick, shapeless tunic over her head, and belted it at the waist so it bulked outward. Loose britches slid on over her hose, and billowed out from her boottops where she tucked in the cuffs. With her broad shoulders, rough skin, and ragged blond hair, she looked more like a young man gone soldiering than a noblewoman of Cathan.

"If those papers are good, we shouldn't have much problem," she said to Cirque.

"Unless we meet that officer and his men," Cirque answered. "The inquisitor's papers offer more latitude than most, and the inquisitor's hood will cover my face. I took all of the soldiers' papers. Several of them will pass for the two of you. As long as you're with an inquisitor, no one will question you too much, I think." Cirque pointed to a tree branch, where the dead inquisitor's robe now hung. The blood had been careful-ly scrubbed away, and the fabric repaired and reshaped to more closely approximate the Helleinen warrior's size. "I sewed while you slept," he explained, "and I washed it in a trailside stream yesterday. Luckily there are no injunctions against inquisitors carrying blades in this land."

"Let's see the papers," said Elise. They spent the rest of the morning looking at their identification and practicing their roles. Falorn chafed at the delay, expecting to be attacked any minute, but Cirque and Elise both seemed to feel the risk worthwhile.

Elise had to explain the contents of the identification papers to Falorn; the bulky documents far exceeded his reading abilities. Each contained a detailed description of the bearer, the location of his author-ized living quarters and workplace, and detailed notes on any travel away from home. Travelers' documents had to be signed and countersigned by authorized officials or soldiers at checkpoints located every few miles. Anyone attempting to travel beyond areas called for in his duties, or any-one who skipped a checkpoint for any reason, would likely be arrested and held for questioning by an inquisitor. However, the inquisitors, because of the nature of their duties, commanded a greater freedom of travel. Higher-ranking civil and religious authorities expected similar or greater privileges.

"Won't they wonder about Sbashe?" Falorn finally asked.

"They might," Cirque answered. "I hope they will not ask an inquisi-tor. Such questions are not safe."

"As long as we don't meet another inquisitor."

"There is little enough danger of that here. When we come to more populated areas we will have to take further precautions."

Falorn sighted the first border outpost early that afternoon. The four of them skirted it by working their way through the wooded hills which still surrounded the road. Four guards watched the road vigilantly but only occasionally glanced at the forest. Two horses stood tethered outside the lone guardhouse, a fortified building large enough to hold a dozen sol-diers or more in comfort. Smoke rose from the building's chimney.

Elise looked longingly at the guardhouse. Cirque finally put a hand on her shoulder and gently led her onward.

"Doubtless they have prepared an ambush there," he told her. "The survivors must have passed this outpost and alerted the soldiers. The offi-cer will have reinforced the guards." Reluctantly, Elise followed him.

They walked through the woods for most of the day, until the forest thinned into a rolling meadow, dotted here and there with wildflowers. Huge rocks interspersed the lush grass. Hills framed a small, walled city against the horizon.

"We will have to leave the forest," Cirque told them. "If we leave now, perhaps we can be away from here before darkness. And someone must see us if we are to draw pursuit away from Ryal and your foundlings."

Elise smiled grimly, and checked the draw of her bow. Falorn tested his sword in its scabbard, and felt his chest to be certain his cards were safe.

Why do you do that? Sbashe asked. *You already know they're there.*

It's a nervous habit, I guess. At least it started out that way. Now I mostly do it just because I'm used to it. I think I'd know right away if something happened to one of the cards.

They walked for an hour through the damp grass before the soldiers revealed themselves.

A dozen horsemen cantered from concealed places behind the rocks. The horsemen drew sabers and spurred forward.

Elise turned to face the approaching riders and calmly raised her bow. "Don't let them bother you, Falorn," she said. "These are amateurs." She let fly her first arrow. It lodged in a man's arm. He tried to pull up too suddenly and his horse reared, throwing him to the ground. Elise's second shot hit a horse in the chest. Puzzled, the animal slowed to a walk, then stopped entirely.

Falorn's first two shots missed. By then, the horsemen had drawn close. He recognized the same officer he'd hit the day before, now wearing gilded armor and a billowing red cape. He aimed carefully and loosed another arrow. It hit the officer square in the face, lodging next to his left eye. The man didn't scream at all, just fell from his horse and rolled over twice, coming to a stop facedown in the grass, buried under his cape.

The horsemen reined in when they saw their officer down. None of them tried to check on the fallen man; first one, then all of them turned and galloped back toward the city.

Elise took careful aim with her bow and dropped two more soldiers out of their saddles before they rode out of range.

She spent the next half hour catching the three unwounded, riderless horses. As they rode away into gathering darkness, Falorn wondered when more soldiers from the city would come to the aid of the crying, wounded men still lying in the grass.

They rode north for the next day, avoiding people as much as they could. They cut across fields and skirted roads and checkpoints, until they could be certain not to encounter anyone who recognized the names on their stolen papers. Cirque wore the inquisitor's hood over his head to conceal his Helleinen features, or at least distort them in shadow.

"I think it will take some time to organize further pursuit," Cirque assured them. "There would be few soldiers in such a backwater province, and we have killed both their military and their religious leaders. They will send out messengers, but descriptions will be confused and incomplete. If we move quickly and avoid soldiers, we should be safe."

Over the next three days, they stopped at farmhouses twice to buy supplies. Cirque's inquisitor's robe encouraged ready obedience, and Falorn overpaid in silver for what they took. He hoped the silver would encourage the farmers to keep quiet, lest the tainted money be taken from them. Although Cirque told him that Ilessan law forbade common free-farmers from owning silver or gold, the peasants took Falorn's specie readily enough. Falorn had Seven Kingdoms coins—taken from the pouches of people who'd tried to kill him—but he thought it best to conserve those coins for more populated areas where the silver would not pass.

In the middle of the third afternoon Elise held the horses as Falorn and Cirque pulled a flat log ferry across a sluggish river. While Falorn hauled at the thick cable, he felt a sudden surge of heat at his chest. The heat didn't grow or spread much, although it flickered a little in intensity. It took Falorn a minute to realize what caused the new warmth. *I've felt this before.* His mind filled with memories of the Hellein warrior, fighting and dying in front of him.

"Cirque!" he said. "There's someone else nearby with a lion card. Someone's looking for us."

"Can you tell which side of the river they're on?" Cirque asked.

"Behind us, I think. I'm sure of it, actually," replied Falorn.

"Good. We must move quickly." Elise checked the horses' fittings as Falorn and Cirque hauled the ferryboat toward the approaching shore.

As they neared the riverbank, horsemen began to ride from the trees on the far side, passing over the trail Falorn and his companions had just crossed. More than forty men emerged from the woods. Most of them wore chain mail and rode tremendous warhorses, even bigger than the one Falorn had found with the dead man who'd borne the first lion card.

One of the riders, a tall, gaunt-looking man with thinning gray hair, pointed a gloved hand at the ferry and began to mutter odd words, which carried strangely out over the river. A brown-haired man in a green and black cape jockeyed his mount over to the thin man. He struck the man's hand upward, just as the pointing rider shouted a triumphant note.

Something crackled in the air over Falorn's head. The air seemed suddenly alive. His hair nearly stood on its end, bursting with energy. A tall tree on the bank in front of them exploded into two. Wood flew in all directions, splinters flying into the water nearly as far as their boat. Flames licked at the shattered wood.

"You fool," said the brown-haired rider, his voice carrying out onto the water. "Are you trying to kill them in the middle of the river? How will we get the cards then? Let them land, then kill them."

"They will escape," the gaunt man said, his voice deep in the suddenly still air."

"Nonsense. There is no escape for them. Only delay."

Falorn heard no more. They mounted and urged their horses into the rushing water at the river's edge even before the ferry reached shore. The soldiers on the far bank had crossbows, but they held their fire.

"They're out of range and they know it," Elise said, spurring her mount forward through the trees. "These men are disciplined."

"How long will it take them to get across?" Falorn asked, crouched low to his horse's head while he waited for more lightning to strike.

"Depends how much those wizards mind getting wet. Soon, I think."

"I think not," Cirque said from behind them. "The flames are beginning to catch." Falorn risked a glance backward. Smoke had begun to spread in a thin haze at their backs. Tongues of flame here and there licked and worried at branches like so many cats grooming wooden paws.

"That won't slow them for long," said Elise, "but it might buy us half a day or so. Time to hide."

"We can't hide," Falorn said. "They can find me as long as they have the other lion card. All we can do is run."

"There is no hiding from them," Cirque said. "Look." He pointed upward. There, far in the sky above them, a giant eagle soared lazily. The wind currents carried it in a broad, looping glide above them. The bird looked far too big for a normal eagle.

"That's another wizard, isn't it?" Falorn asked. "It's a shapeshifter, like Ryal."

"Very likely."

They rode on through the woods, with the eagle overhead all the while. Only after the rain began to fall on them in great waves of cold spray did they lose sight of the creature.

They dared not take shelter. Instead, they rode on through the woods in the downpour. By the time the last of the thin forest lay behind them, the horses were exhausted, the animals' canter slowed to a gentle walk.

Falorn felt a change in the soaked earth. Something clattered beneath his mount's hooves.

"A road," he called out. "I've found a road."

The horses seemed to gain strength once they abandoned the muddy ground. The downpour continued as the animals walked on, barely slackening as the square shapes of darkened buildings rose up around them. Shutters sealed any light within the buildings. Nothing broke the darkness of the town, and Falorn could hear only the sound of rain and hoofbeats on the slick clay surface of the road.

Cirque dismounted and gestured. Puzzled, Falorn followed the Hellein, leading his mount. They walked around a two-story wooden structure, and stopped at the front of a long low building behind it.

"It's a stable," Falorn said, to no one in particular. Cirque waited by the locked double doors. Letting go of the horse's reins, he stepped up to the door. Water poured over his head, cascading down from the tilt of the slate roof. Falorn tried to focus on the lock in spite of being so wet.

The familiar blue did not appear.

He spent a minute looking at the mechanism and then swore to himself. *Mother of Kerion! It's already unlocked.*

After a hurried meal in the stable, they took new horses and left their own behind. Rain scoured them as they rode on the empty road through the town. The animals' hooves thumped on wet clay.

Morning found them still on the road. Thick drops of rain continued to fall. Water dripped from their cloaks and down the horses' necks. Sbashe's fur glistened with reflected water. On both sides of the cobbled road, the ditches had turned into roaring torrents.

Cirque rode up beside Falorn, splashing through puddles as he drew their wet mounts together.

"Can you still sense the other cardholder?" he asked. "Did we lose them yet?"

"I can feel them faintly," Falorn replied. "They're probably holed up someplace dry right now, but they're still out there."

9

Flight

✦⋮✦

Over the next two weeks their pursuers never quite caught up with them again. Falorn saw the riders twice, both times on hilltops a few miles behind. The giant eagle became a permanent fixture in their lives, soaring lazily overhead in good weather, fading away when the sky was overcast. They rode constantly, taking new horses wherever they could find them and sleeping mostly in the saddle. Somehow, Sbashe kept up, running tirelessly beside them, never appearing the least bit fatigued.

They avoided checkpoints when they could, and rode through them when they had to, clearing soldiers from the road at swordpoint. A dozen or so cavalry units pursued them in addition to the wizards and their escort. Somehow, Cirque always seemed to know which way to go to avoid pursuers. They doubled back often, and cut through hills, woods, and underbrush. At other times they brazenly rode into garrisoned towns and bought supplies. Cirque slid easily into Seven Kingdoms accents when he spoke; no one ever took him for anything but an inquisitor.

"We can get to Northfall this way," Cirque said, "but no further. We will have to take a ship from Northfall, and quickly. All of the soldiers who are chasing us will converge there. They are not coordinated now, but in Northfall, the regional governor will assign a grand inquisitor and a general to command them. We will not be able to escape them so easily."

"How have we escaped them so far?" Elise asked. "I can't believe no one has caught up with us yet."

"These soldiers follow a manual-of-arms. None of their officers are high ranking enough to dare ignore it. Their careers depend on obedience as much as success. We need only do things that the advice of their training will not prepare them for."

"And you know about their training because . . . ?"

"We Helleinen live a long time. And we can read."

They reached Northfall three days after the meeting date set with Ryal. For the last part of the journey, they followed a great shallow river, until it finally reached the sea. Falorn fretted about their lateness, but none of the others seemed to care.

Ryal will wait, Sbashe told him. *He is a wise one, and he blends even in my people's own caves. No one will find him if he doesn't want to be found.*

I know, but we're putting him in danger, said Falorn.

Less danger than if we arrive dead. Stop worrying.

From the clifftops, they could look down onto the entire city. The road curved between two high flat plateaus and sloped sharply downward. Below, a vast jumble of gray stone and whitewashed houses filled a wide, sheltered harbor. A thin strip of beach divided the buildings—tiny-looking beneath the massive cliffs—from the vast green ocean beyond. Waves broke endlessly among the wooden docks along the beach, and churned angrily at the jetties which extended far out into the dark water at either end of the harbor.

Sheer rocky cliffs rose around the city, like the one they stood atop. Winding trails led up the wall at the far side of the city. A massive castle guarded the peak, its high towers looking far out onto the ocean, its thick walls daring even the fiercest storm to attack. As they rode downward along the paved track, Falorn heard a roaring sound which began to drown even the constant pounding of the surf.

"What is that noise?" he finally asked Cirque. The Hellein just pointed his arm to the right in reply. Falorn saw nothing until they rounded a bend in the road. On the right hand cliff, a sheer wall of water cascaded down the rock face, ending in a billowing fog of spray below. The fresh-water lake beneath the falls had been dammed off from the sea, and a swath of green marked out a park beside it.

"That's beautiful," he said. "Is that how the city got its name?"

"Yes. It's a lovely place. The Seven Kingdoms doesn't deserve such beauty."

"This city is enormous," said Elise. "Is it the largest in the Seven Kingdoms?"

"Far from it. It is larger than Cathan City in your own country, but there are eight or nine as large or larger in the Seven Kingdoms."

They joined in the heavy traffic along the road. Unlike nearly every other place they had been in the Seven Kingdoms, they saw no checkpoints. Soldiers waved the swell of carts and travelers through each of the four monolithic stone gatehouses which guarded the road between the two cliffs.

"Anyone can enter this place," Cirque told them. "Too many people need to travel here for them to try and control their flow. They are much more careful about letting people leave."

"Oh," Falorn said, after thinking about that for a moment. "So we've just walked into an enormous prison."

"Potentially, yes. However, it is a prison which contains our quarry and his cards, and will soon contain our pursuers with at least one more card. Until now, we have been hunted. Now, we can become hunters again." Elise joined in Cirque's grim smile.

"Let's get it done with then," Falorn said to Cirque. "Where do we find Jhodric, anyway?"

"We will have to do some checking to see if my speculation is correct. But I suspect that we will find him there." The Hellein pointed upward and to his left. Falorn followed Cirque's gesture. High atop the cliff, at the pinnacle of the narrow path, stood the thick walls of the city's main fortress. Dozens of flags and pennants flew from its towers. Prominent among them, he could see Jhodric's familiar green banner.

They boarded the stolen horses at a stable and spent the rest of the morning and afternoon wandering the streets. Two weeks of fatigue fell away as Falorn walked through the city. For the moment, at least, he felt no other cards nearby. The lakeside park teemed with swans. Vendors sold stale bread for children to feed the stately birds. Falorn watched the swans glide through the water for a while, until they began to remind him of the bird who had spied on them throughout their long ride. Children waved and pointed at Sbashe's unfamiliar six-legged frame as well, but their parents dared not ask questions of the cowled inquisitor who accompanied the creature.

Falorn marveled at the huge flat slabs of salted fish piled on tables at the seaside market. Vendors used saws to cut thick yellow-gray chunks of the fish to order. Other foodstuffs came from farms and orchards on the hills above the city, or from the galleys that scuttled up and down the coast. Customers scooped wet ladles full of olives from browned wooden barrels, or bought sacks of flour, dried beans, and potatoes from heavy pallets winched off a ship's deck. High piles of fresh and dried fruit covered other tables. Chickens, pigs, lambs, even cattle wandered around makeshift pens and cages, waiting to be sold or slaughtered.

Everywhere he walked in the market, Falorn smelled meat roasting over coals. Every few paces he saw another firepit or wide sheet-iron basket of coals. Children turned big pairs of square gratings on spits, the two iron grates pressed together with meat or fish between them. Roasting chicken, lamb, and beef sizzled as juices dripped out onto coals. Other stands grilled narrow fish each as long as his hand. He gawked so much that Cirque finally bought a plateful of the roasted fish for a copper coin. He showed Falorn how to split the fish open and pull the tender meat from the spine. They tasted moist and hot and delicious, not at all salty like Falorn expected.

After they finished the roasted fish, Cirque bought a plate of grilled sausage, a small roasted chicken, thick rolls of bread, and a pitcher of sour red wine. They sat at the edge of an empty dock to eat.

"As long as we are in Northfall, we might as well enjoy the food," he said.

"Have you been here before?" Falorn asked.

"A few times," Cirque admitted. "Actually, you can get food like this all along this coast, if you know where to look. There are fishing villages in Delerian that have similar foods, but the effect isn't quite the same."

"It's safer, for one thing," said a new voice.

"Ryal!" Falorn said, looking up. The stranger who faced him looked nothing like Ryal. He wore the gold-edged black robes of a grand inquisitor with the hood down upon his shoulders. His head was shaven, but a thin black beard sparsely covered his chin.

Falorn's hand began edging to his sword.

"Don't scare him, Ryal," said Cirque. "You were right, Falorn. It is him."

The second Hellein sat down, careful not to catch his robe on the side of the dock.

"Well it took you long enough to get here," he said, picking up a piece of sausage. "I had to have some sort of disguise. Not that I would have bothered if I'd known you were going to traipse into town looking like this."

"What do you mean?" Falorn asked. "Cirque's got his robes. And Elise isn't exactly her normal self, either."

"And Sbashe?"

"Oh."

"It's not that those disguises aren't all right, it's that too many people already know them. And a six-legged dog isn't exactly inconspicuous." Ryal winced, as Sbashe presumably responded to his characterization.

"It should be fine, Ryal," Cirque said. "We will be leaving later tonight, I hope. No one will find us before then."

"They will if you parade yourselves around the marketplace. Finish your food and then come with me. I have a place where you can bathe, and rest safely. We will see about better disguises after you've rested."

They ate somewhat more hurriedly, and followed the Hellein from the market. Ryal took no action that Falorn saw, but when he glanced at Sbashe he saw only a large dog; the extra pair of legs and luminous stripe had vanished.

Ryal and I have come to an . . . accommodation, said Sbashe's voice in his mind. *I will play the part of this . . . dog . . . for a little while if it serves our purposes. They are silly, ungainly, unbalanced creatures though.*

Falorn said nothing, and tried to keep unflattering thoughts from his mind. Certainly the dog in front of him had little of Sbashe's sleekness or beauty. It looked like a fighting dog of indeterminate breed: big and fierce enough to deter questioners without being unusual enough to arouse curiosity. Falorn had seen a dozen just like it as they walked around the city; they had probably served as the models for Ryal's transformation spell.

Ryal led them easily through the winding, close-packed streets that surrounded the market. Soon they found themselves walking along spacious lanes. Narrowly spaced whitewashed houses with thatched roofs gave way to fenced estates, each with a large house and one or more outbuildings.

"The grand inquisitor who lives here has gone away for a little while,"

Ryal said as he turned a brass key in the lock of a wrought-iron gate, "so I took the liberty of borrowing his face and clothing." They walked across a green lawn toward a two-story stone house with a wide, low porch. Falorn could see a carriage-house and stables behind the building.

"Will he be needing his face back again afterward?" Cirque asked.

"Oh, absolutely. He and I got along famously. We talked for a long while, and he kindly agreed to tell me everything I wanted to know about him if I promised not to kill him. He's sleeping in the attic right now. He'll wake up very hungry in about a week, and find out I've dismissed his servants. Otherwise, I've left the place intact. I don't want to take unfair advantage of his hospitality."

"How did you catch a grand inquisitor?" Elise asked.

"Unawares. He was taking a hard-earned sabbatical from his strenuous duties in the service of the Immortal King. He didn't expect company to show up unannounced past the guards and magical traps."

"I see," said Elise.

"Magical traps?" Falorn asked.

"There's nothing in here that will hurt you anymore. Just stay out of the attic." They entered into a lush parlor, filled with heavily cushioned couches and low tables. Falorn immediately felt the lost sleep of the last two weeks resurfacing at the sight of the couches. The thread of conversation wandered away from him as soon as he kicked off his boots and sat down. Within moments he curled up and slept without dreams.

Falorn awoke after night had fallen. A lone candle in a wall-holder dimly illuminated the room. Beyond the windows he saw only darkness. Elise lay on another couch halfway across the room, unconsciously fingering the lone, thin braid in her hair as she slept. He heard voices from the next room, and decided to get up and investigate.

"I hope you slept well," Ryal said to him, as Falorn entered what looked like a small dining room. The two Helleinen sat at a circular table, drinking from silver mugs. Twin silver bowls sat on the floor in front of Sbashe, both empty except for crumbs. "There is a heated bath waiting for you if you follow the hallway to its end. After you've bathed, I'll have food waiting for you."

"Thanks," said Falorn. He set off down the hall without further comment.

Falorn found the Helleinen deep in conversation when he returned from the bath. They spoke in their own language.

Sbashe focused raptly on the two of them, her eyes flickering rapidly from one to the other.

Ryal waved Falorn over to the other side of the table, where several covered silver bowls sat. He watched the Helleinen and Sbashe as he ate thinly breaded hot pastries stuffed with spicy ground meat and fish. They continued to talk animatedly, the three of them lost in a conversation that excluded him.

He finished eating long before their talk concluded. Cirque looked up at him finally, after some sort of decision had been reached.

"It is nearly time to go," Ryal said. Falorn looked at Ryal, and realized the wizard had resumed his normal appearance.

"What about the disguises?" he asked.

"That plan has changed. I will be the only one in a different form. The rest of you will enter the castle as you are. Cirque feels that the time for subtlety has passed. You will make a quick, bold stroke, and then escape quickly."

"Aren't you coming with us?"

"No. I will take you there, and help with your escape if I can. But I can't go in with you if I'm shaped like a giant bird. All I can do is keep an eye out for new enemies and try to warn you if I see them."

Sbashe padded into the room with a tired-looking Elise at her heels. The corget had resumed her normal shape as well.

Ryal left the room while Elise attacked the remaining food. Cirque and Falorn checked all of their packs, securing loose ends and retying knots. After they finished, Cirque led Falorn, Elise, and Sbashe to a rooftop garden.

"We leave from here," Cirque said. Falorn looked around the sculpted hedges, wondering what Cirque meant. On the far side of the roof, an enormous hawk perched.

"Hello, Ryal," said Falorn, walking over to the hawk. He looked at the distant lights from the castle tower, far above them. "That's a long flight. I hope you're feeling strong."

It's a long fall, said Sbashe, *and he won't be the one falling if something goes wrong.*

"We're not going to do what I think we're going to do, are we?" Elise asked. She put a hand on Falorn's shoulder as she stood beside him. "Where were we when these Sart-stricken elves decided on this?"

"We were asleep."

"It is the only way to get into the castle without a fight." Cirque said.

"We have only hours to spare before our pursuers catch up with us. We must not waste them."

"Won't they notice a giant hawk dropping people off on the walls?" asked Falorn.

"There are unguarded places on the walls. They guard against a night attack by sea, or along the road. No one watches the walls where they border upon unclimbable cliffs."

"We know this?" Elise asked.

"Ryal has checked and checked again, these last few nights. He knows how to bring us there safely. I will go first, and guard against any unforeseen dangers."

Cirque walked over to the wall, and picked up a hammock of rope and woven cloth strips. At each end, the rope had been tied off into a wide loop. He laid the center of the hammock down on the ground, and carefully smoothed it with his hands. Only after he checked and rechecked every knot and strip of cloth did he sit down. He held up one of the loops of rope in each hand.

Without a sound, the hawk spread its wings and beat them twice as if stretching out tight muscles. Then it pushed itself into the air. The hawk hovered over Cirque, its wings making only the slightest whirring noise. Talons closed over one loop, then the other. Cirque gripped the side ropes tightly as the hammock lifted into the air. The cloth seat swayed wildly beneath the rapid pulse of the hawk's wings. Falorn heard Cirque mutter something dark in his own language, and then the night swallowed him.

They stood on the roof in silence, listening to the wind's faint howl. All of them expected to hear something, Falorn knew: a commotion at the gates, a disturbance in the town, something that would signal pursuit, or plans again gone wrong. But the night remained quiet and empty.

The hawk returned silently, startling all of them in a sudden beating of massive wings. Falorn looked at Elise's white face and decided to go next. He thought he saw a tear on her cheek and turned away, not wanting to embarrass her.

He lowered himself into the hammock, which hung suspended beneath the hawk at the level of Falorn's knees. The seat swayed beneath him, and he hastily took hold of the ropes on either side.

His stomach dropped out from inside him as they took to the air. Falorn gulped, suddenly short of breath. The hammock rocked madly, shifting with each motion of the hawk's powerful shoulders. Freezing wind lashed at his face and hands. It took all Falorn's strength to hold on as his hands grew numb.

Just as his face began to lose feeling as well, he saw walls below. Ryal had flown high around the castle to avoid being silhouetted for the guards in the towers. Now, the hawk swooped toward an empty length of cold, dressed stone.

The hawk had flown away before Falorn fully realized he was on the ground again. He found himself on hands and knees, shivering desperately. The wall seemed to revolve as he held onto it helplessly. Then it seemed as if his head was revolving instead. He gave into the dizziness and closed his eyes.

He felt himself being carried. Someone set him down gently, and he felt warmth.

"Rest for a moment, Falorn," a distant voice said. "Soon, you will have to fight. Soon it will be time to fight yet again."

10

Good Hunting

"Falorn, wake up."

His eyes opened slowly. He could hear cold wind blowing nearby. Looking around, Falorn found himself in an enclosed hemisphere of stone blocks. Something wood supported his back: the frame of a heavy ballista. A spearlike bolt sat in the weapon's shaft, ready to fire outward at invaders. A dozen more spears leaned against one wall. Next to the other wall, a lit charcoal brazier stood. The heat of the coals, along with the protection of the shelter, slowly began to revive Falorn.

"Wake up, Falorn."

His eyes focused on Elise's face. She still looked terribly pale. "Falorn, are you all right?"

"I'm . . . fine," he said slowly. "I'm just cold."

"That is a rough trip," agreed Cirque. "Come over to the coals and warm yourself. We have other work to do soon."

"Where is Ryal?"

"In the air outside, watching. He cannot turn himself back into his own form without a proper mouth and hands. He will remain a hawk until tomorrow evening."

"Cirque . . . ?" The Hellein looked at Falorn, waiting patiently for the rest of the question. "When you and Ryal talked, did he say anything about the people we rescued? Do you know what happened to them?"

"They are as well as can be expected. You will have to ask Ryal for the details. I know nothing else about them."

After a few moments of warming himself in front of the brazier, Falorn began to feel better. The dizziness finally faded. Warmth from the cards at his chest seemed to spread energy through his veins. As Cirque and Sbashe left the shelter to plot a path into the castle itself, Falorn felt Elise's hand on his shoulder.

"Thank you, Falorn," she said. "Thanks again for going first."

"It was nothing," he said.

"It meant something to me. It gave me time to prepare. This is easier for you, I think. The elves are your friends. You have no quarrel with them. For me, it is much harder to trust them."

"It looks like I had more to worry about. I barely made it through the flight."

"I think the elf was gentler with Sbashe and me."

They walked together out onto the wall, joining Cirque and Sbashe on the darkened flat stone. The wall seemed to extend for miles, with shelters every hundred paces or so. Crenellated battlements lined the outer edge. Falorn had never realized just how big a castle could be; even this outer wall spread around him as thick as ten tall men, and nearly as high. Within the wall's confines, dozens of buildings could be seen by their lights. Dominating all of them, the main keep thrust high towers upward into the darkness. Tall, narrow windows blazed, shedding more light from atop the rocky cliff than any lighthouse. A pair of enclosed stone bridges connected the wall to the main keep.

Even with the uncertain illumination of distant torches, Falorn could see the shadows of sentries pacing the wall where it approached the keep.

"How will we get in there?" he whispered to Cirque.

"We will take one of the bridges, of course. How else?"

"Aren't they guarded?"

"No doubt."

Falorn checked his sword in its scabbard.

"Am I missing something?" he asked. "We aren't planning to fight our way in, are we?"

"No. We walk in. We fight when we have to, not before."

"I'd like to know a little more than that."

"Soon. Now, just follow."

Cirque began to walk forward, with Sbashe at his heels. More reluctantly, Falorn and Elise followed. She gave Falorn a tired look and shook her head, but she kept walking next to him.

Above the noise of the wind, they soon heard the measured click of pacing boots on stone. Cirque continued to walk forward in the darkness. He made no attempt to reach for a weapon, or to conceal himself. He had exchanged his black inquisitor's robe for a bright red linen shirt, tight silk hose, and a pale blue cape that seemed to glow in the starlight. A wide-brimmed hat shadowed his face

"Hold there! Who approaches?" called a voice from the night.

"Nenevander of Syllbythum, Duke Theleries's son," Cirque replied, "out walking the walls with friends. Care to share a skin of wine with us?"

"Not tonight, Lord. I've a duty to be clearheaded on watch."

"The night air will keep your head clear. Come, share with us."

"No, Lord. I cannot." They came within view of the guard. He stood against the arched outer wall of a sheltered emplacement, cradling a spear in his arms. He wore no armor beneath his heavy cloak, but a white ivory horn hung at the man's side.

"As you will," said Cirque.

"That's a fine hound you have," the guard said. "I've never seen one like it."

"My father breeds them. They never leave the duchy, save this one. She would die rather than leave my side."

"A hunter, isn't she?"

"None better."

"Well, good hunting, then. Pass, friends. Enjoy your circuit of the walls."

"Thank you. Would that all soldiers were as courteous and thorough in their duties as yourself." The guard nodded as they walked past him. They saw the glow of charcoal from within the shelter he leaned against. Another guard sat within, warming his hands. The second man waved as they moved onward toward the keep.

"What was that name you gave them?" Falorn asked as they passed out of the sentries' earshot.

"There actually is such a place. But no guard will remember such a long name, just that a duke's son with a funny-looking dog was walking on the walls. There are probably twenty or thirty men who fit that description here."

Cirque greeted two more pairs of sentries as they continued, giving each the same name. All the guards passed him along freely, with a word of conversation or two.

"They dare not be unfriendly," Cirque explained. "They don't know which young noble might be a Power someday, and they all carry grudges."

Two more soldiers guarded the first of the stone bridges. The causeway arched off into the darkness. Twin doors stood closed against the chill night air.

The men snapped to attention as Cirque approached. They stamped the butts of their halberds against the stone and looked straight ahead into the darkness.

"Fine men," Cirque said. He put a hand on the door. "What lies within?"

"Only storage rooms and servants' quarters, Lord. Nothing fit for your sight."

"Fit enough to get me out of the cold, though, and to take me back to the keep?"

"Yes, Lord."

Cirque pulled the door open, and they stepped into the torchlit stone causeway.

If Falorn hadn't seen the bridge from outside, he never would have believed how high and precariously it hung above the ground. Wider than his father's inn, the stone floor remained firm and unmoving in the wind, as if anchored to the strongest foundation.

As they passed into the keep the hallway narrowed, and doorways began to dot the corridor. Few of the rooms to either side had doors in their frames. Falorn looked in one as they passed, and saw endless heaps of old wooden furniture, dust covering once-elaborate carvings. Several rooms contained shabby piles of bedding, and a few sleeping servants. Other servants walked in the hall. Cirque called to one of them, a balding man of about fifty.

"You there!"

"Milord." The servant dropped to his knees and bowed low.

"Do you know how to find Prince Jhodric's chambers?"

"His Grace? Yes, of course, milord."

"Take us there."

"Now, milord?"

"Of course, now."

"Yes, milord." The servant rose and began quickly walking down the hall, glancing back now and again to be certain Cirque and the others still followed him. A heavy iron-bound door brought them into the keep itself. They found themselves walking through crowded halls, filled with well-dressed men and women despite the lateness of the hour. Falorn realized that he, Elise, and Cirque looked not at all out of place. Even Sbashe drew minimal attention; he wondered how rare exotic animals were in a city as large and wealthy as Northfall.

They walked through an enormous room floored with a checkerboard of black and pink marble blocks. Two columns of pillars supported a high, vaulted ceiling, punctuated by round windows of intricately stained glass. Plumes of water sprayed upward from a startlingly white fountain in the room's center. Broad hallways trailed off in four directions. White stone stairways flanked each hallway.

Without pausing, their guide led them to one of the stairways. They climbed upward for two flights before exiting onto a narrower hallway, this one floored in polished black marble. Dark wooden panels covered the walls, punctuated at intervals by a gilt-framed portrait or a bust on a granite pedestal.

Few servants walked on this level.

Falorn barely kept himself from staring at the sealed doors they passed. Each bore carvings of a royal couple: throned, or walking, or falconing, once even making love, their bare legs entwined like serpents. The doors had been carved by dozens of hands, in many styles. Some looked very old, others quite recent.

At the end of the empty hall stood an unadorned pair of double doors.

"We are here, milord," the servant said. "May I have your leave to return to my quarters?"

"In a moment," Cirque replied. "Where is the Duke? Is he here?"

"Why . . . no, milord. As you can see, there are no guards. His Grace the Duke was summoned away this afternoon, in the presence of the whole Court. He and his family left this evening for the Forbidden City."

"I had not heard. We were called away on other business this afternoon. Duke Jhodric asked us to call on him at this hour."

"Of course, milord." The servant bowed again.

Cirque looked at the man absentmindedly. "Go," he said, "you are dismissed."

"Milord," the man said, and scurried back toward the stairs.

"Damn," said Cirque, as the servant vanished from sight.

"What's the Forbidden City like?" Falorn asked.

"I think we are about to find out," said Cirque. "It's a pity it's not on any of our maps. They keep its location secret from people who don't belong there, like us. I have some good guesses about where to look, though."

"That servant is going to call the guards," Elise said. "For the love of Marré, don't you think we ought to leave here?"

"Very much so," answered Cirque. He gestured toward the double doors. "Shall we see if our absent friend the Duke has a balcony in his chambers? Perhaps it is time for us to once more take flight."

They spent the last few hours before morning in an empty tax-barn a dozen miles southwest of the city, in the direction where Cirque hoped to find the Forbidden City. Their newly stolen horses cropped at the edges of stacked hay bales while Falorn carefully brushed the animals' sweaty flanks.

"These horses need to rest," he told the others. "We can't leave now unless we want to walk."

"We'll just have to hope no one's on our trail yet," said Elise. She sat atop on of the bales, carefully waxing a bowstring. Her arrows lay neatly spread beside her, their fletching newly checked and repaired. Sbashe had curled up in a corner. The corget looked far more doglike asleep than awake. One of her ears twitched slightly as she dreamed.

"They will be on our trail shortly, if they are not already," Cirque said.

"I think Elise is right," said Falorn, looking up from one of the horses. "We won't know which way to go until Ryal gets back anyway. We may as well try to rest a little."

"If we must." Cirque looked darkly around the barn. He had discarded the hat before their departure from the castle, revealing the angular planes of his face. In the lanternlight, he looked less human, somehow. "I will keep watch if you like. I do not think I will sleep these next few hours. I have much to think on; this evil country makes me thoughtful."

What is it that you're thinking about, Falorn wondered. *What secret are you keeping that makes you hate this country so much?* Something in Cirque's tone reminded Falorn of his father: something about the maddening "I know something that I'm not going to tell you" smugness of the Hellein's words. *And there's a sadness, too*, Falorn realized.

Falorn finished grooming the horses and found himself a nest amid the haystacks. He burrowed beneath his cloak and closed his eyes, but for a long time lay awake, wondering. He shared only a little of Cirque and Elise's dislike for the Seven Kingdoms. *Ilessa is a beautiful country, despite its rulers. I can understand Cirque and Elise's blind hatred, but I can't really empathize with it. But I will have to take the cards from Jhodric to stop the man from trying to kill me,* Falorn knew. *Sooner or later, I'm going to have to confront the wizard with the card as well.*

The soldiers in Tasaria had shocked him. But like Sbashe, Falorn still felt a curious detachment from the people of the Seven Kingdoms, totally unlike Cirque and Elise's more personal, visceral feelings. *They were determined to kill the soldiers, but wouldn't have given it a second thought if Thea and the other children had died. I'm the other way around, I guess. I would have been just as happy to let the soldiers live, but was prepared to abandon the quest to save the life of a handful of children whom I'd never met.*

He felt a warmth beside him as his mind began to wander toward dreaming. Elise's hand stroked his shoulder once, gently, stopping halfway down his arm. She snuggled close to him; he felt the rough fabric of her undertunic against his back. He sighed gently and let thoughts fade from his mind. At his back, Elise breathed slowly and regularly. He reached his free hands up to touch her hand on his left shoulder. Her fingers clasped unconsciously around his. He held her hand as they drifted into sleep together.

Falorn, Cirque, and Elise resumed riding in the morning, while Sbashe ran beside them. They rode away from paved roads and other well-traveled areas, cutting through woods and fields when they could. At night, Ryal and Cirque worked on sheaves of captured and stolen passes by candlelight and magical illumination. After three days spent in woods and rocky meadows, the Helleinen finished preparing the disguises intended to get them into the Forbidden City, if they could find it.

In the middle of the next afternoon, the giant eagle reappeared above them, gliding placidly through a clear blue sky. That night, strange fires burned in the distance both ahead and behind them, like signals between groups of wizards or soldiers.

They rode through woods and untenanted grass fields. Cirque and Elise worked together in earnest now, plotting misdirections and stratagems to throw off the wizards who followed them. Falorn told

Cirque whenever he felt the other lion card approach, but otherwise the Hellein and the guard rarely consulted him. He took to scouting ahead with Sbashe for hours at a time, looking for signs of the Forbidden City.

At night he mostly talked with Ryal and Sbashe. Elise had no more time for lessons. When he could, Falorn practiced alone.

They worked their way south until the ground began climbing again. In the thick belt of wooded hills, they had little trouble avoiding watchers in the sky above. Now and again, Falorn found a sheltered ledge, from which he could see for many miles in one direction or another. Sometimes he saw a faint crawling train of distant soldiers diligently following, and he would wonder if other soldiers waited ahead, ready to spring like hounds on some flushed-out quarry.

More often, Falorn saw belts of meadow or farmland, criss-crossed by networks of paved roads and small guardhouses. Here and there an unwalled town could be seen. Cathedral spires and fortress towers rendered the towns visible from far off. He saw few small farm-villages of the sort he'd grown up in; people hereabouts seemed to cluster in larger congregations.

After five days of riding in the hidden hills, Falorn found what they were looking for.

The road curved through the hills gently, as if it had formed naturally around the rising slopes. Its builders had laid a bed of smooth stones wide enough for two wagons to ride abreast, as if the road had been designed for chariot races rather than travel. It was the sort of road one built to march armies on.

"This has to be it," Cirque said when Falorn showed the road to him. "The Forbidden City is the only place in Southern Ilessa big enough to need this road. North of these hills, along the seacoast, there are cities like Northfall, but where this leads is nothing but farms and the Forbidden City. We have to follow it."

"What about the wizards?" Falorn asked. "We can't hide from them on this road."

"We will not have to, I hope. We are a day ahead of them, at least." Falorn wondered about that, but he felt glad enough to urge his horse behind the others onto the road. After a week in the half-darkness of the wooded hills, he wanted to ride in the light again.

Above, gliding lazily on the wind currents, soared a giant eagle.

11

Fighting Wizards

Falorn stood over the eagle's bloodied corpse. Next to the stained pile of scattered feathers, Cirque tended Ryal, carefully cleaning the hawk's injured wing and face.

"They have fools for wizards in this country," Cirque said. "If you want to turn into an eagle, you had better learn to fight like an eagle. The fool had no idea at all of how to use his talons. He had no chance at all against Ryal." Cirque shook his head.

The three of them stood in a field of mown hay. Nearby, at the road's edge, Elise held the horses' reins. Sbashe sat beside her, looking up occasionally to sniff at the light breeze.

Falorn looked around the roadside field.

"How long do you think we're safe here?" he asked Cirque.

"I do not know. Do you sense another card nearby?"

"No."

"Then we are safe for the moment." Cirque continued to clean the cuts on the giant hawk's wing. "How do you propose we move Ryal?"

"What do you mean?"

"He cannot fly with a hurt wing. He is exhausted from fighting the other wizard, as well. He cannot turn back into his own form without hands and lips to form the spell. He will remain a hawk until tomorrow. How do you propose to move him when we ride on?"

"We can't stay here," said Falorn.

"I know that," Cirque answered.

"Maybe we can rig some kind of sled behind one of the horses?" Falorn asked.

"That might work. Perhaps we should try that," said Cirque.

Before they had finished bandaging Ryal and rigging a travois to carry him, Falorn felt the familiar sensation of another lion card nearby.

"We have company coming," he said to the others.

"Do you think we can outride them?" Elise asked, turning to Cirque.

"No. You ride onward with Ryal and Sbashe. Falorn and I will delay them. You have no cards, so even if they capture us, they will have difficulty tracking you. Ryal will be able to help with disguises when he returns to his normal form."

"No," said Elise. "He's your friend. You take him. I'm not about to go nursemaiding some sick elf with feathers while you fight. You go on. Falorn and I will catch up."

"As you will," Cirque replied. He mounted his horse and rode off without another word, leading the horse bearing Ryal's travois. Sbashe walked behind the laden horse, watching to be certain Ryal did not slip from the uncertain lashings.

"How long do we have?" Elise asked after the hoofbeats faded away.

"A few minutes, I think. I can feel the card getting closer, but only slowly."

"Let's find some cover. There's no use fighting from the road, or from someplace we can't get away from." Falorn looked around, but saw nothing except open fields. A few farmhouses in the distance—mud-walled and thatch-roofed—offered little promise. He rode a few lengths down the road, and then looked behind him.

"Never mind the cover," he said. "Look." In the distance, a line of horsemen began to take shape as they approached. Falorn checked the string on his bow.

"That won't work," Elise said, touching his shoulder. "There's a wizard with them, maybe more than one. If we stay at a distance they'll kill us."

"You want to *charge* them?" Falorn glanced at her incredulously.

"Getting close is our only chance," said Elise

"Are you out of your mind?" He could see the riders clearly now. They wore mail, and dark green colors. At least a score of them rode behind a man in a billowing purple cape.

"I know what I'm doing. You followed me last time and it worked," she said.

"You charged a whole *army*."

"We won the battle." Elise smiled at him.

"When I woke up afterward, I found out that one of my only friends had been killed and your priests wanted to let me die, too," said Falorn, but he could see which way things were going.

"Alex knighted you," she said.

"A lot of good it's done me," he grumbled, but Elise had already spurred her horse toward the approaching riders. Freeing his hands by tossing his bow and quiver to the side of the road where he hoped he might find them again, Falorn urged his horse after her.

"Elise! Wait," he shouted as he struggled to catch up. She pushed her horse to a gallop, and pointed her sword straight at the leader of the oncoming soldiers.

"*Marré!*" she screamed as she charged.

Something bright flashed in the corner of Falorn's eye. Heat seared his back. His horse reared, nearly throwing him. After a few seconds, he brought the animal back under control. He saw Elise, far ahead. The soldiers had spread out into a loose half-circle. A few rode toward Elise, answering her challenge. The caped man rode straight for Falorn, with most of the armored men close behind. *He's the wizard,* Falorn suddenly knew.

Falorn drew his sword and charged the leader. The man wore no helmet or armor that Falorn could see. His purple cape billowed as he rode. A deep green velvet doublet laced up his chest, and he held a shimmering longsword.

The wizard pointed his sword at Falorn and called out something in a guttural tongue. Falorn ducked low and rode at the man as hard as he could. The hair on his head and arms stood on end; the air crackled with electricity, like the edge of a storm.

Falorn shouted and swung his blade as something broke in the air around him. The sky shattered in his face.

His arm shivered as the sword bit into flesh. Someone screamed.

Then the world went silent.

His horse bucked and plunged. Falorn threw his free arm out to keep his balance. He swept his sword arm as he moved. Green sparks obscured his sight. *I have no idea what I'm swinging at.*

The dancing sparks began to clear from in front of his eyes. Two of the armored men lay dead in the road, their horses nowhere in sight. Less than two horse lengths away, the caped man bellowed and shouted. Falorn saw his cheeks and lips move, but heard no sound.

Most of the caped man's left sleeve lay torn open, and blood welled from a long, deep cut. The wizard looked up, his eyes widening as Falorn closed the distance between them.

The man raised his longsword to deflect Falorn's thrust. His weapon no longer glowed with energy. Its edge looked dented and slightly bent; soot blackened the blade. The man turned a second blow. He fought with fierce desperation, despite the fresh blood flowing from his arm.

Falorn's hearing began to return, in a burst of clattering hooves and swordblows.

He felt a fierce joy, even as other troopers started to close in. This man held the fourth lion card, and it wanted to be *his.*

"Help me!" the man screamed at the soldiers behind him.

Falorn swung again. The wizard's longsword shattered.

The man screamed as Falorn's broadsword dipped and drank his blood. Two armored men closed in as Falorn exulted. His blood sang with victory.

Something must have showed in his eyes. The soldiers turned their horses and fled, with Falorn right behind them. He cut one man down; the other had a faster horse. Soon all of the soldiers galloped wildly away.

Falorn and Elise sat on their horses on an empty stretch of road, littered with a half-dozen dead or badly wounded troopers.

Dismounting, Falorn walked back to where the leader's body had fallen. The dead wizard stared blindly upward. Blood soaked the purple velvet of his cape, and the ground around him.

After only a moment's search, Falorn found the cards. His breath caught as he saw the first one. A thick-maned crimson lion pranced across a flat, scarlet landscape, preening as if all the world watched him. Here and there, patches of rust-colored grass colored the red ground a little. The lion walked alone. Nothing else challenged his dominion over the red ivory kingdom.

Beneath the lion, Falorn spread out four other plaques. Trees covered each of them. A lone blue elm crested the blue grass of a solitary hill, silhouetted against a lapis lazuli sky. A weeping gold willow clutched the utmost edge of an eroding river bank, trailing glistening streamers into the bright shimmer of flowing gold water. A tall green spruce rose out of the thick snow which covered a deep evergreen wood, the sky behind it pale green with the gathering clouds that signified a fresh snowfall to come. Finally, an overgrown hedge of scarlet holly decorated the outskirts of a ruined estate's tumbled walls. Bright, poisonous berries covered the stout bush, looking sweet and irresistible.

With difficulty, Falorn tore his eyes away from the cards and looked up. Elise had finished checking the other bodies and now walked toward him. He tucked the cards into his pouch and replaced the leather bag around his neck. A deep contentment filled him as the red lion joined its fellows, like a purr that spread warmth through his blood and into the marrow of his bones.

"Have you finished with him?" Elise asked, watching him put the cards away.

"Almost." Falorn fumbled at the body, removing a pouch of coins and a gold ring. In his distraction, he almost didn't notice the thick gold links around the man's neck, or the silver tree that fastened his cape; Elise pointed them both out to him. He offered them to her, but she waved his hand away.

"You look a little dazed," she said. "Did he hit you?"

"No. I don't think so." Falorn felt over himself, but found no blood. "What happened with that noise? I couldn't see or hear anything for a minute. I thought they were going to kill me."

"They couldn't see anything either. You hit the man as he was casting a spell. He lost control of it."

"What was he trying to do?"

"You know as much about it as I do. Cook you, I suppose. He got a couple of his own men instead. I'm sure the survivors loved him for that."

"I guess they'll be back soon. We should go and find the others."

"There will be more than just the survivors returning. One of them told me there's a whole army behind them. We'd get out of here quickly; we're certainly not going back the way we came." Falorn looked around. None of the fallen soldiers moved, or made any noise. *He didn't live long after he told her, I guess.*

"We're cut off from Delerian?"

"Northfall, too. We'll be cut off from our heads if we just stand here much longer."

"You're right," Falorn said. His legs wobbled a little as he stood up.

He tried to force the shakiness away, walking over to where he'd dropped his bow and quiver.

"Falorn?" He heard Elise from behind, and turned to look. "Thanks for following after me."

He thought for a moment. "You're welcome," he finally said, unsure how else to respond.

"I get a little carried away in fights sometimes. It's nice to know there's another sword behind me."

"You'd do the same for me," he said, stooping to retrieve the bow. "Now let's go find the others."

They found the Forbidden City with ridiculous ease. Three days after the fight, high black walls loomed before them. All of them now wore priests' garb, with Cirque dressed as an inquisitor. The Hellein had coached them on how to seem convincingly priestly, and their acting and documents had passed muster at a dozen guardposts since Ryal had returned to his own shape. Ryal's spells had subtly disguised them all, masking his own injuries as well as shifting their facial features. Sbashe again wore a dog's torso, no less grudgingly than before.

Ryal looked haggard, both from his wounds and from the strain of holding their disguises in place. He could preserve their appearance for perhaps another day or two, he had told Falorn. After that, he would need a long rest before he could cast even the simplest spell again.

"Will these passes get us into the city?" Falorn asked Cirque.

"I hope so. None of my people has ever tried this before."

"Why not?" asked Falorn.

Cirque shrugged. "No one ever thought it would work."

"That's very comforting, Cirque."

"We do what we need to. None of my people has ever needed to get in here this badly before." Cirque's eyes took on an odd cast. "For years, I have waited for a chance."

Is this about the cards, or is Cirque talking about something else? Falorn wondered. "Do you think they'll sense the cards?" he asked the Hellein.

"Probably, but I hope not right away. With luck, we will find Jhodric and be gone before they realize we are within," said Cirque.

"And then all we have to worry about is the army, and the Immortal King."

"You worry too much, Falorn. Plan what you can. The gods will take care of the rest. Now, there is a city to greet, and revenge to be won."

Revenge for what? Falorn wondered, but didn't ask.

Do not ask that question, Sbashe's voice echoed in his mind. *Never ask him that question.*

Guards in black-colored armor watched from the walls as the four of them approached: an inquisitor, two priests, and a hunting dog. Twenty soldiers stood in the shadow of the massive gatehouse, which guarded the only visible entrance to the Forbidden City's walls. The men-at-arms wore unadorned black surcoats over mail hauberks. Their armor glistened with some sort of polished black coating. Black helms covered their heads and faces; Falorn could hardly tell one from another. A thin line of silver trimmed the lone officer's helm and surcoat. Otherwise, he looked identical to his men. The soldiers wore long, two-handed broadswords with odd, thorn-shaped blades. About half of them carried crossbows as well.

"Passes," the officer grunted at them as they approached. He showed none of the deference of other soldiers they had encountered. *Of course not,* Falorn realized. *This is the Forbidden City. They must be some sort of elite just to be here. These soldiers must see dozens of inquisitors and provincial priests every day. We're nothing to them.*

The officer scanned the passes carefully, reading every description and checking it against their faces and features. He leafed through each of the sheaves of paper, examining every signature and countersignature.

"You're an odd group," the officer finally said. "Your papers look in order, but I've had no word from any of the Temples that you're coming." He paused, making one last, cursory flip through their papers. When none of them spoke, he continued. "I'm not going to sign your papers. Maybe you've got legitimate business, maybe you don't. What I'm going to do is have four of my troopers take you to the Temple Complex entrance and turn you over to the guards there. If you've got legitimate business here, the grand inquisitor on duty will sort it out quickly enough. If not, that's where we'd be taking you anyway."

Cirque nodded, but said nothing in reply. The five of them silently followed the pair of guardsmen who led them through the thick, black stones of the gatehouse walls. Another pair of soldiers walked behind them, with crossbows leveled at their backs. Falorn looked around as they walked through the high arched gateway, which towered far above his head. The stones looked like they had been fitted entirely without mortar.

That's not it, exactly, Sbashe's voice said in his mind. *Many of the stones were placed magically. One key word by the right wizard, and the whole thing would come tumbling down on top of us.*

Isn't that a strange way to build a city? Falorn asked.

There's a reason behind it. If a besieging army ever breached the gate, the defenders would bring the gatehouse down and the walls would be sealed again, Sbashe answered.

How do you know all this?

The guard officer thinks about it a lot. You would too if you had to stand underneath it all day. He thinks someday it's going to all come down on top of him.

Could it fall down by mistake? Falorn asked Sbashe.

It hasn't yet.

Without a word spoken, the soldiers walked them through the gatehouse, and onto the streets of the Forbidden City.

12

A Shared Road

I'm still not sure what's forbidden about this city, but it sure is ugly, Falorn thought to himself as they passed through the gates. He'd asked Elise and the Helleinen about the Forbidden City's name, but none of them gave him much of an answer beyond, "That's just what they call it in the Seven Kingdoms." Now, gray-walled buildings sprouted up from the cobblestones like giant weeds. The randomness of the city surprised Falorn. He had expected something orderly; instead, minarets jumbled against old brick warehouses and rows of narrow, slate-roofed tenements. Alleys cut haphazardly through the misshapen blocks of old and new construction. Few of the twisting streets looked wide enough for wagons; some barely looked wide enough for people. Gray faced every building, everywhere he looked.

The soldiers marched precisely, stepping and turning as if on parade, never looking behind to see if their charges still followed. Somehow, Falorn knew that the two crossbowmen behind took equal pains in carrying out their duties. People scuttled in and out of alleys and twisted lanes: gray- and black-clad people, soldiers and priests, all of them moving purposefully from place to place like so many cockroaches avoiding the light.

A few glanced furtively in the direction of Falorn and his companions, as if curiosity were one of the things forbidden in this overbuilt city.

As they walked, the alleys began to widen. Deeper in the city, corridors had been demolished and rebuilt with new temples and palaces of gray brick and stone. Smooth avenues of rain-polished brick divided the new buildings into gray spheres of influence. The buildings began to grow larger. Single buildings gave way to walled compounds.

The soldiers led them to the largest of all these walled structures, a broad arc of heavily domed stone buildings which rose up out of the very center of the city. Whether the temple complex had been constructed on a natural hill or an artificial one, Falorn could not tell. *For all I know, it might be built on the ruins of previous palaces.* The place reminded him of the summer palace in Cathan—in scope, if not in coloration.

They walked to another gatehouse, where their escort departed. Their new captors looked much the same, although their black surcoats bore scarlet trim to identify them as temple guards. These new soldiers received the four of them impassively, unimpressed by the gate guards' story. Six of the temple men-at-arms escorted them through the gate, all of them armed with swords and crossbows.

Those swords are magical, you know, Sbashe told Falorn, *every one of them.*

Meaning they'll cut us to bits as soon as they realize we're not priests? asked Falorn.

I don't know about that. I just thought you might want to know, Sbashe answered.

Thanks. Falorn glanced at the soldiers' blades. *They don't look very special. Just normal swords, like the one I'm wearing.*

You just have to know what to look for. Your sword is nice enough. If any of these soldiers tells you he wants to trade, though. . . .

I'll keep it in mind if the subject comes up.

The inside of the Temple Complex wound and twisted with the same irregularity as the makeshift streets of the city. All the courtyard and open space had long since been roofed over and filled with more buildings. Stepping within the walls of the Immortal King's palace felt like stepping into a mountain, or a deep underground chamber. *The dwarves would feel right at home in this place,* Falorn thought. *I'll bet it's not hard to find poison here, either.*

They walked deep into the dark, teeming hill of the Temple Complex. Only occasional torches lit the walls, although crowds of priests, soldiers, and gray-robed servants shared the hallway with them, jostling by like so many rats in a sewer tunnel. Here and there, a shard of light slipped into the palace accidentally, through a chink in some oddly reconstructed bridging wall or ceiling, but nowhere did they pass a window or a patch of open sky.

Twice they descended deep, spiraling flights of stairs. Only after they had gone far beneath the surface did the guards stop them in front of a tremendous pair of doors. At the apex of their arch, the doors stood more than twice Falorn's height. Elaborate brass flourishes edged darkly stained oak panels. Each door held a heavy brass knocker in the shape of a dog's head, mounted at eye level. None of the brasswork had seen polish in a very long time.

"You go in there," one of the soldiers said. Those were the first words any of the temple men-at-arms had spoken to them.

"Should we knock first?" Cirque asked.

"I don't expect it matters. The Grand Inquisitor'll be expecting you. He expects everyone. If your story's true, we'll be waiting here to take you to your assignment."

"Of course our story is true."

"I believe you," said the guard, "but I'm just a soldier. The question is, will the Grand Inquisitor believe you? The Grand Inquisitor to His Majesty the Immortal King sees things no one else does. He's touched with immortality himself, they say."

"I am certain we will feel honored to be in his presence."

"Feel what you like. He terrifies me. All the gods won't help you if you're lying."

"We have nothing to hide," said Cirque. He lifted the clapper on the knocker to his right, but then put it down without sounding it. Instead, he reached for the door handle and pulled the right-hand door outward.

Darkness filled the room. Only gradually did a light begin to shimmer outward from a distant wall. All of the furnishings took on a slight blue cast in Falorn's eyes. He and the others stood in a room as large and high-ceilinged as the Queen of Cathan's dining hall. To his left, books covered the entire wall—shelf after shelf of leather-bound volumes, extending all the way to the chamber's vaulted ceiling. Long wooden tables stretched across the wall to his right, covered with beakers and jars and other implements of brass or glassware.

In front of him Falorn saw only darkness. Slowly, a shape began to coalesce as the dim light rose. First a wooden, high-backed chair appeared, with arms like lions' paws stretched outward in front. Then the figure seated within the chair began to take on clearer form and definition.

Falorn drew in a breath. The thing in the chair was eight feet tall, at least. And it was not, *could not* be human. Leathery skin covered it like a pig's hide, but with a greenish cast. The face had a pig's flattened snout, and flared nostrils. Its eyes glowed in the dimness, like luminous orange coals at the bottom of a dead-looking pile of ashes. Long, curled horns sprouted from the sides of its forehead, where a human's temples might be. The horns looked like the rams' horns Falorn had seen in the mountains. It had ears like a wolf, and wisps of wiry black hair grew in patches on the back of its head and neck.

"Foolish creatures," the thing boomed out in a deep, deep voice. "Do you really think you can fool *me*?"

"I . . . I am not certain what you mean," said Cirque, haltingly. The Hellein's hand crept toward his sword, but stopped halfway there.

"Don't think to fool me with your pitiful lies, or to impress me with your children's toys. I know exactly who you are, and exactly why you are here."

"You do?" asked Cirque. It looked like he had meant to say something else.

"Of course I do. And soon, you will die slowly for what you have done these last few weeks. Soon you will beg for the human mercy which I entirely lack."

Why is that man in that ridiculous costume? asked a voice in Falorn's head.

What? He's going to kill us, said Falorn.

Him? How? Sbashe seemed honestly baffled.

I don't know—rip our heads off maybe? Does it matter right now? Do you know a way out of here? asked Falorn.

Rip your head off? Him? He can barely reach your head.

What are you talking about? Falorn asked.

The short man in the ratty chair in front of you. What do you think? Why are you all so afraid?

What do you mean "short man"? That thing's hideous, and it's an arm's length taller than I am.

Oh. I keep forgetting, Sbashe said. *You can't see through magic, can you?*

I can't see magic at all, much less see through it, said Falorn.

This is magic. We're standing in a bare stone room about twenty feet square, with two doors on the far wall. There's an illusionist—a kind of wizard—sitting in a chair between the doors playing with your minds. He does have a sword, but otherwise he looks pretty harmless. Why don't you kill him so we can get on with this search for the cards?

Falorn looked around. Cirque and Elise looked cowed, with no thought of their weapons at all. He wondered if they saw the same thing he did. He hoped Sbashe knew what she was talking about.

I do, came an assurance in his mind. *Now will you kill him already?*

Can I have some help on this? asked Falorn.

If you need it. This is your quest, though. Don't expect me to do all the work. The last words came accompanied by the image of a playful nip, the kind sheepdogs give to their charges to get them moving.

Falorn looked at the creature on the chair. Its glowing eyes focused only on Cirque, as the clear leader of the expedition. With a quiet sigh, Falorn drew his sword and began walking forward toward the towering wooden chair.

"What are you doing?" the voice boomed at him.

"Falorn! Don't," he heard Elise's voice from behind.

As he drew close, the creature seemed to contract, and its shape reform. The chair shrank, and became an old padded armchair, its velvet cover faded and worn. A thin man, a head smaller than Falorn, jumped from the chair to meet the attack. A broadsword seemed to spring into his hand, as if he had never sheathed it at all.

That sword is magical, by the way, Sbashe told him.

Thanks. You might have said something before, Falorn said.

There was no reason to. I thought you'd be quicker, and he wouldn't have a chance to draw it.

The thin man met Falorn's attack and parried it easily. He followed with a slashing series of counterattacks which Falorn fought off with little trouble. The man moved quickly, but Falorn had reach on him, and the lion cards gave him endurance as well. The man attacked again with an overhand stroke. Falorn reached up to parry, his mind thinking ahead to a step inward and attack.

Falorn's sword shattered when the magic blade hit it squarely. Metal splinters flew. Falorn stepped in to attack, and found himself holding a hilt and a hand's length of jagged blade.

The lions took over his blood and veins, overwhelming his shock. He dropped the blade and leaped at the man, tackling him before the thin man could bring his blade back down. They hit the floor together, the illusionist on the bottom. The wizard's head thumped into the stone flags. He stopped moving, stunned.

Falorn stood up, dazed. He shook himself. His head began to clear a little. He looked over at the fragments of his sword scattered across the floor. He shook his head again. Stooping down, he picked up the illusionist's broadsword.

Falorn looked back at the fallen wizard and saw Cirque standing above the man, wiping blood from the blade of a knife.

"Did you have to do that?" Falorn asked. "He was down."

"And now he will stay down." The Hellein shrugged. "In the Seven Kingdoms, that is the way we must do things. There is no mercy between their people and mine."

"Not *now* there isn't. You didn't have to kill him."

The Hellein shrugged again. "Someday you will understand, if you live to be even half my age. There is a great deal of vengeance which I have yet to exact." Falorn saw the feral gleam in Cirque's eye and said nothing further.

With the wizard's death, the room's illusions had vanished. The walls were formed of rough-cut blocks of crudely cemented gray stone. Behind them, the wooden double doors remained the same impressive artifacts. Falorn noticed that Elise had barred the entrance from the inside, sealing the guards from the room—although he doubted they'd heard anything through the thick wood. In front of him, the wall contained two doors, just as Sbashe had described. A faint blue aura edged one of the unadorned wooden portals.

Is that left door magical? Falorn asked Sbashe.

You're learning. It is. He looked back at the others. Cirque gripped Ryal around the middle as he walked. The wounded Hellein leaned heavily on Cirque, and held his shoulder. Despite his disguise, Ryal looked worn and pale. Elise stood with her sword drawn. She looked warily from side to side, as if she expected an attack to spring from the walls at any moment. She avoided Ryal's eyes.

Sbashe, did you tell them about the illusionist?

I thought it best not to.

Why not? Falorn asked.

Elise's mind is closed to me. That makes it . . . unpleasant to communicate with her. She is hiding something—from me or from herself—and

I prefer not to pry. I talk with her only in great need. Ryal is hurt, more so than he wants you to know. To communicate with him, I must take on some of the pain he is masking with his mind, and impair my own abilities. Cirque, I can talk with. But he has his own reasons for traveling in this country, and they are not the same as your reasons. You are here in self-defense. He is here for revenge. His thoughts are very dark at this time, and I do not wish to share them. For those reasons, I prefer to talk with you.

Thank you, said Falorn. *I'm flattered that you choose to talk with me.*

I enjoy your conversation. Your thoughts do not disturb me. It has been a long trail behind and will be a longer trail ahead. I am glad of company to share the road with, Sbashe said.

Thanks for sharing my road, answered Falorn, deeply flattered.

Well, speaking of roads, were you planning on trying one of those doors?

Yes. Of course. Falorn realized he'd been standing still, doing nothing. He walked toward the right hand door—the nonmagical one.

"Falorn, what are you doing?" asked Elise.

"Would you rather go back the way we came?" He wanted to get out of the illusionist's room. The dead wizard's body on the floor reminded him of questions he didn't want to answer, both about himself and about the Helleinen.

He swung the door open quickly, sword in his hand. The broadsword felt natural, as if he'd used it for months instead of picking it up only moments before. For a moment he felt a sense of invincibility, armed with a magic weapon and the cards. *Watch it,* he told himself. *The last person to use this magic sword just got beaten by an unarmed man. And besides, even the chamberpot-washers in this place seem to carry magic swords.*

I couldn't agree more, said Sbashe's voice in his mind. *If you die here, I'll have a long trek back to the mountains alone.*

I'm glad someone will miss me, Falorn said.

What about Sera? You think of her often; I know her image from your mind. Surely she will miss you.

I only wish I knew, Sbashe. Sometimes I think she would, and sometimes I think she doesn't care about me at all. I don't know if she thinks about me at all, or if I was just convenient.

Maybe someday I'll be able to tell you, Sbashe said.

Maybe. If I ever see her again.

You will, I think. She has come into your life too many times to leave it now.

Do you know that? Is that some sort of magic sight, or are you just hoping like I am?

Just hoping, I'm afraid. But time will tell.

Behind the door lay a short hall, with three open doorways leading from it. Falorn walked cautiously onto the wooden floorboards of the hallway; they seemed like the first things he'd seen in the whole city colored anything other than gray. A narrow opening at the end of the hall proved to be a dumbwaiter, somewhat more elegant in its construction than the one he'd climbed through in the Baron of Golden Reeds's castle.

Falorn looked into the first doorway. He noticed Sbashe beside him, although none of the others had yet followed him into the hallway. He found himself looking into a wide bedchamber. Fluted wooden pillars supported a silk canopy, which overhung a large bed of polished boards and brass. Matching chestnut-colored tables sat on either side of the bed. To one side of the room, a massive cabinet dominated the wall. The other side contained little besides a brass bathtub, a washbasin, and a bucket. A woven rug covered much of the floor.

Is this real? He asked Sbashe.

Yes. The room has the taste of magic, but there are no illusions here.

Let's leave it then. Leave him the privacy of his bedroom, said Falorn.

He's dead, Falorn.

I know that. But we're not here for loot. If there aren't any cards here, I don't want anything else.

You have his sword, Sbashe said.

That's different. He broke mine.

At least look around.

Falorn poked through the room halfheartedly, but found nothing of interest. The cabinet contained clothing, mainly silks and velvets, as well as black inquisitor's robes trimmed with cloth-of-gold. He wandered across the hall to the other two rooms, joined by now by Elise and the Helleinen.

The first room he dismissed quickly. It looked like a workroom of some sort. The vials and beakers largely duplicated the illusions he'd seen along one wall of the outer room, although Sbashe assured him of the objects' reality. Several jars of clear liquid cooked slowly over a small clay stove. A row of cages lined the top half of one wall, above a file of cabinets. He found the cages vaguely disturbing, but spent little time investigating them. Instead, he opened the connecting door between the two rooms and entered the third of the wizard's chambers.

He paused for a long moment before he could walk more than a few steps into the room. It reminded him too much of Sera's old room in her father's castle. After the initial startlement, the resemblance began to fade. The room actually shared little in common with Sera's, except for the rows of books. Shelves and bookcases covered every wall. Hundreds of thick leather-bound volumes competed for space with smaller, cloth-jacketed books. Interspersed between the books, odd curiosities sat on the shelves. Some of the objects baffled Falorn, such as a ball held within a brass frame which allowed it to spin freely. Odd patterns of blue, green, and brown covered the ball, as well as captions in neatly lettered black ink. He spun the ball idly, then stopped abruptly at the sight of familiar words. Two brown areas bore the captions "Cathan" and "Calathan." An uneven blue line between them had been labeled "Calambria." All three words had figured prominently in his lessons, and in Elise's lost history book. He spun the ball again, before moving on from the mystery of the spherical map.

Other objects looked more familiar. A bleached goat's skull looked out at him from a gap between books. An empty wasps' nest filled one of the skull's eye sockets. Pots of colored ink sat here and there, as well as on the pitted top of the round table in the room's center. An open book sat on the table's center, along with two closed volumes. Someone had been writing in the margins of the volume, and Falorn could see numerous crossed-out places and corrections in the neat script letters of the book's text. The marginal notes and corrections had been made in a different hand, with less of an eye toward precision. He recognized only a few words within the text; he could pronounce others, but the lengthy collections of letters meant little to him. He could make out a few of the marginal notations. "Wrong, all *wrong*," one of them said. Another read, "Use 2 cups, not 1," with an arrow pointing to a place in the text.

Falorn glanced at the other books on the table. He gasped as one of the volumes flashed bright blue. *I know that book!*

He reached over and gently opened the cover, just to be sure. The image of a green lion looked up at him, and somehow the proud creature seemed to be *smiling* at him. His breath quickened. Blood pounded in his face and chest. He flipped a page and saw four tall trees, twins to the ones in his pouch. His blood sang. He looked at the words on the page, but the letters swam away from him, shifting like tiny fish darting away from his touch and understanding.

Falorn? He heard a voice, and realized it had been calling within his mind for some time. *Falorn? Are you all right?*

Yes. I am, he answered, wrenching his mind away from the book. He closed the cover, and shut the ornate brass clasp. *I think we should go on now, though. I found what I came to this room for.*

I'm glad. The others want to move on as well. They have found a path farther into the temple, but they could not wake you.

I'm awake now. He wished for the pack they had left at the gate with the horses. Instead, he took off his cloak and carefully wrapped the book within it. He strapped the bundle with his sword belt, reluctantly discarding his Delerian-made scabbard, which did not fit the wizard's blade. Tucking the package under his left arm, he stood up. He picked the sword up off the table before following Sbashe from the room and back through the hallway to the illusionist's outer chamber.

13

A Taste of Blood

The second door from the chamber now stood ajar. Elise leaned against the wall beside it, her sword drawn. Ryal sat on the floor while Cirque hovered next to him. Much of the color had returned to the wounded Hellein's face. Falorn wondered how much time had passed.

"Ready?" Elise asked him, her expression oddly cold.

"I'm ready," he answered.

"Good. I'll go first. You guard the rear. Cirque has to help Ryal."

"Shouldn't I go first? I have the cards. I have a better chance of see-ing something coming."

"I said I'll go first. I don't care about your damned magic—I think I know a little better than you how to see what's coming. I've been a knight for ten years now, since I turned eighteen. I'm a better soldier than you'll ever be."

Falorn started to say something, then thought better of it. He fell into line obediently at the rear. Sbashe trotted beside him. As they left the room, Falorn took one of the torches from the wall-sconces, tucking his newfound sword beneath his left arm along with the book.

The gray stone passage sloped downward into darkness. Only the torch illuminated the hall. They saw no side doors, and no one else besides themselves in the hallway. After a few minutes, the passage merged into a long corridor sheathed in smooth black stone. The new hallway stretched widely to either side; they all could have walked abreast easily if they chose. The torchlight barely showed the outlines of the ceiling, high above their heads.

Only a few doors broke the symmetry of the long stone hallway, which seemed to stretch far and utterly straight in either direction. A few candles shed small pools of light here and there; the candles seemed to be placed at the tops of high, sculptured cabinets set against either wall at irregular intervals.

His chest began to warm. Falorn felt the flow of his blood quicken.

"Elise?" he called out softly.

"What?" she asked.

"There are cards ahead. We're walking straight toward them."

She said nothing for a moment. He watched Cirque supporting Ryal in front of him. The wounded Hellein could barely walk at all now; Cirque almost carried him. He glanced behind, looking for signs of pursuit.

"You'd better come up front, then," she finally said. "I suppose Sbashe can watch the rear." He walked to her side silently. She wore a hard expression. "I'm sorry," she said as he held her gaze. "I was wrong to say what I did. You've already proven you can fight. I was upset with myself for not attacking in that other room like you did. My behavior wasn't knightly, and neither were the things I said to you after."

"I understand," said Falorn. No other words seemed appropriate.

He stopped to look at one of the candlelit cabinets. The hinged face of the cabinet had been carved of some dark wood in the shape of a full-sized man's nude body. The man looked about forty years old, thick-waisted and bearded. A line running down the center of his body showed where the two halves of the cabinet door would separate to open outward. *It's a coffin*, Falorn suddenly realized. The cabinet held a body within. The carving depicted the features of the man inside. He marveled at the skill of the carver, but also at the oddness of the depiction. The man's body lacked dignity, denied even his clothing in death. This empty, dustless corridor of smoothly polished black stone seemed like a strange place for an underground graveyard.

"Why hide these bodies all the way down here?" he wondered out loud. "Who would rob them? There's nothing to steal."

"Maybe the purpose is not to hide the bodies from robbers," Cirque said from behind. Falorn had thought the Hellein too preoccupied to listen. "Maybe the purpose is to hide the bodies from everyone."

They walked on. Almost imperceptibly, the corridor began to widen. Soon, the torchlight did not reach the walls on either side. Only the occasional candle showed the boundaries of the hallway.

"The cards are very close." Falorn said. He could feel their presence burning into his blood. Part of him wanted to run straight ahead toward them, the call felt so strong. He wondered if whoever held the cards felt similarly. Jhodric and whoever accompanied him doubtlessly knew that Falorn approached.

We have to be walking into a trap. He said nothing however. *Everyone else knows what's going on as well as I do.*

A light shone in the center of the hallway ahead. As they walked closer, the light separated into dozens of tiny pinpricks of candle flame. A death-cabinet more elaborate than any of the others stood in front of them, festooned with lights like a festival altar. It depicted an old, old man, nude like all the others, skin withered into countless wrinkles and creases. Carved arms lay folded across his chest, and his eyelids had closed, although the pose somehow did not look restful. Unlike the other cabinets, Falorn could detect no seam or hinges on this one.

To either side of the coffin stood a ghoulish honor guard. Five armored corpses held weapons ready at each of the cabinet's flanks. The dead soldiers wore no helmets. In the candlelight, Falorn could see skin pulled tight over fleshless faces. Each of the dead men's faces lay fully exposed in the dim illumination of the candle flames, but none had other visible flesh.

Mail byrnes covered the bodies, the armored links extending to mid-calf. Metal rings had been sewn to their hose and gauntlets. Black velvet surcoats fit closely over the dead men's armor, each with a different coat-of-arms embroidered in gold thread. Black capes, also of velvet, swept over their backs. The mail hoods attached to their byrnes had been thrown back on top of the capes. Falorn saw no other rods or obvious props to hold the preserved corpses erect in their armor. *I guess someone wired supports through the bodies,* he thought. *That must have been a hideous job.*

The cabinet and each of the dead honor guards glowed with a faint blue aura. The magic that the card showed him might be what kept the bodies standing, Falorn realized. Or perhaps a spell had been used to preserve the dead in their uncorrupted, if hardly lifelike, state.

Falorn carefully set down the book and now-guttering torch, careful to leave distance between them. Picking up his sword, he walked up to the cabinet, and set his left hand on its face. He had expected to find the cards here. From the coffin itself he sensed nothing, although he still felt the cards nearby.

"What is it?" he asked, out loud but quietly.

Cirque laughed bitterly from behind him. "I suspect we are looking at the remains of the Immortal King," the Hellein said. "Apparently, he was not so immortal after all. After seven hundred years of seclusion within this Forbidden City, even the most faithful worshippers within this empire must have begun to doubt at least a little."

"That's a long time to keep a secret," said Falorn.

"No one can keep a secret forever. One piece of evidence from this corpse, and the secret has vanished forever. The cards are not the only thing to be taken from this country, Falorn. There is something here which can cause much more damage."

"We're not here to damage, Cirque. We're here to take the cards away. I didn't agree to anything else."

"I did not ask you to. I agreed to help you with your quest, but *this* is my quest. This body belongs to me."

"We can't take it with us. Ryal's hurt already, and we still have to get the cards."

"This is more important than the cards. The cards will touch a few people's lives, perhaps win a fight or two. This body will affect what people *believe*. We can bring down a kingdom with this body."

This is insane. What will a body prove to anyone? But he knew better than to say that to Cirque directly. "You're talking about a people's religion, Cirque."

"I'm talking about a false god and a dead king. I'm talking about people who would kill a beautiful girl for no reason at all, just because of her race." Cirque stared at Falorn, his eyes purely feral. "This land owes me the price of my daughter's life. I claim the body of their Immortal King in return for the body they desecrated. Before I finish, they will suffer as she suffered."

Falorn looked into the Hellein's wild eyes and said nothing. He stepped aside to allow Cirque to reach the coffin unimpeded. As he walked a few paces to the side, he felt a surge at his chest.

"We're not alone," he said.

"Quite right," said a voice from behind. Falorn wheeled around, glancing to either side. He and Cirque stood in front of the coffin. Elise, Ryal and Sbashe had disappeared into the darkness.

A lone man stepped into the circle of light. Falorn could see other shapes dimly in the darkness behind the newcomer. The man wore a black velvet doublet, laced over a black tunic. Gold thread embroidered the face of the doublet. He looked like the living twin of the dead honor guardsmen.

"Prince Jhodric of Northfall, I assume?" Falorn asked it as a question, but he already knew the answer. He felt the cards the man carried, just as the man surely knew what he bore. They held cards of the same suit, and the cards desperately wanted to unite.

"The same. And you are Sir Falorn, birthplace unknown. My agents finally put a name on you after that unfortunate incident along the Calambria. That was quite a piece of fighting. It was all to my detriment, but I must congratulate your valor, nevertheless."

"Thank you," said Falorn.

"But surely you realize that there is no hope of any such foolishness succeeding now," Jhodric said.

"I'm not sure I understand what you mean."

"You and your doomed elven friend face eight princes of the blood here. I hold at least as many cards as you do, and I am a much better swordsman." Falorn wondered where Sbashe and Elise had gone. *It can't be too far if they took Ryal with them. If they're trying to escape, I'll do all I can to give them a little more time.*

"There are eight of you to our two. But all we need to do is defeat the eight of you," said Falorn. "You can't call any guards without revealing your secret. How many people even know the truth?"

"The truth is that we are eight pure men of the blood of the Immortal King," said Jhodric.

"The Immortal King is dead," Cirque answered him, stepping forward until he stood at Falorn's side. The rear of the wide death-cabinet guarded both of their backs.

"The Immortal King lives on in the blood of each of us. He reveals His will to princes of the blood, and our servants carry out His commands throughout the Seven Kingdoms. Physical death means nothing. His spirit carries on. The secret means nothing to us."

"Then why keep it a secret?" Falorn asked. "Why not summon the guards down on us?"

"Some things," said Jhodric quietly, "are best kept within the family."

His sword slid from its sheath as he stepped forward. The dim figures behind him began to advance as well, taking on shape as they entered the circle of candlelight.

"I'll take Jhodric," Falorn whispered to Cirque. "I think he's wrong about the cards. I may not know how to use them as well, but I think I have more of them."

"Do it," said Cirque. "I will hold off as many others as I can."

Something hissed in the air. One of the men to Falorn's left stiffened and fell. The man next to him stopped and knelt beside the fallen man. He turned his head and looked down. An arrow pierced his jaw. With a choked moan the prince went down, legs twitching spasmodically.

"Get them!" Falorn yelled, and charged forward. Cirque ran beside him, sword swinging. Out of the corner of his eye, Falorn saw a shape spring out of the darkness onto one of the men on the right. A scream pierced the darkness and echoed through the tunnel, dying away slowly.

Got one, Sbashe's voice purred in his mind. With it came the taste of delicious throat's blood from a startled quarry. He saw another man struck by an arrow as he reached Jhodric, and their swords met.

Jhodric cut and parried faster than anyone Falorn had ever fought, in war or practice. He shed Falorn's blade effortlessly, and made the younger swordsman struggle to fend off his counterstrokes. The lions filled Falorn's blood with the challenge of the attack. Falorn concentrated on his opponent's blade, and gave the cards their head.

The two of them danced across the circle of light forever. Neither blade touched flesh. Jhodric barely seemed to move as he pressed Falorn. With the slightest of motions, the prince sent his blade spinning into attack after attack.

At first, Falorn could do nothing but defend against Jhodric's assaults. But as the fight went on, Falorn's blood warmed. After a long while, he began to launch tentative counterstrikes. Then he attacked in earnest. Nothing he could do came close to penetrating the Jhodric's guard, but gradually the pace of the prince's swordplay began to slow.

Falorn found himself smiling. *I'm enjoying this fight*, he realized. *I'm an innkeeper's son and I'm holding off a prince in a swordfight.* Falorn shook his hair like a lion's mane, and felt no dampness. *I'm not even sweating.* He felt no fatigue at all. Muscles rolled and flew like whipcords with each effortless motion of his blade.

After an eternity, Jhodric's stroke slowed. The prince moved economically, stepping only as he had to. Sweat flowed down the older man's face, flattening his straight, bowl-cut hair to his scalp. The prince looked only thirty years old or so, despite his pure white hair. But Falorn had lions in his soul, prancing with the joy of the hunt, and the anticipation of the kill.

His cards aren't helping him, Falorn realized. *They can't or they aren't.* He scored on the prince's arm, his blade flashing out and opening a long cut. *Where are the others? Why haven't any of the other princes jumped in to help him? This fight has gone on forever.* His blade slid beneath Jhodric's feint and bit into his side. Blood dampened the black velvet of the prince's doublet, a wide stain which spread along the man's ribcage.

"You've killed me!" Jhodric cried out, and stumbled. "You've killed a prince of the blood!" Falorn held his ground. The prince's sword shot up. Falorn beat it aside. His own blade streaked across Jhodric's throat. Falorn stepped back and assumed a guard position. He barely noticed as the man's longsword hit the smooth-polished blackness of the floor.

"Now I have," Falorn said.

None of the Seven Kingdoms nobles stood. Elise and Cirque held blades warily, as if waiting for Jhodric's body to rise again. Laying his sword down, Cirque drew a knife and knelt beside the prince. He looked up a moment later, shaking his head. The Hellein reached within the prince's tunic and withdrew a small leather bundle, cutting it free with his knife. He tossed the bundle to Falorn, who caught it without thinking.

Falorn's chest nearly exploded in an outpouring of warmth. Lions capered and pranced around him, nuzzling his side and leaping up to bat playfully at him with velveted paws. He stood in the thickness of a forest, and serpents wound themselves affectionately around his ankles and calves. A gathering storm on the horizon promised warm, needed rain.

Falorn? asked a voice in his mind. *Is this going to start happening all the time? Are you losing your mind?* The animals faded gradually away. He found himself sitting on a stone floor, the forested knoll gone.

I'm fine, he told Sbashe, after his mind refocused. *I hope it won't happen anytime important. But it probably will keep happening until we deal with these cards.*

Then we will have to deal with them quickly.

Fine with me. Falorn unfolded the leather bundle and gently slid the ivory plaques from within. He held a dozen cards in his hand. He felt his blood pulse again as the lions welcomed the new cards, and the serpent greeted a kindred spirit. A long green serpent wrapped around the limb of a spidery verdant tree prepared to drop on a pale green faun grazing below its perch. A green nobleman with a serious expression looked outward from a tower window, scanning the green band of the horizon for an expected messenger bearing urgent news. A pair of twin blue unicorns nuzzled one another at the top of a blue cliff, gazing at the azure vista of an enchanted world. A gold chalice sat proudly in the center of a high gold altar, its surface rippling with some priceless gold liquid which seemed almost to reflect Falorn's image back at him. Four horses pranced and capered across the surfaces of their cards: blue, green, crimson, and gold. The last four cards held apples, each full and delicious and succulent, each bearing secrets, knowledge, poison, or death. *These were the cards Sera stole from her father,* Falorn remembered. *Some of the ones Jhodric's men took away from Sera when they kidnapped her.* The apples tugged at his appetite; he craved food, wondered how long it had been since he'd eaten.

Now stop that. You're making me hungry. Put them away, said Sbashe.

Falorn tucked the cards obediently into his pouch. His stomach rumbled hopefully.

Ryal sat on the floor nearby, husbanding his strength. Elise walked among the dead. She had nearly finished recovering her arrows from the bodies of the nobles. None had survived, Falorn discovered without surprise. Several bore suspicious knife wounds to the throat. *How many princes of the blood can there be in the Seven Kingdoms?* he wondered. The empire was poorer for eight of them now.

Falorn checked his sword once he felt satisfied about the cards' safety. The blade remained keen and unmarred. Blood had shed in droplets from the polished weapon, rather than collecting in the runnel that ran down the center of each side.

"So much for the princes," Cirque said. "Now, I think, it is time to deal with the king."

Falorn stood up to watch. Far from tiring him, the fight had brought energy with it; the new cards felt like a lightning stroke to his spirit. He felt horses champing at the back of his mind, and probing fingers at the edges of his appetite. *Not much help in a fight, though,* he realized. *A prince of the blood may have an edge over an innkeeper's son, but I'll take my chances wagering lions to beat apples any day.*

The cards seemed to coexist easily. The lions held a sort of primacy in his spirit, but each suit of cards filled a different niche, like a hundred aspects which, put together, might form a whole personality. They all shared a deep thirst for wholeness. The more he had, the more he felt their deep desire to be together. He didn't feel it strongly enough to let it affect his actions, and certainly not enough to kill or die for, but it gnawed at the back of his consciousness nonetheless.

Cirque reached the carved front of the death-cabinet. He tapped it twice with the butt of his sword, perhaps expecting a hollow echo. The pommel thumped against the carved face with satisfying solidity.

"How does it open?" Cirque said after an exasperated moment of examination. "There is no hinge or mark of a door."

Falorn thought back to the rooms above. "Maybe there's an illusion on it," he said. "The coffin *is* magical. Try opening it like the others."

"Magical, is it?" the Hellein mused. He probed the center of the cabinet's surface with his blade, and found a seam readily.

"It and the guards. I think the magic is what keeps them standing."

"Cirque, wait!" Ryal cried out, struggling up from the floor. "The spell on that coffin is not illusion! It's necromancy!" At the same time, the lid of the coffin creaked as Cirque's sword levered its two halves apart.

A blue flash filled the chamber so brightly that Falorn thought they would all be blinded. No one else seemed to notice. Even his own sight quickly returned to normal, without even affecting his night vision.

It's magic, not light. You can see it. Sbashe seemed curious.

The thief card shows me things in blue, things that it thinks I ought to see for myself. I'm trying to learn to get better at looking, said Falorn.

Magic is worth looking at. Look at this.

It's going to kill us. "Cirque! Look out for the guards!" Falorn yelled. The armored bodies began to move—stiffly at first, but with increasing fluidity as they got the feel of their long-held weapons and advanced in defense of their dead king.

Their swords are magical. Can you see them? asked Sbashe.

I had guessed that anyway, Falorn answered.

Cirque parried the first pair of attackers. Falorn jumped forward to fend off another who threatened the Hellein's back. The creature still jerked as it moved. Falorn timed the motion, feinted, and cut through its guard before the corpse could respond. The wrist flew cleanly from the guard's body; its sword clattered against the stone with the hand still attached. The creature continued to advance.

"I can't hit them!" Cirque called out from behind him. "I hit them and my sword just bounces off."

"They can't be hit!" Elise shouted. "My arrows aren't doing anything!"

"Get clear!" yelled Falorn. He hoped they could hear him over the clash of swords. "I'll cover you, just get clear. Only magic can hit these things."

With a familiar noise of splintering metal, Cirque's sword shattered. Falorn wheeled, swinging his blade to hold the handless guard off while he looked toward Cirque. The Hellein dove to the ground, and Falorn found himself fighting three opponents.

None of the corpses moved as swiftly or as accurately as Falorn could, but they fought with the tirelessness of the dead.

"Leave the body," he called out to Cirque. Falorn stood a few feet in front of the coffin, holding off all of the guards. Dried pieces of flesh and skeleton flew, but they fought on, undiscouraged and uncaring.

"No," said the Hellein. "Never. We have come too far, and my child has been too long dead." He pried at the cabinet face with the ruins of his blade. The doors creaked with each handspan they opened outward.

Falorn's knee stung. An armless ghoul bit him, piercing flesh beneath his tunic. Falorn yelped. He swung his sword hilt. The pommel crunched into fleshless bone, crushing its skull with the blow. His shoulder ached. He felt blood flowing. The press of creatures in front of him showed no sign of thinning. Only the armless ghoul with the shattered skull had ceased fighting; he still faced nine attackers.

"I have it," Cirque said from behind him. "We can leave now."

"How? How are we supposed to do that?" Falorn asked.

He swung his blade endlessly, with little effect. Even if he failed to tire, so did his opponents. They had spent generations resting for this fight. He dropped a second ghoul, cutting it into four pieces before it finally stopped attacking.

The press began to thin. He heard Elise in the rear, crying out to Marré and swinging a blade. Pictures began to appear in his head. The lions redoubled their efforts, overjoyed at the vision of skulls crushed or pulled apart by the pressure of tearing canines and powerful jaws.

Soon, only two of the things remained standing, and then none. Hands continued to writhe and grasp long after the arms attached to them had been hacked apart. Elise leaned forward, supporting herself on the long blade pried away from the first creature's severed hand. After a moment's rest, she sighed and straightened, pausing to stretch tight muscles in her back and shoulders. She checked and sheathed her own blade before removing one of the dead noblemen's swordbelts. Using the dead man's belt, she slung the captured longsword over her back.

"It's a Marré-cursed awkward weapon," she said, shrugging at Falorn. "But at least it hits them. I'll get rid of it once we're out of here. I know a weapons-dealer or two in Cathan City who will trade half their shops for an enchanted sword, especially if it's got an exotic history."

"Is this exotic enough?" Falorn asked, waving at the bodies and the still-twitching pieces of the Immortal King's last guards.

"They won't believe half of it." She walked over to Ryal, who leaned precariously against a distant wall. "Come on," said Elise, extending a hand, "You can lean on me. It looks like your friend has his hands full."

Falorn looked back at Cirque. The Hellein staggered away from the cabinet. A thin corpse lay across his shoulders. The body looked freshly dead, like an old, old man who had finally given up living only a few minutes before. "Are you going to carry that all the way back to Delerian?" he asked Cirque.

"I thought we might find horses somewhere along the way."

"I hope so. And I hope it doesn't get too warm."

"How *do* we get out?" Elise asked. Ryal had an arm over her shoulder, and walked against her like a drunken soldier.

"If you'd left any of them alive, we might have asked," said Falorn, more with exasperation than his earlier horror. He wouldn't have chosen to kill the noblemen, but they would never, ever have allowed him to leave this underground chamber alive.

"If we'd left any of them alive, we'd just have to kill them now anyway. And I'm too tired now," Elise said. "You're the one who finds all the secret passages. There's bound to be a bunch of them in this hallway. These nobles couldn't have guards saluting them at every turn on the way in here; they must have had secret ways in and out."

"And I am certain," said Cirque, "that they must have a secret way out of the city. This would be their last refuge, if someone attacked the city. They would need their own way to smuggle their secret out."

"Better get looking," Elise said, smiling wryly.

"I will." Falorn checked his blade and went to sheathe it, only belatedly remembering that he no longer had a sheath. He walked over to where he'd set down the book and the now burnt-out torch. Blood from a nearby corpse had stained his cloak, but the pooled liquid had not penetrated through to the book's cover. He tucked the book back under his left arm. Still holding the sword, he concentrated on finding ways *out*.

Traces of blue began to appear in the floor almost immediately, drowning out the dim illumination of the candles. His head no longer throbbed; the headaches he had gotten before had vanished. The blue thief seemed to draw strength as he did, increasing along with the total number of cards he held.

"This way," Falorn said, and began to walk. He limped slightly from the cut on his knee, but the pain in his shoulder had already subsided. The others followed him, all but Sbashe burdened by load or injury.

Once he had found the entrance to the passageway and got them safely started, he walked over to Elise to help her support Ryal.

"I want to thank you," he told her. "You saved me twice in that place."

"Maybe," she answered. "But you might have won either fight without me. It would have taken longer, but you're a fine swordsman when you get started."

"Thanks," Falorn said, "but it's really the cards."

"Some of it's the cards. But they found you for a reason. You work as hard at swordsmanship as anyone I know. You weren't born to it, but you have the talent. You take to it better than many bred to the sword. If the cards vanished tomorrow, you'd still handle a blade better than most. Maybe not well enough to take two flags in a day, but better than most."

"Thanks. It may come to that."

"It may," she said. "They're yours for now, but these cards have their own desires. You never know when they'll change their minds."

"I know it. That's why I want to learn all I can while I have them. I want to have something left after they're gone—if I live that long."

"I think you will. You're too stubborn to die. Stubborn and innocent," said Elise.

"What's that supposed to mean?"

"Wait a few years. You'll know." She looked at him fiercely, then abruptly broke eye contact.

He let her take the book and the torch that provided their light as he transferred Ryal's weight onto his unwounded shoulder. The wizard winced, but otherwise gave no outward signs of pain. Falorn bore as much of Ryal's weight as he could, and hoped the long, looping tunnel that took them ever deeper into the earth would come to an outlet soon.

14

A New Course

They found the tunnel end by smell, long after the candle burned out. The strong scent of fresh manure filled the passageway for what seemed like hours before Elise announced that she had discovered a ladder leading upward.

Light shone downward through a trap door after Elise ascended the ladder. Falorn came next, carrying the barely conscious Ryal. Their magical disguises had faded while they walked, before the candle flame faded away and finally died. Sometime afterward, Ryal's wounds had reopened. They could do little to properly retie the bandages in the darkness.

As soon as they lay Ryal comfortably on the straw that covered the floor of the stone barn, Falorn helped pull Cirque—still carrying the immortal corpse—upward into the light. As soon as the Hellein and the corpse cleared the ladder, Falorn climbed back down to help Sbashe. After a little assistance, the corget scrambled upward with surprising agility.

This is no way to travel. Who thought of these things? The corget asked.

Someone with long fingers and fewer than six legs, answered Falorn.

You should try it sometime. Why travel with that silly human gait of yours?

Because sometimes, in the middle of your travels, you run into a ladder.

Not if I can help it, Sbashe answered.

They surfaced in a narrow stone barn. A single row of stables lined the opposite wall, while the wall next to the trapdoor contained only a few stacked bales of hay. Falorn poked around the slate floor for a moment, and quickly found a second trap door. Beneath it, a short stairway led into a small, dug-out chamber—the size of a generous grave, but no larger.

"I think I've found supplies," Falorn called out. "They may catch us before we can get out of this barn, but we won't starve to death."

He heard a whistle from Elise. "Wait until you see these horses," she said. "They were planning on a *fast* escape if something went wrong."

"That was considerate of them," said Cirque, looking up from Ryal and the bandages.

"I'll say," Falorn said, from halfway down the dugout stairs. "Maybe we can get out of here before that body starts to rot."

"I think if it hasn't rotted after seven hundred years, we're probably safe for a week or two." Elise walked over to the barn's single, wide door as she spoke. She peered through the crack without opening the door, or even removing the bar. "It's about an hour after dawn. We were in there overnight."

"No wonder I'm so hungry," said Falorn.

You're hungry because you stared at those stupid apples, Sbashe's voice answered in his head.

Falorn and Elise carried boxes and already-loaded saddlebags up from the dugout, while Cirque continued to tend Ryal. After they finished preparing everything except actually loading and saddling the horses, they sat down to eat.

"We should move quickly," Elise said, echoing everyone's thoughts. "They may not find the princes' bodies for a while, but they *will* find them. Other people know we went into the city, and they'll wonder when we don't leave."

"We can't forget the rest of the wizards out there, either," said Falorn. "The two we killed weren't the only ones after us. They may not have cards to track us anymore, but that doesn't mean they can't catch us."

Cirque looked up from his food. He seemed to consider his words for a moment before putting down his food and speaking.

"This is the situation," he said. With his index finger he made a small circle in the dust. "We are here, approximately. North of us is the sea, and to the south are mountains, including the ones we climbed over to get here." He drew lines a handspan above and below the circle. "To the east is Delerian. Much of that border is blocked by swamp, forest, or—further to the south—a spur of the mountain range. The Seven Kingdoms extends far to the west, much farther than we could go without being captured."

The blond Hellein paused, and took a swallow from the jug of red wine that sat on the floor between them. He drew a line across the right side of his diagram, and began speaking again.

"The routes to the east have been cut off by now. We came through Tasaria, and caused a stir. There are only a few other passes through the mountains to Cathan, and the garrison on this side will have been bolstered with better soldiers, and probably wizards. They will be looking for us, and they will have descriptions. We cannot count on Ryal's magic, not until his wounds have healed and he has rested.

"There are two passes through the mountain spur into Delerian, but both of them are strongly garrisoned. The swamp and forest are well patrolled on this side of the border, and difficult to cross. There is a long stretch of open border, but it is guarded by castles and an army of occupation. There are frequent raids into Delerian by Seven Kingdoms soldiers.

"Even if we wanted to try the route east, we know that an army of some sort has been assembled to pursue us. We must assume that all routes east of the Forbidden City have been cut off, including the road northeast to Northfall. No doubt, they expect us to travel in that direction."

"Do we have a choice?" Falorn asked. "Why not just travel off the roads?"

"That would mean we would always move more slowly than the Seven Kingdoms troopers pursuing us. If there is a coordinated force under a single commander—and I expect there is by now—we would find ourselves very quickly surrounded. In any event, if we move very quickly, we may have another option."

"What do you mean?"

"Northwest of here is the seaport of Westfort. It is not as large as Northfall, but it is a major center of commerce. If we can ride to Westfort before the roads are cut off, we can escape the Seven Kingdoms by sea."

"By sea?" asked Elise. "The sea is north. We need to go south. The

Seven Kingdoms and Delerian are at war and there's no commerce between them. There's nowhere to go. Where are you planning to take us?"

"I thought we might go to the University, at Letz. It would seem to be a good place to find out more about these cards of Falorn's. From Letz, we can easily find a ship back to Delerian; everybody trades with Letz, and the island enforces its neutrality in all conflicts. We will be as safe there as anywhere in the world. After we return to Delerian, I can arrange for you and Falorn to return to Cathan, and for Sbashe to return to her homeland."

"The University. I hadn't thought of that." Elise stopped, as if mulling the idea over in her head. "It's a good idea, if we can make it. What sort of ride are we looking at?" She and Cirque began discussing the details of the trip. Cirque had been to Westfort once, many years before, and he began mapping the route from memory while Elise quietly asked questions and pointed out possible problems to plan around.

After a few minutes, Falorn's patience came to an end.

"Cirque, what is a 'University'? And what is Letz?" *And why would I want to go back to Cathan, where the queen wants to take my cards?*

"My apologies," said the Hellein. "I thought everyone knew of the island city. I forgot that you had not traveled before this summer. A university is a place where scholars and students gather to learn and work together. There are many institutions which call themselves universities, but usually when people speak of 'the University,' they are talking about the University in Letz, and particularly its College of Magics. It is the best-known place of learning in the world, or at least in all of the world where I have traveled. Some of the world's most learned men and women live and work on the island of Letz, in the city that bears the same name. If there are answers to be had, we can find them in Letz. The answers may be expensive—but if they can be found, they can be found there.

"Letz is more than the home of the University, however. The island is located centrally in the tradeways across the North Sea. From Letz, ships can easily reach any of the lands and great cities which border the sea: Denborel, the largest city in the world; Mestarel, the key to the desert trade across the Great Salt Sea; Merindia; the Rohnan Empire; most of the Seven Kingdoms; and of course, Delerian. For that reason, everyone sends ships to Letz. The city wars with no one, and no one dares war with a city that holds the key to the North Sea trade, and a city that houses the world's most powerful wizards."

"So we'll be safe there."

"As long as we have money, yes."

Falorn glanced over at the laden saddlebags waiting to be placed on the horses' backs. Some of them were filled with gold. The princes of the blood had not planned to spend their exile in poverty, if for some reason escape from invaders or from their subjects became necessary. "It sounds too good to be true," he said. "People have been trying to kill me since the day I left home."

"They will try to kill you for a while longer yet. There is still a great distance to travel before we reach the island city."

"It's good news, though."

"*This* is good news," said Cirque, patting the corpse of the Immortal King beside him. "Eight dead princes of the blood are good news. From Letz, we can begin to spread that news. The rest, I care nothing about."

Falorn felt a slight chill as the Hellein turned back to planning. The warmth of the cards quickly swallowed his misgivings, but as he got up and began to pack the horses, he could not help feeling new uncertainties about the directions his friends wanted him to travel in.

Falorn had never ridden a horse this fast before. The mare tore across the road like a tornado. She seemed to anticipate his every move and react before he could even nudge her with his knee.

Warmth filled his chest, despite the autumn breeze. Visions of horses prancing occupied his mind, blue and green and gold and crimson horses playing. His own mare frolicked alongside them.

They had taken all twelve horses from the barn's stalls, and loaded them with most of the cached supplies. After cutting across a broad, fallow field, they joined the northwest road out of sight of the Forbidden City, and rode hard along it, hoping the speed of their horses could outdistance any pursuit. They had changed into fresh clothes from the stores in the barn. In his gold-trimmed black velvet doublet, shiny tunic of black silk, and heavy black wool cape, Cirque looked very much the part of a grand inquisitor. No checkpoint guard dared to question his credentials closely, particularly given the obvious urgency of the valuable cargo he and his escort carried draped over one of their long-legged racehorses. Cirque explained the preserved body as that of an outlaw wizard arrested for treason. No one seemed surprised that a grand inquisitor would be carrying such a cargo, and in such a condition.

They hardly stopped at all over the next four days. Switching horses repeatedly, they rode long into each night, and camped only when they feared one of the beautiful animals would lame itself by running in the darkness. They avoided camping at cities and checkpoints when they could, although late one night Cirque ordered a tired-looking junior officer to allot them the top floor of the guardhouse he commanded.

The Hellein assured them that wizards and soldiers pursued them closely, but Falorn saw no signs of anyone giving chase. None of the guards along their route seemed terribly suspicious, or even particularly alert. They traveled far west of the territory where Helleinen raiders might be expected from Delerian; the soldiers on the northwest road watched for highwaymen or runaway serfs, not regicides. A grand inquisitor returning to his home territory with quarry in hand might be a memorable sight, but ordinary guardsmen seemed loathe to interfere in any way with the performance of a grand inquisitor's duties, or even to draw his notice.

Eight days later, they entered the city of Westfort.

The city predated the existence of the Seven Kingdoms. It had grown up around the West Fort, which guarded the mouth of the Green River before the Kingdom of Gatterin had been incorporated into the larger confederation. The weathered stone cathedral across the river from the old West Fort served Acouros, chief god in this land long before the birth of the Immortal King. Priests in Gatterin now worshipped both deities— and openly called the Immortal King the son of Acouros—but in the hearts of the upper priests, Acouros reigned alone in the heavens.

Cirque knew that much about the city, and they learned a few more details from shepherds they questioned on the outskirts of its walls. By the time they rode past the battered walls of the Fort (twice taken by siege and repaired by its new masters) and over the spindly stone arch that bridged the river and led to the cathedral and city proper, they had a fair idea of where to look for a ship.

For a trade center of such importance, Westfort had few inhabitants. Perhaps ten thousand people lived within its walls, and a few thousand shepherds and cottagers in the hills which surrounded the city. The region's gravelly soil sustained few farms. Most of the city's food supply came downriver by barge, or from the shepherds' herds. The people of the city supported themselves by craftwork and manufacturing; Westfort's guildsmen joined wood and fitted brass and forged steel, producing finished goods to be poled back upriver, or carried on long galleys all along the coast and out to sea on fragile carracks, to other trade centers beyond the Seven Kingdoms' borders.

Trees were not scarce, but the poor soil stunted their growth. Guildsmen used the local pine woods for furniture and floorboards. They burned coal for warmth and cooking, and they built their houses from stone. A stone seawall had been built as well, to expand the natural harbor at the river's mouth.

Cirque rode straight for the seawall, asking for directions once to ascertain the location of the harbormaster's office. Once they found the small, whitewashed hut, Cirque went inside alone. He and the harbormaster spoke privately for several hours, while Falorn and a boyishly dressed Elise bought new clothing and necessary supplies at chandlers' shops and the seaside market. Ryal had healed enough to watch their horses with Sbashe, but could do little else.

At the end of Cirque's discussion, their twelve beautiful mounts and half the contents of one saddlebag had changed hands. An hour later, the five of them had boarded a ship outbound for Letz with the evening's tide.

"Amazing, with all of the guards and papers in this country, how easily corrupted its petty officials are," Cirque commented as he and Falorn watched the harbor recede from behind the railing which lined the ship's stern. "Humans are so adaptable . . . and sometimes so predictable."

Falorn gave the Hellein a sour look, but said nothing. Something in Cirque's eyes still looked very far away, watching a girl's death that likely had taken place before Falorn's birth.

Falorn expected to feel seasick on the ever-shifting decks of the round-hulled carrack. He felt sound as ever, though. They sailed through placid seas with a favorable wind. Falorn wondered if he could ensure that the weather and wind continued by using the storm cards. After looking at the fragile craft's narrow masts and carefully joined hull planks, he decided the experiment would be best conducted from shore, or at least postponed to a moment of more pressing need.

The five of them occupied the ship's only cabin. The cheer with which the captain and mate had joined the common sailors in sleeping under the canvas deck-canopy surprised Falorn on the voyage's first night. When Cirque explained that the value of the horses and gold he'd traded the harbormaster exceeded the carrack's worth, he better understood the captain's desire to fully earn his share of the money.

The cabin barely held all of them and their supplies. Falorn and Sbashe spent the warm nights bunked on deck, or talking with the sailors who spent the night watch walking the deck while the ship lay at anchor.

"What are you looking for?" Falorn asked one man, on the third night at sea.

"Pirates," said the man. He spat tobacco juice over the ship's rail and looked around carefully before continuing. "There're pirates in these waters. Not many this close to Letz—tha wouldn't dare—but enough a' them."

"Where are they from? Countries at war with the Seven Kingdoms?"

"Na. A few might be, but most aren'. No one'd dare. Navy'd take care a' any fool'd try that. Most every pirate in these waters comes fra Sterwen."

"Sterwen?"

"It's an island, out there someway." The sailor waved vaguely west. "There's a thousan' islands out tha' way, and the pirate city's on a hidden one. They take a tithe a' the ships that cross these parts, take the ships and crews too. They never take too much, or too little. But the pirate king gets his share a' the North Sea cargo, wherever he is. Someone always has to watch for the men a' Sterwen."

"What do you do if they come? Do you fight?"

"Na!" The sailor seemed genuinely surprised at the question. "They kill anyone who fights, kill the whole crew a' tha ship. If they come, ye give 'em wha' they want. Sometimes they take a sailor or two, if they need crew. The others pay ransom. I pay good money in guild dues so the' pay my ransom if I'm taken."

"What if you don't have money?"

"I don't know. Somebody has to row the pirate galleys, I guess."

Two hours after dawn, on the morning of their sixth day at sea, they drew within sight of the island of Letz.

"You know this part, Councilor. Some of it you were present for."

A strange expression came over the interrogator's face. "Please continue as if I had never been there. Some of the details of what your son did in the city may be very important."

"I only know them secondhand."

"That makes them no less important. Tell me what you know."

A salt breeze came through the window as the wind shifted. Below them, men unloaded cargo from half a world away.

His son had left on one of those ships.

The man interrogating him had had the power to stop his son from leaving, but hadn't done so at the time. A decision he much regretted, in retrospect.

He wondered if misdirection would help his son. Falorn seemed to have passed beyond the interrogator's power to find him, and telling the boy's story was unlikely to make him approach any more closely.

It might keep his father alive a bit longer, however.

"Falorn never knew he was of noble birth, Councilor," he volunteered to the bulky interrogator. "He knew I was an inkeeper and may have suspected that I'd been a soldier, but never knew that I'd once had a title and lands. His skill with a sword wasn't all the cards' doing; there was fighting in his blood."

"Perhaps," the interrogator said, "or perhaps not. The cards are what brought him back here and somehow, even after the . . . accident, he was able to salvage more magic than he should have. Magic that belonged to someone else."

The glint in the interrogator's eyes also belonged to someone else.

He wondered if his son had any idea of the dangers he'd left behind when he departed Letz for the last time.

15

Dining

Late afternoon sun warmed Falorn as he stepped onto the dock. The island felt warmer than the Seven Kingdoms had, despite the faint seaside breeze. Cirque had insisted they would carry their own baggage, somewhat to the crew's relief. Their bundles and spare saddlebags now sat in a heap on the salt-weathered planks of the pier.

A small, black-bearded man in faded blue trousers and a loose homespun tunic sat on a piece of timber where the docks met the shore. He stood up and approached them as they finished disembarking.

"Good afternoon," the bearded man said affably. "Are you looking for a place to stay in the city?"

"Maybe," Cirque answered warily. "Did you have a place to suggest?"

"I did, in fact." He glanced at Cirque, but his gaze focused on Falorn. The man's eyes glittered, deep and sea-green. "It wouldn't do to have a cardholder sleeping on the streets, or at a traveler's inn."

"It might," said Cirque, but the man ignored him; his eyes never left Falorn.

"Who are you?" Falorn finally asked. *And how do you know that I have a card?* He could sense no cards on the man.

"Sorry. I meant to introduce myself right away. I'm called Geary, of Tide Street. I am a member of the faculty of the College of Magics, here at the University." He ran a hand through his black hair unconsciously. "My duties include the curatorship of the University's collection of cards. I and several of my fellows have anticipated your arrival since your ship drew within sight of the University towers. We thought someone should come to the docks to welcome you into the city." The professor extended a hand.

Not much of a welcoming committee, Falorn thought. *But at least no one's attacking us, so I guess it's a big improvement.*

"Thank you," said Falorn, accepting the offered hand. "My name's Falorn, of Tidewater, I guess."

"*Sir Falorn*," Elise whispered to him. Falorn shrugged.

"Welcome, Falorn. And welcome to all your companions. I have a coach waiting, if you please. If you would like to dine, we can prepare quarters while you eat."

"That would be wonderful," Falorn said. He shook his head when Cirque seemed ready to object. At Geary's whistle, a red two-horse carriage approached. The driver, in plum-colored livery, stepped down from his perch to help with the luggage. Geary helped carry their bags as well. His eyes widened slightly at the sight of the sailcloth-wrapped corpse Cirque carried, but the professor said nothing.

Falorn climbed into the carriage, surprised at the comfort of the cushioned wooden benches within. He began to revise his opinion of their welcome. All of the travelers fit easily, with plenty of room for Sbashe to sprawl on the carpeted floor. Padded fabric covered the walls as well. Silk-tasseled curtains had been drawn back from the windows.

"The coach is not mine, I'm afraid," Geary told them as the wheels began clattering over the smooth, old cobblestones of the city streets. "It belongs to another faculty member, who you will meet presently. We'll dine at his home tonight."

Falorn looked out the windows as they rode up and down the hilly streets. At first, the carriage passed small shops and cottages of mortared stone and whitewashed planks. Geary asked mild questions about inconsequential things. Elise had nearly finished describing the sea voyage when Falorn noticed the streets begin to flatten somewhat. They had risen well above the level of the harbor.

"Many senior faculty members and merchants live in this area," said Geary. Falorn watched as the houses grow larger. Most had lawns and wrought-iron fences; attached stables and servants' quarters became more common. The taverns and shops did not disappear entirely from street corners, but they acquired a more discreet character. They looked like the sorts of establishments an innkeeper's son from Tidewater could never hope to enter.

I thought you were a knight, Sbashe said. *Can't you enter wherever you want?*

I suppose, answered Falorn. *I keep forgetting.*

"Do you live nearby?" Falorn asked Geary.

"Gracious, no! My home is more modest, I fear. I rent quarters on Tide Street—three rooms and a shared library, with meals included. We will be visiting the home of Councilor Lawes, of Crewe Street."

"I thought you said he was a professor?" Elise asked.

"He is a professor. He is my mentor at the University. But he has been elevated to the City Council these last twenty years. All the councilors are professors."

The carriage turned through an open gate, onto a gravel path. The path bisected a wide, green lawn, which fronted a tall, white-columned house. Falorn saw footmen running down from the mansion's porch to meet the carriage. Quickly, a plum-liveried servant opened the carriage door, and he felt himself being helped downward.

The moments that followed passed by in a daze of images. Servants walked them up the marble stairs onto the columned porch. A pair of stiffly posed guards in burnished helmets stood at either side of the wide double doors into the house. The guards held halberds, with gold flourishes on their silver blades. Plum-colored velvet doublets covered their chests, laced over red silk tunics. Matching burgundy tassels hung from their halberd shafts. Gold braid covered the guards' shoulders and the cuffs of their tunics.

Someone opened the doors from within, and another herd of liveried servants led them into a hallway within, led by a white-haired over-servant with gold braids at his shoulders and gold buttons instead of laces binding his doublet. They walked on hardwood floors, polished until they shone and waxed to a slippery smoothness. The walls of the hallway had been painted the same gleaming white as the mansion's exterior, but a pair of oil paintings hung on the wall to Falorn's right. To his left, a red couch and two small round tables sat against the walls. A cut-crystal vase on one table held fresh flowers. Falorn glanced at the paintings as the servants led him past. One depicted an older man in sailor's dress. The man leaned on a saber, and a knotted red cloth held his hair back from his face. The second painting showed a carrack running ahead of a high sea. Only wisps of sails remained on the ship's mast. Crewmen scurried across the deck, trying to save their vessel from the force of the gale.

They walked on through a bewildering series of halls, so quickly that the lavish furniture barely registered on Falorn's consciousness. He noticed a servant lighting candelabra and chandeliers with a long, candle-tipped pole. Much of the house glowed with a faint, ambient blue, as if the furniture and walls themselves bore enchantments.

They came to a halt in another splendid chamber. The top half of the walls had been painted the same white as most of the other rooms they'd seen, but a mahogany plate rail divided all four walls into upper and lower halves. Below the rail, the walls had been papered with a thin yellow fabric printed with maroon-colored flowers. Oval serving dishes of painted porcelain lined the rail, no two of them bearing exactly the same pattern. A rectangular table of polished dark wood filled the center of the room, surrounded by two dozen matching armless chairs. Red cushions had been carefully knotted onto the chairs' backs and seats. Four wide cabinets of the same wood sat against the left wall, while a pair of sideboards lined the right wall, one on either side of an open doorway. A high crystal chandelier hung above the table's center. The room glittered with the flames of hundreds of wax candles.

Servants bustled in and out of the room, setting porcelain plates and elaborate silver implements on the table. Others began to set dozens of covered silver dishes on the sideboards. A heavy-set man carried a huge tray of breads into the room, setting it on the chest-high top of one of the cabinets.

At the sound of a small bell ringing, all motion ceased. The servants assumed stiff poses, much as the guards on the porch had.

A door on the far wall opened, and an odd-looking man entered. He wore a plum-colored knee-length coat and white hose over his painfully thin frame. A double row of gold buttons ran down the coat front, and gold braid outlined the shoulders, lapels, and cuffs. His white wig left a slight cloud of powder in the air behind him. He rang a small brass bell as he walked into the room.

"All rise for the Honorable Councilor Lawes," the man called out in a thin, reedy voice. He stood aside and bowed deeply as the Councilor entered the room.

Lawes had to be one of the heaviest men Falorn had ever seen. He stood only a few inches taller than Falorn, but weighed three or four times as much. He walked easily, despite the thickness of his thighs and belly. A perfectly tailored red coat stretched across his enormously broad chest, its high collar wide enough to accommodate the bulge of his swollen neck. A white silk cravat ruffled outward from the collar, obscuring the first of the paired gold buttons which ran in a double row down his chest.

Only a thin fringe of gray hair remained on the councilor's head, where it had not quite disappeared from behind his ears. He had a ruddy complexion and oversized features, which seemed to somehow match the scale of the rest of his body. His large brown eyes seemed to take in the whole room at a glance, as if his powers of observation had grown in proportion to his mammoth frame.

"Welcome!" he said, in a booming voice. "Welcome to my home. Welcome to my city. I am glad you have made it here with your precious cargo."

Falorn knew Lawes meant the cards, but he glanced at Cirque in spite of himself. *I wonder what the servants did with all of our things?* Falorn thought to himself. *I wonder what they did with the corpse?*

"Please," the councilor continued, "be seated. I don't like to stand on ceremony here. Allow me to offer you a small meal, by way of introduction." He turned to the man in the powdered wig, who had finally risen from his bow. "Selden," he said in a whisper, which nevertheless carried through the room. "Would you please be kind enough to show our other guests into the dining room. I would like to begin presently." The steward bowed once again and disappeared through the door behind his master to retrieve the rest of the guests.

Events began happening too fast for Falorn to follow. Too many things about the dinner felt utterly alien to him. A servant at his shoulder quietly inquired about his name. The man wrote it carefully on a strip of paper and glided away. A moment later, he heard Elise insisting the servant add Falorn's title to the slip. Other guests began filing in—more than a dozen men and women of varying ages and shapes. None of them dressed with the formality of Lawes and his servants; Geary's loose tunic and comfortable britches seemed more the norm for both genders. It occurred to Falorn that he and the others still wore their shipboard clothes.

"I would like to introduce my guests," Lawes boomed. "Most of you know each other, but for the benefit of the newcomers, allow me the indulgence of mentioning all of your names." He began to roll off a series of titles, honorifics, and long names, pointing to each person in turn. The man really did have a beautiful voice, Falorn realized, but none of the names registered in his own mind. Falorn's eyes widened when the councilor pointed his way, and listed his own name and title. He followed with what seemed like a somewhat embellished description of Falorn's role in the battle at the Calambria River. Falorn blushed when he realized all eyes had turned to look at him. He didn't breathe again until Lawes turned his attentions to Elise and the Helleinen, favoring each with a somewhat lengthier description, including a list of titles Falorn had not known the Helleinen possessed. Even Sbashe received an introduction, although the corget seemed indifferent to the attention.

A young male servant with long, tied-back black hair guided Falorn to his place at the table. The servant stood at his elbow while others served food. Falorn knew enough not to begin until after Lawes took the first bite, but after that he found himself at a loss.

"Use this," the servant whispered in his ear, pointing to an oddly tined silver fork as the fish course appeared on the table. The young man continued to prompt him throughout the successive waves of food and drink.

When the last course concluded, the meal evolved into a series of conversations, interspersed with occasional toasts. Crystal decanters of port flowed as freely as the beer in his father's inn; Falorn drank little, but his head spun anyway, overwhelmed by a thousand introductions of people, customs, and mannerisms.

He spoke at length with the middle-aged woman beside him, but neither her name nor the conversation registered in his mind. He caught snatches of other conversations, but could remember only bits and pieces at the end of the meal.

The two men at his right chattered together all night, barely taking notice of Falorn at all. *They must both be professors at the University*, he decided. The one had just returned from some sort of trip, and described it at length to his companion. Falorn followed little of the narrative. He paid closer attention to the man's account of a long sea voyage, plagued by storms and great serpents.

". . . And finally, I got to the convocation," the man was saying. "Mind you, I was three months late, but I was there, and ready to give my lectures. They gave me a house to live in, and I found two beautiful women waiting in my bedroom that night, a blonde and a brunette." Falorn drifted into another conversation for a moment, but the man to his right had caught his interest. He tried to listen without turning his head.

"As you can imagine after that," he heard the man tell his companion, "I only barely made it out of bed the next morning. But I wanted to give them a show, to really give them something for their fee. So I throw on a cloak with a high collar to hide the bite marks. I run all the way down to the lecture hall, and it's packed. The room is overflowing with people. There must be two hundred of them there, and I can barely breathe because I just ran all the way from the house.

"Finally, I get my breath back and I start to lecture. I want to tell them everything I know, and it was one of those days when everything seemed crystal clear in my mind—which was pretty amazing after the night I'd just had. I talked for six hours, and it seemed like seconds. Nobody said a word the whole time; not a whisper, not a cough, not anything. And I figure they're all just as caught up in this as I am. I'm getting more and more excited. So I build to a big finish, and make the final point which is going to leave them all stunned. I wait for the room to explode, and *nothing happens*. After a few minutes there's sort of a quiet applause, but you would have thought none of them knew what I'd been talking about for the last six hours.

"Afterward, I have a drink or two, and finally I get up the nerve to talk to the convocation organizer. 'What happened there today?' I ask him. 'Didn't you like the speech?' He looks at me kind of funny, and finally he says, 'It's not that at all. You just weren't quite what we expected.' 'Well, what did you expect?' I ask him. 'Some other kind of necromancer?'

"He gives me the damnedest look. 'Necromancy?' he says. 'This is the Society of Necrophages.'"

The man's companion exploded into laughter, and slapped the speaker repeatedly on the back. Falorn wasn't quite sure what the punch line was supposed to have meant. He kept listening, hoping for another clue.

"So what did you finally do?" the companion asked.

"I stayed and lectured, of course. They *did* pay my way. I have to admit, I didn't eat much, though."

Both men burst into laughter again.

Falorn awoke half-covered by white satin sheets. Light poured through two large windows which overlooked the bed. He did not remember leaving the banquet or falling asleep. He reached instinctively to his chest, but the cards remained in their place.

His clothes hung neatly on a wall-hook, with his sword hanging beside them. On the floor, he saw his boots, newly polished. His possessions remained in their bags on a nearby table. Aside from the bed, table, and two stools, the whitewashed room contained no furniture.

He clambered from the soft feather mattress and pulled on his britches. He could see the rear of Lawes's mansion through the windows; the councilor must have placed them in a guest house for the evening. Falorn turned around at the sound of scuffling beneath the bed. Sbashe emerged slowly, stretched languorously, and blinked several times.

Well, good morning, Sbashe said in his mind.

Good morning to you, too. Did you sleep well?

Very well, the corget answered. *Anything dry and not rocking would have been better than that ship, but the Councilor does keep a fine house.*

That he does. Falorn vaguely remembered stripping off his clothes and collapsing into bed after the banquet; he certainly hadn't left things as neatly as he'd found them upon awakening.

Where are the others? he asked Sbashe.

Here, there. I wonder how the councilor liked boarding that corpse of Cirque's?

At least it hasn't started to smell.

Yet. Just wait.

Someone rapped lightly on the door.

"Come in," said Falorn, and Geary entered.

"Sorry to disturb you," the professor said. He wore a dyed-green leather doublet over his tunic this morning. He looked older in the bright morning light; Falorn noticed a touch of gray in his black hair and neatly trimmed beard.

"It's no disturbance at all."

"Good, good. I thought you might like to visit my offices at the University this morning. We have quite a collection of cards there."

"I would love to." Falorn wondered how much he could trust Geary. *I could be walking into another trap. No one in my life seems to be what they say. Even Cirque used me to help pursue his own hidden plans.*

If it helps at all, Sbashe said, *he's telling the truth. He really isn't planning to trap you. He studies the cards, but he's so scared of them that he never touches them with his bare hands.*

Are you sure? Falorn wanted to believe the corget.

I'm not the one who's feeling unsure of everything. Of course I'm sure.

Falorn hurriedly finished dressing. He turned to speak to Geary as he walked to the table which held his other possessions.

"I hope Councilor Lawes isn't upset with me," he said. "I didn't get to thank him for his hospitality, or talk with him for more than a few words last night."

"No, no, not at all. It's he who owes you; he told me so himself. He didn't expect much of you on your first night in the city. But new guests are a diversion for the regulars at his table. You'll meet him again soon, and I promise, you'll like him. Most of the others you'll get to know as well. I don't suppose you caught many of the names?" asked Geary.

"No. I'm sorry." Falorn smiled wanly. "I was having so much trouble with the forks that I lost track of everything else."

"No matter. There's always time for names later, and forks are important. The councilor entertains often, and he has already promised to invite you again."

"Should I bring these with us?" Falorn asked, gesturing to his bags.

"Only if you like. You won't be staying here tonight, but Lawes will have them sent to your new quarters. You needn't worry about the safety of your money; Councilor Lawes has four estates as large as this in different cities where his ships trade. There are kings with a great deal less money than he."

"Oh! I wasn't worried," said Falorn.

Were, too.

Not now, Sbashe.

He thought about leaving everything, then remembered the book at the last minute. He tucked it under his arm and followed Geary out the door. Sbashe trotted easily behind him.

"Are the others coming with us?" Falorn asked, as they walked down a flight of stairs and through a parlor to the guest house's front entrance.

"Not this morning. There are too many other things to do in Letz, and only you seem to have a direct interest in the cards. They will join us for dinner," said Geary.

"Where are they?"

"Your Helleinen friends have gone to consult with a healer, accompanied by a letter of reference penned by the councilor. The swordswoman has gone with Lawes's understeward to help find suitable accommodations for the lot of you."

"That's a good idea."

"You will be safe here, Falorn. No one carries their fights to Letz.

Not even your friend Cirque will be allowed to do so. I don't know who your enemies are, but you are safe from them here."

Falorn wondered if that could really be true as they walked toward the red carriage, which stood with its team at the ready on the gravel path. Another question suddenly occurred to him.

"Geary, what is a necrophage?"

"A cannibal—someone who eats human flesh. Why? Do you need one?"

"No. I just wondered."

16

A Winter's Tale

The coachman kept his team on the level streets above the hilly portside of the city. They soon rolled next to a narrow brick wall, perhaps twice the height of a man.

"Those are the University grounds, beyond that wall," Geary explained, after they'd paralleled the structure for about ten minutes.

"It must be enormous," said Falorn.

"Bigger than you could imagine. There are a number of gates, but we will enter by one near the College of Magics's buildings."

"They need all this space just to teach magic?"

"No, although some schools of magic can use quite a lot of space. There are two other colleges within the University as well, and hundreds of disciplines. Magic is not the only thing we teach."

"What are the other schools?" Falorn asked, mostly because he knew Geary expected the question.

"The College of Rhetoric teaches languages, literature, history, geography, philosophy, composition, music, public speaking, logic, and similar arts. The College of Martial Arts teaches war and fighting, horsemanship, falconry, tactics, any weapon you might care to learn, and any other purely physical arts. The College of Magics teaches all of the schools of magic, as well as alchemy, geology, botany, engineering, painting, illumination, and other arts which involve making or unmaking things." Falorn only understood a few of the terms Geary used, so the professor began to explain some of the University's disciplines in terms he knew. They turned through a high, gently curving arch somewhere in the middle of Rhetoric, and entered the University grounds.

Wide, brick-lined paths led between red brick-and-mortar buildings, although grass covered most of the grounds. Before Geary could finish expounding upon the various schools of magic, the coachman brought their vehicle to a stop in a sheltered courtyard sandwiched between two of the tall structures.

"This way," said Geary, as he led Falorn and Sbashe through a narrow door at the end of the closer building. "We won't use the main entrance. This is closer to my office, and will probably be a little easier for you. Sometimes the guards are uneasy about letting nonstudents into the building."

They walked three flights of wooden stairs.

"These stairs are just temporary," Geary told him. "They've been doing work on the building these last few years."

At least it's not a ladder, said Sbashe's voice in his mind.

Geary led the way down a cramped third-floor hallway, to three doors that opened off a cul-de-sac. The floorboards displayed signs of water damage. Geary noticed where Falorn's eyes focused.

"There used to be rugs," he said, "but they took them away for the rebuilding." He produced a brass key from one of the recesses of his tunic and unlocked the center door. "This is my office. The door on the right is a workroom, and on the left is a little museum we built for the cards."

Books and papers covered every horizontal surface in the office. A small desk had been literally buried under a mass of parchment. Two large bookcases overflowed onto the floor. The office also contained two chairs—one behind the desk, and the other holding a tall stack of leather-bound volumes—and a dead plant, which sat on the sill of the lone window.

"Have a seat, please. Move the books if you like." Falorn gingerly complied. Flakes of leather drifted from the ancient bindings, joining the dust and piled parchment on the floor. Sbashe found a sort of nest in a corner, next to one of the bookcases, and sat down. Carefully, Falorn set his own book in his lap. Geary eyed the volume with interest.

"May I?" he asked. After a short hesitation, Falorn set it on the desk in front of the professor. With the utmost care, Geary unclasped the bloodstained cover and began examining the pages. Falorn looked at the upside-down letters and images, but they seemed not to dance for the professor as they did for him.

"This is a remarkable find," said Geary at last. "This book is much older than the cards are. It describes the methods used to create them. Only a master wizard could even begin to try the things it describes, but it gives many details of how the cards that keep finding you were manufactured. Have you read it?"

"I've looked at some of it. The words don't stay still, and the pictures move around like the cards do. It's hard for me to make out words when they *don't* move. I couldn't read any of it." Falorn's face reddened a little. He looked down at the floor so Geary wouldn't see.

"There's no shame in that, Falorn. I would be pleased to help you to understand what's inside. All I ask is that you let me study it as well. If you want, I can even have one of my journeyman students help you with your reading."

"Elise was helping me."

"You can have more than one teacher, if you like," said Geary.

"I should ask her first."

"However you prefer. But we have other things to talk about. Why don't you tell me how you came into possession of these cards, and I can tell you a few things that I have learned about them."

Over the next few weeks, while autumn descended in earnest, Falorn told his story to the professor. At Geary's request, Falorn talked to Lawes as well. As Geary had promised, Falorn found himself liking the enormous councilor.

Falorn spent a great deal of his time in the shabby room that contained the University's card collection. The glass-fronted cases in the empty office next to Geary's contained sixteen cards, and several other illuminated books devoted to their study. Falorn flipped through each of the dusty volumes, but found himself disappointed in their contents. The words refused to dance, and the illustrations sat lifelessly on the page, their dull colors failing to approach the vibrant cards against his chest. None of the books had the magical properties of his own volume, which Geary had been unable to explain. But as the days went on, the professor had been able to explain many other things.

When Falorn revealed the full extent of his own cards, Geary told him that he might be the most powerful of the cardholders. "I thought no one person held more cards than the University's collection," he said, a little wistfully, "and then you come to me with twenty-five of them in your hands."

Geary had begun writing his own book on the cards. The University supported his work—although, Falorn came to realize, with little fervency. As he spent more time in the College of Magics, he realized that not all offices were as small and cramped as Geary's, nor was every building perpetually under construction. The University housed many dangerous treasures with far older pedigrees than the cards, and with far more interesting histories. In the world Falorn had recently escaped from, people fought over the cards because of their ability to win battles or influence princes. Neither of those things mattered much in the University, where princes regularly came begging for knowledge. The cards were important to Geary, and to his patron, Councilor Lawes. Someday they might come to be more important to the University as a whole, but until that time, upgrading Geary's office was not a University priority.

True to his word, Geary began to tell Falorn more about the eighty-four cards, and he personally began to help Falorn with his reading. Falorn suspected the latter effort was as much to keep him on the island and cooperating with Geary as for his own benefit. Nevertheless, he came to like the effusive professor, and did all he could to help the man with his book. At the same time, Falorn continued to practice every day, both with his weapons, and with his increasing abilities to use the cards.

Between his own practice and the things Geary could tell him, Falorn began to get a sense of the cards' strengths and limitations. They really did only augment latent abilities; a person with no affinity for animals would not be able to make much use of the horse cards, even if by some mischance he came to possess them. They worked best on his own person, or on things which affected him directly. He could use the storm cards to stir a breeze around his face, for instance, but he had little success when he attempted to shift the paths of distant clouds.

Sbashe spent most of her time with Falorn. She used her ability to see magic to aid in his experiments with the cards. Otherwise, after an initial flurry of exploration, she had only limited interest in the University and the city. Sbashe never talked to Geary or any of the other professors.

Elise and the Helleinen pursued their own studies. The money captured from the Seven Kingdoms allowed for ample instruction, as well as a more than satisfactory standard of living. Elise had rented them a house and engaged several servants. Falorn never felt comfortable having other people do work for him, but Elise insisted that he use his time to learn. He suspected that she harbored secret ambitions of getting him to act more appropriately to his new station in life. She bought him new clothes as well. They cost far more than he would have spent, but they fit magnificently, nearly as well as the clothing Ryal had magically altered for him. He wore the new garments when they dined at Councilor Lawes's mansion, or when they attended the theater or other entertainment together. When he studied or practiced he dressed the same as ever.

Ryal's wounds healed fully, after a convalescence spent befriending several professors of transmutation on the faculty of the College of Magics. These wizards afforded Ryal a sort of visiting professor status, and he spent most of his time working with an assortment of wizards and journeyman in their workrooms or in the University's impressive library. By more-or-less mutual consent—influenced somewhat by plaintive looks from Geary and from Ryal's new partners in sorcery—they chose to winter over on the island.

The decision to stay dissatisfied only Cirque. He had not been allowed to spread the word of the corpse in his possession. Lawes and other members of the Council had made it clear that the body would be confiscated if he tried to use it in any way which threatened the city's neutrality. He finally sent the corpse to Delerian by ship, in the care of a merchant captain recommended by Lawes as trustworthy and discreet. Both Falorn and Elise paid the same captain to arrange to have packages sent onward from Delerian to further destinations. Elise sent a detailed letter to the Queen of Cathan describing the fall's events. Falorn's package contained a painstakingly written letter to his family, as well as a few of the gold coins he had come across in his travels. The letter had few details, since many people beside his family would read it, he suspected, even before whoever his father asked to read it for him. He doubted the money would get through, but if it did, it would ease the winter months somewhat. He would send more money and a fuller account of his adventures when he found a reliable way to do so.

I wonder how my father feels about my leaving. I wonder if he ever regretted any of his secrets and lies. The thought seemed uncharitable, though, given how prosperously things had turned out for Falorn so far.

At the end of the winter, he realized he had been gone from his father's house for nearly a full year.

They were ready to leave by early spring. Falorn would have been happy to remain in Letz, but Cirque, Ryal, and Elise all had duties to return to at home. And even though she never said so, he suspected Sbashe wanted to return to her native mountains as well, now that she'd satisfied herself that Falorn didn't pose a threat to her people. Falorn did want to return to the island when he had seen his companions safely home, and he told Geary as much.

It's funny, Falorn realized. *This is the first place I've been since I left home that I've been really comfortable, and one of the few places where no one is trying to kill me. It's odd that it's also the first place since home where I've made the choice to leave—where I'm not being pushed by someone else's sword. I'm leaving to fulfill obligations, but it's my choice this time.*

That would have felt more satisfying if the island didn't feel quite so hospitable. After so many betrayals elsewhere, Falorn couldn't help but wonder whether some of the hospitality was an illusion.

"I'm glad you'll be coming back," the professor told him, while they sat privately in his office. "Otherwise you'd have made a liar of me."

"What do you mean?" asked Falorn.

"There was a certain amount of sentiment on the Council to prevent you from leaving."

"Why? Why would they do a thing like that?"

"Well . . . the cards may not be the most important magical relic on the University campus. But they *are* powerful, and there was a feeling they could easily fall into the wrong hands if they left the island."

The wrong hands, Falorn suspected, meant any hands not inclined to eventually donate them to the University's collection.

"You mean they wanted to take the cards from me?"

"No, no, of course not. It's not you anyone is worried about. But there are a number of wizards who have already tried to take them from you. I think you have at least two groups of magical enemies, since the things that attacked you when you found your first card seem unlikely to have been sent by the Seven Kingdoms wizards you've described. They sound like *sendings*. They look and feel real, but they can't cross running water or carry anything away from their victims. One or more wizards probably ambushed one of Jhodric's knights, but you took the card away before they could recover it. Why would Seven Kingdoms wizards be ambushing one of their own princes' men?"

"Maybe," said Falorn, thinking. "But I lost the book then, too. And I found it again in the chambers of a Seven Kingdoms wizard. I think it may have been someone else who killed the green knight."

"True. I can't explain everything. But I think it is possible that you may have more enemies than you know," said Geary.

"Well, let me count them. There's Sera's father, the Duke of Roicenet. There's the son of the Duke of Iron Eagle, along with his father's army. There's at least one group of wizards—less two whom we killed—and if you're right, there may be a second group of wizards. There's a city of angry dwarves, if I ever try to take the pass that crosses near their city again. There are a lot of priests in Cathan, and some more in the Seven Kingdoms. There's an archbishop in Windford. I haven't made a very good impression on religious authorities anywhere, I guess. There are the soldiers in Golden Reeds, assuming some of them survived the holy war. If they didn't, there is a swamp in the world where I may actually be welcomed. But that swamp and this city are about the only places I can sleep soundly at night."

"So stay." Geary smiled encouragingly.

"I can't. I need to help Elise and Sbashe and the Helleinen get home. They helped me capture the cards from the Seven Kingdoms. The least I can do is help them get back safely."

"The Queen of Cathan will want your cards if you enter her country again."

"Then maybe I'll have to add her to the list, too. I'll be all right. I'll have good friends along with me, and the cards to help. And without cards of their own, the wizards will have trouble finding me."

"Some of them do have cards of their own."

"Unless they're in a suit I have, they won't help. I've tried all winter; I can only sense cards similar to ones I already have. Even that doesn't work from more than a few miles away."

"I still think you're taking a big risk," Geary said.

"I know. But this time it's a risk that *I've* chosen to take, not one that someone else is forcing on me. After I've gotten everyone safely home, I'll come back."

"I hope so. I'll worry while you're gone."

"Geary?"

"Yes?"

"Can I ask you the truth about something?"

"Of course."

"Did the councilors want my cards?"

"It was pointed out to me that they would make a fine addition to the University's permanent collection if you wanted to donate them. And I attempted to secure council permission to make an offer to buy the cards from you. Unfortunately, the council wasn't able to grant it. They would love to add the cards to the collection, but they do not place the same value on them as the princes and wizards who have been chasing you."

"Thanks for telling me."

"Hurry back, Falorn. We'll miss you."

He clasped hands with the professor, then embraced him before leaving the office. Sbashe rose from her unobtrusive seat by the bookcase and padded softly after him.

You didn't tell him everything, did you? said Sbashe. It wasn't really a question.

What do you mean? asked Falorn.

You didn't tell him that you want to try to find Sera before you come back.

I didn't think he'd understand.

I'm not sure I understand, said the corget.

I need to talk with her again. Even if she doesn't want to have anything to do with me, I want to hear her say so. I saw her so little after the battle, and both of us had other people trying to pull us apart. I just want to talk with her again and see how she feels.

Do you love her? Sbashe asked.

Love her? I don't know. I haven't really thought about it. In fact, Falorn had avoided thinking about it.

How can you ask her how she feels when you don't even know how you feel?

I don't know. I'll figure it out before I find her, I guess.

I don't suppose you've told Elise about any of this? Sbashe asked.

No. Not yet.

I think it would be a bad idea to tell her, said Sbashe.

Why? I might need her help.

I just think it would be a bad idea.

But I thought you couldn't read her mind, Falorn said.

I can't. I still think it would be a bad idea.

Well, I don't need to tell her yet, anyway. I'll wait until later when I have to, at least.

Remember that her loyalties are not toward you. You forgot that was true of Cirque, and his actions surprised and hurt you.

I guess so. But I don't want to always think my friends are going to betray me. Cirque had other reasons than the cards for going into the Seven Kingdoms, but he would never have hurt me.

If you say so, the corget said.

Falorn walked along the docks with Elise and Sbashe. Their chests of supplies had already been stowed in the fore cabin of the ship that would take them to Delerian, and from where he walked, Falorn could see Cirque and Ryal standing on the deck. They waited only on the tide.

A light drizzle dampened his clothes, but Falorn didn't mind. At Elise's insistence, he had packed the silks and velvets into a chest. He would wear them in court at Cathan if he ever found himself back there, but until then, he intended to remain in his familiar, everyday boots and clothing.

Neither of them spoke much as they walked. He and Elise had spent much of their free time in Letz together. They took their meals in each other's rooms, or dined together in dozens of taverns or more pretentious eateries. They'd watched plays together, and visited the circus twice. He had a genuine affection for her, but somehow, their friendship retained an uneasy edge. He wondered how much they trusted each other.

He never stopped thinking of Sera for long. He hadn't mentioned Sera's name to Elise in months, but somehow, she seemed to know his thoughts.

Hours later, as the ship tacked into the horizon at the beginning of its southward journey, they stood alone on the deck together. He held an arm around Elise's shoulder as she leaned close against him. She sighed, and stared out at the horizon. The drizzle continued to dampen them, but the thin clouds above seemed unlikely to menace them with anything further. They stayed on the deck together until the sun went down, without a word spoken.

"Naturally, the hospitality was an illusion."

"Not entirely," the councilor said. Oddly, the stout man seemed to want to talk. "Geary knew the cards attracted each other—you've said as much—and it had occurred to him that letting Falorn leave the island was tantamount to putting out bait for the cards' return. But he did not know what would happen when the cards came together. Nor did he know that by that time, so many of them had come together that the process was essentially unstoppable."

"I did not know that either, Councilor. When we split the cards up after . . . after the sorceress's defeat, it was thought best to separate the cards as much as possible, and it was known that they wanted to come together, but not that the process would accelerate after a certain time had passed, or that there was a point beyond which it could not be stopped."

"You were not supposed to know that," the interrogator said.

The words made little sense, coming from the large councilor.

The room fell silent, except for the cawing of the gulls outside. The stevedores had finished their loading and unloading for the moment.

"Perhaps you should continue your story," the interrogator said. "We will come back to matters on the island soon enough."

17

Shackles and Cossets

On the second day, they spotted other sails, far off against the horizon. The captain tried to run ahead of the distant ships, but the sails grew markedly larger as the day went on. By sundown, details of the two approaching ships could be seen.

Neither of the approaching craft flew any sort of flag. Banks of rowers augmented the oncoming ships' sails. They lacked the rams and shallow drafts of true galleys.

The two ships would catch them before darkness fell.

Armed men crowded the rails of both craft. When the outcome of the race became clear, the merchant captain ordered his sailors to drop anchor. Aside from the captain, only Falorn and his companions carried any weapons longer than a knife. With the ship halted in the water, many of the sailors began to pray, in accordance with a dozen different religions and rituals.

Falorn remembered his discussion of pirates with the sailor on the trip from the Seven Kingdoms. He hadn't planned on a trip to Sterwen, but if he had to make one, he didn't intend to do so in chains. Elise, Cirque, and Ryal might have relatives who could ransom them, but he didn't. And Sbashe would be lucky if she wound up sold to some rich man's private menagerie.

Falorn ducked into the cabin where the others waited.

"Can we find a way to hide?" he asked, looking at Ryal. "Is there some way you can disguise us, or give us some sort of hiding place?"

The Hellein thought for a minute. "I think so," he said, "if you don't mind close quarters for a while. Bring food and anything really valuable. We will need to get belowdecks before anybody notices us. Leave the rest of the chests." Falorn took his remaining saddlebag of coins, along with one of their sacks of food. He ignored Elise's halfhearted glare as he left the chest of clothing behind.

A hatchway leading down into the hold sat on the deck in front of the cabin door. They hurriedly climbed through it, and into the darkness below. The captain had left only a few feet of crawling room above the bales and wooden cases stacked end-to-end in the ship's cargo space. In some places, the crates reached all the way to the unfinished planks that formed a rough ceiling. At Ryal's direction, the five of them crawled toward the stern end of the cargo bay, where the goods had been piled first, and most thickly. Sbashe's claws scrabbled against the crates as she struggled for purchase, but otherwise they moved in near silence.

A loud bump shook the whole craft as they neared the cargo hold's end.

"One of the pirate ships has come alongside," Elise said. "They'll be boarding any minute."

"We have a few minutes before they come down here," said Ryal. "They will want to secure the ship's crew before checking on its cargo." The Hellein ran his hands carefully over the timbers of the back wall, as if comparing the texture to that of the nearest crates.

None of them dared to hurry Ryal as he began to speak in an odd language. He continued to touch the rear wall as he spoke. Occasionally, he made a sketching motion on the surface of one of the cargo boxes as well.

They could hear footsteps and shouting on the deck above them.

A crate next to the wall began to make a soft, slopping noise, like rum shaken against the side of a jar. The boards on the box's corner began to elongate, stretching and darkening like thick molasses running onto the floor. More and more of the box oozed downward. Another crate near the wall joined it.

Soon all of the boxes leaning directly against the wall had begun to flow outward. The liquid wood began forming into a wall against the second tier of crates. Slowly, a new level of timbers grew upward, only inches thick but to all appearances identical to the rear bulkhead of the cargo hold. Between the two walls, the vanished crates left a gap of perhaps three feet.

Ryal paused in his motions to gesture quickly with his head. They all climbed into the gap, careful to step only on the few patches of bare floor, and avoid the still-oozing crates. Ryal climbed in behind them. From within, he continued his motions. The false timbers grew upward until they reached the ceiling.

The loud footsteps above them continued while Ryal finished his work. He said a few rapid words, and snapped his wrist in an abrupt motion. A globe of dim yellow light appeared on the rear bulkhead, illuminating their tiny hiding place.

"They will see nothing from outside," Ryal said. His face looked very pale, even in the dim light. Sweat soaked the Hellein's black hair, even where his braid hung downward. He sat, and accepted the wine flask Falorn proffered. After a quick swallow, he spoke again.

"From the cargo hold, this will look like the rear wall. The wood is real, and until they unpack the hold, they will not notice any difference. We will have to leave the ship at that time, but that will be days from now."

"How much is it safe to talk?" Falorn asked.

"Talk quietly if you like. No one can hear unless they are very close."

They sat in silence while the noises continued on the deck over their heads. Someone opened the hatch to look within the hold, but they heard no one climbing inside. A few people shouted, but the voices quickly went silent. After an eternity, the clanking of chains drowned out the footsteps, and soon the ship began to move again.

"I hated to leave them up there," Elise finally said.

"We had to," said Falorn. "If we fought, all we would have done is gotten the crew killed. There were too many."

"I suppose you're right. We can't have mad charges in every battle," said Elise.

"The last one worked out better for you than for me," Falorn said, trying to echo her wry smile.

"It worked out better for you than for Calathan and the Seven Kingdoms."

"I still spent a few weeks in bed afterward," said Falorn.

Elise nodded and sighed. "I wonder what will happen to the sailors."

"The pirates will ransom them," Falorn said. "That's what one of the sailors told me on the way over. The sailors pay into a guild fund so they'll be ransomed."

"That's odd. I wouldn't think the Seven Kingdoms would pay ransom. It seems like the sort of place that would send a naval squadron and put the pirates to the torch, even if a few of the sailors died in the process. They don't do things by half measures; with a navy the size of theirs, you'd think the pirates wouldn't touch them."

"We're not on a Seven Kingdoms ship, though." Falorn supposed that was an important distinction, even if it didn't feel that way at the moment.

"It's a ship out of Letz. The threat is the same," said Elise.

"I don't know. We'll find out more than we want to know, soon enough."

The ship sailed for eight days. They could tell day from night only by the clatter of the anchor chains falling toward the water when darkness fell. Despite the crowding in the small chamber, the air remained fresh. A small well in the planks held their wastes, which Ryal somehow contrived to have the wood absorb. Falorn asked the Hellein how he kept them from suffocating in the closeness of the hidden room, but Ryal only shrugged in response.

After the fourth day on the ship's new course, the sea grew rougher; they seemed to be riding ahead of a storm. By the time the wind and water calmed, they had all been thrown around inside the little chamber.

On the afternoon of the eighth day, they heard greater activity from above. The ship shifted frequently, as if tacking into a harbor. Finally it came to a stop, but the anchor chain only played partway out before striking bottom. After a last rush of boots and voices, the noises subsided.

"The harbor must be shallow here," Ryal said. "If this is our destination, I think we must be on our way soon. I want to be far from this chamber when the hold is unpacked. In fact, I would like this chamber itself to be gone, so they don't know a wizard has landed on their island."

"Can you undo the spell?" Falorn asked.

"I have to, if we want to leave. There's no other way out. Don't worry, though. It's much easier to undo a transmutation than to do it in the first place. Objects remember their true forms, and want to return to them."

Falorn felt a stirring at his chest, a change in the normal warmth.

"We'd better leave here quickly," he said. "Somebody has a card nearby. He's going to figure out we're here soon, if he hasn't already."

Ryal nodded. He began to chant and motion with his hands once again. The procedure went more quickly this time. In a few moments, the wall had begun to ooze away. They had to clamber through the beginnings of an opening quickly, or risk being caught in the reshaping boxes of cargo.

Except for Ryal's magical light on the back wall, nothing illuminated the cargo hold. They could do little but lie in the thin crawl space atop the crates and bundles, and wait for him to finish. Soon, even the light snuffed out, as reappearing boxes covered over the rear bulkhead.

After a pause, the illumination re-formed, this time cupped in the palm of Ryal's hand.

"This light will last only a day," he told them, "and I will be casting no more spells for some time. This has not been as much strain as getting captured by pirates would have been, but it has been draining."

"We will do without magic," said Cirque. He had spoken very little over the last eight days. Falorn had spent much of the time talking with Sbashe and practicing his reading. He had left his book about the cards on loan with Geary in return for several more portable chapbooks of history and poetry. At least, the letters in the small paperbound volumes did not dance in front of his eyes, although he still struggled with the meanings of many words.

Elise had helped a little with the reading, and spoke a little with Cirque, mostly about military strategy. Cirque spoke only enough to keep a polite conversation alive, albeit in a malnourished way. He and Elise finally settled on round after silent round of some arcane card game, occasionally joined by Ryal when he wasn't resting from his exertions. None of them offered to show him how to play, and Falorn didn't ask. They seemed to be playing for some sort of stake, although he didn't know what had been wagered, or how they tallied winnings and losses.

Night had fallen by the time they emerged silently onto an empty deck. Not even a single sentry remained on board. Falorn could hear a cat mewling from the galley, and wavelets lapping at the base of the hull, but aside from those noises the night remained silent.

The ship lay near the outer edge of a natural harbor. A crescent-shaped beach of white sand reflected the full moon's light. Small huts lined the edge of the beach. From hills a few miles away, a castle overlooked the harbor. A broad swath of jungle separated the hills from the beach, broken only by a narrow dirt road.

Light spilled from broad windows in the white-walled palace. Nothing could be heard except for birdcalls and low animal noises from the jungle. Sound from the castle did not carry as far as the harbor.

Falorn still sensed the card's owner, somewhere within the glittering lights of the white structure.

"We have to go there," he said, pointing from the ship's deck.

"Are you insane?" Elise asked him. "We have to find a boat and get out of here."

"This is not the time for raiding," said Cirque.

"You're the one who wanted me to get the cards in the Seven Kingdoms, to get them out of the wrong hands. You'd rather have them in the hands of a pirate?" Falorn asked.

"I had other reasons to go into the Seven Kingdoms as well," said Cirque. "The cards were secondary."

"The body will wait. It's safe in Delerian. But we can't leave here without that card," Falorn said.

"Why not?" asked Elise.

"If I can sense him, he can sense me. I had to learn that the hard way once already. Whoever it is knows at least one of my cards is here. He probably thinks it's safe in the hold. Don't you think he'll come out to check if it suddenly seems to be leaving the island?"

"Don't you think he'll come out to check if it starts walking toward the castle?" Elise asked.

"Of course he will. But he might come out alone," said Falorn.

Cirque drew his sword halfway from its sheath and checked the blade.

"We had better be on our way, if we want to raid the castle and still leave the island before daybreak."

"Shouldn't someone find a boat?" Ryal asked.

"Does any of us know how to sail a boat?" asked Falorn.

"I do," said Ryal, "although it has been a number of years since I sailed beyond the sight of land."

"I've sailed on lakes," Elise admitted.

"Falorn and I will go to the castle while you two find a boat. We will meet on the beach at moonset." Cirque seemed very sure of his words. Falorn looked up at the night sky. About three hours of moonlight remained.

I hate it when he ignores me, said a voice in Falorn's mind.

Come with us. We're going to need you, said Falorn

Let's see if he notices I'm along, answered Sbashe.

It took a little while to find a way to shore. The pirates had taken the ship's boat with them, but a search of the deck turned up a small dinghy. They used ropes to lower the small vessel to the water. Elise climbed down the anchor chain to secure the boat and keep it from drifting. After that, the ropes served to guide Sbashe downward as well. Falorn, Cirque, and Ryal clambered into the boat without incident.

They rowed to shore through smooth water, more like a lake than a sheltered harbor. Falorn felt no breeze at all. In moments they landed the dinghy and went their separate ways along the fine, smooth sand of the beach.

He walked quickly past the huts, heading for the break in the trees where the path began. Something caught his eye behind the last of the flimsy cottages, a strange heap of round stones. He stepped closer to look.

"Mother of Kerion!" he cried out.

"What is it?" Cirque asked, coming up behind him.

"Those . . . those . . ." Falorn pointed, unable to finish.

Cirque looked at the pile.

"They're heads!" Falorn finally finished.

"So they are." Cirque walked over to the pile so he could examine the severed heads more closely. He picked one up from the top layer. "This appears to be our late captain. I suppose the others are the rest of his crew."

"But . . . they were going to ransom them. . . ."

"It appears the sailor you spoke with was misinformed," said Cirque.

"We could have fought. I didn't want to get them killed. I could have stopped. . . ."

"Perhaps you could have saved them, perhaps not. You can do nothing for them now. Their heads are no less happy piled here than anywhere else." The Hellein tossed the captain's head back on the pile.

"But we can't just . . ." Falorn couldn't finish the sentence.

"If you want me to help you get this card for you, we need to go now. If you prefer not to, I will go help Ryal find a boat so we can leave this place. The choice is yours, just as the choice on the ship was."

Falorn turned and walked toward the path without a word. Cirque followed in equal silence.

Sbashe's voice in his head was a little more comforting. *You couldn't do anything for them, Falorn. All that would have happened is we would have died, too.*

We could have killed some of them, at least.

Not enough. You thought the sailors would be ransomed.

Someone's lying to those poor sailors in the Seven Kingdoms, said Falorn.

Maybe. They may have a separate arrangement than this ship from Letz did. All you can do now is remember what you're here for and get the cards. Don't let yourself be distracted by questioning yourself or thinking about revenge.

Revenge? I never said anything about revenge.

The thought is lurking in your mind, Sbashe told him.

You're right, of course. Falorn sighed.

Of course.

The night air cooled him as he walked through the trees into the hills. He strode quickly with Sbashe at his side; he didn't really care if Cirque followed or not.

He felt the card come no closer as he closed the distance to the palace. He could hear noise now, spilling out over the surrounding hills. The tinkle of music reached him, odd tunes played on unfamiliar instruments. The castle walls glowed white in the moonlight. The structure had been built for comfort, not defense; light flowed from dozens of windows and open doors. People milled about on terraces overlooking the hills and harbor. He kept to the side of the road, although he doubted anyone could see him from the brightness of the palace.

Eventually, he left the road; it showed signs of looping around into open ground in front of the palace. He began climbing the hill to one side, hoping to find an empty terrace to enter. By now, he used the thief card unconsciously, reaching for handholds which would have been invisible a year before. *It's been quite a year*, he thought to himself as he climbed. Sbashe flashed an agreement into his mind. She seemed to have no difficulty keeping up, despite the steepness of the hill. He saw no sign of Cirque. For all he knew, the Hellein had gone back to rejoin the others.

About halfway up the hill, he realized the card felt very close. He shifted direction slightly to bring himself nearer as he reached the base of a sculpted terrace. He heard voices above.

"Damn you, are you trying to kill me?"

"What are you talking about? You're drunk."

"I gave you three women and a chest of gold for these cards, and they're no good."

"They're as good as the others you showed me. I even gave you the letter I got with them. I lost a good man getting those things for you. Don't try to cheat me."

"A good man! Pah! I've killed better men than you for serving my breakfast too cold . . . but you—you accuse me of cheating you! Me!"

"No, I would never say such a thing."

"Then tell me why this thing is getting hot. You're trying to kill me, that's why! Isn't it?"

"No! I gave you everything!"

"Your fool magic went off too soon, didn't it? Tell me what you've done to my cards!"

Falorn heard a choking sound by way of answer, then only a faint gurgle.

He threw himself over the terrace rail lightly, landing gently on his feet.

A burly man with a shaved head looked up to face him. On the ground between them lay a thin man, with a long, curled mustache and a crushed throat. A curved knife remained sheathed in the dead man's belt. Next to the dead man's head lay a large pouch. Falorn could feel the heat of a card from within the leather sack.

The big man clenched and unclenched his hands repeatedly. He stood half a head shorter than Falorn, who had grown some in the past year. The man wore billowy orange pantaloons and no shirt, exposing broad shoulders and a thick, shaven chest. Beaten gold bracelets jangled on his wrists, and gold loops hung from both ears. A wide, curved sword hung from a rope belt around his hips.

"You killed the wrong man," Falorn said quietly. *I want to kill this man*, he thought to himself.

"He had it coming. Smugglers are all the same. They get used to stealing from behind people's backs. It makes them think they can do it to anyone," said the pirate.

"I've come for those cards," Falorn told the man.

"The fool things are cursed."

"That's not your problem anymore," said Falorn.

"Do you know who you're talking to?"

"I don't care. I'm taking that card and leaving."

"Go ahead. Take all of them if you like. See if you get off this patio alive." The man laughed and turned his back on Falorn. He walked toward an open doorway, which led into a brightly lit ballroom; Falorn could see garishly dressed men inside, drinking and toying with young women dressed in filmy, transparent clothing, or in nothing at all. Many of the women bore the marks of chains on their legs. A table filled the room's center, its top covered with chests and coffers and glittering coins. In a far corner, next to a wide staircase leading upward, sat another pile of severed heads.

Falorn held his ground. He watched the back of the man's shoulders as he walked. When the shoulders tensed, Falorn stepped forward and drew his sword. Time slowed down. Falorn swung before the man had halfway completed his pivot. A thin-bladed knife dropped to the ground unthrown as the man sank to his knees. Black liquid coated the knife blade. The man's hand crept to his open throat, as if disbelieving the blood which poured down his suddenly-slick chest. He tried to make a sound, but nothing came from his severed throat and windpipe. No one in the ballroom seemed to have noticed anything amiss.

Falorn turned and picked up the sack, ignoring the dying man behind him. He wiped his blade on the thin corpse's tunic before replacing it in his belt. He quickly swung back over the rail and started making his way back down the hill.

Nicely done, said Sbashe's voice in his mind.

Thanks, I guess.

What's wrong? asked Sbashe.

I . . . I wanted to kill him.

What's wrong with that? He deserved it. He killed that other man without any remorse. Sbashe seemed bewildered.

I've never wanted to kill anyone before, said Falorn.

We all have to make exceptions now and again. If you had to want to kill someone, he was a good choice.

I don't want to leave those slaves behind in that building, Falorn said.

Don't you think you're getting a little carried away in this? First you don't want to kill anyone, and now you want to take on a castle full of pirates by yourself.

I know. I know we can't. But I don't want to leave them. I wouldn't want someone to leave me.

They beheaded the males. They wouldn't have left you.

You know what I mean.

I do. But it's more important that we get the cards away from this island before some pirate king kills you and takes all of them. You can come back for the slaves. With a lot more help. And without me.

Thanks a lot, said Falorn.

Any time.

They returned to the trail at the hill's base. In a little while the path took them to the beach. Falorn heard no pursuit behind, only the noise of breakers along the sand. A few feet offshore, Elise and Ryal sat in a longboat, its mast already stepped up, although they had left the sail unhoisted. Cirque stood in waist-deep water, holding the boat in place.

Falorn and Sbashe began running when they saw the boat ready. They splashed through the water and climbed in quickly, with Cirque following after. Elise and Ryal unstopped the oars, giving two to Falorn and Cirque. The four of them began rowing somewhat unevenly toward the mouth of the harbor, while Sbashe looked outward from where she sat up in the prow, on top of a heap of piled supplies.

"Did you get it?" Elise asked, after they had finally all gotten the hang of rowing together. The harbor lay well behind them by now, although the moon had not yet entirely vanished from the sky. A slight breeze had come up, enough that Ryal had begun looking at the sail hopefully.

"I got it. I think there's more than one here, but I haven't looked yet."

"How can you be sure you got all of them, then?" Elise asked.

"I know." They rowed in silence for a little longer. Cirque sat on the bench next to him. Now and again their elbows brushed accidentally. Elise looked at him oddly.

"Falorn, what's wrong?"

"Nothing. Nothing I won't get over." Cirque looked like he might say something, but the light-haired Hellein thought better of it.

Elise did not pursue the subject. Part of Falorn wanted to tell her about the heads and the slaves, but he finally decided not to. Maybe someday he would go back when he could do something, but until then, he saw no point in getting her upset. What he'd seen burned within him though, more fiercely than the warmth of the lion cards in his chest. He had hoped killing the pirate would make him feel better, but he felt only a burning hatred for all the gold-covered pirates he had seen, in their hall with their cosseted, shackled ladies.

18

The Dreamer's Journey

❖❖❖

"Where are we going?" Falorn asked, long after the moon sank below the horizon.

"From the stars, I think we're not far off the coast of Rohn," said Ryal. "A few days sail to somewhere civilized." The boat slid silently over the water, past the ghostly outlines of islands which rose ahead and then quickly faded into the night. Ryal tacked expertly to use every puff of breeze. Falorn's hands still ached from rowing, although he felt the blisters already subsiding. The cards he wore could heal him outwardly, Falorn knew, but the anger within him would take longer to die down.

In the morning, he finally opened the pirate's leather sack. Five small, bulging pouches lay inside, along with a narrow wooden box. Spreading a blanket over his lap, Falorn emptied out the first of the small leather bags. A few pieces of gold sparkled in the sunlight as the contents clinked out. Mostly, a dull carpet of brass and tarnished silver coins covered the blanket's center. Dozens of faces stared up at him, dead kings and princes from six or seven lands. The second and third pouches contained much the same proportion of gold, silver, brass, and copper coins, a genealogy stamped in worn metal.

He replaced the coins and opened the other two pouches. The first contained lumps of raw gold, ranging from heavy nuggets as large as his thumb to small, powderlike grains. He sifted the precious grains between his hands for a moment before replacing them; a chance breeze or ocean swell could blow a knight's ransom into the water.

The fifth pouch released an avalanche of gems and precious stones. The faceted stones glittered and shone in his hand, reflecting the sunlight in a hundred colors. Falorn recognized a few of them, diamonds and rubies and sapphires and emeralds and garnets and others that he'd seen before. But most of the stones looked alien to him, curiously cut and shaped, shining in unfamiliar colors. Some glowed in shimmering iridescent hues, as beautiful as the stripe on Sbashe's back. A pair of smooth round stones seemed to draw their energy from the heat of his hand, glowing with a lustrous, rich red which deepened and intensified the longer he held them. Part of him wanted to marvel at the stones like a child with new playthings, but he poured them carefully back in the pouch instead.

He noticed Elise watching him. Neither of the Helleinen seemed to be paying much attention; Ryal had eyes for nothing but sea and sails, and Cirque's mind was focused elsewhere, beyond the endless green wavelets through which they crested.

"You had good hunting," she said.

"I guess. That's not what I went hunting for. There were other things I would have rather brought away from that place." He thought of the slaves and said nothing more, for fear of saying more than he wanted.

"There are always other things. Sometimes you take what you can." She eyed the empty expanse of bench at his side and he gestured for her to sit beside him. Elise moved into the space, although her eyes looked wary.

"It's not like I have any use for the money I've already got."

"It can go quickly, Falorn. Hold onto it. You're a landless knight. If you want to keep your freedom, be careful with your money. There are a lot of knights who spend their lives fighting some rich noble's wars in return for a place at the table and a corner of a barracks-room."

"I've got pretty simple tastes."

"You've got rich enemies, too. And one or two expensive friends." He wanted to ask what she meant but decided not to. He sat looking out at the sea for a while.

They sailed across an eternal curtain of green. Islands surrounded them like links in an endless chain; they passed one after another, never straying too far from land, never landing, never seeing another ship. Here and there Falorn could see a lonely hut or the ruins of an ancient stone castle.

He wondered if Ryal could follow the links of the chain all the way to the coast and safety, or if the islands led elsewhere. Once he began to think of the islands as a chain, he could no longer associate them with freedom and escape in his mind. He expected the pirates to find them among these rock-strewn island waters. He only wondered how long their search would take.

"What's in the box?" Elise finally asked him, ignoring his dark mood. He looked down at the smooth wooden rectangle in his lap. Inlaid patterns in lighter wood formed a ship and sea monster, circling around each other on the dark walnut surface of the polished box. The brass hinges and clasp looked dull and flat from lack of polish, but the wood glistened as if newly carved and lacquered.

"I don't know."

"Well, open it and find out." He knew he would find at least one card within, but had no idea what else to expect. He probed the clasp with his fingernail, and it swung open easily, not locked in any way. A layer of folded parchment covered the top, old letters with broken wax seals. Falorn took the letters one by one from the box, unfolding each slip of translucent parchment carefully. They all seemed to be written in the same hand, a dense, curved, flowing script. He could make nothing of the crowded paragraphs; the individual characters in the writing failed to separate before his eyes.

"Here, let me," Elise told him. He handed the sheaf of letters over quietly. She looked at them slowly, reading every one fully before commenting at all.

"Your late friend was a pretty important pirate," she finally said. "He captained his own ship and owned shares in four others that are mentioned here. These letters are from his agent and, I suppose, old friend— someone he trusted, at least. The captain didn't dare leave Sterwen for long, so he had this agent dispose of a lot of his loot for him, and pick up things he wanted that couldn't be pirated easily."

"He called the man a smuggler, if he's the same one I saw him kill."

"I don't know if he was the same man or not, but this one was definitely a smuggler on the side. That's what this letter is about." She waved one of the parchment leaves. "These letters are written over a two-year period. In this first one, he writes about trading silver plate and fabrics for slaves and gold, and arranging for their transport to Sterwen. He was keeping twenty percent of the profit for his part in the deal; a lot of this is an explanation of his expenses and who he dealt with." She flipped through the rest of the letters.

"This is the one that's important to you," said Elise. "It's pretty recent—only a couple of months old. The captain had a card or two by then, it would seem. His agent heard about some more, and was arranging to acquire them. This letter accompanies goods that he is bringing from the city of Windford. According to this, the goods had only recently passed out of the hands of Archbishop Garrister of the Church of the Golden Wasp."

"Garrister!" Memories of the grisly auto-de-fé he had witnessed in Garrister's city crossed his mind unbidden.

"You knew him?" Elise asked.

"Zaren knew him. I met a few of his followers." Falorn shuddered.

"I don't think you'll need to worry about him much, anymore. I gather the cards passed from his hands with a certain amount of violence."

"He was no stranger to violence."

"I imagine not, as an archbishop," said Elise. "The letter says there is a signet ring attached, to verify the authenticity of his cargo."

Falorn felt around the inside of the box without looking down. He avoided the flat bundle that warmed to his touch, and picked up the cold metal oval instead.

The gold ring bore a wasp's shape on its face. Falorn laughed dryly as he handed it to Elise. He reached into a pouch at his belt as she examined it, his hand emerging with its twin.

"I've seen that ring before," he said. "See?" He showed her the matched gold band.

"Where did you get that?"

"I told you, I've encountered a few of Archbishop Garrister's followers before. I met the man with this in Roicenet, the same day I met Sera." He found himself thinking back, although the expression on Elise's face immediately soured. She recovered quickly though, and handed the signet ring back to him. He put it into the pouch at his belt, along with its mate.

"Can I have these?" she asked, looking at him oddly. It took him a moment to realize she meant the letters.

"I guess so," he said after thinking for a minute. "I can't read them, and I don't really have any use for them. I was going to give them to Geary for his book about the cards, but if you can use them. . . ."

"Thank you," said Elise. She leaned over and lightly kissed him on the cheek.

While she read through the letters again, Falorn looked down at the small rectangular bundle remaining in the box. Slowly, he picked it up. The binding thread untied easily in his hand; he had become more facile with knots in the year he'd owned the blue thief card. He unfolded the cloth, which proved to be a soiled silk handkerchief, bloodstained in one corner.

Eight cards lay within. Two of them matched the serpents he already held. A red snake undulated across the surface of the first plaque, cutting silently through a field of crimson grass with graceful, sidewinding motion. On the second card, a golden viper writhed within the branches of a gilded beech tree. The tree bark shone with reflected sunlight, and the serpent's golden eyes shone as well, ready to beguile or strike at some helpless passerby. Both snakes stared at him with uncanny, inhuman eyes. On the third card, a pair of winged green stallions pranced on a lush, grassy hilltop, as like as brothers. Next to the twin stallions, the sharp face of a green noblewoman dominated the fourth card. She stared at a lustrous malachite tabletop in a room of green-tapestried walls. The noblewoman looked sad, and weighted with the consciousness of her nobility.

The next four cards matched one another, one in each of the four colors. The first showed the spire of a tall blue cathedral, its intricate stonework reflected uncertainly in the ripples of a blue lake which faced it. A thick arched door of lapis-fronted wood stood open at the top of the blue marble steps which fronted the cathedral. The doors stood open and inviting, as if anyone could walk inside and be welcomed by all the thousand gods. Falorn felt a deep warmth fill him, even deeper than that of the lions who had untamed his blood.

The second card in the quartet depicted the green face of an ivy-fronted monastery sitting amidst endlessly lush green fields. Green trellises twined with ripening grapevines adjoined one wall. Olive-robed monks walked the fields and the walls, doing the work of the gods. Falorn thought of the frenzy of his own life, and felt himself longing for the quiet meaning of the monks' existence. Only a lion's growl within his mind pushed his eyes forward to the next card. He felt a sadness within himself that he had not recognized before.

Another monk graced the third card, but this one wore red. He looked downward at a rose in his hands, contemplating the redness of its petals. He had not cut the flower from the rosebush, but held it by its short stem instead. A thorn had pricked him, and Falorn could see where a rivulet of red blood slowly ran downward along the monk's wrist. An odd smile played on the monk's red lips.

A golden bishop looked out at him from the last card. The bishop's robes and torc glittered with a golden sheen. He held a staff of shimmering, polished wood, topped by the head of a gilded lamb. His free hand lay palm upward on an altar of beaten gold. A thick golden beard covered much of the bishop's face, but Falorn could sense the cleric's great age and wisdom. He felt himself longing for guidance, for someone to tell him the right steps to take on the journey that had consumed the past year of his life. He looked again into the bishop's golden eyes, and prayed for the wisdom within.

A lion growled again from within his mind. Abruptly, the sense of longing began to recede. He felt dizzy as his eyes struggled to refocus; blue sky swam around him. Someone held him as Falorn fell and fell and fell. After a moment he recognized Elise's touch. He leaned desperately against her until the ocean and clouds regained their equilibrium around him.

"I'm sorry," he said. "I didn't think that would happen." As he talked, he opened the pouch at his chest and tucked the cards within. He didn't want to look at them again. He hoped once they joined the others within they would affect him less.

"It's all right," she said. "You've been through a lot."

"I think I'll be fine now." He still leaned against her for support, but his body had regained its attachment to his conscious mind. He felt the pressure of the empty wooden box in his lap. He looked around at Ryal and Cirque setting the sails, at Sbashe sitting upright in the bow, as if memorizing the features of every island they swept around.

He wondered which of the cards had belonged to the Archbishop of the Golden Wasp. Any of those last four would lend enough fervency to drive a man to power, or away from it. Only the hold of the lions restrained his own impulses, as if the cards were jealous of each other. Falorn finally decided the archbishop must have held the serpent cards instead, more to satisfy his own sense of the man than out of any rational thought. He didn't think the four religious cards would have let go of the man that easily, even if it meant being reunited with their fellows. He knew the letters probably recorded which cards the man held, but for some reason he didn't want to ask Elise to read more of them to him. He enjoyed the feeling of her sitting beside him, her hand on his shoulder. He put the thought of the letters out of his mind and turned to watching the dancing greens and blues of the sunswept water around them.

After darkness fell, Falorn lay on his cloak in the bottom of the boat and tried to sleep. He closed his eyes, but his mind plunged and bucked like an unbroken horse. Lions prowled restlessly inside his head, and other shapes stirred around them. He felt a restlessness in all the cards.

Finally, he dreamed.

He walked within the high smooth walls of a stone-clad monastery. He met no one else within the walls. As he passed from cell to cell, through chapel and library and reliquary and scriptorium, he saw no other living thing. The place looked as if the monks had only just left, or hid when Falorn approached. Open ink bottles and other signs of recent work lay neatly in their places.

He passed out of the monastery's buildings, and into the courtyard gardens. A wide gate stood open, looking out onto a sandy beach. Within the yard, everything flowered and bloomed. Falorn walked among the vines and shrubs, stopping to admire particularly striking blooms. A thick smell of musky roses filled the air. The scent reminded him of a lost night long ago, in a distant city, with Sheanna, the beautiful black-haired circus performer and gods knew what else, who might have seduced the cards from him and ended his part in the whole drama of the cards within its first few days, if they hadn't been disturbed by soldiers.

He touched one lush red bloom, its petals wide and full. Slowly, he ran a finger across the silky smooth edges of the flower, around its base, along the quivering stem. Something stung him sharply. When he pulled the thorn from his finger, the stem shuddered backward, as if drawing away from him. Droplets of blood ran freely from his hand; the rose seemed to draw forward again slightly to absorb the moisture.

Falorn turned from the rose garden, and he saw a green lion standing in the midst of the courtyard, in the direction from which he had come. He walked back toward the creature, which stood quite still, only tossing its thick mane as its eyes tracked Falorn's movements. The lion shifted slightly as Falorn drew close. He put out a hand and touched the creature's mane, running his fingers slowly through the soft green thickness of the lion's hair. He scratched behind its broad ears, and the lion arched its back. It stepped forward and began to pace slowly toward the monastery's open gateway. Falorn walked alongside, his right hand unconsciously stroking the lion's ears and mane.

Falorn and the lion walked across the beach, toward the rolling green of the surf. Morning sun warmed them both as they crossed the sand. The lion tossed his mane at the water's edge, but continued to walk forward. Falorn followed the creature into the water. He expected the surf to feel cold, but it didn't at all. It felt warm on his skin, and gently soothing. They continued to walk forward long after the green water swallowed them completely, closing them off from the sun. Falorn found he could still see; the water had a hazy quality, like sunlight passing through thick, green glass. The lion seemed to be following some sort of path that Falorn could not see.

After they'd walked for a while, Falorn realized he *could* see the road. The wide path of shells and smooth sea-stones stretched forward in gentle waves across the softly rolling sea floor. He and the lion seemed to be the road's only occupants. Then Falorn looked up from the road and realized he traveled alone; the lion no longer walked beside him.

He continued to follow the road. Soon, others joined him. Four not-quite-human men trailed behind Falorn. Pale skin sparkled and glittered in the sea water, as if flecked with gold. Scales grew more thickly on their faces, and on the backs of their hands. Narrow stripes along their ribs pulsed slightly when the creatures breathed. Each of them carried a long, three-pronged spear of some black metal.

As he continued down the path, the creatures behind him grew less and less human-looking. Soon, Falorn wondered where he'd seen the resemblance at all. They swam more than walked, and their scaly faces looked more like fish than men. What he'd taken for leggings proved to be layered scales on the lower halves of their bodies. They followed silently behind him as he walked along the sea floor. He wondered if they saw him as a guest or a prisoner.

After a walk of many hours, the path turned upward, and Falorn began a shallow climb. The road sloped up to a giant palace of living rock. Pebbly walls of pink and white could barely be seen beneath layers of fluorescent-tendrilled creatures living on the coral surfaces. Brilliantly colored fish darted around the walls, jetting back and forth with seeming randomness. The four creatures who followed him swam now, instead of walking. Their green-scaled legs seemed unsuited to land, with long, webbed feet and thickly bunched thigh muscles.

Falorn continued onward, finally passing through the open gates and into the undersea palace. Tendrils swirled on the living walls around him. Brightly lit fish swirled around his head like so many windblown autumn leaves. The path split repeatedly, trailing off in many directions. Corridors twisted away like so many sinuous tentacles, but Falorn unerringly followed a single strand of the walkway, as if the four swimmers guided him from in front rather than following behind. Many of the hallways lacked floors or other walls; they seemed intended for creatures who swam rather than walked.

He passed onward through gleaming treasure rooms stacked high with gold from a thousand wrecked ships. Tarnished silver lay in blackened piles. A massive bell of worn green brass sat in the path's center. Falorn had to walk around it, stepping over a heap of golden serving plates. He touched nothing in the treasure rooms, although he marveled at the wealth they contained. He wondered how many thousands of drowned men had contributed to the wealth within this living palace.

Treasure chambers gave way to a wide, curved corridor, carpeted in soft, thick moss. His feet sank into the lush emerald pile as he walked, though his pace did not slow. He followed the bend in the walls, careful not to touch any of the bright leaves and tendrils that flashed and swirled along the corridor walls. When the carpeted hall began to slope upward, Falorn knew he had nearly reached his destination.

The walls curled around a wide doorway, bordered in thick, bare bones. The bones had come from some great sea creature; the largest of them stretched overhead like an overturned ship's keel, planed from whalebone instead of spruce.

Falorn stepped upward through the doorway. The four swimmers remained close behind him, tridents extended as they glided effortlessly through the water. He had reached the throne room. Ahead of him, curled on a giant chair of linked whalebone, a naked woman reclined.

Long golden hair rippled in the water around her, flowing like a waterfall in cascades around her shoulders and back. Deep green eyes danced as brightly as the sparkling fish who darted everywhere in the palace's softly lit waters. She had pale skin on her slim upper body, light pink at her small nipples and thin lips. Slender arms rested on emerald-scaled hips. A long, powerful tail looped around twice, ending in a strong-looking gray-green fluke. Her scales shone with the deep glow of gemstones, even in the diffuse light.

"Welcome, dreamer," the mermaid said. Falorn bowed low in front of her. With a touch at his shoulder, she motioned him to rise. Warmth spread through his body at her touch, as if the cards felt a kinship with her. Lions frisked and played in his mind.

"I am glad you answered my call. I wanted very much to meet you. You have stirred the waters hereabout a great deal."

"I hope I haven't caused any harm," Falorn said. He wondered how he could speak underwater, but the words came easily from his mouth.

"Not to me or mine," the mermaid answered. "There is trouble where you are going, and you carry trouble with you, but you have brought no trouble to this place or my people."

"I don't understand."

"Perhaps that is your strength. Many people understand a little about the cards you carry. They have powers to help and to hurt, and powers to twist their owners. To understand them, to force them to do your bidding, is to be seduced by them. You seek no control of them at all. When you came to this place you walked alongside the lion. You did not force him to carry you on his back. For that reason, the cards gather around you. And because the cards gather around you, others will try to kill you."

"But what are they? Why do they want to come together like this?"

"The answer to that lies behind you, not ahead of you," said the mermaid.

"You mean at the University?" Falorn asked.

"Perhaps. The road ahead is an evil one. You are traveling into a storm. It would be best for you to turn back before you reach the shores of Rohn. There is a disease in Rohn, a disease that goes all the way to its head. It is a sick land, and you would not want to be caught in its purging."

Falorn thought of the last time he had seen Sera, and of the sad man who had made him a knight.

"I have to go there. I only want to stay for a little while, but there's someone I need to see."

"I understand," she said. Her fluke twitched slightly, sending a cloud of tiny fish streaming away from her. Falorn had expected her to be angry with him. She looked at him, and her eyes reflected all of his life. She smiled wanly and shifted her tail.

"If you look for her, you will find her," the mermaid said, "and if you find her, you will never lose her again. Think deeply before you make the choice to look for her." Falorn flushed at the remembrance of Sera. Something inside him ached as he thought of her, as if the mermaid's words had stirred up a loneliness he had thought buried until now.

"I think I have to go find her. There are things I need to tell her, things I couldn't say the last time I saw her." *I'm still not sure I know how to say them,* Falorn realized.

"Take care to choose the right time for saying them, young dreamer. There are storms ahead of you. Your words will save you or drown you, and the ones you love will share your fate."

"I'll be as careful as I can."

"Would you like some words of counsel?" the mermaid asked

"Yes, please."

"You may have them freely, for the pleasure of sharing your dream and the dreams of your lions. The storm has already broken over the shores of Rohn. If you go there, stay no longer than one night in any place. Find what you are looking for and take it away with you quickly.

"You will reach the place you are looking for before long," she went on. "Let your boat follow the currents; they will take you where you need to go. As soon as you land, leave the boat and the shore as swiftly as you can. The storm that scours Rohn now comes from my lands, and it does not spare those along the shoreline." Her smile widened a little.

"I have a gift for you as well," she said. "I will not see you again, but I want you to have a remembrance of me and my people. Not everything that comes from the sea is evil, and many of the evils that do strike from the sea, men bring upon themselves. Wear this, and sea-folk will know that you have my favor." She reached to her wrist and took off a thin, glittering band. At her gesture, Falorn held out his left hand, and she fitted the bracelet around his wrist. It fit snugly, a thin band of silver scales as soft and supple as velvet.

"Thank you," he said, falling to his knees in a deep bow. Falorn wanted to give her something in return, but he carried nothing with him in his dream. He thought of the finely crafted box lying in the boat on the water's surface. That would make a fine gift, he knew. He owned little else that the mermaid might want. Reaching down, he felt wood and brass at his fingertips. Falorn picked the box up and presented it solemnly, holding it forward with both hands for the mermaid's acceptance.

"I accept your gift, young dreamer. Few of my treasures are freely given to the sea. I thank you for yours. If you will, I will give you a few words more."

Falorn bowed his head to listen.

"You walk through a storm, but storms alone will not hurt you. Beware instead the treachery of things you have come to count on.

Things are not always what they seem, and people are not always what they say, or what you want them to be. If you are to survive the storms ahead, you must learn to see people truly, and to hear what they truly tell you. Trust only yourself. Love others as much as you may, but trust only yourself and what you know to be true. Anything else can betray you: friends, lovers, walls, weapons . . . even cards."

"Thank you," Falorn said, wondering at the dark words in this place of soft light and emeralds.

He awoke to the first pink glow of dawn in the east. Warmth at his shoulder proved to be Elise, curled beside him. She slept uneasily, her short blond hair disarranged. She didn't wake as Falorn sat up to watch the sunrise.

He looked around the floor of the boat for the box in his dream. At first he thought Elise must have moved it. Then he looked at his left hand. The first rays of sun glinted on the thin band of silver scales, wrapped around his wrist as smoothly as skin itself.

19

The Storm Front

❖❖❖

No one mentioned the silver band on Falorn's wrist, but Ryal quietly
accepted Falorn's suggestion that they allow the current to carry them.
The boat moved forward as quickly as before, and in nearly the same
direction. On the second day, they sighted land, but the currents carried
them onward, parallel to the distant coast. Only after two more days of
sailing did they draw closer to the shoreline, within hailing distance of a
seaside village. There, the currents ceased to pull them, and Falorn
helped the others row through the choppy surf and toward shore.

Stubby wooden piers poked out into the water from neat stone bulk-
heads, but no boats floated in the town's small harbor. Except for sea-
gulls, nothing stirred at all. As their boat drew closer, open doors and
unshuttered windows became visible on many of the whitewashed single-
story houses. Nothing moved on the streets except for the shorebirds.

In the distance, on a bluff overlooking the village and surrounding
countryside, stood the walls of a massive castle.

They rowed to the longest of the piers. Cirque looped a rope around
a jutting piling, and pulled them easily up to the planks of the dock. None
of them spoke; the last few days of the trip had been quiet ones. Falorn

wondered if all of them had different reasons for being in Rohn. Sometimes he even doubted his own motives, though the silver band at his wrist reassured him somewhat.

He stepped out of the boat alongside the others, carefully taking supplies as Ryal handed them upward. Sbashe watched the streets carefully while the rest of them repacked their weapons and supplies for the hike ahead of them. Aside from windblown shutters and the squawk of gulls, the village remained quiet and motionless.

This place is dead, Sbashe's voice said in his mind. *I don't hear anything or smell anything. Everything might as well have been washed into the sea.*

Everything might have been, said Falorn.

"Where are the boats?" Elise asked, the first thing any of them had said out loud since landing.

"Gone with the people," Cirque replied.

"You think they took the boats and left? Why not just go to the castle if there's trouble?" Elise asked.

"Maybe the trouble came from the castle. That's the palace of the God-Emperor himself. I've seen paintings of it." Cirque looked unimpresed at the edifice.

Elise looked up at the stone walls and said nothing. They could see an open gate from where they stood. No guards patrolled the walls, or at least none who could be seen from the village.

"Let's go," said Ryal. "If we want to get out of this country, we need to go to the castle. The God-Emperor can help us get back to Cathan, and from there Cirque and I can double back into Delerian without having to pass through the Seven Kingdoms."

"Are you sure we should go there?" Elise asked, shading her eyes with one hand.

"I'm sure we don't want to insult the God-Emperor by not paying a call on him when we visit his country." Cirque's words didn't really address Elise's question, Falorn realized.

"I suppose," she said. Cirque's face seemed to echo her doubts. Falorn said nothing. He had his own reasons for wanting to visit the castle, and the others already knew his feelings.

They walked through the few wide streets of the village. Nothing stirred on the cobblestones except the shorebirds. He looked into a few windows, but the neat, empty rooms within yielded no clues. Dishes remained on their shelves. Brass pots hung next to fireplaces. Only the people, animals, and boats were missing. He wondered if the storm the mermaid spoke of had already hit the coastline.

Leaving the village behind, they began walking the wide gravel road to the God-Emperor's castle. Only as they came closer did Falorn begin to realize the size of the walled palace. Sandstone walls towered high into the air, higher than the walls of the queen's Summer Palace in Cathan. Dozens of high, turreted towers poked into the sky above the walls, like the teeth of a long-dead sea monster's jaw, washed up on the beach and bleached almost white by the sun.

A cool breeze touched their backs, a reminder of the endless northern sea behind them.

The place can't be empty, Falorn said to Sbashe. *There has to be someone there.*

There are people there. I see a few movements on the walls. The place only seems empty because it is so big.

A emperor in an empty, open palace. It seems strange, said Falorn.

It's a strange world, Falorn. There's nothing in it that isn't strange. If something seems normal, you're not looking hard enough.

I'll have to start looking more closely.

That's a good idea. In the company you keep, your own senses are the only thing you can trust.

Falorn started to protest, but instead fell silent. A part of him still trusted the Helleinen and Elise, he thought. But he had not told them about the dream, and he wondered how much they told him of their own intentions. Cirque's insane need for vengeance in the Seven Kingdoms had shocked Falorn and endangered all of them, but it hadn't seemed to come as a surprise to Elise. He didn't think any of the secrets they kept would harm him, but he had the mermaid's warning as well as Sbashe's to make him cautious.

A few men stirred on the walls. The guards walked their circuits only sporadically, eyes cast out to the sea when they looked outward at all. A lone pennant fluttered atop the tallest tower, a long red triangle with no symbol on its empty field.

A heavy, timbered drawbridge extended over a deep moat. Spikes filled the pit below, many of them covered with moss or lichens. Chains ran from the outer edge of the drawbridge to twin openings high in the stone walls of the gatehouse, each link as thick as Falorn's arm. The drawbridge chains needed oiling; flecks of rust had begun to mark the iron.

Cirque led the way as they walked across the drawbridge unchallenged. The guard postings looked deserted. Falorn could see a broad, paved courtyard beyond the walls. He looked up uneasily as they passed through the gatehouse walls. A pair of spiked portcullises had been raised into cavities in the ceiling, one at either end. Iron-bound doors leading to the drawbridge mechanism sat open and unattended. Falorn glimpsed enormous iron wheels and cogs as they walked past the empty rooms.

Pebbles clattered down a stairwell as Falorn stepped into the courtyard. He wheeled, drawing his sword by reflex.

"Sir Falorn! Welcome! Thank all the gods you've come!" It took Falorn a moment to place the man rushing down the stairs toward him. The man wore no armor or sword. His cloak bore a pattern of black owls on its red field. A black beard tufted the base of his round face.

"Kennemen?"

"Of course. Welcome! You and your friends are welcome to the God-Emperor's house."

Falorn sheathed his sword and stepped forward to embrace the Rohnan knight. Kennemen had lost weight since Falorn had met him in Alex's headquarters along the Calambria. He still strode with the same quickness, however. Falorn had to rush to keep pace with him as they walked through the nearly silent courtyard toward the central keep at its far end. Workshops and storehouses looked disused, their fronts boarded up as if secured for a storm. A few sentries looked down from the walls, most of them wearing Kennemen's black owl symbol. Falorn glanced behind to make certain that Elise, Sbashe, and the Helleinen still followed closely behind.

"What brings you to these shores, Falorn?" the knight asked him as they walked. "This is far from the banks of the Calambria and glory."

"A storm carried us, Kennemen. We've come a long way from home."

"Long indeed. But you're the knight without a home anyway. Just glories following you. Lord Alex thinks very highly of you, you know. Speaks of you often . . . never stops, does his Lordship."

"I'm honored. Is he here?"

"He never leaves this place anymore. That's why I'm here. I won't leave his side, not even if he wants it. Dark River is at his service, no matter how dark things get."

Falorn touched the knight's shoulder and stopped walking. They had nearly reached the tall iron-bound doors of the keep. Kennemen stopped walking and turned in response to Falorn's gesture.

"What is it?"

"You're one of Alex's household knights, aren't you?"

"Of course. Need you ask such a question?"

"Where are the God-Emperor's men? Why are you the only one here?"

"There are others here. My men stay to serve Lord Alex and guard his brother's castle. The army is . . . elsewhere. Fighting at the borders. Maybe gone, by now. The storm that brought you carried ill tidings ahead of it."

"What's happened here?"

"I should not speak of our plagues to a foreigner, but perhaps you can help. Creatures rise from the seas to comb our villages, carrying away everyone that doesn't flee inland. Our fishing fleets are destroyed, and our navy has disappeared as if hurricanes had swept our coast clean from end to end. At our inland borders, vile creatures emerge from the forests and pull down whole towns." Kennemen's face colored as he continued to speak.

"I was with Lord Alex when he led the army to the relief of the countryside. Along the coast we found empty villages, with the people gone. He left the seacoast behind and turned inland. At the borders, we found people still in their homes. They'd been pulled apart like pieces of chicken. The soldiers supposed to protect them had run away.

"Lord Alex scourged the countryside, looking for the monsters, and we found some of them. They'd got most of the soldiers who'd run away, and Lord Alex couldn't send out small detachments for fear they'd get those, too. He had to leave men behind wherever we went, to keep the monsters from coming back. Wherever we went, we were a little too late. There weren't enough men. Lord Alex asked his brother for every man he could put in arms and armor." Kennemen shook his head.

"What happened?" Falorn asked him, when the knight didn't continue.

"The God-Emperor called him home. He sent out every trooper he had, emptied every garrison, but he called his own brother out of the field and put other generals in charge of the fighting. Lord Alex came home at his brother's command, and he hasn't left the castle since. He left all of his other knights behind to help with the campaign, but I wouldn't leave his side. I will guard my Lord and my ruler as long as I and my men shall live."

Falorn turned so Kennemen could wipe his face without audience.

When he looked back, the knight had composed himself. As they reached the door, Falorn finally willed himself to ask his other question.

"Is Sera still here?"

"The noblewoman who brought Lord Alex to Cathan? She's here if she still lives. She's been imprisoned for treason. Her head would be gone if the executioner hadn't fled with most of the other castle folk. She's under a sentence of death."

"How can that be? What did she do?" Falorn asked. Part of him felt surprised, but after some of the things he'd seen Sera do and say, it was hard to be all that startled at the news.

"I don't know. No one who knows is still here, or is still talking. I don't know if Lord Alex accused her, or the God-Emperor himself, or someone else, but she's a dead woman. Best you don't ask about her again, especially when you speak with Lord Alex."

"But. . . ." *That makes no sense*, Falorn wanted to say, but stopped himself.

"You have to understand," Kennemen said, turning from the opened door to face Falorn, "Lord Alex is very upset by the events of the past year. Very upset. You might be able to help cheer him up, since he thinks so highly of you. I ask your promise to do what you can."

"I'll do what I can," said Falorn, "but I don't understand what . . ."

"Then I think we do understand each other," Kennemen replied. He turned and walked swiftly into the cavernous entrance of the keep, leaving Falorn and the others to hurry along behind him.

Somewhere in the middle of the enormous, empty palace, Falorn decided to slip away from Kennemen. *I suppose he'll think I'm breaking my word.* When a passage forked, he turned the other way, leaving the red-clad knight to hurry on alone. The others followed behind Falorn without question, although Elise looked at him darkly when he glanced backward.

Falorn worked his way downward as quickly as he could. He didn't really know where to look for Sera. He knew that royal prisoners usually went into dungeons, and dungeons usually lay beneath castles. He hoped the same held true for castles as near to the sea as this one. He dared not wait any longer to try and find her, however. The mermaid's prophecy swam just below the surface of his thoughts; they had to leave this place as quickly as possible.

They passed through silent kitchens. The huge ovens sat cold and empty, their doors gaping open. Falorn felt sure they had taken a wrong turn when he glimpsed a hint of blue from inside one of the spacious pantries. The glitter disappeared in a moment, but not before Falorn saw the stairway leading downward.

Below the kitchens lay the darkness of the castle's wine cellar. By the light of Elise's torch, Falorn could see endless rows of casks and barrels, each with its burnt-in castellan's inscription. Wooden trelliswork covered the far wall. Thousands of bottles filled the spaces between the criss-crossed slats, each bottle tagged with a slip of white paper and the castellan's wax seal. *I wonder how many wine-stewards assembled this collection, over how many generations? I guess the last steward ran away along with the rest of the castle folk.* Falorn thought of his father's carefully assembled collection of a few dozen hoarded bottles and sighed.

He walked between the dark rows of casks, looking for passages which descended further. He soon found a door, even without the familiar blue flash. The smell of damp wood gave it away; all of the casks and barrels had been elevated to keep away dampness.

The door wasn't hidden, just tucked away in a corner of the cellar. He felt a little surge of pride at finding it without obvious help from the thief card.

The lock yielded with a little help from Falorn's knife, and the half-rotted wooden door opened outward. A damp corridor lay beyond the crumbling entryway, so narrow in places that Falorn had to turn half-sideways to walk through it.

The passage ended in another ruined door, so warped that Falorn had to pry it open with his sword. He found himself in an empty guard-room, its undecorated stone walls covered with racks of spears and old, battered swords. Elise lit another torch from a supply piled in one of the room's corners, and set it in a wall-sconce. Three more doors led from the irregular five-sided room. Clearly they hadn't come in by the main entrance. One stood ajar, revealing an upward-bound staircase beyond. A second showed signs of the same decay that had crippled the passage from the wine cellar. The third door, iron-bound and built of stout timbers, had been barred from within the guardroom.

Elise smiled grimly at him as Falorn looked at the door. He saw only darkness behind her eyes.

"What's wrong?" he asked her.

"Nothing. It looks like you found what you wanted." She shifted the torch to her other hand. "Let's go already so we can get out of this place. It's time we were getting back to Cathan."

Falorn hesitated as he reached the door.

Go on already, said Sbashe. *I'll follow behind you. I want to leave this place, too, although I'd as soon not go to this Cathan place, from what I've seen of it in your mind.*

I'm not staying any longer than I have to. But I have to find her, Falorn said.

I know. But the others are only following you to be polite. They'd all rather be elsewhere.

I thought you couldn't tell what Elise was thinking.

I can't. But I'm not blind. Open the door.

Falorn lifted the heavy bar, struggling a little with its weight. None of the others offered to help him. The door opened only slowly, its six-inch timbers turning ponderously on greased iron hinges. Wide stairs of worn slate led downward into the darkness, capped at their edges by silvery-green lichen. Falorn heard water dripping below, and the faint scratching of rats' claws on a stone floor. He stepped uncertainly onto the first stair, his boot-sole barely gripping the slick surface of the stair's tread.

Elise's torch dimly lit the way from behind him, but he felt confident of his direction now. He wondered how the cards affected his steps; he felt their warmth, but saw no telltale blue glow.

The stairwell ended a dozen feet below in a wide hallway floored with dark stone. Three broad stone tables filled much of the hall's center. A series of heavy wooden doors dotted the walls on either side. About a dozen paces separated the evenly spaced doors. Each door contained a flat iron plate, which could be slid aside to create a small window. Heavy wooden bars had been slid through iron rings built into the front of each door, sealing them all. A few bore chains as well, and heavy iron padlocks.

Falorn could hear no sound in the hallway except for the noise of his own footsteps and breathing. Elise and the elves remained standing on the stairs. Only Sbashe had followed him all the way into the dungeon.

He brushed a hand against one of the tables without thinking. It came away stained with old blood and hair. Walking from door to door, he slid aside each iron plate in turn. He could see nothing in the darkness within each cell; he focused on listening as hard as he could.

On the fifth cell he heard movement. He glanced backward. The others had moved from the stairs, but they stood quietly. Elise held the torch passively, her face expressionless. The noise had come from within the cell. Reaching down, Falorn slid each of the two bars out from its bracketing pair of rings. He leaned each of the bars neatly against the wall.

Are you planning on locking the cell again later? Sbashe asked within his mind.

No. I just . . . oh, never mind. Grasping one of the rings, Falorn pushed the door slowly inward.

For a moment, he saw nothing. Then his eye made out a lighter patch in a corner of the cell. He stepped down into the darkness. Straw crunched under his boots as he crossed the small stone chamber. He knelt down, and touched the thin figure gently on one shoulder.

A face framed by brown hair looked slowly up at him. Eyes glittered in the near-darkness.

"Well, it took you long enough," Sera said.

Falorn had to help her out of the cell. She had lost weight; her legs seemed barely able to support the rest of her body. In the torchlight, her skin looked pale, with irregular smudges that might have been soot or bruises. Her hair reflected unevenly in the flickering light, its ends ragged, its surface greasy and matted.

"Come on," Falorn said, "It's time to go home."

Sera made an empty coughing sound that might have been a laugh.

"Home?" she asked. "Where's that? With my father? Here?"

"Someplace else," he said, trying to be soothing. "Someplace other than here."

"Where did you have in mind?" said a man's voice, from the top of the stairs. Falorn looked up. He saw only shadows at the head of the stairs. The voice sounded familiar. He had heard it once before, from behind a secret panel in a castle on the Calambria River. "I don't think you are going anywhere just yet," the deep voice said. "You are trespassing in my country. There is a price yet to be paid before you can leave."

Falorn glanced at the Helleinen and Elise. Cirque had his blade out. The Hellein looked upward at the head of the stairs as if calculating the odds. Ryal's face held a troubled expression. Elise's eyes looked stormy in the flickering torchlight.

"Do not think to escape," the God-Emperor's voice said. "I have quite a few soldiers up here, with crossbows. You would not make it halfway up the stairs." His laugh sounded emptier than Sera's. "My brother will walk down the stairs and collect the cards from you. After that,

Rohn will hold enough cards to sweep these foolish creatures back into the sea, and you along with them if you fail to heed my words."

He paused, then laughed again. "If you would like to resist, go ahead. You are welcome to cross swords with the finest swordsman in the world. You might even hold your own for a moment or two. I do hope so. Alex *so* hates to kill his inferiors. And when you are the greatest swordsman in the world, *everyone* is your inferior. Isn't that right, Alex?"

Falorn heard no answer from the top of the stairs, but a familiar figure appeared in the doorway a moment later. A thin, black-hilted sword hung at Alex's side.

20

Reunions

"Why did you have to come here?" Alex asked. "Why are you going to make me kill you? You started so bravely." He seemed to pay no attention to Elise or the Helleinen. Instead, he stared at Falorn with intensely blue eyes, pale as the morning sky.

Falorn made no move to draw his sword. Sera leaned against him heavily, unable to support herself. He felt the presence of other cards in the room, both from Sera and Alex. Idly, Falorn wondered why they had left her with cards while imprisoning her. Then the reason hit him. He looked up at the blue-eyed swordsman with a new wariness.

"Why did you do this to her?" Falorn asked.

"Falorn," Sera said, her body tightening against him, "it wasn't him. He didn't have anything to do with it."

Falorn's gaze never left Alex's eyes.

Alex finally broke away from the stare.

"We all do what we must do," he said.

"Why her? She trusted you," said Falorn

"She trusted no one. She merely found it convenient to travel with me. My brother suggested another use for her."

"As bait for me." Falorn knew the answer before he said the words. *That's why she still has her cards. So I would be sure to find her.*

"Yes." Sera slumped against Falorn momentarily, but he doubted anyone else noticed. She quickly straightened as much as she could without losing his support. When she spoke, her voice sounded harsh and choked.

"Alex, I . . . I thought . . ." She seemed unsure of her words, and fell silent.

Falorn wondered what she had almost said. He glanced at Sbashe standing at his other hip.

You don't want to know, said the voice in his mind.

That's what I thought, Falorn answered.

"If you want the cards that badly, you can have them," said Falorn. "Just let me take her and the others and go."

Alex looked at him curiously.

"You can't mean that," he finally said.

"Why not? They won't do you or your brother much good."

"They would win the war. With the cards in the God-Emperor's hands, the sea-creatures could never dare rise up as they have. Without the sea-creatures, the border garrisons could hold against the things in the forests. The land would be at peace again," said Alex.

"You don't really believe that, do you?" Falorn asked.

"No." Alex's eyes clouded over. "There are deeper troubles in this land. The cards would only hold them back a little."

"If I give you the cards, will your brother let us leave here alive?"

"No, of course not. You have to die."

"How could you?" Sera asked.

"I have no choice. Sera, I did all I could to spare you until now. I asked you not to come. After we got here, I brought you food every day, even when my brother would have let you die. He only needed the cards you carry, not you."

"It's not a very honorable thing to do, is it? To kill all of us so your brother can rob us?" asked Falorn.

"I'll fight you fairly. If you want, I'll fight all of you at once. That will give you a little chance, at least."

"I don't want fairness. I want to live." *I wonder what Zaren would do if he were here now*, Falorn thought.

"I'm sorry," Alex said. "I don't much want to live at all. I don't want to kill you, either. But I have to do my duty."

"Alex, you can't," said Sera.

"I have to," he said. His face looked worn, as if he carried the weight of many deaths. "I wish you hadn't come with me. I asked you not to."

"If I'd thought you were going to throw me in a cell and then kill me, I wouldn't have." Sera took a step forward, staggering as soon as she left Falorn's side. Alex stepped back, eyes sweeping the room to be certain none of the others used Sera's movement to cover an attack. When Falorn moved to help her, Sera waved him away. She took another halting step forward.

"I thought you cared about me," she said. "I thought you cared about Falorn. I trusted you. I went to you when I needed help before the battle. After the fight I left with you because I thought you needed me. You were so lonely, I couldn't bear to see you go away alone again after all you'd done for me and Falorn."

"I *was* lonely. I am all alone in the world. Believe me, Sera, I don't enjoy doing this," Alex said.

"You didn't care about us at all. The whole thing was a setup so you could get the stupid cards for your brother." She swayed on her feet. "You pretended to be my friend so I'd come back to you when you needed help. You planned to betray me all along."

"That's not true. I liked you very much, Sera. I gave what I could freely. When I left, I warned you what would happen if you got close to me. It was your choice to come back, not mine."

"You *liked* me? What happened?" Sera was almost crying.

"I still like you. I've had to get used to thinking of you in the past tense these last few months."

"When you decided to kill me?"

"That was not my choice."

"Does your brother ask you to kill everyone you care about? Or are we special?" Sera asked, bitterly.

"I have not been wise in my choice of friends over the years," Alex admitted. "This has happened before. I pray it will not happen again."

Falorn stepped forward as Sera fell to her knees. He crouched behind her, his hands on her shoulders. Tears left ragged streaks on her gray-smudged face. Falorn looked up into Alex's sad eyes.

"This will keep happening, as long as you have a brother instead of a soul." He touched the pouch hanging from his neck. "Here they are. All you have to do is cut off my head and take them. Maybe you can get both of us with one swing and save yourself some effort."

"I don't want to do this," Alex said.

"That's what you keep saying. It's not going to stop you, though, is it? Would you like to know something? I've never even seen the God-Emperor's face. Your brother wants you to kill us, and he doesn't even have the decency to look us in the eye. He's not even up there in the guardroom anymore, is he? He's just waiting in his throne room for you to cut our heads off and bring him the cards, and he knows you'll do it. You'll do whatever your damned brother wants, wait hand and foot on him in his empty throne room while his whole empire falls to pieces."

Falorn stood up. Sera sobbed quietly at his feet. He could see Elise and Cirque with their swords out. Ryal stood a few paces away, near one of the locked doors. All three of them looked resigned. Sbashe still hovered near his left hip.

It's all over, isn't it? he asked the corget.

"Get out," Alex said.

"What?" Falorn asked.

"I said, get out. Leave, now. I won't kill you here. Go, before I change my mind." Alex stalked to the far end of the dungeon.

They left quickly. Ryal supported Sera's right side, while Falorn held her on the left. Elise and Cirque walked behind, as if waiting for Alex to change his mind and pursue them. Falorn walked numbly up the stairs and through the now-empty guardroom. He could hear the world's greatest swordsman quietly sobbing behind them.

They saw Kennemen once on the way out, but the knight retreated from the dark expression on Falorn's face. No one tried to stop them from leaving, even when they followed Sera's feeble directions to the stables and saddled a half-dozen horses. They saw no grooms or stablehands in attendance, although someone obviously cared for the animals.

Most of the mounts seemed skittish and aggressive, but Falorn's acted as if he'd ridden it for years. He'd chosen the biggest horse of all, a tremendous, sleek warhorse, all black except for a single white sock. The stallion nuzzled his hand as Falorn adjusted the saddle.

"I think we're going to get along well," he whispered to the stallion. "I hope you don't mind carrying two for a while." The warhorse nudged him again, and he felt something warm at his chest. The four horses in his pouch approved of his choice, he supposed. He'd picked the stallion for its size, and because it looked like it might be the God-Emperor's favorite horse; he counted on the cards to help him ride such a beautiful animal.

Falorn murmured soothing words to the horse as they rode from the stone bowels of the castle and out into the light once more. He held Sera in front of him, guiding the horse with his voice and the barest touches of his knees. The animal seemed instinctively to move as he wanted. Its muscles rippled as they rode, shining in the springtime afternoon sun.

Cirque and Elise acted as outriders, their swords ready. Both rode on warhorses only slightly less impressive than Falorn's. Ryal had chosen a smaller mare. He guided another pair of horses by leads: a spare mount in case one of theirs went lame or Sera regained enough strength to ride, and a pack-horse, carrying the results of a return trip they'd made through the pantry on their way out.

No one pursued them from the castle. The stoneworks fell further and further from sight as they made their way inland, following a course set by Elise. In the remote distance, Falorn thought he saw mountains.

They camped after darkness had fallen. They now followed a wide, unpaved road which seemed to run in a straight line from nowhere to nowhere. A copse of trees near the road's edge offered shelter for the night; they had passed only empty villages during the day, and none of those in hours. Dust from the dry road covered all of them, and their horses as well. Falorn spent more than an hour brushing his mount before joining the others around their small fire.

Sera sat on an old, dry log, staring through the fire into nothing. She held a cup in front of her, half-filled with now-cold stew.

"You should try to sleep," Falorn said, putting an arm around her shoulder as he settled beside her. She nestled against him; he could feel ribs beneath her thin tunic. "You'll need rest to get your strength back."

"I've had months to rest," she said. She had scrubbed her face, but it showed little life, except in her eyes. "I've done nothing but rest since I got to Rohn. Dungeons are very restful places."

"It's over now, Sera. You're free," Falorn said.

"Am I?" She looked up. Tears welled at the edges of her eyes. "What am I free from? Where am I free to go? We're free like Alex is free. All we do is follow what these cards want us to do, just like he follows his brother. The cards wanted him to free us, and he did. Now we're going the thousand gods only know where, just because the cards want us to go that way."

"It's all right, Sera," he said. "I don't think that's why Alex let us go. And that's not why we're going back to Cathan. We're going there so we can get Elise home, and because from there the Helleinen and Sbashe can get home without having to go through the Seven Kingdoms."

"Where are *we* going? They're all going home, but what happens to us? Do we just ride around and pick up cards until someone finally kills us?"

"Maybe. I'd like to go back to Delerian with the Helleinen for a little while, if that's all right with you." She shuddered a little, whether from fear of the Helleinen or from cold, he couldn't tell. He spread his cloak over both their shoulders before continuing. "From Delerian we can catch a ship back to Letz. I have some friends there, and we have plenty of money. I think we would be safe on the island, at least until we figured out where else we wanted to go. And people there will know what to do with the cards."

"You've been to Letz? To the University?" Sera asked.

"It's been a busy year. I missed you."

"I missed you, too. I thought a lot about you when I was locked up. I never should have left you behind after the battle."

She might even mean that, Falorn thought, *especially after how things turned out for her.*

"It's all right, Sera. We're together now. Everything else is past."

"Thanks." She smiled wanly. "Thanks for coming to get me."

"I'm never going to leave you again." He remembered the mermaid's prophecy as he spoke.

Sera seemed startled at his words. She glanced around, her eyes focusing briefly on Elise, who had pointedly ignored her all day. She looked back at Falorn, wild-eyed. After a moment the tension seemed to ebb away from her, and she settled back against him.

"You never left me," she finally said. "I left you."

"It's all past, Sera. We can be together now."

"I hope so," she said. "I really hope so." She fell asleep as she lay against him, but her breathing remained shallow as a wild animal's throughout the night.

Something attacked their camp before morning.

Falorn awoke a second before Elise's warning shout. He leaped from his bedroll, nearly tripping over Sera as he drew his sword and rose.

Shadowy figures ran at them from the trees. Something loomed, nearly on top of him. Falorn took two steps forward and swung his blade. Yellow liquid sprayed from a hooded creature's arm. It kept coming, barely slowed by the wound. Falorn stepped back and swung again. His sword cut cleanly through the hood, which looked brown in the predawn light.

He pulled his sword free. Fresh liquid stained the blade, yellow-green like the blood of an insect. The thing kept coming at him. It reached forward with a clawlike hand. Falorn kicked out as it came too close for him to use his sword. He felt a shudder as his boot connected with the thing's chest. It toppled backward; he stamped downward, caving in its breastbone. As he moved his leg, the creature reached upward. Cold fingers closed over Falorn's calf.

"Oh, die already!" he shouted, plunging his sword into the thing's face. It convulsed and stopped moving.

He looked around for other attackers, and saw none. Two other creatures lay on the ground where Elise and Cirque had felled them. Sbashe stood over Sera's prone form, protecting her in case anything got through the others' guards. A noise at his feet distracted Falorn before he could spot Ryal.

The creature began to steam. Yellow smoke emerged from the holes where he'd cut its cloak. As he watched, it seemed to shrivel away. Soon only an empty cloak remained.

"It's a sending," said Ryal. "It's partly here, and partly with its creator. He sees through its eyes, feels what it feels. If you kill it, it fades away, back to its creator."

"That can't be much fun for the wizard controlling it," Falorn ventured.

"I understand the experience is . . . painful. I doubt we will see more pursuit today. But I think we can assume the wizards are back on our trail."

Late that afternoon they saw a pair of giant eagles, high in the sky and far away.

Falorn still held Sera in front of him as he rode. She sat passively in the saddle, only staying on the horse's back at all because of his hands on her waist. He couldn't think of much to say, so he just held her quietly, glad of the contact after the months spent away from her.

When he saw the birds, Falorn slowed his horse until he found himself alongside Ryal.

"It looks like they learned from the last time," Falorn said. "They're not flying alone anymore."

"Maybe it's just as well," Ryal answered. "That last fight took a lot out of me."

They rode quietly for a while, until Falorn finally broke the silence. "There's something I've been wondering," he said.

"What's that?" Ryal asked.

"How many wizards do you think are following us?"

"I don't know. At least five. Probably a lot more. There are two of them in the sky now. Those two are transmutationists, since they're in bird form. There are at least three summoners, whose sendings attacked us this morning. The summoners might be a master and two of his journeymen, or they might be three fully trained wizards. Either way, they will be too exhausted to chase us much for a while. Since the transmutationists wouldn't be following us without other support, I expect there are others trailing us, probably with soldiers as well."

"Are we sure they're all together?"

"What do you mean?"

"I've been attacked by sendings before, and I've been trailed by giant birds before, but not both together. Sendings just like these attacked me when I found the first card, even before I met Sera. I didn't see any giant birds until the wizards in the Seven Kingdoms started to chase us."

"I'm not sure I see your point."

"Why would transmutationists need to expose themselves if we could be followed by sendings? And if they're going to attack, why not all do it at once and overwhelm us? Why such a small attack?"

"The summoners might be too exhausted to follow closely now, but the question about the attack is a good one. It doesn't make any sense to only attack with three sendings if there are other wizards about."

"I think there are two groups of wizards after us. The ones with the sendings may have been what killed the green knight where I found my first card—I guess he was one of Jhodric's men. I don't know who they are. The others are probably from the Seven Kingdoms, maybe part of the same group that chased us before. Whther they serve whoever took over for Jhodric or decided to keep hunting us on their own after he died, I don't know. We know he gave cards to his followers to use in tracking us, and they had plenty of time to regroup."

"Can you feel other cards nearby?" Ryal asked.

Falorn thought about it. He felt a faint presence, like something moving at the edges of his vision.

"There's something out there . . . a few somethings, actually. None of them are very close."

"They will be, soon enough," said Ryal.

"We'll worry about it when it happens. Let's just ride now. Talk about death too much and soon you'll sound like Alex." Sera tensed at the sound of the name, but said nothing.

"Best we not talk of Alex or his brother," Ryal said, "at least not until we leave this country."

"We can't leave it soon enough for me," said Falorn.

"I feel the same way. This feels like a dying, cursed country. The sooner we leave it behind, the sooner I can return to my homeland."

"Yes, it will be nice," said Falorn. He wondered if he would ever find another home. He never regretted leaving his father's inn, but he missed the sense of belonging that came with his curtained-off corner of the attic. He suspected a part of himself would always feel like a stranger, no matter where he went.

They continued down the endless dirt road, occasionally looking upward at the eagles which still followed them at a distance. When they camped for the night, they found a defensible hollow. Elise and Falorn strung their bows while the Helleinen prepared a cold supper; they dared not build a fire.

Sera shivered as Falorn lay down beside her. He drew her against him and pulled his cloak over both of them. She stopped shaking after a few minutes, as her body warmed. Falorn held her closely to him, stroking her back with his hands. The muscles felt tense and knotted. They didn't loosen at all when he stroked her back with one hand, holding her tightly against him with the other.

"Why did you come back for me?" she asked, very quietly. "After all the things I've done to you, why did you come back?"

He thought for a minute before answering.

"I missed you," he said, finally. "And I didn't want to lose you forever."

"Is that really the reason?" she asked. "Not because of the cards?"

"It's not the cards. I don't care all that much about the cards." He knew as he spoke that his words were not as true as they once had been, but he said nothing more. Falorn kissed her forehead, and Sera smiled faintly in response. She closed her eyes, but her breathing remained shallow, even long after he thought she'd fallen asleep.

Eventually, he slept himself. In Falorn's dreams, lions patrolled the edge of their camp, guarding the perimeter against all challengers. He slept well, but when he awoke, he sensed that the pursuing wizards with their cards had drawn closer during the night.

21

Milestones

The next two days passed rapidly. The weather remained clear, the skies cloudless and blue. Falorn saw deer and bear, in addition to smaller game animals; their presence this close to a road bespoke a lack of hunters in recent months. Falcons and small birds of prey filled the sky, but Falorn saw no eagles.

Each morning, the wizards' cards felt a little nearer to Falorn's own. Despite the absence of people along the road, he and the others made cold camps at night. They traveled by day, riding along the road until it gradually dwindled away to nothing. Afterward, they followed the twisting dirt paths that led from village to village. By that time, mountains had drawn within view along the southern horizon.

After the road faded away, they found signs of life in the sporadic farm villages they passed. People kept to themselves in fields and shuttered houses, avoiding the travelers as much as possible. A few inns sold them thin stews and watered beer, although none offered lodging. Refugees from the seacoast and borders filled the villages, glancing suspiciously at the riders and looking more than a little lost.

The ground grew rougher as the road faded away. Cultivated fields gradually surrendered to wilder land, lingering only in patches where rougher terrain had given up its hold. Rust-colored rocks lined the path, here and there rising into tall, iron-filled cliffs. Scrub trees clung to soil-covered patches of rock.

On the third afternoon, the ground on the left side of the path began to slope sharply downward. Falorn soon found himself riding along the side of a ravine. High cliffs walled off the sky to his right. A few paces to his left, the rock gave way to open air. A thick canopy of treetops colored the land green a hundred yards below. Falorn saw occasional glimpses of blue river water through the carpet of green.

He felt the presence of cards close behind them on the trail. Falorn saw no pursuers, but the rock face twisted so frequently that staying out of sight behind them would be no great feat.

"Someone's coming," he called out. "There's someone on the trail behind us."

Cirque turned on his saddle. His horse continued to walk forward slowly.

"How close are they?" Cirque asked.

"I'm not sure. Very close, I think," Falorn answered him.

"How many cards do they have?" Cirque fingered the hilt of his sword.

"More than one," said Falorn. "Not all of the ones that have been behind us, though."

Cirque turned to Elise and muttered something. She nodded and took the reins of his horse. The Hellein dismounted and strode to the back of their little train, drawing his sword as he walked.

"Best look for shelter," Cirque told Falorn as he walked past. "There may be more of them ahead. The trail is certainly narrow enough for an ambush."

Falorn looked around the thin path. The rock wall a horse-length to his right climbed upward steeply. Sharp outcroppings thrust outward at irregular intervals. Scattered rocks lay where they had fallen at the base of the cliff wall, some of them larger than his mount. A few feet to the left of the trail, the ground sloped downward, quickly turning to a sheer drop into the woods below. Here and there, patches of darkness blended into the face of the wall, revealing the mouths of shallow caves. None of the others seemed able to see the caves except Sera. She sat upright in front of him, and nodded at his gesture.

I see them, Sbashe said in his mind. *Those caves aren't deep enough to fight in, though. Not unless you want to end up at the bottom of a cliff.*

We're already at the bottom of a cliff, Falorn answered, looking up.

At the bottom of two cliffs then. You know what I mean.

Something moved at the top of the rock wall. Falorn saw a flash of red cloth. At the same time, he felt a stirring at his chest.

"There are more of them up above!" he called out. Falorn spurred his horse toward the cluster of caves. He could see Cirque running forward from the rear of the train. Sera's skin felt warm beneath his hand as Falorn held her in front of him. She clutched his hand against her stomach and stared straight ahead at the rock wall.

Hooves echoed on rock as the stallion pulled up inside the mouth of the nearest cave. The rough stone chamber extended deeper into the cliff face than Falorn had thought, perhaps thirty feet of irregular, low-ceilinged oval. He dismounted quickly and walked the horse to the rear of the cave. Sera clung to the stallion's neck with difficulty.

"Stay here," Falorn said to her. "Stay on the horse, as far back in the cave as you can. It's the safest place."

"Don't worry about me," said Sera.

He turned and ran toward the front of the cave. *I hope she stays clear,* Falorn thought to himself. *She's got way too much talent for getting into the middle of things, and not quite enough for getting out of them again. And I don't know what we're about to get into here, trapped under a cliff.* Despite the mermaid's promise, Falorn felt a pang in his stomach at the thought of losing Sera again.

The others had gotten their own mounts into the cave. Ryal seemed to be deep in thought at the chamber's center. Both Cirque and Elise stood at the cave mouth with swords drawn.

Falorn's hair stood on end as he came to the front of the cave. His skin tingled with a familiar sensation.

"Get down!" he shouted, at the same time Ryal yelled out something from behind. Falorn threw his body at the floor. The air crackled. Horses whinnied and reared in panic as thunder broke around them. A stone chip cut Falorn's face. Thunder cracked again, a little farther off. The cave shook.

He heard shouting outside the cave, along the path. Weapons clattered. Someone screamed. From the front of the cave, Falorn could see nothing.

Where are they? he wondered. Falorn huddled close to the ground, hoping to avoid any more thunderbolts thrown by the wizards outside.

He held his sword in front of his body, ready to leap up and fight as soon as anyone appeared in the cave mouth.

An eternity passed. Outside, the noises continued. None of the sounds seemed to come any closer to the sheltered chamber.

They're fighting each other, Falorn finally realized.

Is that a problem? a voice in his head asked.

No, of course not, Sbashe. I expected them all in here.

It's not much of a cave for that kind of crowd, the corget answered.

No, it isn't. Falorn pushed himself up to hands and knees and looked around. The horses shook uneasily, their ears twitching at the noise beyond their enclosed space. Only his own black stallion seemed unconcerned. Sera had dismounted and now stood beside the massive horse, stroking its muzzle.

Outside, swords and other steel weapons blended with battle shouts and screams. Now and again he heard an unfamiliar sound, a hiss or sizzle in the air which didn't fit with the other battlefield noises.

Gradually, the sounds decreased. After an hour, only a few moans disturbed the air beyond the cave. Falorn waited another hour before he crept out onto the path again. Elise and Cirque followed a short distance behind him.

Two armored men lay a few paces from the cave entrance, weapons and helmets fallen on the ground beside them. Hideous burns covered both men's heads and torsos. The dead soldiers looked like they had been struck unawares while fighting one another.

Other figures lay scattered along the path like breadcrumbs thrown out to feed geese. Some wore armor, while others seemed to have carried no weapons at all. Many had been burned beyond recognition. Falorn could feel the presence of several cards on the path, but he felt nothing from the cliff above. The wizards at the top must have died in the fight or fled.

Someone moved a few paces away. Falorn drew his sword and walked over, stepping quietly over bodies along the way. The wounded man moaned as Falorn came close. The man wore no armor. Blood covered the front of his laced velvet doublet. He had thick blond hair and a badly-trimmed beard, both whitening from middle age.

"Help me," he said, faintly. "You must help me. . . ."

Falorn leaned over him. The man waved feebly. To Falorn's surprise, he saw that the man held a card in his left hand.

"Help me . . . and the card . . . is yours. . . ." The man gasped deeply.

Blood bubbled at his stomach, where the doublet gaped open. Falorn doubted he would live long. The man reached his right hand upward toward Falorn.

"Please. . . ." Falorn took the hand, wondering what the man wanted.

An unfamiliar voice thrust into his mind. *You are mine. I will have you, as surely as that sword has taken my own body.*

Wha . . . ? Falorn struggled for his own mind. Something seemed to be scooping his consciousness away, drawing his being out from the corners of his soul one at a time.

Fool. Your mind is open and your body is young. I will have them both, and your cards to go with them. Falorn felt his vision fading in front of his eyes.

Without warning, his eyes cleared. The blond wizard slumped in front of him. His hand slipped lifelessly out of Falorn's grip. Sera knelt behind the dead man. She twisted her knife once, and then pulled it from the wizard's back, wiping the blade on the rear of his ruined doublet. The card had disappeared from the man's left hand.

"I thought you would have learned about talking to these people by now," she said.

"I didn't think . . ."

"Don't worry about it," Sera said. "It's the least I could do after all you've done for me."

"Thanks."

They searched the rest of the path and clifftop, but found no other signs of life. However, they did find five horses who hadn't fled in the confusion or died in the ravine below. Within an hour or so, the horses had been loaded with captured weapons, money, and jewelry. Ryal eyed several rings oddly; no one objected when he asked to keep them as his share of any loot. Falorn halfheartedly suggested they say prayers over the twenty or so dead bodies that remained on the trail, but no one took up his idea. Instead, Sera started to push the corpses into the ravine. Ryal and Cirque soon began to help. After a few moments Elise grudgingly joined in as well. Falorn said nothing, but did not offer any assistance.

They rode along the rest of the cliffside trail with no further signs of pursuit. Gradually, the pathway meandered downward into the valley, and the thick forest growth seemed to rise upward to meet them. They camped against a sheltered rock wall inside a canopy of deep green, surrounded by trees on three sides.

Falorn felt someone approaching as he groomed his horse. He turned from the stallion as Ryal stepped close.

"I thought you might want these," the Hellein said. "I found them when we searched the bodies." Ryal handed Falorn four thin plaques. The cards at Falorn's chest surged in anticipation.

"I can't take these," said Falorn. "You found them. They should be yours."

"I don't want them. You're the one the cards are looking for, you and Sera. If I keep them, you might be pulling them off my corpse tomorrow."

"I don't think. . . ." Ryal placed the cards into Falorn's hand before he could finish the words.

"I don't want them, Falorn. I want you to have them."

"Then I suppose I'll have to take them." Inwardly, Falorn found himself glad to have the new cards. The lions at his chest exulted. Heat raced through his blood.

He looked down at the four thin pieces of something that wasn't quite ivory. The first two held nobles. A noblewoman clad all in blue sat on a sapphire-colored bench, amid a blue grove of azure-leafed trees. A few paces in front of her, blue water played from a fountain inlaid with speckled turquoise. The grove lay within a castle courtyard; Falorn thought of the grove and courtyard in his dream, but the blue castle's grounds looked different.

A golden king sat within the second card, amid his glittering court. He wore a crown of gold filigree. Cloth-of-gold robes covered him entirely, leaving only his thin hands and bearded face visible. His blond beard glittered, as if spun from gold thread. Courtiers surrounded him, all in shades of gold. Their faces reflected irregularly in the polished, beaten gold of the king's tall throne.

The third and fourth cards each held a set of twins, companions to the blue and green twins already nestled within his pouch. On the first, a matched pair of crimson hounds raced through the red grass of a fallow field, chasing some invisible prey. Falorn saw no huntsman or other keeper in the card's framed image; the long-eared hounds ran alone, their company shared only by the hidden quarry they chased.

A pair of golden bears occupied the final card. Well fed and sleek-furred, they lay curled up together in a golden-walled cavern filled with glistening straw and dried, golden autumn leaves. The bears' sleep looked peaceful. Falorn felt himself settling down just from gazing at the card, his muscles relaxing and his body starting to sag.

A stallion's wet nose poked him back into wakefulness, and reminded Falorn of unfinished grooming. Only after he placed the cards alongside their fellows in his pouch and began to comb knots from the horse's mane did it stop staring at him and turn its attention once more to the feed in front of it.

Ryal watched the whole process, looking faintly amused.

A thought struck Falorn as he finished brushing the blackness of the stallion's coat. He turned to Ryal, running through the cards once more in his head as he did so.

"That last card makes forty-three," he said. "I have forty-three cards now."

"Is that a special number?"

"Geary told me there are eighty-four of them. That means I have more than half."

"Congratulations. At the rate you're going you'll have all of them soon."

"I don't think so," said Sera. *She must have been practicing with her thief card*, Falorn thought to himself. He had missed her approach entirely, even through she now stood right beside him. "I have a few that I don't plan to give up."

I'm surprised the God-Emperor left her with more than one, Falorn thought. *Wouldn't one have been enough to use her is bait in a trap for me? But I suppose if he wasn't so arrogant he wouldn't allow his brother to hold onto them, either. They're just a vehicle to power for the God-Emperor, just like Alex is. I suppose he doesn't see any contradiction in combining the two.*

He reached out to touch her shoulder. She flinched momentarily, but then put her hand on top of his to keep him from removing it.

"No, that's fine," she said. "I'm just not used to human contact yet after all that time in the cell. When something brushed against me there, it was usually a rat."

'That's all over now, Sera," said Falorn. "We're almost out of Rohn now. No one will ever lock you up again."

"I know," she answered, moving closer so her right side brushed against his left. At his right, the stallion whickered. "It will just take me a little time to get used to freedom again. Thank you for all you've done." She glanced at Ryal, as if her thanks included him as well. *She still avoids the Helleinen whenever possible*, Falorn noticed, *but she seems to fear them less. I guess that's a good sign.*

"I would never take your cards," Falorn told her. He could sense their heat, radiating from the space between her breasts. Two of the cards he knew—the crimson temptress and the crimson thief she had taken from his table in Cathan the night she fled to find Alex. He could feel a third card, another thief, calling out to the blue card in his pouch. Falorn wondered if the cards talked to each other in some way, or if they just hungered to be together.

"I know you wouldn't," Sera said, almost purring into his ear. She spoke very quietly, so that Ryal couldn't hear her. "But if you're not careful, I might take yours."

"You wouldn't do that," said Falorn, forcing a laugh.

"I would, in a minute. I don't think the temptress controls me any longer, but it pulls at me, more strongly than you can imagine. I like you a lot, and I owe you everything I have, but I would still take them from you if you ever let your guard down. And with two thieves I could do it, too. Don't ever give me the chance."

Maybe I should just offer the cards to Sera if they mean so much to her, Falorn thought. Something stopped him, though. He remembered how he felt every time she left him. *If I give her the cards, she'll leave me again*, he knew. *I'll never see her again.* He remained unsure of his feelings for Sera, but he knew that he didn't want her to leave him once more, for all that the two of them had no real claim on each other.

He wondered if she would really steal the cards from him, after all they'd been through.

Try leaving them lying around sometime when your lives aren't in danger, said Sbashe's voice in his head. *Then you'll know.*

Then I'll know, Falorn echoed, but actually, he already knew. He checked the laces of his pouch with his right hand while at the same time he pulled Sera more closely against him with his left. Ryal had wandered off toward the campfire to leave the two of them together.

"This will all be over soon," Falorn whispered, as much to himself as to Sera. "Soon, this will all be over."

She nuzzled her head against him, and didn't reply.

22

An Unexpected Meeting

Two weeks later, Falorn looked downward into a sprawling valley, green with the spring's first crop, already well on its way to harvest. Behind him lay nothing but mountains. Sera, Cirque, and Ryal followed on the trail a short way back, with Ryal leading their pack-horse.

Elise had ridden ahead that morning, as soon as they had clearly crossed the border into Cathan. She had promised them a hot meal, a bath, and a minimum of bureaucracy would await at the nearest garrison town. As she spurred her horse, Falorn saw life in her face that had disappeared during the previous part of their journey.

Sera saw it as well, and tightened her grip on Falorn's arm.

He watched as Elise picked her way carefully down the trail, increasing her pace to a canter as the pathway widened and cleared.

Shaking his head, Falorn brought his mind back to the present. The town Elise had referred to lay a few miles downslope, where a small river forked and divided the fertile valley. Falorn could see brightly colored roofs and the smoke of cookfires, although many details of the walled town vanished in the glare of the late afternoon sun.

"Let's go," he said to Cirque, pointing with his right arm as the

Hellein spurred his horse close. "If we hurry, we might be able to make it before full dark."

"That is unlikely," Cirque replied. "Especially if we want to keep the horses from going lame on this slope. There will be light from the city after dark, though. We can ride into the night if it means a rest and good food afterward."

All of them had cheered up as Rohn receded, falling farther away on the other side of the mountains. Only Elise had anything to look forward to in Cathan, but they all entered the country in happier moods nonetheless. In the last few days, Elise and Sera had even exchanged a few words, the first time the two women had spoken in Falorn's recollection. Elise had resumed nightly archery practice with Falorn as well. He hoped it signified better things to come. He valued the Cathanese knight's friendship, and had missed her conversation.

A pair of cavalry troopers rode out to greet them as they passed a mountain village, which lay alongside the path Falorn and his companions followed. Sheep wandered freely along the village's lone street, and the troopers had to slow their mounts to a walk in order to avoid the animals.

"Sir Falorn," the first trooper began formally. She had weathered skin and wore a battered half-helmet. When he looked at the woman's light mail and black-trimmed green surcoat, Falorn realized he knew her.

"Risylla?" he asked. "You're the soldier who met us when we first came to Cathan, aren't you?" The second trooper, a young man with a thin black beard, looked at Falorn curiously.

"Yes, I am," she answered. "I was a junior officer then. I command half a troop of the Queen's Own Guard now. Sir Elise asked me to guide you to Forkingriver, since it will be dark before you can get there, and the path can be treacherous at night. She also remembered that I had met you; she read my first report."

Reading, Falorn thought to himself. *That's what I miss. I've hardly been able to practice reading since we landed in Rohn. To these Cathanese soldiers it's nothing, but here I am a knight and I can barely spell my own name.* He pushed the thought out of his mind.

"It would be a pleasure to follow you . . . . Lieutenant?"

"That's right," she said, brightening a little at his use of her proper title. Falorn was glad to get the rank right from his memories of the Cathanese army camp.

They reached Forkingriver an hour later. A second pair of mounted guardsmen waited beyond the town walls. The four troopers guided the way through a small postern gate by torchlight.

Falorn smelled the streets before he saw them. Mud sucked at his stallion's hooves, splattering the horse's coat and Falorn's britches. He followed the soldiers through dark, narrow lanes. Flickering lanterns lit the town, glowing from the overhanging second stories of thatch-roofed houses. Rain had fallen recently, and muddy water ran freely down the center of each street, carrying with it all of the town's waste. Low shapes moved along the wet lanes, like scuttling hunchbacks, or deformed children. Only after a moment's concentration could Falorn make out the outlines of hogs running freely in the muddy avenues.

Few people walked on the dank streets in the darkness. They passed two taverns with well-lit fronts and plank walkways. Neither spilled any noise beyond its doors. Falorn felt uneasy at the quietness of the town—quieter than the spring nights in the mountains he had become used to.

The stallion seemed to sense his concern. The massive horse walked nervously, and nearly nipped at one of the soldiers' geldings.

The narrow lane they followed discharged onto a square filled with standing pools of shallow water. At the rear of the clear area sat a square building constructed of gray stone slabs. Guards with torches stood on the building's tile roof. Falorn heard flags flapping in the night breeze, but the darkness blocked his view of them.

Risylla led them straight to the wide stone-faced door, which slid open before they reached it. She dismounted, her boots splashing on wet cobblestones. Falorn and the others followed her example, and led their horses through the doorway and into the fort.

The building's ground floor contained mostly stables and storage rooms. Grooms took their horses, and Risylla led them up a narrow stairway and into a hall above.

Elise sat at a central table in the hall, surrounded by a dozen or so soldiers, and by other men and women in silks. She had bathed and changed, and now wore a green suede doublet over pale hose. Although she carried no weapon, she looked as much the knight as she had in the Summer Palace where he first met her.

Falorn felt conscious of his travel-stained clothing as she waved them over to the table. He stepped forward reluctantly. Sera followed closely behind. The Helleinen and Sbashe hung back in the doorway; Falorn noticed a pair of scowling, gray-robed priests sitting at the long rectangular table.

"Falorn, welcome!" Elise called out. "I was just recounting your part in the raid. Come, eat, there's plenty of food." Someone cleared a space along one of the benches and Falorn sat. A plate of food appeared in front of him, although he never saw the hands which put it there. He began to pick at the food as he half-listened to Elise talk. After a few bites of stew and soft, crusty bread he found himself eating in earnest. The surroundings seemed to fade away; Falorn had to concentrate to see more than colors, or to hear words instead of merely sounds. The accumulated fatigue of weeks on the trail began pulling him under like river currents, aided by the strong, dark wine which filled his pewter mug. He caught only snatches of conversation, and said nothing himself.

Elise talked forever, as animated and happy as she had not been since their landing in Rohn. When her eyes focused on him, they glimmered with the same vibrancy he remembered from his first days at the Summer Palace.

"After a year away," Falorn heard her say, "it's nice to be back among friends."

He woke up on a straw mat in the corner of the hall. Light poured in through wide, unshuttered windows.

Well, it's about time, he heard Sbashe's voice say from within his mind. The corget sat upright about ten paces away. She had cleaned herself thoroughly, erasing all traces of the mountain trails from her fur. The iridescent striping on her back glowed in the late morning light.

How long have I been asleep? Falorn asked.

Long enough. Elise and the soldiers are doing whatever it is that soldiers do. The Helleinen are wandering the town. I promised I'd watch you.

Where's Sera? he asked, sitting up slowly.

Look in the corner. Falorn glanced over and noticed the brown-haired woman sitting quietly, hands wrapped around her knees. He could see her eyes, but she seemed not to see him. *For some reason*, Sbashe said, *she didn't want to go with the Helleinen or with Elise.*

Falorn wondered whether to comment on Sbashe's sarcasm as he got up. He stretched, then walked over toward Sera. *I must smell terrible*, Falorn realized. *I need to find a bath soon.*

"Sera?" he asked quietly.

She looked up. Her eyes took a moment to focus. She had cleaned up somewhere, but still wore some of the same tattered clothes they had carried through Rohn.

"Oh, hello, Falorn. I was just thinking."

"I didn't mean to interrupt. I wanted to ask you where to find the bath. After that, I thought we might look at the town if it's safe."

"It's safe enough, I think. As safe as anywhere. The bath's that way." She pointed, and then disappeared into her own thoughts again.

That afternoon they wandered the muddy streets of the town. Daylight treated the houses unkindly, exposing rough boards and peeling paint. Most of the houses looked old and weathered, as if unevenly maintained. His father and the other folk Falorn had grown up with would never have tolerated that sort of disrepair, he thought as they tracked through the soggy streets. They had a way of forcing neatness on people that Falorn had always resented. Now, seeing the alternative, he wondered whether his father had been right.

Toward evening, Elise and Risylla joined them. The young lieutenant eventually guided them along the darkening streets to a tavern for dinner. Falorn smiled as Sera and Elise exchanged pleasantries; he really wanted the two of them to get along.

"This is the best place to eat in all of Forkingriver," Risylla said as the four of them sat down at a table in the Forked Dove. A cloud of tobacco smoke permeated the air, as if the light-colored wood in the paneled walls exuded the bitter tang. The room contained eight round tables, stained dark with years of animal grease. Half of the tables contained other diners, fifteen or sixteen people in all, in commoner's dress like Falorn and Sera wore. On an elevated platform in one corner, a piper sat on a stool. His thin-sounding tune dissipated in the smoke; Falorn tried to listen, but he could not follow the melody at all. None of the other diners paid particular attention to the knights and foreigners in their midst.

A serving maid brought small, earthenware cups of mead and a bowl of flaky-crusted bread. Falorn sipped at the sweetly sour liquid in the mug. Sera drank only a little. Elise and Risylla seemed much more accustomed to mead. The maid soon brought a glazed roast duck, a plate of spiced pork, and a platter of steamed cabbage. Falorn ate slowly, used to lighter fare after months of travel. None of the other visitors seemed to be eating anything quite so elaborate, he noticed.

"They were lucky here," he heard Elise say, replying to some comment of Risylla's. "How many did they lose?"

"Twenty men, maybe a few more. Some others crippled. A small harvest last year, but this year was better. No fighting at all in this part of the kingdom."

"They came through the war as rich as before."

"It's always been a rich town."

Falorn stopped listening to their words. He hadn't thought about the war dead much. Many of them must have been village levies like the ones who'd died under his and Elise's command, though. He wondered how many sad little towns like this there must be scattered across Cathan. He hoped death never meant as little to him as it seemed to mean to these Queen's soldiers.

After two days in Forkingriver they moved on, now escorted by a dozen cavalrymen. Ryal had cleaned and mended Falorn and Sera's garments with his sorcery, much as he had done in Delerian. Sera thanked the black-haired Hellein gravely, and seemed deeply touched by his kindness. Otherwise she spoke little, and always stayed close to Falorn's side.

They rode hard for six days, stopping each night in travelers' inns, where they always seemed to be expected. Falorn supposed that Elise had sent riders ahead to prepare their route and inform the queen of their arrival, but he still found the ready hospitality at each inn somewhat disturbing, like a spider showing sudden friendliness toward a prospective visitor to its web.

Late on the seventh morning after they left Forkingriver, Falorn began to recognize the countryside. By early afternoon, they rode within sight of the Summer Palace walls.

"Her Majesty will want to see you right away," Elise told him. "She'll want a full story of what happened in the Seven Kingdoms."

"Won't she want to talk to you first?" he asked. "After all, you're her knight. I'm just an innkeeper's son who wandered into the whole mess." *I wonder if I'll ever get used to speaking with queens and kings*, Falorn thought to himself. *I've only barely gotten used to speaking with other knights.*

"She'll want to talk to you first. She's already read my letters. Her Majesty can talk with me anytime. You are a knight, remember—a foreign knight, but still a knight."

No thanks to the queen, Falorn thought, scowling in spite of himself. He'd thought often the last few days of the men who had died under his command. *I'm probably not cut out to be a knight,* he realized, *no matter how many people I killed when I let the cards take me over. Maybe the queen was right and Alex was wrong.* The thought failed to cheer him.

He continued to brood silently nearly all the way to the edge of the Palace walls.

Once more they seemed to be expected. The gates opened with no greeting or challenge, and silent grooms waited to take their horses and packs as soon as they passed through the outer walls. Falorn's stallion shied and whinnied when a stablehand took his bridle; only a quiet word and pat on the flank from Falorn settled the huge horse.

Soldiers of the Queen's Own Guard arrived to escort them away, taking the Helleinen and Sera to their old tower quarters, and Falorn to the Queen's chamber as Elise had predicted. Elise herself joked with the guards for a few minutes, and then wandered toward the practice yards.

"Come join me later if you can," she called out to Falorn as she walked off.

He looked at her back briefly, until one of the guards quietly urged him onward.

"Time enough to talk later, Sir Falorn," the guardsman said. "Her Majesty would like a few words with you now, and it's best not to keep her waiting."

"Of course not," Falorn said, and followed quietly into the complex of interconnected buildings within the Palace walls.

The guards brought him to a chamber he hadn't seen before. The soldiers remained outside as he slipped through one of the elaborate oak doors, its face covered with inlaid garlands of tulips carved from half a dozen different light-colored woods.

Sunlight poured downward from a glass-paned ceiling. A slate-paved path wound through the wide, octagonal room, cutting between hundreds of potted trees and flowering plants. The air smelled of jasmine and a thousand herbs. Insects buzzed between flowers. Falorn stepped onto one of the irregular slate tiles and began tracing his way through the foliage. He had to brush leafy branches and tendrils of vine from his face as he walked. The air felt very warm, like a wet summer day.

In the center of the room, he found a small, round atrium. Four high-backed white wicker chairs with oversized arms overlooked the gardens from within it. The queen sat alone within one of the chairs. She waved Falorn over when he hesitated on the path.

"Don't be afraid," she said. "This is my solarium—my own private place within the Summer Palace. Do you like it?"

"It's . . . it's beautiful," he said. "I've never seen anything like it. Where do the plants come from?"

"From all across the world. These days, most of the new plants I get are presents, sent by ambassadors or foreign princes who want some favor of the Queen. Once, my own knights went questing for them, looking for the world's brightest flowers and most beautiful plants to fill their Queen's garden and brighten her days."

"It's remarkable," said Falorn.

"Of course it is. Come, sit here in one of these chairs." She waved to the three wicker seats in the pavilion. "I would like to talk with you about your journey and return."

"Yes, your majesty," he said, remembering suddenly that he'd forgotten to call her by her title before. She didn't seem upset. He stepped onto the wooden floor and over to the nearest chair.

As quickly as he could, Falorn told her the story of their year's journey. He left out only his dream-visit to the undersea kingdom, and the precise number of cards he had found. The queen seemed not to notice his omissions, or the thin silver line at his wrist. She prodded him to say more periodically, but seemed to barely listen as he spoke.

"You did fairly well, all things considered," she finally said, cutting off the end of his tale. "You brought back what you left for and other treasures besides, although it cost the life of Tirya Huntmaster, one of my most able servants. But you have brought troubles with you as well."

"Your majesty?" Falorn finally asked when she seemed disinclined to say more.

"Your friend and mentor Alex of Rohn has come visiting, on behalf of his brother the God-Emperor of Rohn. They threaten war because of you."

"War?" he asked. *What could she be talking about?* he wondered to himself. *This doesn't make any sense at all. They're allies, not enemies. The only thing they don't see eye to eye on is the cards.*

He listened guardedly as the queen went on.

"You made a powerful enemy in Rohn. I can protect you from them, but not without a substantial cost. I would expect a gift from you in return. I would like the cards you brought back with you—all of the cards you have with you. In return, I will confirm your knighthood; I will make you a knight of Cathan. When things calm down, I might even be able to grant you a piece of land to build a home on."

That's not a very generous offer for so many cards. It occurred to Falorn that the queen didn't seem to realize exactly how many cards he now held. *Surely Elise's report would have told her, though.*

Falorn's look must have betrayed him.

"Your reluctance is not surprising. You have grown used to the cards. They have given you a measure of power, and helped you to gain a fair degree of wealth. Why not take a week or two to think about it? Walk around the palace. Think about what you would be gaining as one of my knights. Decide if you really want to be alone on the road again, with everyone in the world trying to catch you. The choice is yours."

Not that she really intends to give me a choice, he knew. *That's fine — I'm not planning to give her much of a choice either. But there's no point in telling her that before I have an escape planned.*

Belatedly, it occurred to Falorn that he should have planned an escape *before* fate sent him back to Cathan. He suspected it wouldn't have helped, given how the cards clearly found ways to come together.

"Thank you, your majesty," he said, trying not to react to her words. "I will think carefully about what you have said."

"Please do. Those cards are meant for the games of kings and queens, I think. But there are other rewards that might come to a knight who plays his cards wisely."

"Your majesty." Falorn stood up and bowed. He walked away very carefully after her gesture of dismissal. He felt like he had disturbed a poisonous snake, which only waited for another movement to strike. The queen continued to smile until he lost sight of her in the foliage.

Why didn't she just order me to give them to her? he wondered as he stepped back into the hallway. The guards stood where he had left them, and now they silently walked him toward his tower room. Halfway up the stairs, the reason came to him. *I'm not one of her subjects,* Falorn realized. *I'm a foreigner, knighted by a foreign prince. She can ask me to do something, but she can't order me.* He started to smile as he left the guards behind and stepped up to the door of his room.

Of course, she can always have you killed and take them, said a familiar voice in his mind.

Sbashe looked up at Falorn from where she lay on a woven rug in the room's center. He looked at the table and its pair of narrow chairs, all as he remembered them. His pack sat unopened on the table. Falorn stretched, then looked over at the bed, wondering if he had time for a nap before anyone summoned him anywhere.

He froze.

Alex of Rohn sat on the bed looking at Falorn, a long, thin-bladed sword unsheathed across his lap.

23

Blood and Promises

"I'm glad you made it back," said Alex.

"How did you get in here?"

"I asked the guards to let me in," Alex said.

"And they did?"

"Of course."

Falorn wondered if he should try for his sword. He doubted he'd even get a hand on his weapon before Alex killed him. The cards stirred uneasily at his chest, as if troubled. He could feel a similar stirring where Alex sat, as if the prince of Rohn's cards reflected his own inner disturbance.

Don't try it, Sbashe's voice said in his mind. *Let him talk. If he wanted to kill you he'd have done it already.* The lions subsided at his chest, and the other cards with them. Falorn felt a sudden sense of calm, despite the heat which had begun spreading through him, stronger than the cards' normal warmth.

"Aren't you going to ask me why I'm here?" Alex asked. "I've come a very long way to see you."

"If you wanted to kill me, you could have done it in Rohn."

"Yes, that's true. I've thought about killing you many times since that day."

Falorn said nothing.

Alex looked down onto his lap for a long while. When he looked up, tears rimmed his eyes, and he held the sword's hilt in his right hand. His face seemed to twist slightly, as the swordsman fought for composure. Falorn saw lines at the edge of the older man's eyes and mouth

"Do you see this blade?" Alex asked, in a voice that wasn't quite level. "I never named it, but I've killed four hundred thirty-two men with this sword. It's not the only sword I've ever had. Do you have any idea what it feels like to only be known for killing? Did you ever wonder what it's like to be the best in the world at killing, what kind of horrible person must be inside of such a deadly killer?" As he spoke, Alex's voice became flat and calm.

Falorn held his silence. He found himself staring into the thin steel blade of Alex's sword, fascinated in spite of himself.

Alex stood up, sheathing his sword with a metallic scrape. He adjusted his belt, as if uncomfortable with the feel of the sheathed blade on his hip. The swordsman's hands slid along the tooled leather until they stopped against a worn brown pouch. Falorn watched, fascinated, as Alex untied the knot which secured the pouch without looking down. The strings quickly loosened. Alex lifted the pouch up, holding it level with his eyes. He opened his mouth to say something, then closed it again, frowning. Without a word he tossed the pouch to the floor at Falorn's feet. Turning quickly, Alex strode from the room. The door slammed behind him.

Falorn stood quietly for a while, somehow unwilling to move. Sbashe finally disturbed him.

Well? she asked. *Aren't you going to open the pouch? You are curious, aren't you?*

No, Falorn answered truthfully. *I already know what's in it. All of the cards from Rohn.* He could feel the pouch's contents burning on the floor in front of him, like glowing coals waiting to spread their heat and consume him.

Alex wanted you to have them, Sbashe said.

No. Alex wanted to be rid of them. They really don't bring anything but trouble, do they?

They've brought you a great deal besides trouble. You're carrying a pouchful of gold. You're the honored guest of a queen.

I'm only a guest because she hasn't thought up an excuse to make me a prisoner yet. She wants to take the cards from me.

Of course she does. So does almost everyone else you know. But the cards want to be with you for some reason. Alex didn't want to get rid of his cards. He thought you should have them. He's a very sad man.

I know he is, said Falorn.

He really does care for you, you know. He thought the cards might help you. He's given up a lot for you.

Falorn walked over to the window and stared out into the gardens below. The open shutter rocked slightly from the breeze, clicking gently against the stone wall. *It sounds almost like a bird, clicking and clicking*, Falorn thought. He didn't want to think about cards, or Alex, or anything else.

Maybe I should give them to the queen, he thought, directing the words at Sbashe. *Maybe that would solve everything.*

Do you think that would stop her from killing you? Sbashe asked.

No. Not really. Not if she thought I might threaten her.

Why hurry? She'll give you a little time to make your choice, if she thinks you haven't made up your mind. In a day or two you may have more options. Things might become clearer.

You're probably right.

He tried to put the politics of queens and princes out of his mind. He took a step toward the door, thinking to find Elise. Maybe he could work some of the frustration off on the practice field.

He stopped, in spite of himself, and looked down at the small brown sack at his feet. Reaching down, he took it in both hands, and lifted it to his face as Alex had done.

A lot of people have suffered for you, he thought. *I suppose I'll be next.* Shaking his head, he worked open the pouch's strings.

He counted nine of the thin plaques inside. The cards at his own chest seemed to sing in recognition, as if overjoyed to be that much closer toward completion. Warmth played through his whole body. Falorn's fingers tingled as he withdrew the new cards from Alex's discarded pouch.

A beautiful, scarlet-haired princess stared out at him from the face of the first card. Her eyes glinted like the deepest garnets. Waves of red hair flowed around her softly rounded face and across the shoulders. A coronet set with glittering rubies crowned her head. She stood at a windowsill, looking outward at Falorn from a red tower much like the one in which he stood. Behind her, he saw hints of a red room lined with books and treasures. *I wonder if I'll ever have a room like that, or like Sera's old room in Roicenet,* Falorn thought. *Someday, it would be nice to have a place of my own where I could just sit and do what I wanted, without anybody trying to kill me or rob me or tell me what to do. I wonder if I'll ever have that? I wonder if anyone ever has that? Sera certainly paid a high enough price for everything she had in her father's castle.* He looked more deeply at the card, and thought he could detect a pensive sadness in the woman's garnet eyes.

On the second card, a nobleman in blue rode at the head of his knights, armored for battle. A blue standard billowed in the air above the heavy-set, bearded nobleman's head: a light blue dragon sleeping on a field of darker blue. The baron held an axe in his left hand, close against his hip. His right hand pointed outward, as if showing his knights the way to an invisible enemy. All around them, blue grass grew, thick and lush except where the warhorses had trampled it.

A crimson prince stared out from the third card. He looked arrogant and angry, more closely akin to the baron and his fighting men than to the princess who stood at her tower window, waiting for someone to return. The prince's coronet bore a single ruby twice the thickness of a man's thumb, and carved in the shape of a skull. He wore red fur. A ruby-hilted knife hung at his belt of tooled cordovan leather. His eyes burned, red and searching. Falorn felt afraid to look at the card too long, lest he be caught in the grip of that red, red flame.

The next two cards held a blue knight and a golden knight, companions to the green knight that had belonged to the dead General Stennet and to the golden knight Falorn had taken from Rorik Iron Eagle. Each knight sat on a warhorse, fully armed and armored. A squire rode behind the golden knight, his cloth-of-gold tunic matching the knight's surcoat and gold-chased helm. The blue knight rode alone and bareheaded, with his helmet tucked beneath his left arm. Long indigo hair swirled outward behind him, caught in the breeze as he rode. A grim smile touched the blue knight's face, as if he felt glad of the direction he traveled in, but knew of dark things ahead.

The last four cards held swords, one each in blue, crimson, green, and gold. Each blade looked different, and none bore ornamentation. A green longsword not unlike his own sat on a cushion of green velvet. The sword had a long hilt covered with green leather tape, and quillons which tapered outward slightly at their ends. The red broadsword had an oversized grip, as if it needed two hands to wield the heaviness of its wide steel blade. The blue saber's curved blade thickened at the head, to give more weight to a killing downward stroke. Blue wire covered the hilt closely, and a pointed metal stud capped the pommel. The golden sword had a long thin blade, very like the one Alex bore. Falorn felt a pang as he realized the extent of the Rohnan prince's loss; the cards had not given Alex his skill with a blade, but they had given life and spirit to it, as if his sword had been granted a soul of its own. Already Falorn could feel a new awareness of the weapon at his hip, a new understanding of the strength and ferocity that had gone into the forging of its folded-steel blade. Like the lions and the other cards that followed their lead, the sword seemed to sing and rejoice in its newfound companions. The blade wanted to be freed of the confining leather, to swing in the air and be kissed by the warm blood of life.

Falorn shuddered as he put Alex's cards into the pouch beneath the other plaques. Part of him felt fuller for their presence, but he wondered how soon they would become stronger than his own will.

He looked up as he drew the pouch's string tight and replaced it against his chest. Sbashe lay curled up on the carpet, seemingly asleep. Falorn quietly opened the door and stepped outward, not wanting to wake the corget while chasing his worries around the castle.

He heard voices as he entered the hall. He found himself standing silently outside Sera's door, listening.

"What do you mean you gave them away!" Sera shouted. "You had no right!"

"The cards were mine by right," Falorn heard Alex say. "I chose to give them to him."

"If they were anyone's by right, they ought to have been mine, after everything you've done to me. If you were going to give them away, the least you could have done is give them to me," Sera said.

"I have hurt you deeply," Alex agreed. The room fell silent.

"Why did you do it?" Sera finally asked. She sounded more sad than angry, nearly as sad as Alex himself.

"I thought if I gave him the cards I might prevent more fighting," Alex answered, although Falorn wondered if that had been what Sera asked about. "I have been the cause of enough fighting already. It is time to put an end to it. I will leave here tonight, and I will never return to Rohn or Cathan."

"Why did you have to tell me this? Why didn't you just leave?"

"I thought if I had to leave . . . you might come with me," Alex said. "I know I hurt you, but I hoped you might give me a chance to make it up to you. You cared for me once. Without the cards to drive me, I can try to be the man you thought I was."

Falorn held his breath outside the door, listening for Sera's answer. He thought he could hear her sobbing within the room. Finally, her crying subsided. In spite of himself, Falorn couldn't help thinking that Sera had told him almost the exact same words Alex had just used. *I'm still not sure if the cards actually change people, or just make people more of what's already inside them. I want to blame Sera's cards for every betrayal—but then I'd have to blame them for the times she's loving, too, wouldn't I?*

"Get out," she finally said to Alex, in a half-broken voice. "Please leave now. You've done enough to me already. Don't ask me for this, too."

"I won't," he said, his voice deceptively steady. "I won't ask you for anything again. But I'll think of you, and what I did to you, forever."

"Please, go."

Falorn slipped away from the door before Alex could open it and see him. Silently, he returned to his room, stripped off his boots and sword belt, and lay down on the bed. For a long time, he stared up at the ceiling, waiting for his eyes to close and sleep to take him. After he had fallen nearly asleep, he felt warmth beside and against him, as if someone else had joined him on the bed.

When he woke up, he found himself alone on the bed. Morning sun streamed through the open window. Sbashe sat upright beside the window, ears perked outward.

Falorn sat up, instinctively checking the pouch at his chest. He heard the sound of trumpets from beyond the palace walls. Quickly, he pulled on his boots and sword belt, half-drawing the blade from its sheath to test its looseness. The sheath he'd had made for the sword in Letz never felt quite right to him. he missed the way the Delerian-made scabbard had held the now-shattered blade he'd left behind in the Seven Kingdoms. *I suppose it's just my imagination*, he thought. *I don't think there's really any difference. The old sheath was just special to me because of where I got it, and the blade was the first sword I ever owned.*

Someone knocked on the door.

"Come in," Falorn called out. The door had already begun to open. Elise stepped through, wearing a gray velvet tunic he had never seen before over black britches. She wore her sword in a new scabbard as well. Her face and hair looked freshly scrubbed.

"We have unexpected guests arriving," she said, waving vaguely in the direction of the wall.

"Who?" Falorn asked.

"Old friends of yours, I gather. Our lady Sera wasn't happy to see them coming. There are about a hundred armored men, riding under a flag of truce and a gold and scarlet banner. Sound familiar?"

"No . . . or, yes . . . it does. That's probably the Duke of Iron Eagle's flag. I imagine he's looking for me and Sera." Falorn thought back to his first encounter with Rorik Iron Eagle and his father the Duke's soldiers, when he'd been brought into the young noble's tent as a prisoner. He supposed Rorik would not have forgiven Falorn for his theft of Rorik's cards and fiancee. He had hoped they would stop pursuing him after the fight in the marsh castle with the Baron of Golden Reeds and with Sera's father. To his embarrassment, he had nearly forgotten Rorik in the events of the last year.

"That's who Her Majesty thought it might be, as well. She's asked that you and Sera stay out of sight until the Duke's intentions become clear. She says that she still considers you under her protection," said Elise

"Thank you. I'll do what she asks, of course, and I'm sure Sera will as well."

"Her Majesty also wondered if you had given any thought to her proposal."

"Yes, I have. But I will need more time to decide. Some things are very hard to give up."

"I'm certain she'll understand. Take all the time you need." Elise leaned over and kissed him gently on the cheek. Then she wheeled and strode from the room. The sheathed blade of her sword clattered on the stone floor as she walked.

Falorn walked over to the tower window. He could hear the trumpets, but the window looked down onto interior courtyard, rather than outward over the walls.

I take it you don't like this Rorik much? Sbashe's voice asked in his mind. Falorn thought back to his own feelings of helplessness, while he watched Rorik's men killing the outnumbered Helleinen in the forest clearing. He said nothing; Sbashe would see the images clearly enough.

Sera doesn't much like Helleinen either, you know. They scare her.

I imagine they do, said Falorn.

Not just because of what she did. There's more to it than that.

The door opened, interrupting the words flowing into Falorn's mind. Sera walked in, red-faced and only partially clothed. She wore a faded red knee-length tunic, but no hose, belt, or doublet.

"Falorn, I'm scared," she said, reaching out to him. He held out an arm and gently pulled her close, holding her against his shoulder while she quietly shook.

"I thought they were gone," she finally said. "I thought we were rid of them for good."

"They don't have us yet," Falorn said, trying to sound soothing.

"I know," said Sera, leaning into him. "I'm just tired of running."

"Me too. It won't be much longer." He wondered where the Helleinen were. They might all have to run soon, and the best chance he could think of might be to go to Delerian. Sera would hate it, but no other place within reach offered any safety at all.

Before long, Elise returned. The Helleinen entered the room along with her.

"Her Majesty would like you to come to the grand courtyard, where she and His Majesty the King will meet with His Grace, the Duke of Iron Eagle. She gives her word that no harm will befall you today."

Elise grudgingly allowed Sera to dress before they all walked down the steps and through the halls leading to the courtyard. As they emerged into the sunlight, Falorn could see rows of mounted troops drawn up, surrounding a pair of gilded wood thrones that had been carried to the center of the yard. Behind and to either side of the thrones, Cathanese knights and soldiers in polished armor sat on carefully groomed mounts. Gold and blue ribbons garlanded the animals' manes and tails. In front of the thrones stood five ranks of armored horsemen in scarlet and gold, each rank twenty soldiers wide. A pair of riders in gilded helmets held their mounts slightly forward of the other horsemen. Falorn recognized Rorik instantly. An older man, twin to Rorik save for a more weathered face and a gray mustache, he took to be the Duke of Iron Eagle. A sack hung from the Duke's saddle bow. Falorn could not see the king and queen from where he stood behind the thrones, but he assumed they sat within the great chairs.

The Duke's horse pranced and shied at its bit nervously. The older man stilled it with a touch. He reached for the sack as he started to speak.

"Your Majesties," he started, bowing his head respectfully to each, "as you may know, you are harboring folk who have dishonored my son and my house. They have done you no wrong, but I ask that you turn them over to my house for justice, in the name of honor and fellow nobility. You would have the gratitude of the Duchy of Iron Eagle, which is, as you know, a powerful one."

"Your people are a grand folk," the King said. "Iron Eagle is a beautiful land to pass through. I rode through it once, and have never forgotten its beauty."

"Thank you, Your Majesty."

"Is your mother well? I met her when I was much younger. She gave me sweetmeats." The king seemed lost in another time.

"She lives, though she is not well. My mother is a very old woman now."

"So she must be. Time passes slowly over those of us who rule, but pass it must. Even kings grow old."

"Indeed, your majesty. Although you are far from old to my eye."

"Thank you, Your Grace."

"You are quite welcome. About the people I asked after, Your Majesty?"

"They are quite safely held," the queen interjected. "My husband and I will certainly consider your petition on the basis of its merits. Remember when you claim the privileges of nobility that those you ask for are noble as well, one by birth and one by valor on the field of battle. I would ask you now to please tell us of the injustices you claim need redress—unless you would prefer to submit your case in writing, Your Grace?"

"Your Majesty, I could not speak in detail of all that has happened in the presence of so many. As you know, the Lady Sera was promised to my own son and heir Rorik. She spurned him in his own camp and robbed him at swordpoint, with the aid of the companion who still accompanies her." The Duke stared at Falorn. Rorik's eyes burned at the spot beside Falorn where Sera stood.

"A girl and an unarmored man robbed your son in the midst of all his soldiers? I had not heard that story."

"I ask Your Majesty to give them over to me in true justice."

"I have heard that Rorik and the Lady Sera never had her father's permission to wed, and he refused to dower her if they did wed. You quarreled over it, I believe."

"Your Majesty, that is true. I quarreled with the Duke of Roicenet over his daughter and . . . other matters. But that quarrel has now been ended. Roicenet is no longer concerned with his daughter's fate."

"And why is that?"

The Duke unfastened the ties which held the sack closed. Reaching inside, he pulled out a black-haired head, its beard still matted with blood. The neck had been severed jaggedly, as if torn from the body instead of cut. Falorn felt Sera stiffen beside him; he dared not look at her or touch her for fear of attracting further attention.

"Your Majesty, Roicenet no longer expresses any feelings at all toward the fate of his daughter. Were she and her companion to join him in this sack, I would feel justice had been served. You would have my gratitude, and that of my family and my folk."

"I see. If you will give me a written grievance, my husband and I will examine the merits of your case and render judgment presently. I must confess, however, that I am reluctant to turn over for execution a pair of nobles who have rendered me nothing but useful and loyal service."

"But Your Majesty! You cannot allow them to run about together like a pair of dogs in the gutter, leaving my son cuckolded! To be left for an honorable marriage elsewhere is one thing, but to fling dishonor in his face is intolerable!"

"Very well. That is not an unreasonable request. Falorn, step forward."

He walked forward through the space between the two thrones, kneeling down when he came within sight of the king and queen. The royal couple wore matching blue satin robes, trimmed with rich ermine. They looked hot in the warm morning air.

"Falorn, have you given any thought to that small matter I asked you about?"

"I am thinking about it, your majesty. I have not come to a decision yet," Falorn said.

"I would prefer that you think with more alacrity. But since you are not of my people, I will not compel you in this matter. There is this other affair, however. Do you know this man?" she pointed at Rorik Iron Eagle, who glowered at Falorn from the back of his horse.

"I have met him, your majesty. He turned his guards on me and I fought three of them."

"Did you rob him, as he says?"

"He had property taken from me which I hoped to regain. I did so, and took a few things of his after his men attacked. His claim . . ." He reached for words, and decided to speak simply. ". . . it's not untrue."

Falorn saw Sera flinch at his words. He tried to keep his eyes focused on the queen.

"Did you take a woman who was promised to him?" the queen asked.

"Sera came with me of her own free will, your majesty. I did not know of any promise at that time. There is no promise between us now."

"That, young knight, is precisely the nature of the problem." The queen glowered at him, unhappy with his answers. "Duke Iron Eagle is due some redress. You have rendered a great service to this land, and I will not punish you for misdeeds committed elsewhere. But I cannot permit you to dishonor another nobleman while you live in Cathan. You will marry the Lady Sera within the next seven days, or I will turn her over to the duke and his son for punishment. If you leave Cathan before that time, I will consider you to have flouted my will, and will do all I can to assist in Duke Iron Eagle's pursuit of you. As long as you are a nobleman in this country you will display behavior appropriate for a nobleman, or you will not long enjoy that status. Do I make myself clear?"

"Yes, your majesty."

"Will you marry the Lady Sera?"

"Y . . . yes, your majesty . . . if she is willing."

"Of course. She may, of course, consider the alternatives. You may go now. One of my knights will see to it that you and your intended are summoned in plenty of time for your betrothal feast tonight. You will have to do without a dowry, of course, but under the circumstances, you might consider her life dowry enough."

"Your majesties." Falorn bowed low to both king and queen and returned to his place beside Sera.

"Well, Duke Iron Eagle, does that satisfy your honor?"

"Your Majesty, it will have to do for the moment. But only blood will fully satisfy my family's honor. If I must, I will wait to see that blood shed, but I will have it."

"Perhaps you will, Duke. For now, I would be pleased if you and your son saw fit to stay around for the betrothal and wedding as my guests," Falorn heard her say as Elise and soldiers of the Queen's Own Guard led he and Sera back within the structures of the Summer Palace. "There may yet be blood enough for us all."

24

Festivities

Falorn remained silent on the walk back up to the tower. Elise and the half-dozen guards who escorted them up the tower stairs joked with each other as they walked. They made no move to take his sword, but Falorn knew now that he was a prisoner in Cathan. The queen had found her pretext.

Sera walked into her room without a word to Falorn. Elise accompanied him into his chamber, where Sbashe awaited him. The corget had taken to acting more like a pet since they arrived in Cathan. The results were both successful and disappointing to Falorn: No one in the palce seemed to pay any attention to her anymore, but that included Elise and the Helleinen, who should have known better.

The guards loitered in the hallway outside. Falorn saw no sign of the Helleinen, but supposed they remained in their own room. Elise sat at the lone table, and reached for the jug of thin red wine which sat there.

"I'm sorry it worked out this way, Falorn," she said, as she poured two glasses full. "You did the honorable thing. I just hope you don't regret the choice you've made."

"It was no choice at all. I owe her my life, Elise. And I do care for her."

"Enough to spend your whole life together? Or just until she disappears again?"

"For as long as she'll have me," said Falorn.

"That's not much of a thing for a knight to say."

"I'm not much of a knight."

"I think you are. You are brave and noble, a better knight than many people I've known from better families. You have nothing to be ashamed of, Falorn." She touched one of his cheeks, and he found to his surprise that she wiped away a tear. "I care for you very much, Falorn."

"Thank you, Elise. You mean a lot to me. I . . ."

"Shhh," she said, "don't say it. You'll be married soon. There's no room for other women in your life."

"I didn't mean . . ."

"I understand." She reached for a glass. "Let's drink to your future—and your wife." The glass lingered near her lips, while her eyes looked at him with a wistful expression.

Falorn picked up his own mug. Something smelled odd, as if mint leaves had been crushed into the wine.

"Elise! No!" he shouted, diving across the table. She fell backward as he slammed into her. Her cup flew out the window, while his own spilled beneath him. Wine sprayed across the stone wall and floor.

She looked up at him angrily, hand at the hilt of her knife. The door opened and a woman of the guard looked in, sword drawn.

"What's going on in here?" the guardswoman asked.

"Poison," said Falorn. "Someone tried to poison Elise with fool's mint. I recognized the smell."

"Falorn," said Elise, "someone tried to poison *you*. The wine was on your table. I just happened to pour the glass. That would have been the last toast you ever drank."

"Why would. . . ." He stopped the words before they finished. Dozens of people wanted to kill him, many of them within the Summer Palace.

"I don't know," Elise said, answering his unfinished question. "Who do you know who likes to use poison? I'm sure there must be somebody who fits that description, among all the people who want to kill you."

In spite of himself, Falorn looked at the wall which separated his own room from Sera's. Elise caught his glance and smiled sadly.

"She didn't know what would happen this morning, of course. There was no way any of us could have known. A very happy marriage the two of you are going to have."

"You don't think that . . . ?" The idea spun around in his own mind. It had a certain degree of sickening credibility. *I can't believe it, though. I just can't believe that Sera would do something like that.*

"I don't know, Falorn. You have a lot of enemies. Maybe there's another one who would do a thing like that. I just don't know." She walked over to the table and picked up the spilled jug. It still contained half a measure of wine. "Unless you mind, I would like to take this out of harm's way. I'll send someone to clean the mess on the floor."

"Thanks," he said to her back as she left the room.

He realized something a moment later.

Sbashe, who else has been in this room? Falorn asked. *You were in here all night. Did you see anyone come in?*

Only Sera. She came in late last night, after you fell asleep. She was lonely, and upset. She lay down beside you and went to sleep. After that I fell asleep myself. She left before I woke up.

No one else? Falorn asked.

No one else that I saw. I've been wandering around the palace while you were out making wedding plans. The kitchens are very nice in the afternoon, especially on a feast-day.

Sbashe, someone is trying to kill me. Didn't you see anything?

Someone is always trying to kill you. I wouldn't worry about it.

What if it's the woman who's about to become my wife? Falorn asked.

You'll work it out between you, I'm sure.

You're awfully calm about this. You don't think she did it, do you?

I have no idea. She certainly knows a thing or two about poisons, and she was in your room, and she's already tried to take your cards a few times. It certainly could have been her. But she wasn't thinking about poisoning when she came in last night. She was looking for a friend. Unless she changed her mind after I went to sleep. . . .

A knock sounded at the door.

"Come in," Falorn said. Sera poked her head shyly into the room.

"Are you sure it's all right?" she asked. "I just heard about what happened. I heard the guards in the hall talking."

"It's all over now. Elise took the poisoned wine away and nobody was hurt. Come on in."

She walked over and laid a hand on Falorn's chest.

"Please be careful," Sera said. "I don't want to lose you. You're the only one who's ever done anything nice for me. I don't have anything left except you."

Falorn wrapped his arms around her and pulled her close.

"It's all right," he said, stroking her hair gently with his right hand. "I'm not going anywhere. I'll never lose you again."

"It's funny," she said. "If you'd asked me how I'd feel about my father dying, I would have said I'd be glad, after all the awful things he did to me . . . all the awful things he did to everyone. But I just feel empty."

"It's all right," he said again.

"I hated him . . . really hated him. But the sight of his head like that. . . ." She trailed off, and there didn't seem to be any good answer Falorn could make.

Instead he held her quietly against his body for a long time. When Falorn looked up, Sbashe had left the room, leaving them alone together. He led her to the bed without letting go of her. They lay together, bodies touching, still fully dressed. Sera buried her head in his chest. Rhythmically, Falorn rubbed her back and sides. Both their thoughts floated elsewhere.

Later that afternoon he cupped her chin, so she had to look upward and meet his eyes.

"Will you really marry me?" he asked.

"Of course."

"I'm not much of a catch, you know. An innkeeper's son who's been knighted won't do much for you socially."

"Neither will a dead father who liked to Hook people. We'll survive. We have some money. Maybe I'll even learn to be an innkeeper." Sera smiled so that he would know she was joking. He wondered what lay behind that smile. "Besides," she added, "I can't leave you while you have all those cards."

"I like you a lot, Sera. More than I've ever liked anyone." She laid a finger across his lips.

"Later, Falorn. We'll have all the time in the world to talk about this later."

When Elise came back to the room, she brought an army of servants with her. A tailor and four seamstresses bustled about, measuring and cutting rapidly. A young maidservant provided the seamstresses with endless lengths of cloth, strips of ribbon, buttons of silver and brass, bits of lace, and bobbin after bobbin of brightly colored thread. Two other servants armed with a tub of steaming water went to work on Sera's hair, while a valet grilled Falorn about his favorite styles and colors.

Elise leaned against a wall away from the crowd, and watched the proceedings with amusement.

"This is just for tonight's pre-nuptial dinner, you know," she told them. "You have days of this to look forward to before the wedding."

"But you're one of the queen's favorites," Sera replied, smiling grimly. "You have a lifetime of it to look forward to."

Elise's grin faded a little.

"That's all too true," Elise finally answered.

An hour after sunset, Elise finally pronounced the servants' efforts suitable and dismissed them for the evening. She laughed quietly at the sight of Falorn and Sera in formal Cathanese clothing.

"It's about time we got you two out of those traveling clothes," she said. "Fine pair of nobles you are, always wearing half-ruined leather rags."

"You're one to talk," Falorn answered. "You never wear all these silks and tufts and things." He pulled at the puffy sleeves of his shimmering yellow tunic.

"But I'm not the one getting married, am I?"

"No," said Falorn, after a moment's thought. "No, you're not."

The three of them walked down the tower stairs together. The two women talked, as if trying to pretend the coldness between them didn't exist, or at least didn't matter anymore. Falorn found it hard to believe that only a few hours before one of them had all but accused the other of poisoning. *It can't be true. I won't believe it.*

Perhaps half the space on the dining hall benches held people. Falorn saw gray-robed priests of Sart immediately, and scowled in spite of himself. Ryal and Cirque sat in a far corner, their backs to a bare stone wall. Falorn glimpsed Sbashe's ears beneath the table where the Helleinen sat.

Mostly, the cavernous room held soldiers. Dozens of guardsmen surrounded the king and queen. Knights filled the royal table and spilled over onto two others. The Duke of Iron Eagle and his men had a table of their own, filled with loud officers and troopers. Rorik Iron Eagle sounded drunk already. He stood beside his father and sang loudly and off-key. Periodically, he upended a drinking horn over his mouth. Dark red wine poured in rivulets down his neck and along his broad shoulders.

Falorn followed Elise's lead to a table near the room's center. Sera no longer walked beside him, he realized abruptly. He tapped Elise on the shoulder, but she only shrugged in response to his question.

Rorik continued to sing, now joined by many of his father's troopers.

Falorn could make out only a few of the words. It sounded like a war tune, hardly auspicious for an ostensibly prenuptial feast. *I wonder if Rorik knows any other sorts of songs?* He tried to imagine Sera married to the drunken nobleman, and failed utterly. *But then, I can't really imagine her married to me, either. I didn't think this would be the way everything would come out, when the mermaid told me that I would never lose Sera again. I don't want to lose her, but this wasn't what I wanted either. She's a duke's daughter. It's not fair that she's being married to an innkeeper's son at swordpoint.* Falorn smiled to himself, darkly amused by his own thoughts. *I never expected my life to be fair, but somehow I always thought it was different for nobles. Maybe I should be happy that the highborn have their troubles, too.*

After an interminable chorus, Rorik's song finally ended. The Cathanese knights and ministers applauded politely. The King seemed on the verge of speaking as the room quieted. Instead, Rorik began to pound on the table with the hilt of his dagger.

"Got somethin' t'say," he called out, "Everybody listen. The woman I wanted is goin' t'someone else, and I'm goin' t'make a speech. Everybody listen." Rorik pounded the table again. "Need somethin' t'drink first." He reached back expectantly. Someone pushed a fresh horn of wine into his hand. Rorik leaned back and poured it down his throat. He straightened, wobbling slightly. The horn clattered as it hit the floor.

"Got somethin' t'say," he repeated again. "I never thought I'd see this night . . . never thought I'd see . . . I'd be . . ." Duke Iron Eagle tugged at his son's wrist, trying to get the drunken young nobleman to sit down. Rorik ignored his father. His face colored suddenly. His body shook as he continued to speak. "I never . . . I'd be . . . thought I'd be . . . somethin' t'be said . . . but I . . . never thought I'd be . . . poisoned."

Rorik croaked out the last word and pitched forward. His head struck the table hard.

No one moved for a moment. Then a dozen nobles and officers rushed forward. Duke Iron Eagle cradled his son's head as Rorik thrashed and convulsed. One of the guard officers retrieved the drinking horn and sniffed the dregs inside.

"Fool's mint," the soldier called out, holding the horn aloft. "The Duke's son's been poisoned."

Falorn surged forward with the rest of the hall's occupants, pushed along with the crowd. The duke sat in front of him, holding Rorik in his lap. Falorn thought back to the dwarven mountain where they'd found the fool's mint. He wondered if anyone had taken some of the poison. He wished he knew where Sera was. *Could it have been one of the Helleinen? Cirque swore to kill Rorik, for what he did to their kinsmen. But why poison him here, or now?* Suddenly, he remembered the antidote Ryal had given him, still tucked safely within one of the pouches at his belt.

He looked at Rorik's eyes, already turning upward in his skull. Falorn felt the lions at his chest. He thought of the Helleinen warrior he'd never been able to talk to, who'd fought so valiantly and whom Rorik had ordered killed for the sake of one of those lions. The Hellein had died in Falorn's arms, looking much the same way Rorik looked now.

Falorn forced his eyes downward, away from the stricken nobleman. *Kerion forgive me*, he thought, *I can't save him. I can't do it.*

Three hours passed before he saw Sera again. Two guardsmen held her, pinioning her arms behind her. Only the queen and a handful of her guardsmen stood in the unfurnished anteroom along with Falorn and the troopers guarding Sera. The Queen's Guards all held drawn blades. Falorn's own weapon remained sheathed. They had allowed him to keep his sword, but the soldiers watched him closely.

"Where were you when Rorik Iron Eagle was poisoned?" the Queen asked Sera, wasting no time on preliminary questions.

Sera said nothing. Her face bore a wide, fresh bruise.

"Sera, I hold your life in my hands. Iron Eagle wants your blood, and I'm inclined to agree with him. I'm only going to ask you once more. Where were you when Rorik was poisoned?"

Sera held her silence.

"Perhaps I can refresh your memory. One of my knights says she saw you hand the man that last flagon of wine. Do you remember that?"

Sera looked downward at the floor. When she looked up to face the queen again, her eyes held nothing. She remained silent.

The queen finally broke the stare in disgust. She muttered something under her breath before looking over toward Falorn.

"This . . . poisoner is what you were going to marry," she said. "We'll be rid of her in the morning. I'm going to give her to Iron Eagle, I think. He wants your blood as well, you know."

"I supposed he would, your majesty," Falorn answered.

"What do you want me to do about it?"

Falorn remained silent, waiting for the queen to speak again.

"I can protect you," she finally said. "You did me a service and I have not forgotten it. It will cost me a great deal, but I can protect you. You will live as a knight on my lands. Even after all that has happened, I will not give you to him."

"Your majesty, at what cost?"

"Give me the cards tonight, and you will go free in the morning."

"And my friends?"

"What friends? You come to me with a dog, a poisoner, and two elves. The dog you can keep. That one goes to Duke Iron Eagle." The queen pointed at Sera. "The elves I will give to my priests. They keep asking for elves."

"Your majesty, the others did you a service at the same time I did," Falorn said. "They fought for your country, as did I."

"You are not in a position to bargain for any lives other than your own. Do not waste my good will on a pair of elves. Keep your dog and your gold and count yourself fortunate."

"Your majesty, I cannot."

"Give me the cards, Falorn. Do not trifle with me."

"I'm sorry, your majesty." Falorn looked at the queen, expecting to see anger in her eyes. But her face showed him nothing at all. "I can't."

The queen paused, and then sighed.

"Very well," she finally said. "You have made your choice. I will not have your life for it, although I feel that would not be improper. In view of your past services, I will grant your life, and that of your so-called 'friends.' You will take your poisoner, your dog, and your pair of tame elves, and you will remove yourselves from this country. You may take the horses you rode in on, and the supplies you brought with you, but nothing at all of this land. I hereby order you exiled from Cathan. You re-enter this land only at peril of your life. Go."

She turned and strode from the room. The guards filed out behind her, none of them paying any attention to Falorn at all. He might as well not have been in the room. Last of all, the two troopers holding Sera released her and walked out as well. Falorn caught her before she sank to the ground. She stood against him weakly, holding his side for support.

"Oh, Falorn," she whispered to him, "what have you done?"

25

Burning Roses

They left three hours after midnight, riding as swiftly as their Rohnan warhorses would carry them. Falorn's dark stallion seemed hungry for the road, and anxious to be free from the confines of the Summer Palace. He could barely hold the animal in check at first; the stallion galloped away from the dark Summer Palace like a night wind carrying storms toward the looming mountains. After a few moments of trying to hold the warhorse back, Falorn gave the animal its head; he and the others shared the stallion's desire to escape.

Falorn had time for only a few words with Sera in the rushed moments before they began their ride into the darkness.

"I didn't poison him," Sera had whispered into his ear, although they stood alone in the room together.

"Why didn't you tell the queen that?" Falorn asked.

"I couldn't, Falorn. I just couldn't. She wanted to know where I was, and I couldn't tell her."

"Why not?"

"Later. I'll tell you later. We have to go now, before they change their minds." She leaned against him for support, but Falorn could feel a deep strength welling up from Sera, as if the warmth of her cards wanted to reach out and touch him somehow. He felt new echoes as he held her close. He wondered if the new cards Alex had given him made him more aware, somehow.

Why would they change their minds? he wanted to ask, but instead they rushed off to join the others and begin their ride. He didn't doubt that the queen would kill him if he came within her power again. By morning, he suspected that the Cathanese ruler would share Iron Eagle's desire for blood.

He talked to Sbashe as they raced through the moonless night. The corget seemed in the mood to talk as she ran; strange pieces of the night scenery entered his mind along with Sbashe's thoughts.

She didn't do it, did she? Falorn asked.

What do you think? asked Sbashe.

I don't know. I don't know what to think. She knows how to use poison, and she had reason to use it on Rorik, I guess. But someone tried to poison me, too. Why would Sera want to poison me?

For your cards, maybe?

She wouldn't do that, said Falorn. *She might have taken them, once—I don't know, she might still take them. But I can't believe she'd try to kill me for them.*

The thought has crossed her mind, Sbashe said.

She could have killed me before if she wanted to. She's saved my life instead, more than once.

Does that answer your question, then?

No. Not really. I don't want to think she could do it, but that doesn't mean anything.

That's too bad, said Sbashe.

What do you mean?

I don't know if Sera did it or not, either. She slipped out of the dining hall just after you and Elise entered, and I lost the trace of her mind. I don't know where she went or what she did. If she poisoned him she hasn't been thinking about it much, but aside from that I don't know any more than you do.

Except that she keeps showing up in places right before people are poisoned. Falorn couldn't avoid the obvious.

That was enough to convince the queen.

The queen was looking for a reason to blame her for something. I guess I should be convinced, too. But I don't want to believe it.

What does Sera say? Sbashe asked.

She told me she didn't do it.

Would she lie to you?

I don't know. She might if she thought she had to. Sometimes I think everybody lies to me. I just don't know what to believe.

Then don't believe anything.

That's what Cirque says. He says I trust too easily, said Falorn.

You are who you are. Some people see you for the person that you are. But other people will only see you for the cards that you hold. There is nothing that you can do to change that.

And which one does Sera do?

Sometimes one, sometimes the other. Sometimes a little of both. She really does care for you, you know.

I care for her, too.

I know, Sbashe answered him.

At dawn, Falorn spotted a lone rider following them. He gestured to Cirque, and the Hellein nodded, gesturing that he had spotted their pursuer as well. The horses had slowed to a steady walk by now, their desire to run having faded away with the night's darkness. Falorn tested the looseness of his sword in its scabbard, and touched the leather pouch at his chest. The cards warmed him, although the night's coolness had not yet dissipated.

The sun rose, brushing away the last of the pre-dawn mistiness. The lone rider continued to close the distance between them. Ryal began to mutter something ominous, but a faint shake of Cirque's head stopped him. The two Helleinen talked briefly in their own language, coming to some agreement which they did not share with the others. Gradually, Falorn made out Elise's features in the distance. She rode a chestnut gelding, and carried a pack, sword, and bow. No other riders followed behind her.

When they stopped to rest and water their horses, Elise caught up. Cirque looked on warily as she walked her lathered mount up to them. One of Cirque's hands had crept to his sword. Ryal stood a few horse-lengths away, his eyes focused on the Cathanese knight, his lips pursed.

"I mean no harm," Elise said, noticing Cirque's wariness. "I came to warn you, not to bring you back."

"Warn us of what?" Falorn asked, when Cirque seemed about to respond.

"The Queen is sending a party of soldiers to catch you as soon as you cross the border. She won't attack as long as you're in Cathan, but once you're in the mountains, they have orders to track you down and bring your cards back."

"What are they planning to do with us?"

"You're to be killed."

Cirque stepped forward, sword drawn. He stood between Falorn and Elise.

"Why do you tell us this?" the Hellein said, interrupting.

"I owe you too much. Some things must be repaid."

"And your loyalty to your queen?" Cirque asked.

"I have no choice. She asked me to lead a group to kill you, and I couldn't; not all of you, anyway. My only other choice was to come here and warn you."

"So your queen's soldiers will catch you here? I think not."

"They won't catch us. They needed this to track you by." Elise held up something, which caught the sunlight in a flicker of blue. Falorn saw a coil of thorns across the card's face, blue vines covered with deadly barbs, and a single, exquisite, blue rose. Elise replaced the card within her tunic and stared at Sera, ignoring Falorn and the Helleinen.

But that's not a suit I have, thought Falorn. *Unless I have so many cards at this point that any of the others can be used to find me.*

"Why would the queen go back on her word?" Falorn asked. "She exiled us, but she said she would let us go. Was she planning all along to kill us and take the cards?"

"Certainly she was," said Cirque. "That is the way of queens, as you will discover."

"No," Elise said. She rubbed the neck of her winded mount as she spoke. "No. She had every intention of letting you all go as a last reward to Falorn. She would have even let the cards go. The situation has altered, however."

Elise continued to stare at Sera, who returned her gaze with a dark intensity.

"What's going on?" Falorn finally asked. "What happened?"

"You didn't poison him, did you?" Elise asked Sera.

"Rorik? No." Sera's eyes betrayed nothing.

"But you couldn't tell the queen where you were during the banquet, either," said Elise.

"Of course not."

"What is going on?" Falorn asked again. Elise looked at him, finally breaking her eyes from Sera's gaze.

"During the banquet, someone stole Her Majesty's cards from their place in the Palace. The blue thorn which I hold is the only card left in Cathan, except for those you and Sera carry." Elise resumed staring at Sera, who said nothing. Falorn thought he saw a faint smile curl the edges of Sera's lips.

"And yet you are willing to ride with us?" Cirque interjected. "You ask us to believe that you will not betray us?"

"I will ride with you until my debt to Falorn is repaid."

"Elise, you don't owe me anything," Falorn said.

"I do," she said. "If I had been able to repay you sooner, I would not have had to betray my own Queen for you." The edge of a tear touched her right eye. Elise blinked it away hurriedly. "I will guide you through the mountains, at least. Farther if necessary. You will need another sword before this is over."

"We're going to Letz," said Falorn. He'd planned to do so all along, but recent events had confirmed his instinct that a return to the University and its collection was the best thing to do. In the island city they would be safe, at least.

"Then I will see you safely there before my debt is repaid." Elise bowed her head. She seemed to be mouthing the words to a prayer or oath of some sort. When she looked up again, her face appeared perfectly composed.

They saw no soldiers as they rode across the last of Cathan's fertile plains, and entered the rocky foothills which paved the way into the mountains. Green fields gave way to patchy grass, as the soil grew pebblier. Scrub trees lined the trailsides with increasing thickness, growing more gnarled as the road ascended.

Elise and Cirque rode together, as the surrounding hillsides became steeper, guiding the rest of them around the main trails and along rocky sidepaths. The light-haired Hellein and the knight pooled their knowledge grudgingly, although Cirque's right hand never traveled far from the hilt of his sword.

Although Falorn expected tensions to boil over momentarily, nothing of the sort happened. As they entered the mountains, some of the strains actually seemed to ebb. Despite everyone's suspicions, the six of them began to function smoothly together, sliding unthinkingly into the routine which had brought them safely away from Rohn. Elise and Cirque worked together as only two nobles raised to the sword can do, scouting out safe paths while barely speaking to each other. Falorn walked with Sbashe most of the time, guarding the rear. With no one else for company most of each day, Sera and Ryal talked together. Sera seemed to be making an effort to get along with the Helleinen, and she and Elise tried to minimize their dislike for each other.

Falorn saw none of the Cathanese soldiers. Cirque confirmed Elise's story, however; while searching out safe trails, he and Elise saw dozens of troopers, scouting the mountainside for any sign of the fugitives.

On their last night in Cathan, Falorn dreamed of Sheanna, the olive-skinned circus-woman who'd sought him in Roicenet. She sat on a flat stone, brushing her long, black hair with an ebony comb. A thicket of wild roses nearly surrounded the stone. She beckoned, and Falorn walked to her. He knelt before her, and bowed his head as she spread her arms. A thick, musky scent of roses filled the air.

Sheanna took Falorn's hands and placed them on her doublet. He began untying the laced front, while she ran her hands over his chest. As her doublet loosened, she slid her hands under Falorn's tunic. She traced shapes on his chest and side. Falorn gasped. His right hand found her breast.

He found himself lying on the flat rock, with Sheanna straddling him. Pulling his tunic up, she slowly rubbed his chest and stomach. Her hands slid a little lower.

The sky darkened somehow. Strips of branches and leaves covered his vision of the world beyond the rock. Everywhere, Falorn saw rose petals. The thick smell of roses filled his head like rich, deep wine. Rosebushes now grew all around them, Falorn realized, although his mind felt very distant. Roses blocked the sky as Sheanna traced light patterns on his skin. Her fingers felt smooth against him. His body tingled where she touched it. Gently, she touched her lips to his chest.

A lion roared.

Wake up! A voice said in his mind. *Falorn, wake up!* The world felt very far away. Falorn lay back, but the vision of Sheanna had begun to fade. Very far away, someone shouted.

Falorn, wake up.

He opened his eyes. The camp smelled of smoke and roses. Their small, hidden fire had burned down to embers. Sbashe stood beside him, looking down at Falorn's face with a concerned look. His mind felt fuzzy. The cool night air only slowly began to clear it. The fragrance of rose petals lingered at the edges of his mind, along with the tantalizing, dreamlike memory of Sheanna's touch.

What happened? He finally asked the corget.

Someone sneaked into the camp—not one of the Cathanese. Not a soldier, anyway. Sera saw someone crouching over you, reaching for your cards. She shouted and whoever it was ran. Elise has gone chasing after, while Cirque makes sure we didn't alert any soldiers nearby.

I didn't wake up? Falorn asked the question a little woozily.

I tried to wake you, but you wouldn't stir.

Falorn looked to the edge of the camp. Sera walked the outer perimeter, as if searching the ground the intruder had fled over. Something glittered red, at the ground near her feet. Whatever it was glowed scarlet in the night. Falorn rose to his feet, all fatigue vanished. Before he could take a step, Sera picked up the card. It glinted again against the darkness. Even from a distance, Falorn saw red roses growing across the dark red face of the card. He turned away as Sera's hand closed over the ivory.

Did you sense who it was in the camp? Falorn asked Sbashe.

No. The person's mind was dark to me.

An hour later, Elise returned to the camp empty-handed.

Three hours after dawn, they crossed into Delerian. Sera still wore a smile on her face, only lightly concealed. Oddly, Elise seemed happy as well.

"Have you ever been to Delerian before?" Falorn asked her.

"No. Few people from Cathan go to Delerian."

"For the same reason few Helleinen go to Cathan," Ryal pointed out.

"It's a beautiful country," said Falorn. "At least the parts of it I've seen are." Elise smiled almost wistfully and said nothing.

They camped at the foot of a wooded slope, in a sheltered spot Ryal found for them. Moss-covered rocks hid the trees on three sides. A stone-lined firepit nestled beneath an overhanging rock, forming an oven of sorts. Another overhang revealed stacks of dry wood.

Later, the two Helleinen went off into the forest alone, to perform some private homecoming ritual of their own. Elise sat by herself, her back against the wide stone which sheltered the firewood. Bits of wood flew into the darkness as she endlessly whittled pieces of kindling. Sbashe lay on top of the stone, her head moving alertly as she tracked forest noises and unfamiliar scents.

Falorn and Sera sat together next to the firepit. Red coals glowed like burning roses in the oven. Now and again, Falorn tossed a piece of wood into the flames; his mind wandered elsewhere.

Sera touched the silver band which circled his wrist. She glanced up at him, but the look in his eyes seemed to still her curiosity.

"Falorn?" she asked, a little later.

"Hmm?" His mind wandered back to her slowly.

"I've just been wondering, that's all."

"Wondering what?" he asked.

"What happens when we get to Letz?"

"What do you mean? In Letz we can stop running. No one can chase us there," Falorn answered.

"That's not what I mean. We've been running all this time. What do we do when we stop running?"

"We stop running. We have quieter adventures. We go to the theater without people trying to kill us. I finish learning to read. We go swimming. We do all the things that you can't do while you're running."

"Sounds delightful." Her expression belied the words. "What are you going to do with your cards?"

"I thought I might give them to the University. They'll know what to do with them."

"You'd just give them away?" Sera asked.

"Sure. Why not? The people at the University are the only ones who haven't tried to take them away from me. And they won't do me a whole lot of good once we settle down in Letz."

"You're probably right. But if you're going to give them away, why not just give them to me?"

"I can't do that, Sera."

"I know," she said, and snuggled closer.

Falorn threw another stick into the coals, and watched as burning roses consumed it.

26

Private Conversations

"Milord?" Falorn heard a half-familiar voice beside him. He opened his eyes drowsily. His hands gripped the arms of the carved wooden chair tightly, until his eyes focused and he remembered siting down to take an afternoon nap in the hunting lodge. A young, pale-skinned woman stood beside him.

"Milord?" she said again, looking at him out of deep blue eyes. He couldn't place her at first, although the voice sounded familiar. Falorn did not remember meeting her on his last journey to Delerian. Only when he noticed the strip of ribbon binding up her light brown hair did Falorn remember her.

"Thea?" Falorn asked.

"Yes, milord. You remembered me." His awareness sharpened as he awoke more fully.

"Of course I remember you, Thea. I hoped I would see you here."

"Have you come to take me away?" Thea asked.

"To take you away? Why would I take you away? Aren't you happy here?"

"I belong to you. You took me from the soldiers," she said.

"Thea . . . I don't own you. I don't own anyone. I just want you to be somewhere where you can be happy. I couldn't leave you there with those soldiers."

"You don't want me, do you?"

"Thea . . . that's not it. I don't own you. And I'm promised to someone else." *I wonder how true that really is,* Falorn thought to himself. *What does she want? Whatever it is, I can't give it to her.* He wanted to cry, looking at her achingly sincere face. He didn't think she understood anything he said.

"I understand, then," Thea said. She turned and walked away, shaking slightly. Falorn wanted to call to her, but he couldn't think of anything to say which wouldn't make things worse.

The hunting lodge seemed smaller and cozier than Falorn remembered. He settled quickly into the comfort of the building's rhythms and comforts. Sera and Elise felt discontented within the mostly Helleinen lodge, however. The two women shared an uneasiness inside the dark wood building, and spent most of their time outside. Sbashe loved the surrounding woods and hills, and disappeared for hours on end. That left Falorn inside most of the time, talking with Danbhe, Cirque, and other Helleinen leaders about what he had seen. After the first few days in Delerian, Falorn felt less need to run than he had before, less need to force his angers and fears out onto the forested hills around them.

He did not see Thea again.

Although he had hardly spoken with Cirque and Ryal on the trip back, the news that they wouldn't be going to Letz with Falorn still surprised him a little.

"I wish you well, Falorn," Cirque told him, "but we succeeded in what we set out to do. The rest of your story is not our story."

Falorn had never found out what had happened with the Immortal King's corpse once it had been shipped back to Delerian from Letz. There had been no excitement or commotion that Falorn had seen, but Cirque didn't seem particularly disappointed that his fellow Helleinen didn't seem to be furthering his crazy revenge plan. *I hope they buried it,* Falorn thought.

"I understand," said Falorn, although he didn't, really. He wondered why the Helleinen had come with him before, and what had changed now. *Was it all about Cirque's revenge, and nothing else?*

Something about the dark-paneled room seemed to close off conversation after a while. Falorn's eyes kept traveling back to the wide golden sculpture of the family tree on the wall. He lost the thread of the discussion, and only Ryal's gentle nudge at his elbow brought him back to reality.

"We were thinking of taking a walk outside," Ryal said quietly, "perhaps with a stop at the bathhouse afterward. I think we have all been in this dark room for too long."

Falorn nodded in agreement and stood up, stretching his stiff legs. It had rained that morning, and for two days before; he wondered if the weather had cleared.

When they walked outside, bright sunlight met them. Other than a few scudding gray clouds, the storm had passed completely. Across the grassy hilltop, he could see Helleinen and a few humans practicing swordwork on the damp ground. Sera stood watching the swordfighters at work. High above in the sky, a pair of large hawks circled in the updrafts, waiting for prey to break from the cover of the nearby treeline.

The birds' flight reminded him of the wizards who had chased them. *Are any of those wizards still alive?* he wondered lazily. He supposed not, based on the lack of pursuit. *Not that they'd be likely to follow into Delerian, anyway.*

Sera waved as she saw Falorn. He walked toward her, looking at the fighters on the practice fields as he walked. He wondered if he could find a partner for a few hours of sparring; after days inside, he felt like he needed the practice. The confined feeling was beginning to return, on the heels of the news from Cirque and Ryal.

Something flared at his chest as he approached Sera. He felt his pouch curiously. An odd, warm sensation tugged at him from the woods. He wondered for a moment, but then an explanation came to him.

"Where's Elise?" he asked. *She must have gone wandering,* he thought. *I guess none of us will ever get lost as long as we have these cards.*

Sera's face darkened.

"She's in the bathhouse. I'm sure she'd be happy if you joined her."

"You mean she's not . . . then what . . . ?"

"Falorn! Down!" Ryal shouted.

He caught at Sera and dove to the ground. Out of the corner of his eye, he saw something plummet out of the sky—a hawk diving. It grew in size alarmingly as it closed. He hit the ground with Sera beneath him, then rolled, reaching for his sword.

The air flashed around him. Falorn's hair stood on end. His arms leaped from his sides, out of his control. Spots flew in front of his eyes.

"Falorn!" someone called, but he couldn't see who.

Claws raked his face. His head flew back as something slashed at him again. Feeling returned to his hands again, and he threw an arm up to ward off the attack. He had no idea where his sword had gone. Falorn reached for his belt-knife with his free hand.

Something bit into his arm, puncturing it deeply. His sight wouldn't clear. He had the knife free and slashed forward, but at the same time, something raked his face again. More talons bit into the back of his legs. Falorn felt himself collapsing backward. He hit the ground hard, his head bouncing with the blow.

Blades kept cutting at his face, and he couldn't see them. He wondered if they'd blinded him. Screaming, he flailed away with the knife. He didn't hit anything, and the pain kept intensifying. His hearing faded away. He felt himself flailing against the ground as he lost control of his limbs. He still held a knife, but soon even that arm faded from his control. He had only the cards at his chest.

After all other sensation vanished, he felt Sera's hand at his chest. Her hand lay against his skin for a moment, then closed against the pouch. He tried to scream as the pouch was lifted away from his skin. He could hear nothing. After that, something fell heavily against him. Soon, all consciousness faded away.

He awoke in a light-paneled room. *I've seen this place before*, he thought, but couldn't remember when or where.

My mind seems to be working too slowly. The hazy quality of light pouring through the thin curtains seemed familiar, as if he'd spent a lot of time in this place. He saw another bed across the room from his, stacked high with puffy down pillows. A folded comforter lay across the unoccupied second bed, twin to the padded goosedown quilt on top of him. The blanket felt hot, in the warmth of the room.

This is the healer's house, he finally realized. *This is the bed Zaren was in when we first came to Delerian after his boat crashed. Sera was in the other bed. This is where I used to come and visit them. It looks strange because I'm used to seeing the room from the other side, by the door.*

Falorn found himself thinking about Zaren. He still missed the big mercenary, even though the two of them had never gotten to know each other very well. He thought back through the times he and the gruff man had spent together. Only gradually did Falorn realize that he was not alone in the room. He heard a voice beside him, and realized that the soft, almost musical cadence had been going on for some time.

Someone sat in a chair beside the bed, reading poetry aloud from a small leather-bound book. Falorn didn't know the language, which sounded unlike the Helleinen words he'd heard in Delerian. It took him a moment to place the blond-haired Helleinen woman in the wicker chair. Then the sapphire at her throat revealed her, even before she looked up and he saw her face.

"Hello, Nia," he said. His throat felt tight and constricted. A lace-work of cuts across his face stung as he tried to smile. Falorn didn't care about the pain; his eyes seemed to work normally. The cards at his chest purred with familiar warmth. So nobody took them after all. *I wonder what did happen?*

"Hello, Falorn," she said. Nia set the book down on a nearby table as she stood up. She reached over and felt his forehead. Her hand felt cool and smooth. "You are very lucky to be awake. Your gods have looked after you again." She looked at him enigmatically.

"What happened?" he asked. It hurt more to speak the second time. *I must have reopened unhealed cuts on my face.*

"Let me get you something to eat, first," Nia said. She tossed her hair slightly when she spoke. Falorn found the gesture sensual, in spite of his weakness. "While you eat, we can talk."

"Thank you," Falorn said. "That would be nice." He closed his eyes for a moment while he waited. When they opened again, darkness had fallen.

A small, dark-skinned human woman fed him thin broth with a carved wooden spoon. She said nothing, and Falorn found that he could focus only on the carved birds which flew up the spoon's handle. His eyes closed again almost before he could finish eating.

He awoke again to morning sunlight. This time Elise sat in the wicker chair by Falorn's bedside. He turned his head slightly to face her. The rest of his body seemed reluctant to follow his movements, but the pain in his face had lessened somewhat. He wondered how long he'd slept.

"Good morning, Falorn," she said. "Welcome back to the land of the living."

"Have I been gone for long?"

"Long enough to make us worry whether you were coming back. The healer said you would make it, but . . ." Elise glanced around, her distrust of Helleinen things showing in her sea-green eyes.

"It feels like it was a rough trip."

"A few cuts and scratches. It looks like they won't even scar, the way you're healing. It's nothing compared to what you looked like after the battle at the Calambria."

"Thanks, I think."

"You'll be fine." She reached over and tousled his hair. Her thin rat-tail braid tickled his face before she could sweep it over her shoulder.

"What happened? Was anyone else hurt?" Thin lines of pain radiated across his face as he spoke. His skin felt as if it had hardened in position, like drying clay-pools. Elise's face darkened slightly, but she hardly hesitated.

"One of the elves was badly injured in the same blast that hit you. Another was hurt fighting the wizards. There were three of them, all from Cathan. I knew them all by name when they'd been caught. They were sent back to the Queen, with a warning about encroaching on Delerian lands in the future. The elves might have killed them, but in light of all the encroaching we've been doing on Delerian's behalf recently, they thought better of it," said Elise.

"So they weren't the wizards who were following us before? I thought all the cards were gone from Cathan."

"Apparently not."

That's not really an answer, put it's probably the best I'm going to get, Falorn knew. *Did you end up with the card, Elise? I wonder.*

"Did I know either of the Helleinen who were hurt?" asked Falorn

"I don't think so. But you ought to know that Sera was also injured."

"Is she all right?" Falorn almost sat up, but his body wouldn't let him. Pain shot through his ribs and his legs. Elise sat beside him on the bed, and gently held him until the waves receded a little.

"She'll live, I think," said Elise. "She took a hard blow, and she's not a quick healer, but she's still alive. She may wake up before you are walking again."

"What?!?"

"Falorn, please, try to relax. You can't help her here. You need to get better. She's not going anywhere, and neither are you, if you don't settle down and try to rest."

Falorn settled down unwillingly. Eventually, he dozed off, and woke to find Elise gone, replaced by a young-looking Helleinen man who fed him soup and spoke only in a language Falorn did not understand.

The next morning, Sbashe sat beside the bed when he awoke.

Feeling alive again? her voice asked in his mind.

A little, he answered. Actually, he did feel better. The bandaged slashes in his ribs and legs ached less than they had during Elise's visit. He still felt the trelliswork of cuts on his face, but they seemed to have faded slightly as well.

Not quite ready to get up yet, though, Sbashe said.

No. Falorn could feel that from the lingering ache behind his knee. He didn't want to test his legs yet.

Soon, though. Soon you can get up and visit Sera.

How is she? Falorn asked, a little uncertainly. He wondered how much he wanted to know the answer.

She sleeps. I spent much of yesterday with her, but she hasn't wakened yet. The Helleinen healer thinks she will, but she is afraid the healing process will be long—and that worries her.

Why? Are we still in danger here? Falorn asked.

You are always in danger, Falorn. But I don't think the Helleinen will harm you here, and I doubt the queen in Cathan will send anyone else, after the humiliation of her wizards. The Helleinen looted their camp, and sent them over the pass without much more than their clothes and a sealed note to the queen.

Then what's the problem?

The problem is that the Helleinen want you to leave. And they want you to do it as quickly as possible. You have helped them and they respect you for it, but you are a political liability. Danbhe and Cirque think about this a great deal. They wonder if you will feel insulted when they ask you to leave.

Danbhe is worried about insulting me? He threatened to have us all cooked and eaten when I first met him. The Helleinen leader had said nothing about leaving when he and Falorn talked in the lodge. The topic had never come up—had never even been hinted at, as far as Falorn could tell. He supposed the attack had changed things.

You didn't have quite so many cards when you first met Danbhe, did you? asked Sbashe.

No. Actually, we'd just been washed out of a wrecked boat, said Falorn.

Manners change, as do alliances. I don't think they will ask you to leave, but they would probably be happy if you offered to go on your own—and the sooner, the better.

Not without Sera.

I don't think they understand your feelings for her. This latest battle is likely to bewilder them further, Sbashe said.

What do you mean?

There is some dispute as to how Sera received her injury. Ryal saw her lean over you and shield you from a magical bolt after you had fallen.

She saved my life, then. I couldn't leave her. Not again.

Elise has told the Helleinen that she saw Sera trying to remove your cards before she fell. If she bent over you to steal them, only her own bad luck struck her down, not any desire to save you.

But there's no way of knowing that until she wakes up. Falorn remembered the sensation of Sera's hand on his chest after he had fallen, and wondered if he really believed his words to be true.

In another week, Falorn regained his feet. Soon he could walk with only a slight limp. Already, the deep wounds in his side and legs had closed, and the thick pink scars had begun to narrow. His face showed only a few traces of the ugly red lines which had scored it, and each day the lines faded a little more.

He spent most of his days in Sera's white-curtained room, reading haltingly out loud while she slept on. In the mornings and evenings he and Elise practiced together with bow and sword, but the Cathanese woman no longer helped with his reading. He carried on alone, borrowing a book of heroic ballads from Ryal.

Whenever Falorn left Sera's sickroom, Sbashe curled at the foot of the bed, middle legs tucked beneath her so she looked like an ungainly, oddly colored dog. Falorn wondered what conversations had passed between the corget and Sera before her injury, but he thought it best not to ask. Sbashe offered few details.

"You can't wait much longer," Elise told Falorn as they crossed wooden blades in the early summer grass. "They'll find you and the cards if you stay here too long. You need to go on to Letz."

"Who are 'they'?"

"Who do you want them to be? It could be anyone. You have enough enemies. So do I, for that matter. Now that I've left Cathan for your sake, they'll be looking for me, too," Elise said.

"You are a cardholder," said Falorn.

"And you're a beacon," she answered, sliding through his guard and scoring across Falorn's leg. He winced as the injured skin stretched.

"Enough for now," he said, lowering his guard.

"Just think about it," said Elise. "It would be safer for all of us."

"What about Sera? I can't just leave her here like this. She has cards, too."

"Then take them and hold them for her. She can follow us to Letz when she recovers, and you can give them back to her then. She'll be in no danger—without the cards, no one will find her. If you leave money, she'll be able to get to Letz easily."

"I can't do that. I can't just leave her," said Falorn.

"You'd be doing her a favor, Falorn. You might be saving all of our lives, including hers."

"She just needs a little time to heal."

"She needs a lot of time, and we may not have it. You've been very loyal to her and to me, and it's a noble trait, but you have to think about what's the best course to take here. You can't help her by making her a target, Falorn."

"I can't leave her, Elise."

"Just think about it. Please?"

"I can't, Elise."

By midsummer, Falorn had begun to wonder if Elise might not be right. His body had healed completely, the scars fading into his skin until all signs of the fight had vanished from his exterior. Sera, however, seemed to gain strength only slowly. Her body showed no sign of damage, but her breathing remained eerily steady and her eyes refused to open. Despite the healer's encouraging words, Falorn had begun to wonder if Sera would ever return to consciousness. Each day seemed to reduce her chances of recovery a little further.

Danbhe and Cirque visited Falorn frequently, often coming to see him while he sat in Sera's sickroom. They remained constantly polite, but he felt a little less welcome after each conversation. They seemed more remote than before, reminding him of the subtly impermeable gap between human and Helleinen. He rarely saw Ryal.

The sun had just set when Sera woke. Falorn was reading a passage from the *Lay of Moulter's Fall* aloud while the light lasted. He glanced over at Sera and saw brown eyes.

He closed the book as she continued to stare at him silently.

"Are you awake?" he asked, but she said nothing. Her eyes quietly tracked his movements until darkness fully cloaked the room. By the time Falorn lit a candle, she had fallen back into slumber.

The next morning her eyes reopened. This time, she stayed awake for nearly an hour before once again passing into sleep. Falorn stayed close by her bed now, not even leaving Sera's side to practice anymore. Instead, he rolled up the sickroom rug and practiced sword movements in the room's center, on the wide, plank floor. The healer and her assistants looked at Falorn disapprovingly, but said nothing.

Within a week, Sera could sit up in bed, although days more passed before she regained enough strength to feed herself. By late summer, she took her first, halting steps, supported by Falorn's arm. But summer had nearly passed into autumn before Sera spoke again. In that time, she and Sbashe shared conversations, Falorn knew, but whatever passed between the two of them remained private.

Something significant must have happened in their conversations, though: When Sera finally regained her feet, Sbashe told both of them that she would be accompanying them back to Letz. *I want to see how this story ends*, Sbashe told Falorn. *I miss my home, but when I return to it my friends are going to ask what became of you and the cards, and I would like to be able to answer them.*

27

Dark Magic

Snow flurries brushed against Falorn as he helped Sera down the gang-plank and onto the dock. Heavy capes covered them both, hers in dull scarlet and his in untrimmed gray. Ahead of them, Sbashe scuttled easily on the dark wooden planks of the dock, looking back to see how closely they followed. Elise lagged a few paces behind, looking warily through the snow at the cobblestoned streets which lay beyond the docks.

"Don't worry, Elise," Falorn called back to her. "This is Letz. We're safe."

A half dozen hooded figures emerged from the doorway of a chandler's house as Falorn reached the cobblestones.

"Geary!" Falorn called out as he recognized the black-bearded professor. Geary waved, his sea-green eyes flashing in the winter afternoon light.

"Falorn! Welcome back. We knew you were coming when the cards started glowing, but you've brought so many more of them with you. Is this the Lady Sera?" He leaned upward to kiss Sera's cheek. She smiled slightly, as if shy of the attention. "I see the Helleinen didn't make it back. Sad, we'd hoped to have their conversation at dinner. We're happy to receive the rest of your company, though." He made a sweeping gesture to include all of them.

"Come now," he said, turning away from them. "We have a feast preparing at the University. The College of Magics' faculty dining hall is ours for the night. A whole boar is roasting. You are an honored guest." Geary put a hand on Falorn's shoulder as he led the way to a tremendous blue coach. The other cloaked figures followed behind. Falorn wondered if he knew any of them; he hadn't gotten a good look at any faces.

Falorn climbed into the carriage behind Geary. Two blue-liveried footmen assisted him upward into the plush, velvet-cushioned interior. The coach smelled of jasmine. Four gold-plated lanterns lit the space, each shielding a scented wax candle.

"Councilor Lawes was good enough to loan us one of his carriages and teams for the evening. He is hosting the feast in your honor as well. He is very pleased that you have returned. When it became known that all the remaining cards were on a ship only a day beyond the island—well, it reflected well on the School of Magics. Tonight will be the first time since their original dispersal that all of the cards will be assembled together. The University's collection of cards is now within the Lesser Display Hall, adjacent to the Faculty Dining Room. After the feast we will all step into the Display Hall together, and see what wondrous magic emerges when the cards are reunited again."

"Are you certain that is wise?" one of the hooded men asked. "Once again, Geary, please reconsider."

Geary smiled and shook his head as the last person clambered into the carriage. Despite the number of people, the interior held them all easily on its two padded facing benches. Falorn wondered how many streets could hold such a wide vehicle.

"Falorn, I would like you to meet Javin, of Cobweb Row." Geary gestured toward the man who had spoken. "Javin is a lecturer in the College of Magics. He has joined our project recently, along with all of the others you see here. The project has grown a great deal in popularity. We have learned much about the history of the cards since you left us before. Tonight will be the confirmation of all of my theories."

"Or the death of us all," Javin said.

Geary smiled but said nothing.

The carriage left them in front of a building Falorn had never entered before. Even in the dim winter light, the building gleamed. Three marble steps led up to a wide porch of polished white stone. White marble facing grained with black covered the building's exterior as well, broken at frequent intervals by tall, rectangular, stained-glass windows. Four enormous round columns supported a terrace above the porch, where Falorn could see a few people in brightly colored winter capes talking.

The wide double doors into the building swung open before Falorn, Geary, and the others had finished climbing the porch stairs. Two young boys in green and gold livery held the doors. The boys stood very straight as Falorn entered the building. Seven or eight other liveried children scurried around the oak-paneled front hall of the massive structure. Scattered green rugs in a dozen shapes covered the white marble floor in places. A green carpet covered the wide paired stairways which led upward from either side of the hall's far end. Between the stairs, another set of double doors remained closed.

Above the doors, more brightly clothed people milled around on a balconied landing. An open door at the landing's far end seemed to be Geary's eventual destination.

A blond girl in green livery took Falorn's snow-dampened cape for him. He adjusted his tunic and sword belt, one hand reaching for his pouch of cards habitually. *Elise and I are the only people in the building wearing swords*, Falorn realized.

"This way," Geary said, leading them toward the stairs. He pointed toward the closed double doors as they walked by. "The display hall is in there. After the reception, we'll all walk down together. The new cases the University has built for the cards are truly remarkable. Of course, someday we hope you and your friends will allow us to add your cards to the collection as well, so the set can be truly complete."

Falorn nodded noncommittally. He glanced at Sera as they climbed the stairs, but her face showed nothing. People continued to talk as Geary led them toward the crowded room on the landing. Falorn looked around. To either side, marble stairs continued upward, at right angles to the flights they had just climbed. An oak-floored mezzanine surrounded the building's second level, looking downward onto the landing where he now stood, as well as to the entrance hall below. A chandelier made of thousands of pieces of dazzling cut crystal hung from the high ceiling above. Soft light shone from each glittering crystal, enough to illuminate the whole central area of the building. Falorn saw no source for the bright glow. *It's magic*, he finally realized. Decoratively molded plaster covered the rafters and ceiling, forming a criss-cross pattern of elaborate swirls and finely rounded edges which seemed to catch a portion of the chandelier's light and throw it back downward again.

Strands of ivy hung on the walls of the reception hall, garlanding the paneled room. Tall windows admitted feeble winter light through pale-colored stained glass. Dozens of magical lamps augmented the sparse sunlight. A tremendous fireplace dominated the far end of the long, rectangular room. Flames shot up to the height of Falorn's head and higher, but they consumed no fuel that he could see.

Falorn saw a few people he remembered from dinners at Councilor Lawes's house, and in a far corner, the enormous professor himself held court. No servants seemed to be in attendance, not even the liveried boys and girls of the hall below. Instead, people served themselves from three tables heaped with cold meats, cheeses, breads, and enormous ewers of wine. At the center table, the promised roast boar lay on an enormous gilded tray.

"Please pardon the spareness of the food," Geary said from where he stood at Falorn's elbow. "We had no way of knowing when you might arrive. It wouldn't have done to serve stale meats and soggy bread to celebrate your return. The food and wine are good, if plain. Councilor Lawes provided them."

"I'll have to thank him. And thank you, too—this is wonderful." Falorn marveled at the room. After months away, he had forgotten the casual air of magic and wonder that pervaded the University. When he had left, Geary and the cards commanded little notice. Clearly, that had changed.

Well-dressed men and women filled the room, perhaps fifty or sixty in all. Some of them looked as if they belonged to the university, with the clear stamp of scholars or students, but others simply looked like wealthy or well-connected friends of Councilor Lawes.

"Why such a big crowd?" Falorn asked Geary.

"Why, for the cards, of course. Many people are happy to see that you have returned."

Geary walked toward Lawes and the circle of people surrounding the big counselor. Falorn would have followed, but a touch at his arm stopped him.

"Wait," Javin said from beside him. "I would like to talk with you for a moment."

Falorn followed the lecturer to one of the tables, where they each filled a plate with food. Javin motioned toward two empty armchairs next to one of the windows and Falorn nodded. They walked over and sat down. Falorn found himself eating hungrily. Javin picked at his food warily.

"How much do you know about the cards?" Javin finally asked him.

Now what in Kerion's name is that supposed to mean? Falorn wondered. *I'm carrying most of them, so I guess I know a lot, but I'm no professor.* Falorn looked around for Sbashe, but he didn't see her.

"I know a little bit, I suppose," he finally answered.

"Do you know what happens when they all come together?"

"No. Why would anything happen?"

Javin seemed taken aback by the question.

"Of course something will happen. Why else would the cards want to come together so badly? There's a dark sorcery on them, something that will happen when the cards are united again. That's why they were separated in the first place, to break up the evil sorceress's curse on them."

"So what exactly will happen when they come together?" asked Falorn.

"I don't know," Javin admitted. "Nobody knows—that's the problem. All we know is that something will happen—and it won't be something good. Nothing good comes of dark magic, and these cards are the darkest kind of magic."

Something nudged against Falorn's legs. He looked down and saw Sbashe settling down at his feet, looking for all the world like an awkward pet dog. Falorn suspected that Sbashe had been practicing her unobtrusive act.

There's no such thing as dark magic, Sbashe's voice said in his mind. *Javin just made the term up. He really is scared about the cards, though.*

Thanks, said Falorn.

My pleasure. Make sure you have some of the roast quail at the buffet. It's superb.

Falorn looked down. Sbashe seemed to be sleeping peacefully. He looked back up, and found Javin staring at him oddly.

"You don't believe me, do you?" the lecturer asked.

"I don't disbelieve you," Falorn answered. "I just don't see any reason why the cards have to do anything when they come together. I don't know that much about the woman who created them, but I know Geary has spent years studying the cards' history. He would know if there was any danger."

"He's blind to the danger," hissed Javin. "He has glory in his reach.

The cards are shining in their gleaming new cases and he's the darling of Lawes and the other Councilors. Since the attack, everyone in the city wants to see the cards, and everyone wants to listen to Geary's lectures. That doesn't mean his theories are right. He stumbled onto the cards first, but celebrity hasn't helped his scholarship."

Javin's face reddened as he spoke, although he kept his tone low.

"What attack?" Falorn asked. He glanced around for a way to get away from the lecturer, and managed to catch Sera's eye. She saw his pained look and began to walk over to the window.

"The city guard caught four women trying to steal the cards. They . . . seduced one of Geary's students who was supposed to be watching the cards. Geary found the boy drugged and asleep, and all the cases pried open. He gave the alarm, and the guard found the women about to board a boat. Until then, nobody much cared about the cards. But once someone thought they were worth stealing . . . *then* the University started to care about them."

"Who were the women?" Falorn asked.

"They were members of something called the Thorn Cult. They seem to have wanted the cards for some sort of religious ritual. Nobody ever found out for sure."

"What do you mean?"

"They killed two guards before the rest of the watch showed up and trapped them. Then they took some kind of poison—killed themselves right there at the dock while their boat escaped. The guards got the cards back, but the Councilors had to piece the rest of the story together. Someone recognized that they were members of the Thorn Cult by their rose tattoos. But nobody really knows much about them, or about why they wanted the cards."

Falorn thought of Sheanna suddenly. He wondered if he really had dreamed of the olive-skinned woman the night of the attack in the mountains, or if she actually had been in the pass somehow. The mountains at the edge of Delerian seemed a very long way from the circus wagon outside of Roicenet where he had first met her. *But then, you've come a long way yourself.* Even now, Falorn could almost smell the fragrance of wild roses.

He noticed Javin looking at him curiously again, and wondered how long he'd been distracted.

"I knew someone like that once," Falorn said. Suddenly he felt as if roses encircled him.

"Did she try to take the cards from you?" asked Javin.

"I guess she did," said Falorn.

Sera finally reached them. She put a hand on Falorn's shoulder, interrupting the conversation.

"Is everything all right?" she asked innocently. Her hands slid to his shoulders, and she began massaging out some of the fatigue. Falorn suddenly realized how much the sea voyage and the months of waiting in Delerian had worn him out emotionally. He had barely felt any physical fatigue since the lion cards had come to him, but now exhaustion seemed to wash over him in waves.

Javin shook his head slightly and excused himself. Falorn struggled to keep his eyes open. The noise of the room seemed to fade. He felt only Sera's hands, rubbing the stiff muscles of his shoulders.

"Falorn?" He opened his eyes, wondering how much time had passed. The room seemed unchanged. People still clustered in small groups, talking. The light had faded a bit outside, but glowing lamps and the fireplace still kept the room bright.

He looked up, rubbing his eyes. Elise stood in front of him, holding a pair of wine flagons.

"I thought you and Sera might want something to drink. You looked too tired to get up."

"Thanks," he said. "I already have a drink, though." He reached down for his own mug, as Sera accepted one of the pewter mugs from Elise with a faint smile. Falorn sipped the spiced wine from his cup, glad to find it had remained hot. *I can't have been asleep for all that long, then*, Falorn thought, although his mind remained fuzzy. The mulled wine warmed him as he drank. He hadn't realized how cold he'd felt, sitting by the window. Sera drank from her mug as well, reluctantly lifting her hands from his shoulder.

"Drink," said Elise. She put the second mug down where his had been. "I'll go get another mug for myself, and we can toast your success."

"Thanks again," Falorn said. "I'd like that." His eyes began to slide closed again, and he put the mug down to keep from spilling it. He struggled to keep them open, wondering what Lawes and Geary would think about Falorn falling asleep at his own party. He kept trying to pull himself awake, but his eyes and body refused to cooperate. He began to feel cold again, but his body didn't want to move from the comfort of the chair. Sbashe's nearly-still form covered his feet, her sides swelling and contracting as she breathed evenly. Falorn finally gave into the inevitable, and let himself be drawn into a thicket of roses. Thorns cut at him as they wound and grew over his body, wrapping against him like constricting serpents.

Falorn jerked awake. He felt cold all over, and bruised, as if someone had beaten him while he slept. Sbashe blinked up at him, disturbed by the sudden movement. Falorn tried to stretch, but his shoulders felt cramped and sore, sorer than he'd felt since his injuries in Letz. *I couldn't have slept more than a few minutes*, he realized. The sky outside the window looked no darker. Steam still came from the mug of spiced wine beside his chair. Glancing around the room, he saw the same groups of people in the same conversations, although he couldn't locate Elise or Sera anywhere.

Falorn shivered again. He felt to his chest for the familiar warmth of his cards.

He found nothing. His pouch was gone.

28

The Promise of Blood

❖⋮⋮❖

"The cards!" he tried to say, but the words came out as a choked cry. Adrenaline pushed him from the chair. He ran toward the door, scattering people in his way.

Downstairs. They must have gone downstairs. Falorn had already turned toward the stairs when Sbashe reached his side. He didn't stop to look and see if anyone else followed.

The entrance to the display hall stood open. The green-liveried boys and girls had vanished.

Shattered glass littered the carpeted floor. A half-dozen display cases had been pried open or smashed, and the cards removed.

Further inside, the door to a second room stood ajar.

Falorn stopped only briefly in the ruined display chamber. Drawing his sword, he stepped through the inner door. Sbashe followed closely at his heels.

A polished wooden counter lined the entire back wall of the workroom. Matching bookcases covered all four walls. On the shelves of the cases, Geary's collection of books remained undisturbed. Someone had spread the cards out on the countertop. They lay in an irregular pattern. A single, long-stemmed hothouse rose lay on top of them.

Falorn's empty pouch lay on the floor nearby, its bottom cut out. Sera sat slumped in the room's only chair, unmoving. A trickle of blood flowed from her scalp. Elise stood over her, one hand held protectively near the cards. Her unsheathed sword lay across the counter within easy reach. A long-bladed knife sat beside the sword.

"Elise," said Falorn.

She looked up from the cards. He expected to see wildness in her eyes, but she looked normal. An enameled rose pendant hung from a thin gold chain on the outside of her tunic. *She's worn it before*, he remembered. *She's always worn it.*

"You're a member of the Thorn Cult," he said flatly.

"Did I ever deny it?" Elise asked.

"Why?"

"Why what? Why didn't I tell you? You wouldn't have given me the cards if I had. And the Queen wouldn't exactly have let me take them away, would she?"

"You've been planning to take them all along." Sera stirred slightly. Falorn tried not to look toward her, hoping that Elise wouldn't notice.

"I never tried to take the cards from you. We needed all the cards, not just a few of them. I knew you would bring them all together, if you lived long enough. A very wise woman foretold it. After Sheanna failed to take the first cards away from you, I knew you were the boy from the prophecy, even though many of my sisters disagreed. I did everything I could to keep you safe and protect you from anyone else who wanted to take the cards away—including my own Queen. I *do* like you, Falorn. I tried very hard not to hurt you."

"You took the cards," said Falorn.

"*She* took the cards." Elise pointed to Sera, who stirred again slightly in the chair. "I just took them from her. She took your cards very neatly away from you, rubbing your shoulders and all that. After that, all I had to do was follow her when she came down here. I'm sorry you had to wake up and see it. I hoped to be gone by then."

"You can't just take them," said Falorn.

"I have to, Falorn. Ten of my sisters died to get these cards—four in this city. I can't give them up—not for you or anyone else."

"What are you planning to do with them?"

"They belong in a temple, where they can be looked after by wiser women than me. The woman who made these cards did some bad things, but she did a lot of good as well. These cards will help us to honor her memory."

Elise flexed her right hand twice. Falorn noticed her glance at her sword. He wondered if he could still use his sword without the cards to help him. From their place at the table, they seemed agonizingly far away, much closer to Elise's reach than his own. He supposed that two years of drilling and fights had probably made him into a passable swordsman even without the cards, but Elise had been raised to the blade, brought up as a knight. If he tried to draw his blade, he knew she would kill him. And he felt unsure that he had it in himself to oppose her.

"Take them," he said, shrugging. *I'd wondered if I could let them go or not, but I think they've already let me go. I'm more tired and sore than I was, but I still don't feel like the cards are worth dying for. Or killing for.*

He could hear voices approaching from upstairs, but he doubted any of them would be able to stop her. Maybe the city guard could try to trap her like they had the other members of the Thorn Cult, but he suspected she had prepared for that possibility.

He couldn't imagine Elise lying poisoned on a dock. His mind recoiled at the possibility.

"You mean that?" Her face brightened a little. "You would give them up for me?"

"You have a claim on them, Elise. I don't anymore. I never really wanted them. I think I'm the only one who didn't. If they mean that much to you, take them. I won't stop you."

"Thank you," she said. Elise turned warily toward the cards, never quite taking her eyes from Falorn. The ivorylike plaques seemed to have altered their pattern while the two of them spoke. Falorn wondered what had happened to his vision; the colors of the cards shifted and ran before his eyes, flowing among each other like tendrils of smoke above a slowly smoldering brush fire. He heard a growl from behind him and glanced back. Sbashe faced a crowd of professors at the room's doorway, her fangs bared in a feral snarl.

"I'll miss you, Elise," said Falorn. He stepped back a pace to lean his back against the wall. The colors continued to twist and flow before his eyes. He began to feel dizzy; he could still see Elise, but even Sera's form had become obscured by twisting, disorienting colors, expanding to fill the center of the room.

Elise stepped back as well, her right hand instinctively closing on her sword hilt. She took a step forward and reached for the nearest of the cards. A lion roared at the room's center and she jumped back again. The colors began to solidify and coalesce onto Sera's nearly still form. The rest of the room settled back to reality. Falorn and Elise both looked at the table together. He saw her draw her sword hand back. At the same time he reached for the hilt of his own blade.

The cards lay in their assembled pattern on the table, bare plaques of old, dried lizard skin, all color leached from their surfaces.

Sera staggered to her feet. Falorn let his sword slide back into its sheath and stepped forward to support her. Sera's arm lashed out, slamming into his jaw. He staggered back, surprised at the force of the blow. *Does it hurt so much to get hit without the cards?* he wondered. *Mother of Kerion, what's happening to me?*

"I have returned," said a deep woman's voice, totally unlike Sera's. It took a moment before Falorn could believe the voice had emerged from Sera's mouth.

"Who are you?" Falorn asked. To his right, Elise fell to her knees.

"You have returned," the swordswoman said. "After all these years, you have returned. Praise to Marré and all Her kin."

"A thousand curses on Marré and all the demons who spawned her," the deep voice intoned, in nearly a chant. "I have come back, and I long for blood."

"Blood?" Elise asked.

Blood? Falorn wondered to himself. He repeated the word in the same tone as Elise, speaking it under his breath.

"Where is the blood you have brought me? Have my daughters forgotten me? Are you the only offerings you have left to sate the weakness of this feeble body?"

"Offerings?" said Elise. She still held the sword. Falorn wondered if she realized she had fallen into a guard position.

"I have hungered for years. Now I must feed to regain my power. Come. You will do for a start."

The woman in Sera's body took a lurching step forward. She seemed to have little control of her limbs. Falorn wondered how much of Sera remained inside the sorceress's captured shell.

"No . . ." Elise said, as if pleading with herself. "No, it wasn't supposed to happen this way. You were supposed to come back later, in the temple. Not here. Not now. Nothing is ready. I'm not the one who was supposed to bring you back."

"I am here," said the voice, growing deeper. "I am here, and I will have what I was promised. I have suffered, and I will have my own back. Give me what is mine!"

Elise cringed back against the shelf. Then she looked down, lowering her sword until the blade touched the floor. When she looked up, Falorn saw no emotion at all on her face.

"It is time," said the creature in Sera's body. "I will not wait any longer."

"No," Elise whispered softly. "No . . . you must not wait. You must not wait any longer."

Sera's body stepped forward again. She stumbled, swaying almost drunkenly.

"Give me . . ." The woman fell to one knee.

"No," said Elise. "No. Don't let it happen this way. Please. Take me." She dropped to her knees as well, letting her sword fall unnoticed on the floor. A lone tear ran down her left cheek, falling to splash on the rose at her throat. "Please don't let it happen this way."

The woman in Sera's form raised her head weakly. Her lips parted, but Falorn had to struggle to hear her words.

"I . . . have been . . . betrayed . . . again. Again . . . I must leave. You will see me . . . again." The head slumped forward, falling against Sera's chest.

"Why," sobbed Elise. "Why here? Why now? You could have taken me—anyone else. Why did you have to . . ." She stood up, blind to Falorn and the onlookers held back by Sbashe. Tears ran freely down her face. She stared at the faceless cards, in their precise alignments on the counter's surface. The chair still sat where the unconscious Sera had filled it, closest of all of them to the cards and their flowing colors.

When she turned to face him again, Elise's face once again looked composed. All sadness and uncertainty had vanished. She stooped to recover her sword, not once taking her eye off Falorn or the people crowding the narrow entrance. She spared only the briefest glance at Sera, who had begun to convulse where she lay on the bare floor.

"She'll die in a few moments," said Elise. "She drank wine laced with fool's mint upstairs. Only a little—not so much that the smell would give it away. But enough." She glanced at Sera's body again, and for the briefest moment Elise's face slipped. "Too much. I will pay a high price when I see my sisters. Only what I deserve."

"You poisoned her? So you poisoned the others, too." Falorn tried to absorb the idea. He remembered the way Elise had paused at the cache of fool's mint Falorn had uncovered in the dwarven city. Then something else occurred to him. *You tried to poison me, too, but I didn't drink from the cup you brought me a few minutes ago. And you tried to poison me in Cathan as well. You just stayed with me until you could take the cards.* But that didn't seem quite true, either. *I don't know what to believe.*

"Ask her about poisonings," said Elise. "She has far more on her conscience than I do. She goes to her gods far more peacefully than I go to mine." Sera twitched again.

"Elise . . . you can't . . ."

She lowered her sword. Reaching out with her left hand, she touched his cheek.

"I'll miss you, too," she said.

But you tried to kill me. I don't understand.

Then she stepped past him toward the door, raising her sword. Sbashe leaped aside noiselessly. Falorn looked down at Sera again, knowing that when he looked up once more, Elise would be gone.

He knelt down, taking Sera's head in his hands. Bending over, Falorn kissed her lips. She still breathed faintly; he could smell the mint scent as she exhaled.

He shot to his feet suddenly, nearly dropping Sera's head to the floor as he released her.

"Water!" Falorn shouted. "Somebody bring me hot water!"

He groped at his belt, tearing away a pouch. The seam ripped as he pulled the leather open, fumbling for the smaller cloth bag inside.

Someone pushed a flagon into his hand. He grabbed at it without even looking to see who else had come into the room. Muttering voices filled the air around him. Falorn ignored them, falling to his knees again, careful not to spill the precious water.

Angrily, he worked at the strings of the cloth bag. Everything had untied so easily when he had the thief card; he had become unaccustomed to ordinary knots.

Drawing his belt knife, Falorn slashed the bag open, letting Ryal's herbs spill from the ripped cloth into the mug of steaming water. He wondered how much of the herb to use—he couldn't remember the Hellein's directions. Droplets of blood appeared in the water as well. *I must have cut my finger*, he realized.

Falorn stirred the muddy water with the hilt of his knife. Blood swirled at the top, slowly dissolving into the liquid as it browned.

Grabbing Sera's neck roughly, he forced her head back. He squeezed at her jaws with his fingers, forcing her clenched teeth apart.

He tilted the brackish water to her lips, pouring it in her mouth as slowly as he could. Half of it sloshed across her jaw.

"Drink, damn you!" he shouted. "For the love of Kerion, drink it!"

Sera swallowed a little of the liquid as she inhaled. She began to convulse. Falorn forced her shoulders downward against the floor and poured more into her mouth. She coughed, and swallowed a little more. Her twitching increased as he kept pouring. The flagon held nothing more, he realized. He threw it against the wall and lay his head against her chest, sobbing as she shook beneath him.

"Live, damn you!" Falorn cried. "If you love me at all, why won't you live?" He closed his eyes and willed the world away. The cold he had felt before wouldn't come. The murmur of voices continued around him. "Go away!" he called out, but nothing changed. "I love you, why won't you live?"

The coughing beneath him stopped. He wanted his heart to stop. He wanted the beating he heard to leave, to go away and take him with it now that everyone he cared about had gone. He wanted to die.

Falorn sobbed against Sera's chest. The heart kept beating, pounding in his ear.

His eyes opened, and the heartbeat continued. Ever so slowly, his hand reached to her throat to be certain. Faintly, he felt the same rhythm. Sera lived.

Falorn pushed himself to his knees, both hands on the floor for support. The room reeled around him.

"Somebody help her," he said. "She's alive, now somebody help her. I can't lose her again." Falorn swayed backward. The surge of strength he was used to from the cards didn't come, though. He felt stronger than he had been when he'd left home, but not strong enough to keep going after what he'd already been through this night. Falling, he pushed a hand back for balance, but he felt no support. His head fell toward the floor, but he never felt it hit.

"Is he alive?" he heard someone say above him. Falorn heard everything in the room very clearly, although he felt nothing at all.

"He will be fine," said a loud, throaty voice. "Did anyone catch the witch?"

"She had a sword. None of us could stop her.," said the first voice— Falorn recognized Geary's familiar tones. He wondered what the scholar would do with himself now that the cards were gone. "I've called the guard. They have to catch her. "

"What is there to catch?" asked the throaty voice. "Geary, there is nothing left to catch. You might as well call the guard off."

"We can't let her escape," Geary said.

"We have to." Falorn wondered why he heard no other voices in the room except these two. Had all the other people left?

"Why? Why, Councilor? If she escapes, we have nothing."

"We have nothing now. The only thing you have left is a mystery. If you catch her, you will have less than that."

"If we catch her, we will have answers."

"Answers are not what we want," Lawes said.

"What else is there? What else do I have left to search for except answers?"

"If you find her, you will have all of the answers. If you find her, Geary, they will blame you for all that has happened here."

"But . . . but . . ."

"Go on with what you are doing, Geary. Keep searching for your answers. You will be back in a corner of a small, forgotten building in a week. In a month, no one will remember you. Keep searching for your answers. Everything will be exactly as it was," said the councilor.

"But . . . this room . . . the display cases . . ."

"Go, Geary. I will take care of the display cases. Send a student for your books, tomorrow. Tell the guard that you were mistaken about the woman with the sword."

"She cut Javin."

"An accident at the party. Javin is accident prone. He will agree with you."

"Thank you, Councilor." Geary spoke very quietly, as if he barely controlled his own voice.

"Goodbye, Geary. You might want to take some time off. A year or two to study in private. Maybe you should travel a little, follow up on some of your research. The University will approve your request for leave."

"I . . . suppose. Thank you again, Councilor."

"Think nothing of it."

The room fell silent. After a few minutes, Falorn felt himself lifted from the ground and held. Councilor Lawes's steps echoed heavily on the marble as he carried Falorn out into the cold winter air. He felt himself set on a couch of some sort. He must be in Lawes's coach again, Falorn realized. The chill began to revive him a little. The barest shade of sensation began to flow back into his legs and side. He wondered if he should try to open his eyes. Finally, he decided against it. He lay back and tried to savor the feeling flowing back into his worn-out body.

After a little while he heard Lawes return. The Councilor deposited something on the carriage's second bench, and then lifted Falorn into a sitting position. Falorn felt the enormous man sit beside him, and hold him upright as the carriage began to move.

"You are a very lucky young man," Lawes said as Falorn slumped against the softness of the big man's shoulder. "I suppose you can't hear me. You have lost the cards, but I think you have lost the least of any of us. Geary is ruined, now. He doesn't know it yet, but his career is over. Someone will have to be blamed for all this. I wonder if he will ever understand why.

"A lot of people dreamed about these cards. The Thorn Cult, the Golden Wasp sect, kings, queens, dozens of nobles. You have ruined that dream for all of them. They will never know just how little you really cost them. All they will remember is what the cards might have given them if it had not been for you. They will go on hating you long after they have forgotten about the cards.

"The University—the University has already forgotten about the cards. You will forget about them too. You will recover, and go on to do a thousand other foolish things, and this will be just another half-remembered episode of your youth.

"But I—I have lost most of all."

Falorn wasn't sure what to make of those words.

The interrogator seemed overcome by his story.

"You let him go," he said to the councilor. "You had him in your hands, helpless on the floor, and you let him go. Then you let him leave the island, before you even realized you needed him. You gave a pretty speech as the one person who could have helped you get out of the pickle you find yourself in listened without having a clue what you meant. And then you let him go."

The big man looked up grimly.

"Don't mock at me. I will not tolerate you laughing at me." The words came out of the councilor's mouth, but weren't his, somehow.

"You thought my son was just an unimportant boy, but he foiled you, didn't he. He had no idea whose body you'd settled in when the poison drove you out of Sera. But you had no idea you still needed him."

Both of them had dropped that pretense that it was really Councilor Lawes holding him prisoner.

"You let him leave."

"I didn't know he was important. The cards brought me back as intended. Once I had Lawes's body, I thought I could get the rest of what I needed from the University. He had power and money, and this island contains all the tools you could want to reclaim a body."

"But it isn't your body that's the problem, is it?"

"No." The sorceress in the councilor's body seemed almost dejected. "A body is easy to find. But that boy still carries most of my magic inside him. The cards gave me back my spirit, but he kept most of my power, and I don't know how he did it."

"And he has no idea."

"The boy's too innocent to even know why his father lied to him. Do you really think he'll ever know how he kept the magic he took from me?"

"You got your life back. You got your escape. You really have no grounds for complaint."

"And your son has my power! I want him to bring it back! I want *you* to bring him back!"

A long silence was finally broken by the sound of a lone gull cawing.

"He doesn't even know I'm here," the sorceress finally said. "He doesn't know you're here, either. For all of our attempts to use that boy for our own ends, you've ended up as a prisoner of the woman you tried to kill and I've ended up trapped in this body, with nothing left but my anger."

He just nodded.

"What about the Thorn Cult?" he finally said. "They seemed pretty determined to find you."

A look of real fear crossed the sorceress's face. "I don't dare let them find me. They've built all their hopes on an all-powerful witch who's the next best thing to a god. What would they do if they found out their god was helpless and powerless?"

"So all you can do is try to to lure my son back. Would you even be able to get your power back from him if you found him?"

The fearful look remained, straining the bulky councilor's face, but the sorceress didn't answer for a while. Finally, she said, "Finish the story. What else do you know about your son's leaving?"

"Only a little, and nothing about after he left the island. I think you know more of that story than I do."

"Tell me," she said, her tone regaining just a hint of confidence. "You are still my prisoner, even if I am a prisoner in this body. Tell me the rest of the story."

Epilogue

Sera remained confined to bed, but much of the color had returned to her complexion. She looked up at Falorn as he entered her room. Smiling at him wanly, she closed the book in her lap.

"You look a lot better today," he said.

"I feel a lot better," answered Sera. "The healer is going to let me up out of bed tomorrow, at least for a little while."

"That's good."

"Come, sit." She patted the mattress next to where she lay. "Let's talk. We haven't done a lot of talking in two years, have we?"

"We've talked," Falorn protested as he walked over to the bed. He sat gratefully. He still felt weak from the shock of losing the cards, although he gained strength each day.

She started to say something and then stopped. They sat together quietly until the early spring sunlight began to creep away from the bedspread and across the floor.

"Do you think you'll hear from Geary again?" she finally asked.

"I wrote him another letter. He may not have gotten the first one. Or maybe he couldn't understand my writing."

"Do you think he'll ever come back?"

"No." Falorn finally said.

She fell silent again. After a little while her hand crept over to rest on top of his.

"Should I get you something to eat?" Falorn asked, when the room began to darken.

"No. I'm not really hungry."

"You should eat. You need to get stronger."

"I know. But I'd rather you just stay here with me for a while longer."

Darkness gradually overtook them. Sera leaned against Falorn's shoulder and closed her eyes. He lay very still as her breathing slowed and grew more regular. Far into the night, he lay awake, listening.

When his eyes finally closed, Falorn hoped to dream of lions once again, but they didn't come.

When the days grew warmer, Sera joined Falorn and Sbashe in morning walks on the city streets. He walked to market early most days, to buy vegetables and meat for their kitchen. He enjoyed cooking now, more than he had in his days in his father's inn. Falorn liked the quiet time, alone in the small rented house with Sbashe and Sera, but without any cards or enemies or thoughts of magical portents. In the afternoons, Falorn worked out in the narrow brick-floored court behind the house. He didn't feel as smooth as when the cards flowed through him, but the sword still felt natural in his hands. His legs moved easily in familiar motions.

After their evening meal, he and Sera usually read together while Sbashe went off on errands of her own. They found dozens of book-sellers' shops on their morning walks; the presence of the University made books and pamphlets plentiful. He enjoyed reading out loud, although he still struggled on all but the simplest words. Sera read to him as well. Falorn liked to listen to her voice; sometimes the tone so capti-vated him that he lost the meaning of her words altogether.

As she got stronger, they walked farther. By summer Falorn and Sera often wandered the slopes beyond the city, watching the sea break against cliff walls, or looking at the flocks of sheep in the grassy hills. Sometimes Sbashe walked with them, but more often she stayed alone in the house. She seemed more restless, now that Sera could walk easily again. Falorn loved the regularity of life in the city, but he began to feel confined by the island as well.

"Have I changed at all?" Sera asked him one day, as they walked past a row of dockside chandlers' shops.

"What do you mean?" asked Falorn. He rubbed her neck and shoulders lightly with his right hand as they walked. "You're still the same person."

"I don't have the cards any more. I did so many terrible things when I had them. Part of me wants to blame the cards for all the things I did. But another part of me doesn't feel any different. I don't know if I've changed at all," said Sera.

"What matters is that we're here now. What's past is past."

"But I could do something like that again. I hurt so many people. I could treat you like that."

"But you won't. You haven't," Falorn said.

She did, he had to admit to himself. He didn't want to believe it, but she had done all those things. *I just don't know whether or not I can live with that. Or whether she'll just leave me as soon as she gets the chance, in spite of what the mermaid said. But I guess I have to find out.*

She turned to face him.

"Falorn, I'm not sure you know who I really am. You seem to think there's this wonderful person inside me waiting to come out. I'm not sure there's anything there at all. I'm not a good person."

"You are who you are. I'm not asking you to be anyone else."

"But who I am scares me. It scares me so much."

It scares me too, Falorn thought. But instead of saying anything, he slid his arm across Sera's shoulder and pulled her close beside him. She shook against him. A warm breeze from off the water ruffled his hair. Falorn found himself looking at moored ships as he held Sera close against him.

"I don't want to lose you, Falorn," Sera said in a quiet voice. "I've lost everything else I ever had. I don't want to lose you, too."

"I'm not going anywhere without you." Falorn looked at the silver band that still encircled his wrist. "I'm never going anywhere without you." *I wonder if the mermaid told the truth.*

They walked slowly back toward the house.

"It's time to leave the island, isn't it?" asked Sera as they walked through the blue-painted door and into the small front room.

"Just about. I'd like to bring Sbashe home. She's been away a long time."

"That's a long trip."

"I guess it is," said Falorn.

"Did you have any plans after that?"

"I've thought about it a little," he admitted. "I might like to go visit Golden Reeds again. The lizards ought to be happy to see their lost savior return. And I'd like to spend time getting to know them without a prophecy hanging over my head."

"And after that?"

"After that, I don't know. I have plenty of money, so I don't *have* to do anything. I've thought about traveling some more, visiting more of the world. There are still a lot of places where nobody's tried to kill me yet. And at some point I'd like to go home, and visit my family again. I'm not ready to face my father yet, but sometime I will be. He hasn't returned any of my letters, either. If he even got them."

"You don't mind if I come along?"

"I wouldn't go without you. Look . . . Sera . . . I meant what I said in Cathan . . . you know . . . when I said I wanted to marry you."

"Oh . . . Falorn. That's so sweet of you. But you hardly know who I am. You've got a title now, and I have nothing."

It's an empty title, he thought, *given to me by the brother of a man who wants to kill me. Not much different than Sera's legacy, really.* But what he said out loud was, "That doesn't matter to me."

"Why don't we wait? I'll travel with you if you like, but I don't think either of us is ready to get married yet. I'm not sure what life is going to be like without the cards. I need to live it for a while before I make any big decisions."

"You know I'll ask you again." He said the words because he knew she expected him to, but a part of Falorn wondered if they were really true anymore.

"There's no one I'd rather be with right now, Falorn."

"Well, let's start packing then," he answered.

Sera walked over and kissed him on the cheek before she walked from the room.

Sbashe, Falorn thought, as he walked toward the rear courtyard where the corget slept, *wake up and get ready. We're going home.*

"So Falorn didn't know that he carried my powers dormant within him when he left the island," the sorceress said.

"I'm not sure they are still dormant. Between the noble birth he never knew about and his time with the cards, he seems to have had a certain natural affinity for your powers. I hope he's putting them to better use than you did."

"I might have ruled the world with those powers."

The tower room seemed very far from world domination.

"Sera left him, you know," he finally said. "She's done well for herself. She married the Duke of Denborel, and helps rule a city much larger than the one she grew up in."

"You don't mourn for your son's lost love?"

"He's safer without her."

"I thought you said the mermaid promised him they would always be together."

He shrugged. "I wasn't the only one to lie to him. He's been lied to a lot. I don't think he really expected that to come true, either. I imagine he'll be happier without her, once he gets over the initial sadness."

"You know that from experience?"

"As a matter of fact, I do. My own, if not his."

The sorceress didn't pursue the point. "He is not with the lizards, nor in his native land, nor in any other place that Lawes's money could search for him."

"If he learned to use your powers, all of Lawes's money wouldn't find him if he didn't want to be found, even if he stood in this room."

"That is true," the sorceress acknowledged.

The room fell silent again

"Do you think he'll ever come back?" she asked, eventually.

"No." Falorn's father finally said.

He wondered if his son would begrudge him that one, last lie.

About the Author

Leigh Grossman teaches science fiction, fantasy, writing, and book publishing in the English Department at the University of Connecticut. He is the author of twelve published books, and has edited many others, for a variety of publishing houses. He lives in northeast Connecticut, in a big old house with a computer programmer fiancee, four cats, and a robot. Visit him at www.swordsmith.com or www.wildsidegame.com.